Chad in Accounting

Matthew Poirier

D1520614

Dedication

To my beautiful wife Jen, and all of my family and friends who have supported me throughout this process. It's been over 10 years, but I finally did it, it's finally here. Hopefully this book won't be the end of the journey, but rather just the start.

Contents

Stacy in Accounting

If I were a little cuter, and could sing a little better, I could've been Chris Kirkpatrick, thought Chad in Accounting. He thought anything was better than being Chad in Accounting, even being Chris Kirkpatrick—which was saying a lot, considering it was Chris Kirkpatrick for Christ's Sake!

When did he become Chad in Accounting? That was easy, one year ago, when they hired Chad in IT. Before that there was no need to differentiate between Chads. No, that wasn't true. If he were honest with himself, he had been Chad in Accounting starting five years ago, the moment he sat down in this dreary cubicle at this area branch of this huge insurance firm based in this massive office park on the strip, as opposed to the job he had had with a tech firm downtown in the beautiful open space of a converted Baptist church. Five years ago when he was twenty-seven. Five years ago when he weighed thirty pounds less. Five years ago when he didn't have that bald spot on the back part of the top of his head that he was so self-conscious of, which led him to contort himself in myriad ways to keep women from noticing it, not knowing that it was more the contortions and less the bald spot that turned women off and kept him single. Five years ago after Gwen decided she wasn't happy anymore.

He looked at the clock on the lower right-hand corner of his monitor. 2:36. Two hours and twenty-four minutes to go. He went to his e-mail box. It had only been two minutes since he'd last checked it, but you never know. Sure enough, he had something new. Maybe someone commented on his Facebook status. Damn, his mom mass-forwarded another silly video. 2:38. He could maybe kill another five minutes watching it. Anything to kill time was a blessing. Anything other than work, of course.

The video was something a person posted on YouTube of her cat standing at the kitchen sink, sticking his head under the running faucet. Chad watched the cat's ear fold down as it hit the water, and his eye close, like he was a little pirate. The cat had a reason for putting himself through this: the water from the faucet splashing on his head was collecting then running down his nose and dripped off, where he caught the drops with his tongue. He did this for three full minutes before Chad closed the window.

The first thought Chad in Accounting had was: why didn't the cat just drink from the water bowl his owner probably had on the floor nearby? Why was he going through all the trouble to get so little water? The second thought Chad had made him shudder: that cat is a metaphor for me. I'm sitting under the faucet of life, licking little drops off my nose, when there's a bowl of life on the floor somewhere, and I haven't even bothered to look for it. Even Chris Kirkpatrick has found his bowl of life on the floor for Christ's Sake. He needed to share this moment of perspicacity with somebody.

Stacy in Accounting walked past his cubicle.

Stacy was thin and very attractive, with her olive complexion, black hair, and brown eyes; features that looked best in her tight purple sweater vest over her tight white shirt and black mini skirt—none of which she was wearing today, opting instead for an unremarkable sleeveless blue shirt and unflattering baggy gray dress pants, much to the chagrin of her male coworkers.

Though Stacy was engaged, Chad was pretty sure that he and her had this flirtatious thing going on. He couldn't have been more wrong. Chad assumed that because Stacy occasionally chuckled at his bad jokes or put her hand on his back to let him know politely that she wanted him to move out of her way, that this meant he was only one or two cleverly spoken lines from him and her having sex in the copy room, when in fact Chad kind of annoyed Stacy with his bad jokes, and weirded her out with the way he would stand sometimes, unbeknownst to her in an effort by Chad to keep her from seeing his bald spot.

"Stacy, take a look at this thing my mom sent."

What now, Stacy thought, another stupid Kanye West/Taylor Swift joke? It was like a month ago, give it up Chad!

Fortunately for Chad it wasn't another Kanye/Taylor Swift meme.

"See this cat."

Anyone who could see Chad in Accounting at that moment, sitting in his cubicle, trying to angle his head so Stacy wouldn't notice his bald spot, while trying to use his computer in front of him at the same time, would have found it difficult to not grab him and force him to sit correctly, like one might do to a five-year-old who was fidgeting in church on a hot Sunday; and which is what Stacy wanted to do too, but restrained herself.

"Aww, that's cute. That's so cool your mom sent that. All right, I'll see you—"

"See, Stacy, I was... uh... thinking..."

Oh God, please don't ask me out, please don't ask me out. I knew he was going to do this eventually. Ugh, I should never have laughed at his bad jokes. Wait, Stacy thought, I'm engaged, I can just tell him I'm engaged. If he asks me out, I'll just tell him I'm engaged.

"See... I was thinking, the cat... it's like... I don't know... a metaphor for my life... like, you know, the water is life, and I'm the cat, working so hard for the drips here and there, when there's a bowl of life somewhere on the floor that my owners set down that I need to find, you know?"

"Wow, Chad... I never knew you could be so... deep... wow... um, okay, I'm going to get back to my work, but I'll see you later, okay?"

Chad felt his soul drop as she walked away. Stupid, stupid, stupid. I totally freaked her out with that. Now she thinks I'm a total weirdo. And I know she saw my bald spot. What was I thinking?

Stacy, though, didn't think Chad in Accounting was a total weirdo, she felt like she'd just been out to lunch with her girlfriends for Chinese, and happened to get a fortune cookie that really spoke to her, like it knew everything that was going on in her life, what was wrong with it, and how to fix it with one sage line of Confucian advice. She was stunned. For months now she'd been having misgivings about getting married, feeling that she was settling down too easy. She was the cat in Chad's video too. She had fallen into a routine of getting up every day and putting her head under the faucet to get a few drops of water, and she had known for a while that something about it didn't feel right, but she didn't have anyone like Chad put it into perspective for her. Maybe she was wrong about him, like she thought she might be wrong about everything now.

2:52. Chad in Accounting had about two hours to save face with Stacy before she left for the day and had a bad impression of him left in her mind for the night. What would he do? Of course, another Kanye West/Taylor Swift joke. Yo yo yo Chris Kirkpatrick, I'ma let you finish, I'ma let you finish, but Jonathan Knight was the most superfluous boyband member of all time. Stacy would love that.

A couple days after Kanye West jumped on stage during the MTV Music Awards to interrupt Taylor Swift accepting her award, Chad heard Stacy laugh out loud at something on her computer. A friend had posted a bunch of memes on her Facebook wall based on Kanye's rant. She showed them to Chad, and as luck would have it, a few minutes later he found a couple on his Facebook feed too, which he showed her, and she also found funny. He felt like they had made a connection, so over the past month, as much of the rest of the internet world had moved on to other things to make memes of, Chad had been showing her more he'd found—or even worse, had been trying to create his own Kanye jokes, which to Stacy had even less success; but her faint laughter to not sound rude made Chad think he was furthering that connection with her.

Chad didn't get to use his new Kanye joke, didn't get to make up for his gaff, didn't get to leave a better impression in her mind overnight; because Stacy thought about what Chad said for another ten minutes, then told their supervisor she had a headache, her work was caught up, and she wanted to leave early. Chad watched her gather up her stuff, turn off her computer, and give him a quick wave goodbye. There was a smile in that wave, a smile he'd never seen from her before. Wow, maybe I *am* in. As she walked away from him, down the hallway, moving both elegantly and with purpose in her heels, he watched her. He watched as her shape emerged from her baggy pants as they pressed up against the flesh beneath them, and he had trouble breathing for a second. She never looked more beautiful to him, even when she wore her purple sweater vest and black mini skirt.

Driving home from work in his black Jetta, he heard *NSYNC's "Tearin' Up My heart", and was certain that was a sign that Stacy was meant to be The One, reasoning that he almost never heard *NSYNC on the radio anymore, and he had been thinking of Chris Kirkpatrick when he saw the cat video, which was when Stacy and he made the connection that led to her giving him that smile as she left. It was fate. It's funny how we do that, assume that the well-focus-grouped list of music corporate radio deems most playable for a certain block of time during a certain day can be a positive omen telling us the person we're falling for is cosmically ordained to be that one person we're meant to be with; and when we're heartbroken, we feel like the DJ is picking the perfect mix of songs to twist the knife in us that much more, "after the break, we'll have 45 minutes of continuous commercial free rock featuring songs that remind you of *her*." Though Chad would be loathed to admit it, a furniture commercial once reminded him of Gwen, when the booming announcer's voice yelled "one day only!", and it sounded like Gwen's response after he asked her how long they were staying at her parents' one Christmas.

Chad in Accounting lived in a third-floor apartment in an apartment building that was one of a large community of apartment buildings about a mile south on the strip from his job. His apartment entered into the living room, which was off to the right, and was furnished with a faux leather couch and matching recliner that faced the flatscreen TV on the wall next to the door and an entertainment center underneath it. To the left was the kitchen, which had a dining table and chairs that he had never used, instead opting for the glass coffee table in his living room so he could watch TV while he ate. Tonight's meal was linguine and Ragu jar sauce, which he had with a beer. Between the kitchen and living room was a small hallway that led to the bathroom on the left, Chad's bedroom in the middle, and the "guest" bedroom to the right. We put "guest" in quotes because he'd never actually had a guest stay over. Five years ago when he moved in here after the lease was up on his and Gwen's place, this was supposed to be a temporary dwelling until he found something better, and while in that five years he'd become used to living here and had no plans to move anywhere else, he still kept the "temporary" title in his mind. There were no pictures on the wall, no elements of sentimentality; also no books, no plants, no paintings.

He had been in a funk for the better part of the last week or so, after Gwen and Dave posted pictures of their second child on Facebook. The same Gwen who told him that she wasn't ready to settle down and didn't want kids, though for an outsider looking in, it would be the same Chad who couldn't let go, the same Chad who accepted Gwen's add request a year ago, the same Chad who couldn't bring himself to hide her on his news feeds, the same Chad who was thinking how great it would be to change his relationship status to "In a Relationship with Stacy" and have Gwen see that on *her* news feed. Maybe he should've been thinking of that cat and the bowl of water more.

Maybe, but it had been over two years since his last relationship—if you could call it that, it wasn't so much a relationship as it was the last time he'd been with a woman. Her name was Brooke, or Miss Dalbert, as her students called her. She taught French at Oak Grove Academy. Chad met her when he went to an 8-minute dating night at the Sheraton Lounge downtown, something his mother pushed him into doing as a way to get over Gwen.

Brooke was obsessed with Harry Potter. Read and reread the books over and over. The last book Chad could remember reading was *The Da Vinci Code*, a few years before, and he wasn't interested in breaking that streak for a series of kids' books about a wizard or something. On the other hand, he wanted badly to be with a woman, hadn't been finding much since Gwen, and Brooke was somewhat attractive. She was tall, thin, lanky, with pale skin and long brown hair and small blue eyes; she also wore skirts, which was something Chad liked, and something Gwen seldom did.

Brooke saw in him a lot of potential. She was like a house hunter on The Home and Garden Network, and Chad, with his college degree and good job as an accountant, was a nice house in a good neighborhood for a decent price. He was a fixer-upper though too, but Brooke was willing to work with that, because she was getting up there in age—28—and all her friends were settling down and having babies. She didn't want to be the spinster school teacher all her life. Chad might be a little rough around the edges, but he had the raw material that she could mold into a suitable partner. She wanted him to learn French again—something he hadn't done since high school—so they could go to Paris together—a place he'd been once before, on a high school trip that he honestly couldn't remember anything of because he was drunk the whole time. Most importantly, she'd make him into a Harry Potter fan. Once he read the first one, he'd be hooked like her, she was sure of it, and there wasn't much time, because the next movie was coming out that July. He needed to be ready.

The last straw for Chad came when she wanted him to dress like one of the characters for the midnight premier of the film. It came out at that moment, the night of, when he showed up in street clothes, that he hadn't been reading the Harry Potter books she'd given him either.

Chad had been making a decision mentally for the few weeks leading up to that—which was the bulk of their 1-month relationship—that Brooke was not the girl for him. The sex wasn't that good: she only ever wanted to do missionary, and would just lie there, as if sex was something she wanted to get through; and they had nothing in common: she hated sports, hated action movies, and hated beer, all things he loved. The thing that upset him the most, though, was that she was so certain her tastes were superior to his, that Harry Potter was somehow a more worthwhile pursuit than soccer.

She ended it with him though, despite Chad having mentally checked out weeks before, because he didn't have the fortitude to give up her as a girlfriend, even if she wasn't at all compatible with him. Two weeks after the break up, he saw the Harry Potter book sitting on his shelf, and wished he'd just read it and made her happy, because something was better than nothing, which was what he'd ended up with until now. Until Stacy smiled at him when she waved. She could break this sorry streak of sexual futility, he was sure of it. All that afternoon, all that night at home in his apartment, all he could think about was Stacy's smile and her body and seeing her the next day. If Stacy knew the things he was thinking about her, she would've been disgusted; and if Chad knew she would've been disgusted, he would've been devastated. He didn't think once about the cat and the bowl of water.

Stacy thought about Chad too, but not at all the way he'd hoped. She thought about the cat and the faucet and her bowl of water. It never left her mind. The first thing she did when she got back to her apartment was stick her iPod in the docking bay on the desk next to her bed, set it to shuffle, and crank up the volume. It played Ashley Simpson's "Pieces of Me", which she loved. Next she took out a small bin in her closet filled with large, old, white envelopes that she'd received in the mail from the various tourism bureaus of European countries. The top one was from Portugal. She had always wanted to start in Portugal.

She and Todd had a one-bedroom apartment, and their queen-sized bed nearly took up all of the space in their bedroom. There was just enough room on the left to put a small desk for the computer and iPod docking station between the bed and the closet, and that's where she sat, browsing for flights.

When she was 20, she and a couple of her sorority sisters made plans to go backpacking through Europe after they graduated. They bought all kinds of guide books and sent out for all kinds of brochures and information. Between 20 and 22, something happened in her life that made those plans untenable: she met Todd. She told herself she'd still do it someday, though, and kept all of the things she and her friends collected in that little bin. Stacy showed it to Todd after they moved into their apartment, and he asked why she would keep all that dumb shit, and it took a lot of work from her to convince him not to throw it all out.

After her aunt died a few months ago, and Stacy discovered that she was the beneficiary of her aunt's $50,000 life insurance plan, the common consensus was that that money would go toward a house for her and Todd after they married next year. But she thought about that bin and those guide books and brochures and all of those plans—plans that were Stacy's before there was a Todd and Stacy. It took Chad's video to make those thoughts become actions.

She sang loud and obnoxiously to the songs on her iPod while she looked up flights. She hadn't sung like that since before she'd met Todd. There was a flight to Lisbon that would be perfect. She clicked on the button to buy the tickets, but stopped when she needed to confirm her information. Something was holding her back, and all she could do at that moment was lie on her bed and listen to her iPod, while the confirmation screen remained on her monitor, waiting for her to make one click that she was too apprehensive to make.

Todd came home a couple hours later, and she joined him in the living room. He looked more attractive than she could remember him being. His hair wasn't too gelled, his fake tan suited him for once—made him look more Mediterranean. Maybe she was making a mistake. Maybe what Stacy wanted was right here after all. She sat down next to him on the couch and ran her fingers through his hair.

"How come you don't have your hair all spiked up?"

"I went to the gym at lunch and like a fuckin' idiot, didn't pack my gel. I look like a fuckin' moron."

"I think you look hot."

"Yeah, whatev. What did you plan on making for supper?"

"I was just going to eat some leftover Chinese I had in the fridge."

"I don't know how you can eat that fuckin' Chink food. It makes me fuckin' sick."

When did it become an issue for her that Todd only had one adjective in his vocabulary? Fuckin'. Fuckin' fuckin' fuckin'. Fuckin' this, fuckin' that, fuckin' moron. Or the fact that he was racially insensitive? Really, "chink food"? When did Todd go from being funny to being a moron? When out of the four years they had been together did Stacy stop being the sorority girl he met at his frat house? She knew she had to do this.

She stood.

"Todd, I'm leaving you."

There, she said it. It's out there. I'm fucking leaving you, Todd. I'm going to take my aunt's inheritance and backpack through Europe instead of use it to buy a house with your dumbass.

"What the fuck are you talking about?"

"It's a long story, but I haven't been happy for a—" This was harder than she expected, and the fact that Todd was in too much shock to comprehend things made it even worse. "I've just been thinking a lot lately... I don't know... this just doesn't feel right... I don't know... I want more out of life... you know?"

"What're you on the rag or something?"

Todd was not in too much shock to deal with this, like Stacy thought, he actually wasn't taking this seriously. He came from the school that said women were by nature extremely capricious (not a word he'd ever use), and as a guy, he needed to weather these inane mood swings by feigning sensitivity. "What're you on the rag or something?" was Todd's way of showing her that he understood Woman Problems, and he could do the little things he needed to do to placate her feminine capriciousness.

"What? *'On the rag?'* No, it's not that... it's just... I saw this video today... a guy at work showed it to me... with a cat with its head under the water... and I felt like I was that cat... you know?"

"What the fuck are you talking about? And who is this fuckin' guy? Are you fuckin' him?"

"What? No, I'm not seeing someone else, that's not what this is about."

"I bet it's that fuckin' Chad guy that you said is always hitting on you."

She paused, and he noticed that.

6

"I knew it! You're fuckin' that Chad guy!"

She laughed, which made him even angrier. He stormed around the apartment talking about what he was going to do to Chad. Now he was getting it. Todd was from the same school that never considered problems in a relationship could be confined to the two principle parties. Oh no, it was always some other guy messing around, trying to get his girl from him. He needed to stand up and defend his turf. He'd fix this situation quickly. Stacy put her head in her hands and laughed harder.

"You think this is fuckin' funny?"

"Yes, I do. I think it's hilarious, Todd. I'm leaving you because I don't love you anymore, and you think I'm fucking some guy I don't even find attractive. I'm going to pack my things, and you can have whatever I don't take. I want you to know, it's not me, it's you."

"What?"

"Um… I'm sorry… I meant 'it's not you, it's me'…"

She started laughing again. Todd was finally confused. This might actually happen. His Old Lady might actually be leaving him for this Chad guy. His brain shut down, and her finding it amusing didn't help matters.

"Very funny, very fuckin' funny. What the fuck am I gonna to do about the rent? I can't fuckin' afford this place on my own."

"The rent? That's what you're worried about? Here:" she picked up her checkbook and wrote him out her half of the rent for the next two months. "That'll give you 60 days to find a roommate."

He stood over her shoulder as she wrote out the check. He didn't know why he brought up the rent. He didn't know what was going on. Todd was not wired to accept sudden changes, not wired for empathy or to consider that Stacy had her own life to live, not wired to comprehend that Stacy or anyone else couldn't share his *weltanschauung*.

They went back and forth for another 45 minutes. Todd was trying to get to the bottom of Chad. He wanted to know what this guy had that he didn't. Was he rich? He must be, but he works with her, so how rich could he really be? It's not about Chad, Todd, it's about me. Does he get into clubs that I can't? Did he get her a reservation at that restaurant she's always wanted to go to? Todd, it's not about Chad. Me and Chad aren't doing anything. He's not even that cute, for God's sake. Then he must be rich.

Todd's circuits were overloading. None of this was computing. He declared he needed some drinks with his friends. Stacy realized how upset he was, because he didn't take two hours making himself look right before he went out like he usually did. It made her feel sorry for him and what she was doing to him. She wrote a note before she left, telling him what was in her heart, even though she knew it wouldn't do any good. Todd may go the rest of his life and never know why she did what she did. Stacy in Accounting didn't want to be Stacy in Accounting anymore, and somehow, from 21 to 25, not being Stacy in Accounting anymore meant not being Todd's fiancée anymore too.

She didn't think of him again that night until 1AM, when she was lying on the bed in her room at the airport hotel, looking at all the things she'd received in the mail five years ago about all the places she'd be seeing soon, and she thought I bet he'll be getting home from the bars right now.

This fascination with Europe started when Stacy was very young. She was the only grand-daughter of her mother's mother, and Stacy's grandmother regaled her with tales of Paris and London and Madrid and Lisbon and Milan in the 1950s: cafes, country-sides, castles, romance, beauty, losing oneself and finding oneself all at the same time. Stacy was in awe of these tales, wondering why her life in American suburbia was so dull and unromantic, when worlds like these were out there where people like her grandmother had such exciting things happen to them. In high school Stacy took Spanish, but the day before her class was scheduled to go on their trip to Spain, her grandmother died of a heart attack. Stacy was devastated, her grandmother was one of the closest people in her life, and it was this trip to Europe, finally, that her grandmother was most excited for her to experience. She skipped the trip to attend the funeral, but vowed she'd make it back there, and when she and her sorority sisters discussed it a few years later, she obsessed over the idea, taking the initiative to plan everything out, send away for the brochures, and buy up all the guide books. Her friends weren't as serious about it as she was though, and when Todd came into the picture, her drive to make it happen evaporated. Europe felt like a dream world millions of miles away, and Todd was real and in front of her, and what was real was what mattered.

The aunt that passed away was her grandmother's sister, a woman with no kids of her own, who worked for 50 years as a librarian, and kept mostly to herself after Stacy's grandmother died—she was known to her neighbors as The Crazy Cat Lady, not because she had a lot of cats, but because she was kind enough to feed and care for all of the strays in the neighborhood, which, for her neighbors, must've meant she was crazy. Without telling anyone, she named Stacy as the beneficiary in her life insurance policy. Stacy was humbled. $50,000 out of the blue? A woman she barely knew, only really knew of her through her grandmother, would do something that kind for me? There was something about the way everyone in her life immediately appropriated the money for a house for her and Todd that irked her. It was as if money that special shouldn't be spent on something so base and unimaginative, and to do so would have in some way insulted the act of its giving. That's when thoughts of her grandmother and Europe crept in.

She suggested it to Todd, but he wrote it off as ridiculous, that Europeans sucked ass and Americans ruled. It sparked a heated argument between them, as she attempted to defend Europeans, and he accused her of not loving her country enough. She pictured him in Milan or Vienna or Barcelona, as her grandmother had described those cities, and he didn't fit. How had she let herself become used to a guy that couldn't fit in places that were so special?

But she had. It didn't matter how, just that she had, and this was it, Todd was the guy for her, and her aunt's $50,000, whether she liked it or not, would go towards their first house. Then Chad showed her the video of the cat on YouTube. Why should she settle for drips of water with Todd, when there was a whole ocean of life to drink from in Europe? Her aunt gave her this money to live off of, not grow old and die with.

Chad couldn't wait to see Stacy the next day. He'd ask if she wanted to get drinks some night after work. It didn't matter if she was engaged—engaged people broke up all the time, right? He knew that as well as anyone. He imagined her in his head coming into work in something hot that she wore to get his attention, waving at him with that same smile she gave him yesterday. It made him anxious just thinking about it, how would he feel when she actually got here?

His clock on his computer read 9:05. Then it read 10:05. It wasn't like Stacy to be late like this. She was usually there before him, and now she was over an hour late. At 11:11, his supervisor came in with an IT guy, and they went to work on her computer. This was odd.

After lunch his supervisor called him into a meeting with their boss and gave him the news. Chad was crushed. He had been looking forward to so many things he imagined he and her doing, and now none of those things would happen. It didn't even seem real yet, he didn't want to believe it was true.

Almost a month later, when Chad in Accounting had fully moved on from Stacy, a large, younger man with a do-rag on his head and wearing only a tank top and gym shorts attacked him in the parking lot. He accused him of taking his woman away, and asked where she was. The man wouldn't listen to Chad's pleas that he had no idea what he was talking about. He almost admitted to how long it had been since he'd had sex he was so scared and so desperate to prove his innocence. It took security a few minutes to pull the guy off.

It wasn't until he was driving home that he realized who the man was. The same man whose fiancée he had planned on asking out for a drink a month before as if the guy didn't exist. He examined his face in his rearview mirror at a stop light. There was a mouse forming under his left eye, he could taste the blood from the inside of his lower lip, and part of his shirt was torn. Perhaps worst of all, Chad felt sick in the pit of his stomach, because he had been a coward; and after the mouse disappeared, the lip no longer hurt when he ate salty foods, and the shirt was lost forever in a landfill, that feeling of uneasiness from how afraid he was of Stacy's fiancé would continue to haunt him.

Todd heard rumors about what had really happened to Stacy, but it wasn't until after he confronted Chad that he believed them. She only told her parents what she was doing, and they didn't care for Todd, so he never asked them. Eventually her friends found out, and some of them dated some of his friends, and they told him. The only explanation he could gather was that she was a fucking bitch. In his mind he gave her everything, and he did everything he thought she and every other girl wanted, from lifting weights, to wearing tons of Axe body spray, to buying her shit, to not being a pussy. What more *could* she have wanted?

As for Stacy, her trip to Europe didn't go the way she'd planned. On her fourth day in Lisbon, she met an amazing local man whom she fell in love with immediately. He convinced her to move her stuff out of the hotel she was staying in, which proved to be a mistake, because they went to a club together the next night, and he abandoned her. To make matters worse, he had somehow managed to procure her purse from her before he left. She was still unfamiliar with the city, and had no idea where he lived. She spent that night out in the freezing cold, scared, in only the skimpy little dress he'd bought for her earlier that afternoon.

Had she not read all of those guidebooks, she might not have known she could turn to the US Embassy for help, but she did read them, and that's where she went first thing that morning. It was the longest night of her life though. Shivering on a park bench underneath a smelly newspaper, she thought it would never end, that the morning would never come, that the present would never push her forward to the time when she could go to the embassy and leave the purgatory of these cold, black, foreign streets. She didn't even have the comfort of Ashley Simpson on her iPod. That made her cry.

Had Stacy really been thinking clearly, a better move would have been to go to the police for help and end her horrible night early; but she wasn't thinking clearly, and instead feared the police would arrest her for sleeping on the street. She thought about her parents, and how she knew they disapproved of her going to Europe with her aunt's money, but they disapproved of Todd even more, so the idea of her leaving him was more important than how foolish they thought she was for doing this. She thought of Todd and how she wished he was there to hold her, and feeling that made her more ashamed than anything.

The embassy was further away than she imagined, and it was hard to get directions from people when none of them spoke English. Not only that, but her feet were very tired and sore, and she was walking without her shoes on. Any other time she would've felt very gross, but all she felt now was the need to get to her destination anyway she could.

Upon entering the embassy, the only thing she wanted to do was call her parents and get a flight home. She would be returning with her tail between her legs. In her haste to find Chad's water dish, she found this catastrophe instead. But she also found Johnny, who worked in the embassy, and who was not only very hot, but very helpful.

Instead of going home with her tail between her legs, Stacy would stay in Lisbon for almost a year, and as her romance with Johnny grew, and they made trips to see all the cities her grandmother told her about, she always thought about Chad and his video and what he told her. She thought about inviting him to the wedding, but didn't know his address; and when their son was born, his middle name was Chadwick. It would have never crossed her mind that when Chad thought of her, he thought of the humiliation of Todd's confrontation, because when she thought of him, she thought if it hadn't been for him, she'd still be Stacy in Accounting engaged to Todd, and the idea of that life compared to the life she had now made her shudder. In her mind, Chad's epiphany after seeing that video must have affected him the way it affected her, that there was no way there was still a Chad in Accounting as she knew him, and she would sometimes daydream that he was doing something even more amazing than she was. In fact, Chad never thought of that video or what he said to Stacy ever again. That doesn't mean that Chad would always be Chad in Accounting, just that it would have to take something more to affect him the way that his words affected her.

Lisa the Heartbroken

The reason Chad in Accounting had gotten over Stacy during the month between her departure and Todd's attack had more to do with a new woman in his life and less to do with his ability to bounce back after heartbreak. Actually, Lisa wasn't a new woman in Chad's life, but rather someone who lived in his building with whom he was familiar. The weekend after Stacy started her European adventure, Chad bumped into Lisa in the elevator, and she remarked on the Steven Seagal films he'd rented.

"I love Steven Seagal."

"You do?"

"Uh huh. I've always thought he was hot."

She pulled out her lip gloss and reapplied it, not because her lips needed it, but for Chad's benefit. Had her dirty blond hair not been tied back in a ponytail, she would've twirled it in her fingers for him too. She looked at him to see if it was working, and saw him staring straight ahead. What Lisa didn't know was everything she was doing, both on purpose and not on purpose, was working. Chad just didn't know her putting her lip gloss on was for his benefit. It turned him on, as did the way her chest looked under her white turtleneck and open black leather jacket, or how her legs looked in her black skirt and black leather boots, especially how she would spin one foot on its stiletto heel. But Lisa was used to her boyfriend, Lars, who had just broken up with her two days ago. With Lars it was obvious when what she was doing was working, because he reciprocated. Chad instead grabbed his DVDs tighter and stared straight ahead, which was too subtle a form of body language for Lisa to translate. Luckily she didn't give up. She turned and put her hand on his arm.

"I got an idea, why don't you come to my apartment and we'll watch them together?"

Chad's eyes lit up—body language Lisa understood.

"Um… yeah, that sounds good."

The elevator opened and she bounced out of it.

"All right, I'll see you in a few hours. Bring a bottle of wine too."

It all happened so fast, but Chad was ecstatic. Who knows if he would've been less ecstatic if he knew that Lisa really wasn't interested in him, but was only using him to get over her boyfriend, Lars. Probably not. Chad's Saturday night went from watching Steven Seagal movies alone to a date with a hot girl from his building that he'd bumped into in the elevator. These kinds of things only happened in movies. Had he not decided on a whim to go get some Red Box DVDs and beer, he never would've seen Lisa. It was fate, like Romantic Comedy style fate.

The turn of events though also meant getting ready. It meant shaving, taking a shower, picking out clothes. He couldn't screw this up. As much as he preferred spending an evening with Lisa to one by himself, it presented a much greater level of stress.

Lisa wasn't feeling any of that stress. All she could think about was Lars, and the last conversation she had had with him a few days before. It was just like Lars too, the way he did it. He came into her apartment, kissed her on the lips, took a beer out of the refrigerator, sat on her couch, put his feet on the coffee table, and turned on the TV, as if nothing were wrong. When she sat next to him and ran her fingers through his Scandinavian blond hair like she always did, he still didn't let on. It wasn't until she mentioned their upcoming weekend getaway that he broke the news.

"I won't be able to see you anymore."

When she first met Lars, she thought everything he ever said with his Swedish accent was sexy. This was the first thing he'd ever said that wasn't. He continued to flip through the channels and drink his beer, as if he'd remarked "let's see what's on *Judge Judy*."

"What? Why? I... I thought you loved me."

"My mother doesn't like you."

Her insides were falling apart, yet at the same time, what he said wasn't entirely real. Especially the reason.

"You're kidding, right?..."

"No. She said you were uncouth, and as you know, if my mother doesn't approve, she can convince my father to take my money away, and there goes the hedge fund. You understand, don't you? It's nothing personal."

She tried to say "what?", but nothing came out, only tears. She realized at that point that she was still running her fingers through his hair, and she pulled them back violently. That made him turn from the TV and look at her.

"What?"

She shook her head and looked away. All she wanted now was for him to leave and not see her crying. This was humiliating enough.

"We've only been dating like two months, it's not like the end of the world."

"I dumped my boyfriend for you. I thought you loved me."

"Well, no one asked you to do that."

"*You* asked me to do that!"

He shrugged his shoulders.

"You told me you loved me!"

"I just thought that's what you Americans do."

She stopped crying for a second.

"You know, you Americans with your 'hi how ya doin'?' to complete strangers who happen to be ringing you out at the store, or how you know someone for five minutes and he's a friend on Facebook. I figured you just said you loved someone all the time."

"Wait, you never loved me?"

"Well, yeah, I loved you..."

She smiled and started breathing easier.

"I mean, girls tell me all the time 'Lars, I love you', and they kiss me on the cheek and put their arm around my shoulder. That's what I thought you meant."

Now she was close to hyperventilating again.

"What are you saying, Lars?"

"This just sounds like a simple cultural misunderstanding. Like the word 'love' was lost in translation."

"You think this is a joke? I gave up everything for you!"

"You dumped a guy you said you didn't really like anymore anyway. What did you give up?"

"Um… but… you took me to meet your parents, why did you do that if it wasn't a big deal?"

"Well, I was with you, and I had to go see them, so I figured we'd go together. But my mom was adamant after that that I shouldn't see you anymore. It seemed rather fortuitous to me that we found this out early on before things became too serious."

She wanted to kick him out, but he even robbed her of that satisfaction by putting his beer down and making his way to the door on his own. She was glued to the couch, her whole body frozen, and all she could do was watch him leave.

Lisa's friends all told her how he was no good and she needed to move on and she was better off without him, but it still hurt. Lars was like no one she'd met before. He was smart, sophisticated, worldly, and amazing in bed. He wasn't like other guys she'd been with, who had never traveled, might have had money but didn't have any taste, and thought sex was supposed to be like a 2-minute porn video they illegally downloaded from the internet when they were 14. Lisa had fallen for Lars, and she had fallen hard, and for him to say he never really loved her hurt more than she could've ever imagined; and to hear that his mom thought she wasn't good enough, made her feel worthless.

The only problem was, Lisa only knew one way to feel better, and that was through the approval of other men—something that dated back to her youth, when she needed to be Daddy's Girl. She played sports, went fishing, and helped him with the yard work. Her father doted on her and she craved his attention and affection. Then when she was about 12 years old, she developed boobs earlier than her classmates, and guys looked at her in a new way before she was old enough to deal with that kind of attention. Her father changed too. He wasn't comfortable with his daughter blossoming into womanhood, and he thought it would be more appropriate for her mother to deal with these things. He turned his attention increasingly to her younger brother, who at ten was now able to play all the sports, fish, and do the yard work Lisa used to do.

It was devastating to see her father become so distant, and she wanted desperately to get that affection and attention back. She stumbled on how one day when she wore a shirt that no longer fit her. It was tight, showed off her stomach, and was tearing a bit at the center of the collar from the pressure of her chest. Her father was livid. Who does she think she is? Didn't her mother see her? You need to go upstairs and change now!

And from there it started. No longer the tom boy playing sports and fishing, she became a real girl. And the guys noticed; and her father noticed that they noticed. Every day was a constant battle between father and daughter, from clothes, to make-up, to boys Now she had his attention, but she found she kept winning these battles because her mother, so excited to finally have a daughter, took up for her, and her father relented. What could Lisa do to up the ante?…

In high school, she found many opportunities to do that. Senior boys with cars and drugs and money were all drawn to her as a freshman in her provocative clothing and flirtatious personality. She had her pick of bad boys, the badder the better, and her parents joined forces in denouncing her behavior, but by then it was too late. The pattern that would mark the rest of her life had begun. Boys and partying and pissing off her parents.

Lars was the first guy to make her want to give that up though. He was the first one who impressed her, the first one who made her feel like he might be The One—and to find out he never even loved her, the first guy she'd ever truly fallen for, because she wasn't good enough, hurt almost as much as her father not wanting to play catch with her because he wasn't mature enough to handle the fact that his daughter had boobs.

And now here was Chad, in her crosshairs as she worked out her heartbreak.

To an outsider, there wasn't much to differentiate Chad's various outfits, but in his mind the light blue, striped Abercrombie button-up shirt he picked was the best out of all the others he owned, because a girl once complimented him on it. The jeans and shoes he picked were also nice, but probably also no nicer than his other jeans or his other shoes, but again, those items were also given the seal of approval by a woman at one time or another, which was a badge of distinction that elevated them in Chad's closet. After looking at himself one last time, he grabbed a bottle of red wine and the DVDs and proceeded to Lisa's apartment.

That Lisa's outfit was very 2002 meant absolutely nothing to Chad. It was probably one of the things that made Lars' mother think she wasn't fit to date her son—that or how "trashy" or "borderline streetwalker" it was—, but Chad was not Lars' mother. The red halter top that seemed like it would fall off her neck was not trashy to Chad—all he could concentrate on was how the light reflected off her bare shoulders, and how delicate she felt when she put her arms around him to hug him hello. The shiny snakeskin print vinyl skirt wasn't borderline streetwalker either—it made his heart stop as he watched her take his bottle of wine into her kitchen. And of course, he recognized the boots from earlier in the elevator.

Her apartment was laid out differently from Chad's. It opened into a small dining area where Lisa had a long dining table with four chairs around it. From there, one could either go straight to the living room, or take a left into the kitchen, which was like a corridor that had the stove and cabinets on the left side, the sink and more cabinets on the right, and then a doorway on the end to the right that also led into the living room.

Chad sat on her couch while she poured them each a glass of wine. Lisa really had no interest in watching Steven Seagal movies, but she put one on and sat right next to Chad, crossing her legs so the end of her boot brushed up against his leg. At first Chad was nervous, but as the wine hit him, he became more confident and assertive.

That's not entirely accurate. Lisa was leading this dance, but she did a great job of letting Chad believe he was in control. He put his arm around her, but he did it after she moved her right shoulder ever so slightly away from the couch, making it only natural for Chad to put his arm around her and she put her shoulder on his chest. They didn't even make it through the first movie before they started making out.

Now this was certainly better than watching Steven Seagal films alone on a Saturday. Stacy who, right? He even forgot about his bald spot. After a few minutes, Chad figured they had made out enough, and it was time to take this to the next level, so he searched through her halter top until he found her boob. He had to make a conscious effort to not be too rough because he wanted it so bad. It didn't matter, though. Lisa pulled away anyway, tears welling up in her eyes.

"I'm sorry, I can't do this."

14

Chad went to protest, but she was too quick for him, and secluded herself in her room, which was through a door on the other side of the living room from the kitchen doorway. He sat on the couch, laid his head back, and sighed. The movie had finished a few minutes before, and was now at the DVD title screen, recycling the same thirty-second music and animation over and over. He looked around her living room for a bit, hoping she'd come right back out. He saw but didn't take in a framed Marilyn Monroe poster on the wall; a bookshelf filled with various Romantic Comedies and Adam Sandler films, topped with pictures of her and her friends from various special nights out or concerts, with similar pictures near the flatscreen TV on the entertainment center; and *Rachel Ray's 30-Minute Meals* cookbook on the coffee table in front of him. Chad didn't pick up on any of these things, even if he looked right at them, because all he could think about was Lisa in the other room.

I guess I should go say something, he thought.

He approached the door like the person in a horror movie inspecting the basement after he'd heard a noise, and the audience, if they could've seen Chad at that moment, would've been calling him stupid for not running away. He knocked.

"Um, Lisa, are you okay?"

He could hear her crying.

"It's just... it's just a headache... I'm sorry... it's that time of the month and stuff... I'm really sorry... maybe we can do this some other time..."

And with that Chad was spending the rest of Saturday alone in his apartment watching Steven Seagal movies, only now he had a severe case of blue balls.

The next day Chad told his neighbor Miguel all about what happened with Lisa. Miguel was in Chad's apartment playing *FIFA '09*, because Miguel's wife, Julía (pronounced with an "H" sound), wouldn't let him play video games in their own apartment. Miguel, Julía, and their 14-year-old son Richard were originally from Peru, and moved here after Miguel's company, which sold produce in the United States, sent him to work with their American buyers.

They met Chad on the day they moved into the building, when they passed him coming back to his place on their way out to eat, and they invited him to join them. Miguel has been playing video games at Chad's ever since.

During that first lunch, at IHOP because it was nearby, "Hold onto the Nights" by Richard Marx was playing above them. Miguel put his arm around his wife, while his son rolled his eyes.

"This is our song."

"Oh, that's cool."

"Yeah, we met at a Richard Marx concert."

"In Peru?"

"Yes *in Peru*. What, you don't think Richard Marx plays concerts in Peru?"

"Geez, I guess I never thought about it."

"Anyway, we were standing near each other during the opening band, The Tubes, you remember them? *She's a beauty...*"

Chad loved the way he sang 80s songs in his Spanish accent. His wife took over the story:

"By the time he played 'Hold On to the Nights', I knew this was the man that I would marry. We named Richard here after him."

15

"After Richard Marx?"

"Uh huh."

They kissed, embarrassing their son. Miguel and Julía were only 36, which was three and a half years older than Chad. The thought of them having a 14-year-old made him feel very old.

"You need to watch out for that Lisa chick."

"I kind of got that impression."

"No no, that's not what I mean. Julía and a couple other women in the building went out with her for a girls' night out or something a few months ago."

"Okay?"

Miguel paused his game.

"I guess Lisa got stupid drunk, and was making out with all sorts of dudes, including this sketchy bald bodybuilder guy that tried to take her home with him. Julía felt bad and didn't want her to get hurt, so she took her back to her apartment and stayed with her there."

"Wow, what a mess."

"Hold on cowboy, I'm not done. So Julía gets her into her pajamas and into her bed, and decides she'll stay for a little while, just to make sure she's all right. She ends up falling asleep on the couch, and wakes up the next morning and picks up her purse to leave—and finds it's full of water."

"What?"

"It gets worse. It wasn't water."

"Oh no…"

"Oh yeah, while Julía was sleeping, Lisa got up and peed in her purse."

"There's no way. You're full of shit."

"Honest to God. It was like pulling teeth to get her to pay for a new phone and everything too. Let's just say it was the last time Julía went out with her."

"How come you never told me this story?"

"Because you never asked."

There was a knock at the door. Richard had been sent over to retrieve his father. Chad went to Miguel before he left for their perfunctory bro-hug.

"Remember man, be careful with that Lisa chick."

Chad went back to being Chad in Accounting that Monday, but all he could think about was Lisa. The way her hair smelled, her lips tasted, her boobs felt. With Stacy no longer there, he had extra work to do, and less brain capacity with which to do it. Tuesday the longing subsided a little, but only until he got home, when he passed Lisa leaving the building, walking arm-in-arm with Lars. Chad had seen Lisa with Lars before, but didn't know who he was. They both said hi to Chad as they passed, but Lisa didn't stop or introduce him.

If he'd had better prospects for women in his life, Chad wouldn't have dwelled on Lisa as much as he did. But he didn't have better prospects, Lisa was the hottest girl that had given him the time of day, let alone made out with him, in a long time. Seeing her in the arms of another man drove home to him just how much he didn't have and how much he wanted and how much guys like Lars got to have. For some reason he didn't think "I used to get girls like that", or "why don't I get girls like that anymore?", which was the truth. Lisa, unlike Stacy, was right around Chad's age, and ten years ago, he would've slept with Lisa in college and probably not even called her after, and now she had him by the balls. Call it karma for how he'd treated women before, but this was the post-Gwen era, and instead of thinking "I used to get girls like Lisa all the time" he thought "why can't I have Lisa?", and he kept thinking it as he thought of how hot she was and flipped through the digital cable guide bar looking for something to watch on TV and unable to settle on anything.

Wednesday evening Lisa showed up at his apartment. It seemed to be apropos of nothing, and Chad should've been at the very least suspicious, but instead had to hide his excitement at her standing in his doorway asking to come in because he didn't want to come off as desperate, especially since he was.

"I wanted to apologize about the other night. Can I come in?"

"Um yeah, sure, come right in."

She was in her gym clothes, which was a sharp contrast to the clothes he was used to seeing her in. The short shorts and tight tank top were still hot, but the sneakers made her lose about three or four inches in height, and those three or four inches took her from almost as tall as Chad in heels to coming up to just below his chin. It made her less intimidating and more diminutive.

"I'm sorry it's such a mess in here."

She plopped herself down on his couch and let out a big sigh to show how tired she was after a long day of work and working out. Chad's apartment wasn't dirty, he was struggling for a conversation starter, and that felt like something he should say.

"No, it's fine, don't worry about it."

"Can I get you something to drink?"

She pulled out her Nalgene bottle from her gym bag.

"No, I can't stay long."

He sat down next to her.

"I'm glad you came. It's really nice to see you again."

"Really?"

At first he felt stupid for being so forward, but she smiled and he knew he'd said the right thing. He leaned in and kissed her and she reciprocated. Then she pulled away.

"Listen, I'm sorry, I really do have to go. But I want to see you again. Give me your number, and maybe we can get together this weekend."

Lisa was all Chad thought about. Every time his phone rang he got excited, and every time he saw it wasn't her he was disappointed. For some reason Chad didn't consider calling or texting her instead. She said she'd call him, he thought, and he left it at that. She didn't call though. Friday night he spent by himself, watching college football on ESPN, and every little move his phone made in his pants made him jump with the thought that it might be a call. So he put it on the table, and every noise he heard made him think it might be a call too.

Saturday Chad decided to accept an invitation from Miguel to watch a football game between his alma mater, Dodge State, and their bitter rivals, Silverman-Moore. Miguel was unfamiliar with the teams, having grown up in Peru, but one of their customers gave him the tickets, and Richard didn't want to go with him. Chad never mentioned Lisa once, but again, kept checking his phone to see if he missed a call. You'd think Chad would've gotten into the game, especially watching DSU beat up on those preppy rich kids, but even that wasn't enough to get Lisa off his mind. He spotted some of his fraternity brothers sitting closer to the field, and thought he recognized Kovacs with them, but wasn't sure. He hadn't spoken to Kovacs in a year anyway, and that was just a quick conversation when they'd bumped into each other in the mall. He'd lost Kovacs in the split, after Dave took Gwen from him, and he was willing to leave it at that.

Miguel knew Chad was preoccupied, and wanted to take his mind off of Lisa.

"Hey, what're you doing this Wednesday?"

"I don't know, why?"

"Well, I was thinking… Julía has this girl she works with, and, I don't know…"

"Dude, no way, the last time you and Julía tried to set me up, it was a disaster."

"What are you talking about?"

"You know exactly what I'm talking about, Pilar, fat, uni-brow."

"Hey, she got that waxed… and some guys like bigger girls."

"Bigger, yes, 300 pounds, no."

"Pilar is not 300 pounds. And it's not like you're so skinny. You were out of breath coming up the stairs to our seats."

"I'm not 300 pounds, dude."

"Neither is *she*."

Chad looked at him.

"All right, but she's lost some weight recently, now she's like 280. Besides, I didn't know we'd already tried to set you up with her."

"Wait, you were trying to set me up with Pilar *again*?"

Miguel shrugged his shoulders, and they both laughed.

Saturday night and all day Sunday passed without a word from Lisa too. If Chad had only known that all he needed to do was call Lisa during that time and she would've seen him. While Chad was thinking about her, Lisa was still thinking about Lars. He had called a few days after her night with Chad. He never said anything about them getting back together, just asked if she was free and he could visit. She knew she shouldn't have let him come, but she did, and they ended up having sex that night, and she called in sick to work the next morning and they had sex all day too. Chad passed them on Tuesday when they were leaving the house to get something to eat. Then Lars left that night and didn't contact her or answer her calls. She went to see Chad because she was upset about Lars, but when he kissed her, it was too much and she had to leave again. Chad reminded her of everything she didn't want in a man: someone who let her lead, let her dictate the terms of the relationship; and reminded her of everything she'd lost in Lars because he wasn't that kind of man—or drove home the increasingly tangible reality that what she'd lost with Lars she'd never really even had. Chad had no idea he'd lost the game before he ever played.

But she needed someone to talk to. All her girlfriends told her was she needed to move on, and she felt like talking meant complaining and they didn't seem sympathetic. Friday night, while Chad was waiting for her to call, she was waiting for Lars to call, but had Chad called, it would have been a welcome reprieve from the hurt she was feeling. On Saturday she went out with her girlfriends and bumped into an old guy friend, went home with him, but couldn't bring herself to have sex with him, and ran out of his apartment crying. She spent all day Sunday in her pajamas watching a marathon of *America's Top Model*.

Lisa and Chad would see each other on Monday, when they happened to be in the elevator again at the same time, and made plans to have supper that night. This time, Lisa's dinner table in between them kept the physical intimacy to a minimum, and with the help of the wine, allowed Lisa to spill her guts to Chad. She went into everything, from how she met Lars, how he was in bed, how she felt about him, and how much of an asshole he was for what he did to her.

Chad didn't know what to do except pretend to listen. Lars was an asshole, not because he broke Lisa's heart, but because he had had sex with her and Chad hadn't. After a certain point, the words disappeared and all he cared about was how sexy she was and how badly he needed to have sex with her. Whenever we spill our hearts to someone, part of us doesn't care if the other person is listening, because to a large extent the catharsis comes just from getting it off our chests; but the other part of us also takes for granted that the person listening is really listening to everything we say. Lisa was no exception. She felt like she'd finally found someone to talk to, a guy no less, and one that she didn't have to sleep with for him to accept her. Lisa had no idea that Chad would've failed a quiz on what she'd just told him, or that he was only sitting there across from her because there was a faint chance he might get sex out of the deal.

At about 9:30 Lisa declared she was tired and sent Chad off with a quick kiss goodnight and a promise that she would see him again sometime that week. Chad felt like he'd laid the foundation for something good. He would be sleeping with Lisa regularly by the end of the week, he thought, and changing that always important Facebook relationship status soon thereafter. He was so happy Tuesday and Wednesday, he was actually glad to be Chad in Accounting and did his work and a good portion of Stacy's. But Thursday he saw Lars leaving from the building and his heart dropped. Miguel was right, Lisa was bad news, but it still hurt.

This was the mindset into which he entered his Friday evening. He hoped to hear from Lisa, but didn't bank on it. His plan was to order some Chinese and play some video games and try to forget about Lisa for a little while, try to get that feeling out of the pit of his stomach. He had just gotten himself settled onto his couch with the Jade Empire take-out menu, when he heard a knock at the door. Could it be? No, it was probably Miguel. When he made it to the door though, he heard teenage girls giggling outside. It was Amy, the girl from down the hall, and from the sound of it, she was with her friend Brittney. He considered not answering, pretending he wasn't at home, but his TV was up too loud, giving him away.

Chad was used to seeing Amy at his place. Her mother was something of a drinker who ran around with various men, and would sometimes kick Amy out of their apartment in order to have her alone time with them, and when this happened, she would visit either him or go to Miguel's where he and Julía would take care of her. The mother also worked odd hours, which meant Amy and Brittney had plenty of time without adult supervision to do whatever their hearts desired—and more often than not they desired to make videos for YouTube.

Chad assumed correctly that this was what they were up to, seeing them wearing dark, sequined leotards and black tights, with tons of make-up on, and Brittney toting a portable CD player. Chad never knew where they found their costumes and props for all these performances, but for some reason he never questioned it either, just accepted that they had whatever they needed, as if they were cartoon characters making items materialize out of thin air. What he questioned, rather, was why the girls would come to Chad for his opinions on their acts at all, because, without fail, he always told them they were great. The whole thing seemed pointless to him, but he humored them anyway to be nice. He didn't know Amy had a crush on him, and spent a long time making herself look attractive for these performances in an effort to impress him.

"Hey Chad, whatcha doin'?" Amy asked.

"I was about to order some Chinese. Should I even ask?..."

They giggled.

"We wanted to show you the thing we made up. We're gonna put it on YouTube later."

"Will we need a lot of room?"

More giggling.

"No, we'll just do it right here. You sit on the couch."

"Right here" was the area just off from the living room almost into the kitchen, not far from the doorway they were just standing in. The couch was perpendicular to them, and Chad had to sit on the edge and turn his torso so he was leaning over the arm in order to face the show. Having performed for him plenty of times before, the girls knew where the dimmer was, and Chad muted the TV. Brittney put the portable CD player on the ground in front of them.

"Are you ready?"

"Uh huh."

More giggling.

Chad was expecting a current pop song, maybe by Rhianna or Jordan Sparks, but the opening told him something different, like early 90s Freestyle. What? And he kind of recognized it. Was this Exposé? As the girls acted out their choreographed moves to the lyrics, Chad was trying to pull from his memory what the song was. Then the chorus came:

I wish the phone would ring...

Oh my God, he thought, when is this song from? 1990 or something? He did the math out. I know I was in high school. He almost wasn't paying attention to the girls, but by how intently he was thinking, they thought he was really into it, which made them a little self-conscious and miss some of their moves. Had Chad been alone, he probably would've sung along, but with the girls there he was too embarrassed.

The song faded out, and Chad stood and applauded them, to which they bowed.

"Did you like it? It needs a lot of work."

"No, it was great. Where... where did you get that CD?"

"Oh, this?" Amy asked the question, but Brittney handed him the case.

"What, there wasn't any Wilson Phillips around?"

It was easily the best joke Chad in Accounting had told in maybe two months, and it was completely lost on its audience. He inspected the case, looking first for the date—1992, wow, he was like a sophomore then—and then for any other songs he recognized. No "Seasons Change," no "Come Go With Me." Those must've been an earlier album. Wait, here's one, "I'll Never Get Over You Getting Over Me." Winter Formal, junior year. Of course, 1976 to 1992, sixteen years, he was a junior then—or was he a sophomore? He and Julie Sludowski slow danced to that song. Those were the days, it was so much easier then. All you worried about was bad breath or sweaty armpits, or maybe a big zit. It was a matter of finding a girl who was cute enough and without a date. There was Julie Sludowski, he knew her from Track, he asked her to dance, and she said yes.

Chad was telling the girls about his school dance.

"Julie Sludowski? Was she cute?"

"She was okay…"

They played the song. Chad had forgotten how cheesy it was, but it still had the ability to bring him back to that moment, or those days. The girls were slow dancing in front of him. Amy went to dip Brittney, and dropped her on the floor, which led to the girls laughing hysterically. He shook his head and smiled and helped them up.

"What are you girls doing tonight? Is your mom working Amy?"

"She's out at the bars. We're going to go to Brit's in a little while. Her mom's coming to get us."

There was a part of Chad that considered asking the girls if they wanted to stay for Chinese with him, but there was a bigger part of him that didn't feel right spending too much of his Friday evening with two 15-year-olds, especially after what happened with MacKenzie. He hit the mute button to turn the sound back on on the TV after they left, and the volume reminded him that he had originally wanted to feign absence when the girls had knocked. Now he was happy for the brief respite that visit had given him from obsessing over Lisa, even if that respite came with "I Wish the Phone Would Ring" stuck in his head.

Then he got a call on Saturday night at 2AM that he didn't see coming. It was Lisa's number, but one of her friends was on the other line. He muted the rerun of *Cheaters* he was watching.

"She's a mess right now, and she said earlier in the night that you were a nice guy, so you think you could take care of her? We're in her apartment."

This excited Chad. Not that he would be taking advantage of Lisa in her inebriated state, but that he could take care of her and she'd see him as the rock in her life, the guy she could turn to when things were bad—and eventually have sex with.

When he got there, the friends were right, she was a mess. They left the moment they saw him, like a security guard whose shift had ended ten minutes ago, and the person relieving him had shown up late. Lisa was sitting on the edge of her bed, leaned over to the right side, with her face buried down in her blankets. Instead of the red halter top and snakeskin print skirt he saw her in two weeks before, it was a shiny silver halter top and black mini skirt. Her boots were off and on the floor, one of them lying out flat, while the other kind of resembled the position Lisa was sitting in, with the bottom of the boot upright, and the top part that would've gone up her leg folded over and onto the carpet.

Chad put his hand on her back, asked her tenderly how she was, and she groaned. He picked up her legs and swung them onto the bed to get her into a lying position, and covered her in a blanket. He told her he'd be in the other room watching TV if she needed him, and she groaned again.

Chad was elated. Not only had she told her friends about him, but she said such nice things that her friends called him when they needed someone for her to turn to. They'd be having sex in no time. What Chad didn't know was that Lisa was an emotional mess the whole night, which her friends chalked up to her being a drama queen, and she told them something to the affect that at least Chad listened to her, and they asked who Chad was, so she told them about Monday night. Chad also didn't know that he was the third of four Chads in her phone her friends tried before they found him. Anyway, it probably wouldn't have mattered.

What happened next did matter, though. About an hour after he'd been there, Chad heard music in the other room. It sounded like a girl's voice, and he kind of recognized it as a pop song from a few years ago. He went to check on her, but stopped when she came out of her room, completely naked. Chad wasn't sure if he should look or not. Lisa didn't acknowledge him, though, she just found her purse, opened it up, and squatted down over it.

The music was louder with her door opened. He finally recognized the song as Ashley Simpson's "Pieces of Me".

Right after Chad graduated from college, he had an apartment with Dave and Kovacs, and Kovacs would do something similar. After a long night of drinking, he'd try to piss in the closet or the refrigerator, and Chad would have to grab him and direct him toward the bathroom. One weekend away he came home to find the papasan smelled like urine because Chad hadn't been there to prevent the damage. Instead of taking Lisa by the arm like he did Kovacs and directing her to the bathroom, he sat and watched. It wasn't for any kind of perverted reason, he was in shock—plus, he realized at that moment that he didn't even know where the bathroom was in Lisa's apartment anyway. After she was done she went back to her room, and Chad decided that was as good as any time to make his exit.

This wasn't a deal breaker for Chad, but Lisa didn't know that because Chad didn't call her. When she found out what she had done the next morning, she was a little embarrassed; but when she found out from her friends that they had called Chad to babysit her, she was mortified. She was too afraid to call him again, and she thought she knew why he wasn't calling her. Had Chad just called Lisa and told her that what she did wasn't a problem for him, it wouldn't have mattered to her that the only reason why it didn't matter to him was that she was the hottest chick to give him the time of day in a while, so urinating in her purse in front of him with no clothes on was something he could overlook. But he didn't make that call, because he figured if she liked him she'd call him, so they spent the rest of their time in the building together exchanging awkward hellos when they passed each other in the hallway.

The Two Haleys

Chad's parents split when he was 8 and his brother Steve was 6. He had always taken his mom's side in his parents' estrangement, until events in his own life caused him to be more sympathetic with his father's position. A child compares his stern, martial father to his more free-spirited mom, and the decision's easy. An adult who catches the woman he loves and planned to spend his entire life with in bed with one of his best friends, isn't so hard on that father who caught his wife and mother of his two children in bed with his brigade's staff sergeant.

The relationship between Chad's mother and the man she was having an affair with didn't last, and she took her children from where they were stationed in Germany back to her hometown, which is roughly where Chad has lived ever since. She got a job as a paralegal, took the LSATs, went to law school at Dodge State, and became a family law attorney. Throughout this process, she didn't get the support from her family that she was hoping for. Luckily, the older residents in their new neighborhood were much more sympathetic and willing to help out. Foremost among them, Mr. and Mrs. Haley.

Mr. and Mrs. Haley lived right next door. Mrs. Haley was a housewife, and Mr. Haley was a retired civil engineer and World War II vet. They were more like grandparents to Chad and Steve than their real ones were. They took them to Little League games, Mr. Haley helped with Cub Scouts and school projects, and Mrs. Haley would send over dinner on the nights their mother couldn't get home from class or out of work on time.

In college, Chad saw less of the Haleys, pretty much only here and there on his breaks or occasional trips home to do laundry. After graduation when he moved out for good, it was even less, and in the last five years, when he was wallowing in the devastation of Gwen's betrayal, he saw them almost not at all. He didn't really feel too badly about this—or rather, didn't even think about it all—until his mother called him recently to say that Mr. Haley had become very ill, and they didn't know how much time he had left. She wanted him to come home and see him, and he said he would, but then the whole Lisa thing sprang up, and he forgot all about it.

They finally, after over a month, hired a replacement for Stacy. Her name was Haley, which should've been a reminder to Chad in Accounting that he needed to go home and see *Mr. Haley*, but it wasn't. He was too preoccupied with figuring out whether Haley was hot or not. She had light brown hair, almost blond, but not a lot of attention had been paid to it other than it being washed and brushed out. She was thin and attractive, but her outfit wasn't overly flashy, just a long tan skirt, blue tank top, and sandals that were slightly dressier than flip-flops. The face was the most fascinating: almost no make-up at all, but instead of looking pale, she looked clean and natural. It was pretty in a way that was very unfamiliar to him.

Haley exuded this strong, positive energy that everyone noticed right away. She smiled a lot, and when she wasn't smiling, she was looking concerned and genuinely interested in something someone was telling her—like when she asked Chad about the small shiner under his eye he'd received from Todd. It annoyed Chad a little to see her give their supervisor that kind of attention as he explained her job duties to her, but it was very refreshing when she treated him the same way whenever she had a question and their supervisor wasn't nearby. How could someone be so happy? And when he helped her with logging into her computer after the screensaver activated, she was more grateful than he could remember himself being grateful for anything in a long time.

Haley was simply Haley, not Haley in Accounting the way Chad was Chad in Accounting or his supervisor was his supervisor or Jared with the Hyphenated Last Name in HR was Jared with the Hyphenated Last Name in HR; but this wasn't why Chad found himself drawn to her. His eyes were adjusting to Haley's initial unique beauty, and he found elements he recognized in all the other women he found attractive. She had a nice rack, and cleavage was cleavage no matter how much make-up a woman wore. Her hair smelled amazing when he stood next to her to resolve her computer issues; again, very clean and feminine, and intoxicating. Then there were her lips and the way she sucked on the back end of her pen while engrossed in her work. Chad could get used to this.

Of course, it was a no-brainer when Haley asked him if he'd like to join her for lunch, even if he'd packed his lunch that day. Based on her outward appearance and attitude, he expected her to take him to some exotic ethnic restaurant or some vegan, organic food truck downtown or something. She had been craving Applebee's nachos, though, so they went a couple miles down the strip to the one near the mall.

They got the preliminaries out of the way over her water with lemon and his Sprite. Haley was 26, grew up two towns over from him, and had just moved back home after living in LA for the past three years.

"What were you doing out there?"

"I was an accountant for *Love Shack*."

"*Love Shack*? No way!"

Love Shack was a popular reality show where four girls and three guys lived together in a big mansion and behaved in ways that made their parents cringe. Chad wasn't a devoted follower, but he knew about it and had watched it from time to time.

"Yeah, it was a blast."

"Why would you ever leave that?"

She paused, and Chad understood that he may have said something he shouldn't have. It was the first time he'd seen any distress on her face all morning.

"Well... I might as well just tell you... my fiancé was one of the producers, and he had... relations with one of the contestants..."

"Oh no... wait, was he...?"

"Yep, he was the one..."

Chad was star-struck. Haley was linked to one of the greatest scandals in reality show history. Her boyfriend, whom no one ever saw on TV, was caught having an affair with Sebastian, one of the guy contestants, who was supposed to be hooking up with all the women.

Chad's excitement evaporated, though, when he saw Haley start to tear up and go to her napkin. It was very unlike him, but something in Haley made him reach for her.

"I know how you feel, Haley… I mean, I don't know know, but I know… I mean," he stopped. "I caught my girlfriend cheating on me too. Five years ago."

"Really?"

He nodded. Haley had been thinking maybe she'd given too much information on a first lunch with a coworker, but now she felt good at getting it out and having Chad as someone who at the very least understood the betrayal she'd endured. From there the mood lightened up and Haley turned back into the person Chad had gotten used to that morning. They talked about everything, from their local school rivalries—she went to hated Silverman-Moore—to hobbies, to the ins and outs of their place of work. Haley told him all about her new life with her family too, about how she'd missed the birth of her sister's baby two months ago, but now, staying with her mom, she's been a bigger part of her niece's life, and how much fun that's been. As much as she was hurting by what happened with her ex, she seemed even more excited about the new opportunities her life without him could give her. It might have been a good example for Chad, who looked at his split with Gwen as the end of the world, and still hadn't recovered five years later, but he was too preoccupied with making a good impression and getting an "in" with Haley as a potential mate.

As the rest of his first week with her went on, he wasn't the only person positively affected by her presence. The women loved how she complimented their hair or their shoes or their outfits. They also didn't see her as threatening because her more natural and understated appearance made her seem less "slutty." The guys didn't find her threatening either, in part because of her looks, but also because Chad, Stacy, and their supervisor had had a tendency to be less pleasant. When they handed in expense reports or other papers that would mean more work for Accounting, instead of being met with disdain, they now had Haley happy to see them, and in turn, Chad and his supervisor became happier too, because they saw quickly how far it got Haley.

But it was with Chad that Haley was becoming closest to, at least in her mind. She felt he alone best understood what she'd been through, and the process she was going through to get past that. Chad, though, looked at all the attention she was getting from everyone else, and, as usual, assumed erroneously that he was losing ground in her world. He thought for sure when Jared with the Hyphenated Last Name in HR started putting the moves on her that he'd be on the outs. Jared with the Hyphenated Last Name in HR was everything Chad thought was important: smooth, good looking, confident, former back-up quarterback on the DSU football team. After Jared had spent a good deal of the day chatting it up with Haley, Chad went home that night despondent. Why was he having so much bad luck with women?

Haley and he had talked about so many things during that first lunch at Applebee's that Chad couldn't possibly have remembered them all, especially since he was only saying he liked her hobbies to endear himself to her. One of the things he said in passing was that he enjoyed hiking. This wasn't entirely false. He did like to walk out in the woods, he just hadn't done so in a long time. Haley, though, upon hearing this, thought she had a potential peak bagging buddy, someone to really share the outdoors with. That Thursday morning, as Chad was still apprehensive about Jared, she approached him, as energetic as ever.

"What are you doing this Saturday?"

"Um… I don't really have anything going on, why, what's up?"

Yes, take that Jared.

"Well, I looked at the weather, and it's supposed to be unseasonably warm in the mountains this weekend. I was thinking I might hit Mt. Birnbaum. What do you say, you in?"

"Um… yeah, sure."

"Have you hiked it before?"

"No."

"Oh, this'll be great then. Have you done any of the Fifty Fivers?"

"What?"

"You know, the 50 mountains over 5,000 feet in the state. It's 51 actually, but 'fifty fivers' sounds better."

"Um, I did Mt. Minor back in college."

"Okay, that's only 2,000 feet, but that's cool. I know it has a *nice* view."

"How tall is Birnbaum then?"

"6,288 feet."

"Oh wow."

"Do you think you can handle it? If you want, we can always get together and do something else when I get back."

"Oh no I'll be fine. I'm a little out of shape, but not too bad."

Chad didn't know it, but Haley had seen this situation before. People who thought they hiked didn't have any idea of what hiking really was to her. This wasn't just a walk in the woods, this was some serious uphill, and not a lot of fun if one wasn't ready for it. Chad was too worried about missing his opportunity to have a solid "in" with Haley to be worried about what hiking Birnbaum entailed, especially since she was asking him and not Jared from HR. No, he was going to conquer that mountain.

Friday, Chad's mother called and insisted that he come and see Mr. Haley. He needed to be up at 5:30 for his hike with Haley the next morning, but he knew the tone in his mother's voice meant she was telling him, not asking him, to come. It wasn't that he didn't want to see Mr. Haley, the whole thing just felt so awkward, and he didn't have the energy for awkwardness. He felt guilty for not having gone sooner, and didn't really have a logical reason for not having gone sooner other than that guilt.

Mr. Haley was back at his home now, the doctors deciding that would be more comfortable for him. Chad met his mother at their house first before going over. Steve was already there, as he had been seeing Mr. Haley quite regularly, even before his illness. Steve was always the better son, and it made Chad feel that much guiltier.

Ingmar Bergman's films weren't exactly Chad's first idea of quality viewing, so he wouldn't get the metaphor of him looking like a young Alexander afraid of getting too close to his father on his death bed, but anyone who has seen *Fanny and Alexander* would make the connection, and probably wonder to themselves if Chad was going to run and hide in the corner upon touching Mr. Haley's hand. But he made it, the 32-year-old Chad beat out the 11-year-old one, if only barely. His voice cracked initially when he said hello. He caught himself before he asked "how're you doin'?" He could barely hear Mr. Haley ask him how things had been.

He didn't recognize the frail man on the bed in front of him. It had been too long for him to feel the connection, and there was more of him that wanted to be free of the awkwardness than there was of him that wanted to stay and see the man who had had a substantial hand in raising him lying on his deathbed. Then Mr. Haley asked, still barely audibly, if Chad still had that old glove he had given him when he played Babe Ruth. Chad nodded. Mr. Haley's eyes welled up with tears, and he managed to choke out that Chad had grown into a fine man. This finally drove home to Chad how emotional and final this situation was. It didn't drive home how silly he'd been in not visiting for over five years, or not coming sooner when he found out Mr. Haley was sick, but at least it made him feel something, and he had trouble saying thank you with the lump in his throat.

They left Mr. and Mrs. Haley to get some rest and went back to his mother's, where she went to bed too and left Chad and Steve at the kitchen table to have a beer.

"I was going to go hiking tomorrow morning, but maybe I should cancel..."

"No, you're fine. Mom and I'll be here. Where are you going hiking?"

"Mt. Birnbaum."

His brother did one of those slight moves of the head back, almost like a cobra, combined with raised eyebrows that we use to denote a "wow".

"That ought to be fun. I haven't done that one in years. You gonna go up Bear's Head?"

"I have no idea, this girl that just started at work is taking me."

"Oh yeah?"

"Her name's Haley... oh, get this, her fiancé was the staffer that hooked up with Sebastian on *Love Shack*."

"No way! Oh man, I can't wait to tell Sara that, she'll die. Wow... is she cute?"

"Yeah, she's not bad..."

His brother smiled and took a sip off his beer. Chad didn't know that Steve, their mother, and Steve's wife Sara, all discussed how much they wished Chad could find a new girl and get over Gwen. Chad assumed his brother's smile was your run-of-the-mill guys talking about chicks smile, or an excited his brother was seeing a quasi-celebrity smile, but it was his brother's holding-out-hope that Chad's finally moving on smile.

"How have you been?" Chad asked.

Steve shrugged his shoulders.

"Same old same old. I gotta go down to the VA on Monday, get the ol' peg leg looked at, maybe get a better one that's even more like a real leg."

Chad always felt awkward when Steve discussed his missing leg, especially when he joked about it.

"Did you get GI Bill money to go to that culinary arts program?"

"Yeah, so that will be good. It was funny, the other day in class, one of the chefs was talking about how stressful it was working the line at some greasy dive joint he worked at, and how none of us could handle that. So I asked him how he might handle having your convoy being shot at after the front car detonated an IED. He just shut up." He took another sip off his beer and finished it. "I don't know why I get a kick out being an asshole like that." He stood and put on his coat, which was draped over the back of his chair. "All right, I gotta get back and help Sara get the kids to bed. It was good seeing you."

"Good seeing you too."

27

"Have fun tomorrow. And give me a call sometime and we'll go out and get a beer."

He didn't get back too late to get a full 8 hours of sleep, but 5:30AM on a Saturday is early no matter how much sleep one gets. And Haley was there knocking on his door promptly at 6. He opened it to find Miguel out there with her, the two of them speaking in Spanish. They stopped when they saw him.

"Miguel, what are you doing up so early?"

"I'm going to hike a mountain with you guys." Haley laughed. "No, I'm just kidding. Julía's sister is flying in, and I gotta get her at the airport."

He said something else in Spanish to Haley, then hit Chad on the stomach. Haley laughed again, and responded:

"We'll see what happens."

It was a two-hour drive to the mountain in Haley's almost brand new blue Ford Fiesta Hybrid. Chad was in no shape to make small talk. She asked if he'd been out partying last night, and he told her about Mr. Haley. He told her everything, about his mom cheating on his dad, moving next door to the Haleys, and how important a part they were in he and Steve's lives. Haley was genuinely interested. She wanted to learn more about Chad, and Chad being tired and not able to focus or not having the energy to get into things further, made him more mysterious and intriguing to her, like he had some big secrets he was hiding that she wanted to work to uncover.

They stopped at a McDonald's in the ski resort town ten miles out from their destination. Chad didn't really care for McDonald's, and didn't know why Haley, who was all about hiking and the outdoors, would want to eat here either. Then he saw what she was ordering.

"All right, let me get the Number 4... um... oh, with a coffee, cream and extra sugar... um... two breakfast burritos... and an extra hash brown."

"Will that be all?"

Chad couldn't believe it. He was used to women watching what they ate; and it wasn't like Haley was fat by any means. How did she stay skinny eating all that?

"What can we get you, sir?"

"Um... I'll just have two hash browns."

"Are you insane? He'll get a Number Four as well."

"I'm really not all that hungry."

"Would you like coffee or orange juice?"

"What do you want Chad?"

"I... I just want the hash browns..."

"No, you need more calories than that. We're doing 4,300 feet of elevation in 4 and ½ miles. This isn't going to be your morning run, and I'm not carrying your ass down the mountain if you can't make it. You know what, add on a breakfast burrito while you're at it."

Doubt crept in after the McDonald's incident. Maybe he had made a mistake. But Haley didn't look like much of a house. If she could make it up, so could he, right? And he'd heard about people hiking Mt. Birnbaum all the time... though when he really thought about it, they drove the toll road to the top instead of actually hiking it.

It was too late to back out now. As they pulled into the parking lot, Haley remarked that they had made it before the Weekend Warriors. That made Chad even more apprehensive. Haley changed her sneakers for hiking boots, which had Chad questioning his own footwear, even though his sneakers were all he had for something like this. He got out and put his backpack on his shoulders.

"What do you have in that?"

"Huh?"

"In your backpack. What's in there?"

"Some water, food, a coat, hat, sunblock, insect repellent…"

"Leave it. I have all the water and food we'll need 'til we get to the summit, and then we can get more water there. Put the sunblock on now, and then leave it in the car with everything else."

"What? Won't I need it?"

"I have everything we need. You can throw your coat in my bag in case it's windy on the summit."

"Don't you want me to carry something?"

"Nope. Believe me, it'll be a lot easier if I just take it."

Her pack that had everything they needed wasn't that heavy—lighter than Chad's, in fact. It wasn't Chad's macho and chivalrous side that made the thought of her carrying everything on her own anathema, it was more the idea of people on the trail seeing her burdened with all of their stuff on her back and him bouncing up the trail completely unencumbered. If Chad only knew.

The smell of nature in the air was the only thing Chad recognized between this hike and the less strenuous hikes he'd done in the past. Within 15 minutes he wanted to say Uncle. His legs were a mess, he was completely out of breath. How much more did he have to go? How long till it leveled off? He stopped.

Haley planned on him having trouble from the moment they talked at work. She decided after their conversation that she liked the idea of hiking with someone, Chad in particular, over going it alone, even if it meant taking twice as long. Chad didn't know that, and thought he was losing face. He considered feigning an injury.

"Here, have some water. We have all day, so don't worry if you need to stop."

"I don't know if I can make it."

He had trouble talking while he caught his breath and drank from her Nalgene bottle.

"We just started. Believe me, you'll find you have reserves in there you didn't know about. Man, when I did Aconcagua…"

They slogged on. The late-coming Weekend Warriors were passing them, which wasn't as much embarrassing as it was a welcomed respite because he would have to stop and move to the side of the trail so they could fit by. He didn't even have the energy to care when they threw the occasional digs in about him not carrying a pack. Haley made it worse by not being exasperated with him. She was in perfect shape, and could've probably hiked up and down and up again before most of these Weekend Warriors reached the summit, but it didn't anger her to have them passing her in droves. She was enjoying giving this experience to Chad, and by going as slowly as they were, she was able to see things she often missed, liked frogs or weird foliage.

"Look at that tree growing out of this boulder," she'd say, but Chad was so exhausted he could only pretend to notice and utter a barely audible "that's neat."

That was the craziest aspect, to be so winded going uphill that he couldn't speak, that every word felt like he was using priceless energy. In contrast, here was Haley chatting away telling him about something her niece did, or something that happened on the set of *Love Shack*, or more often than not, an anecdote about her trip to Aconcagua. Chad had no fucking idea what an "Aconcagua" was, or why it was such a big deal, or why she kept on bringing it up. On and on, "when I did Aconcagua" this or "on Aconcagua" that. Couldn't she see he was dying here? Didn't she care? He'd had it. He didn't want to be here anymore.

Haley was telling Chad about a big moment in her life. Hiking was a major passion for her, and Aconcagua was one of her proudest achievements, but like a lot of her hiking achievements, they were somewhat bittersweet, because she experienced them with her ex-fiancé. She fell in love with him doing the Fifty Fivers while they both attended Silverman-Moore, and she moved out to LA with him so he could pursue his dreams of working in the entertainment industry, a dream that for him truly reached fruition when he got the job as a producer for *Love Shack*. They planned the Aconcagua trip as a Christmas present to each other to celebrate. She had never been so happy, but it wasn't until after that she realized outside of the hiking, all of her happiness was for his life, not hers. She took a job as an accountant with *Love Shack* to support *him*. What did *she* want to do with *her* life? To that point being his wife would've been enough, and on the drive back from LA in her new Fiesta she understood that whether he was gay or not, whether their relationship had worked or not, living entirely for someone else's dreams should never be enough. It was time to figure out what she wanted out of life, and she was excited for the journey. She did have one thing to hang her hat on for their time together: the hiking, and even though she did that with him, they were still her achievements and her struggles and her rewards. Aconcagua and Rainier and Whitney and the Grand Tetons and all the state high points and 14ers in Colorado and California—all of it was hers, not theirs, and it would still make her happy, even if the memories were with him.

But it wasn't making Chad happy. He slipped while ascending a rockier part of the trail and landed on his hands. Haley came down to him.

"Are you okay?"

"No. I can't do this. We need to go back."

"You *can* do this. We've only been out here like an hour."

"And how much more is there?"

"At this pace? Probably another three."

"And it's all like this?"

"Well, some of it's easier, and some of it's hard, but yeah, we still have some elevation to go. Let's take a break and get some water."

Chad was getting fed up.

"I can't do it. I'm not in shape enough."

"You really wanna bag out?"

"I'm sorry, I know you really wanted—"

"Oh, I'm summiting today no matter what. That's what I came out here for. If you really don't think you can make it, you can head down and hang out at the visitor's center and wait for me. They have a café and an arcade and a gift shop for the Weekend Warriors."

Chad was puzzled. He thought about how far they had already gone, which in reality wasn't far, but having been at it for an hour, it seemed further. He thought about hiking that by himself. He didn't think about being a quitter or what Haley would think of him bagging out or potentially losing her to Jared with the Hyphenated Last Name in HR. It was the hiking by himself that decided it for him. But he also felt betrayed. He never expected Haley to go on without him. With every successive steep pitch or collection of rocks, he resented her more.

Haley was spot on in her prediction of three more hours to the summit. It was long and grueling and emotionally draining, but when Chad got there, he understood a little why Haley had this as her hobby. The whole time they were on the summit, though, taking pictures and admiring the view, Chad knew they still had to traverse that whole length back down. His day was far from over.

And Haley was as happy as ever. You gotta see this, you gotta do that. Look, they have a Post Office up here, you can send a postcard. Chad just wanted to get back down. They needed to eat, and went to a little cafeteria area filled with Weekend Warriors. Chad wasn't hungry. It doesn't matter, you won't make it back down if you don't eat. Chad let out a huge, sulky sigh, like an angry teenager.

"Look Chad, I know you're exhausted and this took a lot out of you, but you did it. Look at all those Weekend Warriors that drove up at the summit sign taking pictures. You made it, and you did something today that none of those people can say they did. You earned the right to stand next to that sign and have your picture taken, and no one can take it away, no matter how long it took you... who knows, maybe this'll be the start of a long hiking career."

"Oh Christ no, I'm never doing anything like this again."

Haley frowned. She had incorrectly assumed that Chad's negative attitude would evaporate the moment he achieved his goal. She wouldn't let him ruin her day, though. Chad didn't know that his sulking for Haley was in the context of her convincing herself that all of her hiking achievements were hers and it didn't matter who was with her. She was determined to take ownership of this experience, which made her defensive.

"Chad, when was the last time you *pushed yourself*?"

"What?... I don't know..."

He went from sulking to feeling inferior—no, worthless might be a better word, or maybe somewhere between the two. Here was Haley, who had hiked all over the world and was carrying all of his stuff up this mountain, and he'd barely made it, or rather, if he'd had his way, he wouldn't have made it. No, he hadn't pushed himself since playing soccer in high school, or maybe intramurals for the fraternity team in college—but he was young then and full of energy, he never felt like this.

Haley saw how this distressed him and she wished she hadn't said anything.

"I'm sorry Chad, all I was saying is, you just did something you should be proud of, instead of sulking and focusing on the negative."

"But we still have all that way to go down."

She laughed.

"It's always easier going down. Gravity helps out."

"I just... I feel like you did all the work, carrying everything. Like I didn't do anything."

"I've been hiking a lot longer than you. It's nothing to be ashamed of. Don't worry about all those Weekend Warriors asking where your pack is. They don't know anything about hiking."

"I didn't ruin your day by sucking so bad?"

She laughed harder.

"I would never let *you* or anyone else ruin my day."

Mr. Haley passed away the next evening. Chad was there, but his whole body was as stiff as board. He couldn't remember ever feeling that kind of pain in his muscles. Every trip up or down a flight of stairs was a potential disaster. When Steve asked how things went, he still felt guilty and embarrassed about Haley carrying all of their stuff and how difficult he made things, so he didn't say much, which made Steve think he was being modest about the accomplishment.

There wasn't much else that any of them could do, because Mrs. Haley's family was taking care of it, so Chad went home to lie down. The moment he hit the couch, though, there was a knock at the door. Chad had forgotten that Miguel was coming by to watch some Serie A, with Peruvian national Juan Manuel Vargas playing for Fiorentina against Roma. He had set the game to DVR on Chad's TV two weeks ago. Miguel came bearing gifts too: some of Julía's world famous ceviche. Chad took a fork and ate it right out of the Tupperware.

"How you feelin' buddy?"

"I don't know if I've ever been so stiff."

"Ha HA! Oh, I'm so sorry my friend. Did you make it the whole way?"

"Oh yeah, though I wanted to quit."

"Yeah?..."

"Yeah, Haley told me if I did, I'd have to go down on my own though, so I decided to gut it out."

Miguel was getting a big kick out of it. He was a little overweight like Chad, but the extra pounds suited him better, especially in his face when he laughed, giving him a cherubic quality that made the laughter infectious, which forced Chad to laugh with him, even if Miguel was laughing at him.

After the game went through the starting line-ups, and Miguel was satisfied that Vargas was playing in his more suited position out on the left wing, as opposed to left back, they fell into a conversation about where Chad was all day, and Mr. Haley passing away, and then Miguel complaining about what it was like having his sister-in-law there. Then Miguel brought up Haley again.

"She's quite the girl, huh? You better not screw that one up."

Chad wasn't so sure. The whole hiking thing didn't feel right, made her less attractive.

"And can you believe she hiked Aconcagua?"

"How long were you outside my door?"

"Only a few minutes. I asked about if she'd done Aconcagua, kind of showing off, you know, and she put me right in my place."

"What, is that mountain some kind of a big deal?"

"Some kind of a big deal?— Oh my God! Hit that! Hit that! Yes!" Fiorentina scored on a header right before half-time. Miguel stood next to the TV pointing at the screen. "Watch this cross! Watch this cross! Boom! On a line right on his head! Whoo!"

He sat back down on the recliner and did a few more fist pumps. What had happened was his countryman, Señor Vargas, at a full sprint with the ball on the left hand side of the field, in one motion sent it into the box, over the defenders, and right into striker Alberto Gilardino's path, from which he redirected it with his head past the keeper. Chad was unfamiliar with Italian soccer, preferring the English Premier League.

"Oh my God that was awesome," he took a deep breath, "okay, where was I? Oh yeah, Aconcagua. You've never heard of Aconcagua?"

"Should I have?"

"It's the biggest mountain in South America, and the biggest mountain in the world not in Asia."

"And you've hiked it?"

"Oh yeah, a long time ago, of course. Back when I was in school, my friends and I used to go on road trips all the time—when we probably should've been studying. It was a different place back then. Someone told me they have Internet access at Plaza de Mulas now, can you believe that?"

Chad could believe that, because none of what Miguel was talking about made any sense. It added to Chad's disillusionment, though. Instead of looking at the Mt. Birnbaum experience as a positive, he focused on how poorly he did, and looked at Haley, and now Miguel, as these people who had experienced so much in their lives while he had done relatively nothing. Instead of wanting to know more about Aconcagua, and through Miguel's story, more about Miguel, he was envious of these people he knew who had so much more to hang their hats on. In fact, Chad didn't know much about Miguel beyond the fact that both of his parents were doctors in Lima. He didn't know that Miguel spoke English so well because his parents had had him sit with English tutors from the time he was five. Or that he spoke French, Italian, and Portuguese in addition to Spanish and English. Or that he was a very bad student who never really took school or a career seriously until he met Julía. He also didn't know that Miguel had been to every country in North, Central, and South America except for some of the islands in the West Indies—and Greenland of course, he always joked when he and Julía were among friends that their next family vacation was going to be to Greenland so he can scratch that off the list.

Chad didn't know any of these things about Miguel because he never asked or tried to get to know him better beyond watching soccer games on the Fox Soccer Channel and playing *FIFA '09*.

On Monday Haley didn't seem like herself. She was very melancholy, and didn't smile or exude any of her positive energy. Chad being Chad chalked it up to her being unhappy with him for their hike on Saturday, but when she ran away from her desk crying, something told him that wasn't it. He considered going after her, but three or four of his female coworkers from other departments were way ahead of him.

Haley was upset, because the evening before, around the same time Mr. Haley passed away, her niece had been dropped on her head by the baby's father, and was pronounced dead at the hospital. Of course, there was no way for Chad to know this. There was also no way for him to know that out of everyone they worked with, it was him she wanted with her at that moment most, not the three or four women who beat him to her.

One of those women came by about fifteen minutes later and took her purse from off her desk. Chad didn't ask her what was wrong. Without Haley there, his work day went back to normal, or rather, the dismal environment he was used to prior to her arrival last week. When he got home that night, he decided on a whim to text her and ask if she was all right. She called two minutes later and told him everything. He didn't know what to do, what to say. What is the right thing to say when something like that happens? I'm sorry was all he could think of. Haley just wanted him to listen, because in her mind, he alone understood what she'd been through, from her fiancé cheating, to how excited she had been to spend time with her niece; and in her defense, Chad should've understood, but he had no idea how to connect those dots. He had a niece and nephew of his own, but only ever saw them on holidays. If one died, it would be tragic, but he didn't know them like she knew her niece, and never would've considered them as a potential means to help get over his heartbreak. Chad couldn't understand that that wasn't the point, in large part, because he had never really listened to anything Haley said, just looked for his opportunities to impress her and make her a potential mate. He'd missed most of the importance that Haley placed on her family in her new life, and how much that had been snatched from her and the ones she loved in one fatal and devastating mistake. But Chad was on the other end of the phone, and Haley felt like he was listening, and it was enough to ease a little of her pain, and she appreciated him for it.

On Wednesday, the local news picked up on the tragedy, because the coroner determined that the infant didn't die from a fall: her father couldn't deal with her crying, and in a fit of rage, hit her head against the dining room table until she stopped. When the police confronted him with the coroner's findings, he confessed, and was arrested.

This was a major topic of conversation when Chad went out with Steve, his wife, and some friends at a bar around the corner from their mother's the next night. Mr. Haley's funeral was earlier in the day, and both brothers were pall bearers, which was hard on Chad, because he was still a little stiff from the hike.

"Can you believe that shit?"

"What a psycho."

"They better give him the death penalty."

"I think those fucking liberals banned it, didn't they?"

"Well, they should bring it back for him."

"Chad, you worked with her aunt, didn't you?"

"Yeah, it was the girl I went hiking with on Saturday. She hasn't been to work since Monday."

"I bet. Did you talk to her?"

"Yeah. She was pretty upset."

"I bet."

Because Steve and Sara were broken up about Mr. Haley's death they never put two and two together to surmise that Haley was the same Haley they were excited about Chad knowing because of her connection to *Love Shack*. Now she was a celebrity to them for a different reason.

Sara put her hand on Chad's arm.

"Steve, we should send her some flowers. We'll give them to Chad and he can bring them into work for her."

"That's a great idea, honey."

Chad had left his car at their mother's, but the walk back there from the bar wasn't a long one, and he declined Steve's offer of a ride in favor of some fresh air. He wondered how Haley was, if she'd ever make it back to work, and told himself he had to remember to give her flowers too, just like his brother and sister wanted to do. As long as that story stayed in the headlines, everyone at the bar with him that night told everyone they knew that they knew someone who was connected with it. "Sara's brother-in-law worked with the aunt," "Steve's brother worked with the aunt;" which spread out to "I know someone who knows the aunt," or "someone I know knows those people."

As Chad was making his way by the Haleys, Mrs. Haley came out to the front door and called him over.

"I want you to take some of this food with you."

She ushered him inside and showed him all the containers filled with food spread out on the kitchen table.

"People kept bringing it over, you know. They think I'm hungry… but I can't eat now…"

It took a second for Chad to understand that she was saying she was too upset to eat, but when he did, she could read it in his eyes. She put her hand on his arm, giving him that same gentle smile she used to give Chad and Steve when she gave them candy for Halloween or told them they could swim in her above-ground pool. It still had the same ability to put his mind at ease.

Chad thought he heard music, and looked around Mrs. Haley and into the living room to see where it was coming from. He remembered the song because it was the same one he heard a couple weeks before when he was with Lisa, Ashley Simpson's "Pieces of Me."

"Are your grandchildren here?"

"Wha—? Oh, that. Ed… I mean Mr. Haley… Mr. Haley always loved the music the kids listened to. He'd keep it on that channel all hours of the day… you know, we got one of those fancy boxes from the cable company, with the HD and stuff… he said the regular cable didn't show videos anymore, so he needed that one."

"Wait, Mr. Haley watched MTV?"

"Oh yes, he loved all that stuff. It used to drive me crazy. Especially that rap stuff. He had one of those iPack thingys… your brother gave it to him."

"An iPod?"

"Yes, that's it… he'd use it on his walks… put all kinds of songs on it…"

Chad went back in his mind, to his thirteenth birthday, when Mr. Haley got him Guns N' Roses' *Appetite for Destruction* on cassette. He just thought Mr. Haley had asked his mother what he wanted, and that was it. It never crossed his mind that Mr. Haley could've been into it too. A pang of regret shot through him. Mr. Haley was much more intriguing than he ever could've imagined, and he would never get a chance to know him better.

Mrs. Haley filled up a few grocery bags of Tupperware. He was uncomfortable when the Ashley Simpson song was replaced by something from Disturbed. It wasn't appropriate to have on in front of Mrs. Haley. He asked if she wanted him to change it.

"No, this will probably be my last night with..." she started to choke up, and then caught herself. "Here, do you have enough, because there's more of... of... of whatever this stuff is."

They laughed, and Chad was thankful for it to relieve the tension. He gave her a big hug and wished her goodnight. As he packed the stuff into his car and drove off, he was struck by how upset Mrs. Haley was, yet at the same time how much she didn't want to show him that. And that image of Ashley Simpson on the TV, there because that was Mr. Haley's favorite channel, and Mrs. Haley watched it as a final goodbye to him.

Chad thought about Haley too, and how odd it was that Mr. Haley would die around the same time her niece did. That was it, just that it was odd. Because Mrs. Haley did a good job of hiding her pain from Chad, he wasn't able to see how devastating Mr. Haley's death really was to her, even if she'd seen it coming for some time now. Unlike Haley's niece, whose killing represented a world of expectation senselessly ripped from her family by a father who couldn't deal with the frustration of his infant daughter crying, a world of first steps, first Christmases, first words, first days of school that will never happen; Mr. Haley's death was the terminus of a sixty-plus-year journey she had had with him, filled with all the Christmases, graduations, marriages, and grandchildren anyone could ask for. For any couple who enter into marriage, this end—one of them dying in old age—is considered the best possible outcome, but for Mrs. Haley, it was no less difficult to deal with. For longer than Chad's parents were alive, Mrs. Haley had had someone who was always there to start her day with, to join her in tackling the world, and to fall asleep next to knowing he would be there again the following day. Mrs. Haley would never compare what happened to Haley's niece to Mr. Haley's passing—in fact, she'd probably feel guilty for being upset when she had had so many good years with him and Haley's niece barely made two months—but as she sat in front of the TV, watching a music video that made no sense to her, the reality that she was going to have to start her day without him was sinking in, as if her soul was in quicksand, and the longer she stayed awake and sat in front of that TV, the longer she could keep her head above the surface.

Haley came back to work on that Monday, and everyone, including Chad in Accounting, as deliveryman for his brother and sister-in-law, made sure she had plenty of flowers. Chad didn't get her flowers personally, though. The day before, when he was walking around downtown, he passed the outdoor adventure shop, and thought he might go in and see what they had. All of the equipment looked foreign to him, but there was a coffee table book about Aconcagua, and a pint glass listing the Fifty Fivers on it. He bought them for Haley, but left them in his car and told her he'd give them to her after work. She asked him if he'd like to join her for lunch, because she needed some Applebee's nachos, and he could give her what he got her then.

Chad was horrible at wrapping presents, so everything he gave came in cute little gift bags. While their drinks came, Haley picked the tissue paper off the top and saw the book and glass. She was certainly happy, but Chad was expecting an enormous show of exuberance, which Haley was still in no condition to display. She also was hurt that he never called or texted or e-mailed to see how she was doing last week after that one conversation, and a coffee table book and pint glass, no matter how sweet, wouldn't make up for that.

"Thank you, Chad, these are very nice…" she looked down and sighed, then picked her head back up and smiled. "This definitely… I don't know… it's not that it's ever a *good* time for something like this… I mean, what the hell, right?... but I really thought I was getting over the hump, and then… I don't know…"

"I'm sorry."

"No… no, these are very nice, and very thoughtful of you… I mean… I have plenty of flowers, huh? And it's kind of fitting that you got me this, because I've been thinking…"

"Oh yeah?"

"Yeah. I want to do something in Mariah's honor—" Chad realized at that moment that that was the first time he'd heard her niece's name. "I was thinking I could maybe make a push to hike Denali this summer."

"Denali?"

"Yes, that's the real name of Mt. McKinley."

"Oh, okay." That didn't really clear anything up for Chad, but he decided to let her continue instead of asking again what she was talking about.

"Eventually I want to do all the Seven Summits… I mean, I already have Aconcagua, so it's just six more, and an old hiking buddy got me in touch with some people he knows that are planning a Denali ascent next summer, so I can get some experience in this winter, link up with them on some less involving treks, and see where I stand."

"Wow, that's really cool."

"Yeah… I mean… the way I look at it, Mariah never had a chance at any of this:" she held up her new Aconcagua book and shook it. "I'm lucky enough to have done everything I did, and I'm too busy feeling sorry for myself because my fiancé was gay and afraid to tell me. You know, what's wrong with me, right?"

Chad went home that night after work and looked up Mt. McKinley on Wikipedia. As opposed to Aconcagua, Mt. McKinley was a completely different animal. Weeks on end in the freezing cold at dangerously high altitudes. Who would willingly put themselves through this? Thanks but no thanks.

Thank You for Your Service, Steve

"Thank you for your service."

When he first started at West Point, Steve never got any thank you for your services. Instead of people wanting to shake his hand, they looked at him funny when he wore his uniform in the mall or at the game. Then 9/11 happened and it all changed. Now he and his buddies were getting front row seats at the Yankees with everyone around them buying them drinks. He wasn't deployed to Afghanistan after the attacks, but he was sent to Iraq a couple years later. His first tour wasn't so bad, but his second tour, when the insurgency was at its peak, that was a different story. He commanded patrols in advanced positions, and there was a sense that every trip out might be his last.

All of his life, Steve felt inferior to Chad—probably a little brother complex—but when he finally had more esteem in many people's eyes, he didn't relish it. That wasn't why he was in the Army either, to one up his brother, or to have people he didn't know want to shake his hand. It wasn't something he thought about. He didn't even know the level to which Chad envied *him*. Every thank you for your service made Chad feel, not only not as successful as his little brother, but also like he was missing something he should've been a part of. He'd actually gotten to the point a couple years ago that he contacted their father to see if he could enlist, which was a mistake, because Chad really wasn't serious about it, and their father, then retired, inundated him with recruiting pitches.

But then Steve lost his leg in the cruelest of ironies and could no longer serve, and with that each thank you for your service that was now given in a tone of the Simple Past as opposed to the tone of the Present Perfect Progressive, twisted the knife of irony in him that much more. He felt emasculated, not completely whole, adrift and purposeless. In a split second, doing something as simple as running to the grocery store, everything changed, and three years later he was still trying to get over the shock that it actually happened, let alone move forward.

While Chad and Steve's father had a distinguished military career, it wasn't their father that made Steve want to enlist in the military, it was Mr. Haley. His only memories of his father brought to mind an overbearing presence that upset the balance of the house, not someone in whose footsteps he'd want to follow. It was later, in America, when Steve was still a child, his Pop Warner football coach was being confronted by the team's parents for his tough practice regimen, and Steve's mother asked Mr. Haley to attend for her. The coach, in an attempt to defend himself, told the group of parents that it was a war out there, and he was just getting his soldiers ready for battle.

"I was in a war, coach, and a bunch of kids falling on the ground in pads is not a war."

There were other issues going on with the team that Mr. Haley didn't know about. The coach had big aspirations for him and his son—his son as a player, and he as a college coach someday—and a lot of the parents thought he was a jackass. Once they heard Mr. Haley shut him up with that retort, they wanted *him* to coach the team instead, which he did. The team didn't win a game all season, but the kids all had a fun time.

From that moment on, Steve idolized Mr. Haley. He was always nice, always helpful, but he knew how to take charge in sticky situations. He was all at once like a dad, grandfather, cool uncle, and best friend. There were pinewood derby cars built, tents erected, oil changes made, fish cleaned; but it was that one line about the coach never having been in a war that stuck out in Steve's mind. He wanted to be able to say that just like Mr. Haley did.

He found out later why Mr. Haley said what he said, during his second tour in Iraq. Carrying a comrade whose legs had been blown off isn't anything like a bunch of kids in pads falling down, and Mr. Haley didn't want anyone else to have to experience that kind of thing. It was for that reason, when Steve told him in high school that he was considering enlisting, and even enrolling at West Point, that Mr. Haley didn't want him to, but he didn't say anything, because he could tell it was something Steve wanted—and because he didn't see the country getting into any wars anytime soon.

"So what you're saying is, I named my kid Dick?"

"Well, no, you named him Richard…"

"But if Dick is short for Richard… ugh… I'm so embarrassed. I should probably apologize to Amy."

"Yeah, probably."

Miguel was playing *FIFA '09*, telling Chad how he and his wife invited Amy over to supper because her mom wasn't around, and they got mad at her after she called their son Dick. They told her that kind of language wasn't tolerated in their house. Both children tried to protest, but Miguel, Julía, and her sister would have none of it.

Chad's mother called in the middle of their conversation. She wanted Chad to talk to his brother, because he was taking Mr. Haley's death pretty hard. Chad thought she was overreacting, since he seemed fine the night of the funeral, but he agreed anyway.

"I can't believe I named my son Dick. Why do you people name your kids after a nickname for your penis?"

"I don't know, maybe the name predated the nickname. How did you not know Dick was short for Richard? Haven't you heard of Dick Clark or Dick Cheney?"

"Yeah, but—ooh, ooh, yes!" His team scored another goal. Miguel had won the championship title in most of the major European leagues in *FIFA '09*, and now he was trying to win the Belgian Pro League with KRC Genk, the computer putting up scant resistance. "But I'd never heard them called 'Richard Cheney' or 'Richard Clark,' have you?"

"I guess you're right."

"I know I'm right…. Oh, I forgot to tell you, Fiorentina is playing in the Champion's League tomorrow."

"You want me to set it to tape?"

"No, I already did, I just wanted to remind you that I'll be over to watch it."

By the time Miguel left, Chad figured it would be too late to call, because he didn't want to wake Steve's kids. The next night he was afraid to call before Miguel came over to watch his game, which he didn't make it over for until after seven because he had to hang out with his wife and sister-in-law, so by the time the game was over, it was too late again.

And on Wednesday, Kovacs showed up. No phone call, completely unannounced. It had been over a year since Chad and he had last talked, and in that time, Chad had only seen him through pictures on Facebook that his wife, Mandy, posted. Kovacs himself didn't do that kind of thing, he usually limited his Facebook usage to one sentence statements about the performance of his favorite sports teams, or how bad his commute was that day. Now he was standing in Chad's doorway, carrying a backpack, a case of beer, and about 15 more pounds than the last time they'd talked.

"Man, I know this is short notice, but can I crash on your couch?"

"What? What happened? Come in, come in."

"Can I get these in your fridge?"

"What?... oh yeah, whatever..."

Chad granted that second request, even though he hadn't officially granted the first one. It took him a second, as Kovacs rearranged the contents of his refrigerator, asking if he needed to keep this or that, before Chad understood what was happening.

"Dude, stop, this is my apartment. What are you doing here? Stop moving shit around, and don't throw anything out."

"I thought you said I could put my beer in here."

Chad shut the fridge and sent him over to the couch, where Chad followed and sat on the recliner. Kovacs had taken one of the beers out of the case and opened it.

"Now, tell me what's going on."

Kovacs took a sip, then made a sour face.

"Do you have a frosty mug or something? These are warm. They only had cases outside the cooler at the store."

Chad put his head in his hands as Kovacs made his way to the freezer, found one of Chad's mugs in there, poured his beer in, tasted it, let out an overindulgent "ahhhh", and returned to the couch.

"That's better. So, Mandy kicked me out."

"Oh geez... finally had it with your drinking?"

"No, I cheated on her. Actually, I've been cheating on her."

"Jesus Kovacs."

"I know, I'm a moron."

"Do I know her?"

He paused, took a sip from his beer, and studied the condensation dripping down the mug. He didn't look back at Chad when he spoke again:

"It was Carol."

"Your dad's wife?"

He nodded. Chad hadn't seen Kovacs' dad's wife in years—at least as long as he'd seen Kovacs's father. His dad owned the local Ford dealership, Carol was the secretary, and Kovacs had been working there since he'd graduated from college, the idea being he'd take over after his father retired at some point in the future.

"Does he know?"

40

"Oh yeah…" He looked up from his glass and saw that Chad wasn't stunned or sympathetic, he was disgusted. "Come on man, you gotta help me out. If I can just crash here a couple of days, that's all I need."

"Why didn't you go to Dave's?"

"You know Gwen hates me. God damn it, I'm a fucking moron."

There was no apology from Kovacs for not having talked to Chad for years, for choosing Dave and Gwen over him after everything happened. Unlike everyone else, who cut Chad out swiftly, Kovacs did it more gradually, so in Kovacs's mind, he and Chad just fell out of touch, as opposed to him making a point of not wanting Chad's company in favor of Dave's. Chad understood the conscious decision Kovacs had made though, and he resented him for showing up out of the blue because he'd screwed up his life and had no one else to turn to.

"You don't have to sleep on the couch, I have a spare bedroom. I'll throw the bed linens in the wash right now."

Chad and Steve weren't always that close, but Chad, Dave, and Kovacs had been best buddies since Chad's mother moved he and his brother to her hometown when he was 8. They were like the Three Musketeers—or maybe the Three Stooges. They played sports together, egged houses together, smoked weed in the basement together, got jobs and got fired together. Then they went to college together, partied together, pledged a fraternity together, went to Cancun for Spring Break together. Then they graduated, got an apartment together, entered the workforce together: Kovacs at his dad's car dealership, Chad as an accountant for a small tech firm, and Dave as a realtor. Slowly, they became adults—or so they thought—and they met women and started to settle down.

Kovacs had been dating Mandy since they met at the fraternity house their junior year. She put up with Kovacs's penchant for being a party animal, because he had a lot of endearing qualities, like his sense of humor and natural charisma. She figured he'd grow up eventually, and actually encouraged his moving in with Dave and Chad after college, so the two of them could ease into a more settled life as a couple, and eventually move in together and get married. He wasn't Kovacs to her, he was Jeremy. Unfortunately he was still Kovacs to himself.

Every group seems to have a Kovacs, and yet, to every group that has a Kovacs, he somehow seems *sui generis*. It's unfathomable to the people in that group that another person like Kovacs could exist on this planet. That there could be another person who has always been chubby, from as long as anyone could remember, but was never quite fat, and actually pretty athletic; that there could be another life of the party the way Kovacs was the life of the party, boisterous, hilarious, self-deprecating, borderline insane; that there could be someone else who could be the subject of so many remember the times or you should've been theres. And much to Mandy's chagrin, Kovacs's identity was too tied into being Kovacs for him to officially settle down and finally be Jeremy.

Like Chad and Dave, who lived with him before, and knew that with the life of the party came the after-party routines of making sure he didn't pee in the closet, or didn't smash the TV, or didn't set himself on fire passing out while smoking a cigarette, Mandy did her best to babysit him, hoping beyond hope that he'd grow out of it. The whole Man Law thing kept them from telling Mandy about Kovacs' one night stands, but she learned about those quickly enough as well—those nights he went out to the game and didn't come home until the next morning, smelling like sex and perfume and all manner of other gross things. He'll grow out of it, she thought, it's just Kovacs being Kovacs.

And she thought he *was* getting better. A big part of that was Dave settling down with Gwen, leaving him without a partner in crime, but she felt like maybe he was caring more about her too. Yes, he spent more time at the office, but he was doing it for their future, and he wasn't coming home smelling like booze and sex and perfume as much anymore either. And she still loved how he could command a room wherever they went. Everyone loved Kovacs, and even though she called him Jeremy, she kind of loved Kovacs too. Then she found out that his "getting better" was actually him having a long term affair with his step-mother.

Steve was not Kovacs, and he was not Chad. He had plenty of friends, he never cheated on his wife, and was very much an adult. His wife and mother knew that, despite the strong face he showed them, he was broken up over Mr. Haley's death, and they were right. Mr. Haley was his best friend. Every time he came home, from both his tours, he would visit Mr. Haley often, and they sat on his porch, not saying anything, drinking beers and listening to the neighborhood. This was Steve's true thank you for your service, and Mr. Haley alone understood that. He tried doing the same thing on his own porch a couple nights after the funeral, found himself close to tears, and had to catch himself because Steve Jr. and his friends wanted him to play whiffle ball with them.

When he enrolled at West Point at 18—accepted to the academy more for his prowess as a long stick middie than anything—the Army and lacrosse was all he knew, and after he graduated, it was only the Army. He went over to Iraq as a 1st lieutenant in 2003, then went back as a captain in 2005. He knew right away that things were different this second time. Dirtier, more dangerous. They had gone from freedom fighters removing a brutal dictator to the enemy, an occupying force that people wanted out. Everyone was on a knife's edge, not sure who to trust, if that kid with the funny looking bag was just a kid with a funny looking bag or someone holding their death in his hands. Steve took pride in defending his country, but he didn't know what this was, couldn't recognize defending his country anymore; all he wanted was to survive this and make it home to his family. He became more withdrawn, chose paperwork over special events meeting visiting celebrities and athletes; would beat himself up working out, trying to burn off the tension that boiled in his veins, only to find it came back right after his shower—and what was worse, he had no other outlet for this tension, he had to keep it inside because the soldiers he commanded looked to him for their own resolve. When his tour was finally up, he didn't know what he'd do if they called him back. Go, I guess, I'm a soldier, it's what I do. But go back to what? Unfortunately, that decision was made for him.

When he was home in 2006, one Saturday morning he offered to run to the grocery store for Sara—Steve being Steve felt it was unfair of her to have to take care of the kids alone while he was away at war, and wanted to help her as much as he could while he was home. Because it was a Saturday morning, the parking lot was jammed, so he decided to just grab a spot far away instead of circling the lot multiple times for something closer.

Since he'd last been home, the grocery store had been bought by a bigger chain, and everything inside was different, he had no idea where anything was anymore, and with people zipping around him he had no time to think. He found a stack of baskets and grabbed one, and looked for an opening so he could zip into the cereal aisle.

He caught the eye of a stout doughy man in his mid-40s, wearing a late 90s era goatee, a camouflage baseball cap, and a black NRA T-shirt—two days after a tragic school shooting had killed a teacher and five kids in the Midwest. Steve already knew he didn't like this guy, even though the guy seemed to like him.

"It's like a warzone in here, geez!"

"I just came back from Iraq, this isn't so bad."

"Hey, put 'er there pal, thank you for your service."

Steve shook his hand, and made sure he gripped it firmly so the man would know Steve didn't like or respect him. Then he left the man and pivoted into the cereal aisle. The kids liked Lucky Charms. When he and Chad were growing up, they got a kick out of generic cereals with funny names, like "Crispy Spheres," which was "Kix" with a cartoon raccoon on the box; or "Toasty Oats," which was "Cheerios" with a giraffe on the box. Steve looked around and saw the generics here, just boxes with pictures of the cereal—enlarged to show detail—with titles in block letters and the grocery store's generic brand in cursive letters. No random cartoon animals. What about the WWF cereal with the Ultimate Warrior on the box, or the Mr. T cereal? He and Chad used to beg his mother to get them those cereals, and now he was Dad buying Lucky Charms for the kids.

A thin teenager with sleeves of tattoos was crouching near the bottom shelf with his back to Steve, restocking the rice cakes. For a second Steve thought he was Private Wilson, but it couldn't be, could it? The boy stood and turned and walked past him. Of course it wasn't Wilson, it couldn't be.

Private Wilson was from Southern California. He and his friends raced tuned out Hondas, until Wilson's father passed, and, looking for meaning in his life, he enlisted in the Army, as his father had done during Vietnam. He was a great driver, Steve trusted him more than anyone to get them out of a sticky situation. One afternoon, while Steve was talking on the phone with Sara and the kids, a patrol had been attacked outside their base. He rushed out to help with the survivors that had returned, and he saw Wilson lying on the back of a truck, a sheet over him. He pulled the sheet down, and saw that the lower half of his body was missing.

"Excuse me, can I just get in here?"

A woman needed to get to the Apple Jacks, and the tone in her voice told Steve that she took it personally that he would decide to daydream about Wilson right there at that moment. He knew needed to get the rest of the things and get the hell out of there. After another 20 minutes of shopping, and 20 more minutes in line, Steve was outside in the parking lot loading their groceries in the back of the SUV. As he was walking to the driver's side, he heard a scream and looked up. A car was speeding at him, and he tried to dive out of the way, but he wasn't fast enough, his left leg trailing behind, and it was pinned between the car and the SUV. The man driving had fallen into a diabetic coma, his foot collapsing on the gas pedal, causing the car to speed out of control. He would ultimately be okay, but Steve would need his leg amputated just above the knee.

If people walked on egg shells with him before, too afraid to bring up the war, they were really cautious now. Not only that, but his Army buddies, one source of support, also didn't know how to be around him, and he didn't know how to be around them either. Everyone was awkward except for Mr. Haley. Mr. Haley was the one person he could go to who understood and wasn't afraid of saying the wrong thing. Those evenings on the porch centered him, got him to a place where he could talk frankly with Sara about how he felt, about the guilt, the emasculation, the lack of purpose in life; got him to a point where he could come to terms with everything that had happened, and define his identity as a civilian. For the last three years, every time he didn't feel right, every time the stress built up inside of him again, one trip to Mr. Haley's porch would set him right, and now he didn't know what he was going to do without that.

Even if he was using Chad because he had no other options, having Kovacs around that night made Chad feel great to be Chad again, instead of just Chad in Accounting. They stayed up late, talking about old times, drinking beers. The next day, Chad was invigorated, and Haley and his supervisor didn't recognize the Chad in Accounting working next to them. It was like Gene Kelly had invaded his body the limber, energetic way he moved around and went about his tasks. It wasn't that he did any more work than usual, he just wasn't moping or acting like everything he did was the worst thing ever. He left his station to use the copier, and his supervisor leaned over and asked Haley if he'd gotten laid, to which Haley laughed and told him to cut it out. Haley was hoping secretly he didn't get laid, because she was attracted to this version of Chad.

Thursdays meant Thirsty Thursdays at The Dirty Sombrero, which meant $1 well drinks before 10, which meant this was Kovacs' regular Thursday night thing, and for this one night, while he was staying at Chad's, it was Chad's Thursday night thing too. Chad had never had a Thursday night thing, or an any night thing for that matter. He could get used to having Kovacs around.

Around 6, as they were watching SportsCenter and getting their pregame in, Amy and Brittney stopped by. Amy was dressed like Alice from *Alice in Wonderland*, and Brittney was in a fluffy bear costume, cartoonish, like a character on kid's show.

"Hey Chad, who's your friend?"

"Amy, Brittney, this is Kovacs. I grew up with him. Amy lives down the hall, and Brittney is her BFF."

They giggled.

"Should I even ask what you two are up to?"

"Welllllll, we're doing this new thing on YouTube, where we take requests from people…"

"And they wanted you to dress up like this?"

"Sorta…"

Chad didn't like the sound of this. Kovacs was trying to figure out why two fifteen-year-old girls would hang out at Chad's place. It really had been a long time since I'd seen him, he thought, and the last thing I wanna do is judge a guy, but this is kinda weird. Plus, Chad of all people should know how weird this is, especially after the whole Hestermann thing.

"What's the sorta?"

"Um… do you think you could get us a strap-on?"

Kovacs coughed up his beer.

"No I'm not getting you a strap-on. Why would you even ask?"

44

"That was the request. Brit would dress in the bear suit with a strap-on, and then I'd—"

"You'd nothing. You need to have that guy reported to someone."

"I don't think it's a guy. The name was like 'bearprincess02' or something like that."

"I'll get you girls the strap-on."

"You will?"

"Shut up, Kovacs, you're not helping."

"What? It's not like I'd be using it *with them*."

"Dude!"

"Why can't he get it for us?"

"How do you girls even know what that is?"

"Duh, we Googled it."

Kovacs was loving this, and the more exasperated Chad got, and the more hopeful the girls got that Kovacs might do them this solid, the more he loved it, and the more Chad became exasperated. He was also relieved to see that Chad wasn't a weirdo that hooked up with young girls. He finally relented, and told the girls he couldn't buy them a strap on either.

"You guys suck. Why can't you just buy it for us? No one will know."

"*We'll* know," Chad said. "You need to have the guy that requested that reported. There are a lot of bad people out there."

"We know, Chad. Plus, it was a girl anyway, not a guy."

"Haven't you told them about Hestermann?"

"Why would I tell them about Hestermann?"

"Who's Hestermann?"

"It's a long story."

"You never told them this? I tell people this story all the time."

"What story? What's Hestermann? We wanna know, we wanna know."

"You tell everyone? That's great…"

"What, you don't want people to know? Dude, you were a hero. Listen to this ladies, Chad here saved some girl's life. She was about your age at the time too. Christ, how long ago was that?"

"Ten years ago. She just turned 24 a little while ago."

"24? Holy shit!"

"Oh yeah, she's getting married this summer. I got the invitation over there somewhere."

"Wow, time flies, huh?" He finished his beer, and went past the girls to get another, having trouble getting around Brittney's bear suit belly.

"You gotta tell us what happened, Chad."

Chad started to, but Kovacs went ahead instead.

"See, me, Chad, and our friend Dave had this apartment after we graduated from college. We lived across the hall from this weirdo dude, Hestermann. He was just a total creep fest. Anyway, so one day I was… where was I?"

"You were helping Mandy buy a car at your dad's."

"That's right… and Dave was… where was Dave?"

"Home doing his laundry."

"That's right, his mom always did his laundry."

"And yours too, asshole."

"Why'd'you call me an asshole?"

"What?... I don't know, it wasn't serious, just an expression."

The girls were getting annoyed.

"Okay, so Chad's all alone, and he goes out to the store to get some stuff, and on his way back, he sees this girl outside of Hestermann's. She tells him she's his cousin, which Chad thought sounded weird because Hestermann was old—"

"Plus, she looked like she was lying."

"Right, which made you suspicious. So he hangs by our door and looks through the peephole and keeps his ears out for anything suspicious. Then he hears a scream."

The girls gasped.

"Yeah, so he rushes across the hall, bangs down the door—"

"Actually, he left it unlocked... I just walked right in..."

"Whatever. He sees Hestermann with the girl, struggling, and he takes the guy out with one punch. Boom, out cold."

"OhmyGod, Chad!"

"Well, it wasn't exactly one punch..."

"Don't be so modest. Now check this, girls. Hestermann had set up an apartment 500 miles away that he was going to take this girl to, and a van with blacked out windows waiting outside to throw her in. Who knows if anyone would've found her after that."

"You really did all that, Chad?"

"Pretty much... and that's why I worry about you taking requests from some dude that wants you to put on a strap-on in some video. There's a lot of weirdoes out there."

Amy wasn't thinking about that anymore, she was thinking about Chad, the guy she had a crush on, being so heroic.

"So what happened, did the guy get arrested? Is the girl okay?"

"Yeah, what was her name, Morgan?"

"MacKenzie."

"I knew it was an 'M' name."

"She grew up and went to college and played volleyball. Her team actually made it to the national championship."

"Yeah, they interviewed him about it when the game played on ESPN2."

It didn't cross Chad's mind to consider that that ESPN2 interview was two years ago, long after he'd been alienated by Kovacs. When they bumped into each other in the mall last year, the last time he'd seen him, Kovacs never even brought it up, instead made it seem like he needed to get away from Chad quickly; and here he was now, telling the girls about Chad being on ESPN2 as if the two of them had watched it together. It never crossed Chad's mind, but it crossed Kovacs's. When he and Dave had heard that the girl Chad saved would be playing volleyball on ESPN2, they watched it, and got a kick out of seeing Chad interviewed. They could tell he'd let himself go, that he wasn't that happy, and they both felt guilty about it, though neither let on to the other that he felt that way. All of that hit Kovacs at the moment he mentioned the show, that he had abandoned Chad because of Dave, and how good it was that after all that Chad was still helping him out and letting him stay at his place, but it was a testament to the kind of person Kovacs was that he never let on that all of this was going through his head.

What Chad did know was that that tale of him saving MacKenzie's life wasn't exactly the way Kovacs told it. It was mostly correct, except for the confrontation with Hestermann. Even now, it was so surreal to Chad, he had trouble convincing himself it actually happened and wasn't just a dream.

Up to the scream, Kovacs had it pretty much right. Chad heard the scream and ran over. The door was ajar, and he looked in. It was like something out of a soap opera or *Magnum PI* episode. Hestermann had a white cloth that he was trying to shove over MacKenzie's face, like a chloroform rag, like Hestermann was some kind of evil villain who had just caught the girl snooping in his evil lair. Hestermann saw him, and panicked, letting the girl go accidentally. She ran across the hall to Chad's apartment and called 9-1-1.

There was no scuffle, no punch, no taking anyone out. Hestermann slumped to the floor and wept. Then he started hitting himself, calling himself stupid. It was still in that surreal zone for Chad, and he stood there and stared at Hestermann, expressionless. It wasn't until he heard the police officer tell him it was okay, they'd take it from here, that he snapped back into reality.

MacKenzie had met Hestermann in a chat room. Before that, Hestermann had limited his dysfunctionality to downloading pictures of young girls and whatnot. But he started using the chat rooms, and he found MacKenzie. He gained her trust, convinced her to run away from home, and set up the rest. MacKenzie on the other hand, had recently moved to the area with her family, didn't have a lot of friends, and used the computer and Internet to pass her time. Hestermann told her he was younger (as opposed to 49, he said 22), told her how beautiful she was, and how good he'd be for her. She was completely smitten, and agreed to do whatever he told her. When she got to his apartment and saw him, she first thought she had accidentally gone to the wrong place, and that's why she screamed when she saw Hestermann, because she was embarrassed, not because she was afraid.

The investigators said Chad saved her life, because Hestermann had put too much chloroform on his handkerchief, and had he placed it over her face, it would've been enough to kill her, as opposed to just put her to sleep. Forget the apartment 500 miles away, or the blacked out van, or anything else he was planning, had Chad not been suspicious—or even if Hestermann hadn't left his door ajar—Mackenzie would've been dead.

But MacKenzie wasn't dead. She would go on to high school, play volleyball, go to her prom, get her license, graduate, go to college, play volleyball there, get her degree in marine biology, and now, next spring, she was getting married. For every major event, Chad was either there in person, or was e-mailed pictures, and he was always sent a thank you card. Chad could never know how her family felt, or how she felt, that they owed every moment, every milestone, to him. Like Stacy, who couldn't fathom that Chad wouldn't have placed the same importance in that cat video as she did, MacKenzie's family couldn't fathom that he'd live a life like the one he'd been living since Gwen left him.

Speaking of Gwen, it's important to note before we move on that it was this incident of Chad being a hero that initially swayed her in his favor over Dave. Chad never knew that. He'd met Gwen at work, and had invited her over for parties and whatnot so he could court her. He had no idea that Dave was courting her at the same time, having met her through him. She really liked Dave, and she was lukewarm on Chad, but didn't know how she could pull off the roommate switch, because she knew Chad had a thing for her and they worked together. Then he became a hero, and she saw things in him she hadn't seen in him before.

There was a huge line outside The Dirty Sombrero, even at 8 PM. $1 well drinks will do that. Kovacs took Chad with him to the front of the line, where the bouncer recognized him, gave him a little bro hug, and told Chad it was nice to meet him. No cover, no ID check, no waiting in line, they just walked right in after saying hi to the bouncer. Chad could get used to this.

At work, they piped the local pop station through the PA, which Chad wasn't entirely fond of, but that day he caught an ad for The Dirty Sombrero. Really, he'd always heard that commercial and just hadn't noticed it before. *Thirsty Thursdays at The Dirty Sombrero. DJ IROC-Z manning the wheels of steel. $1 well drinks until 10. Women always get in free.* There was nothing Dirty Sombrero about the place: nothing Southwest, nothing Mexican. But when he thought of that slick voice over the house music in the radio ad, that was what he was looking at in front of him. Dimly lit, couches here and there, a big dance floor with a few brave souls out there before the crowd hit, waitresses in tight black shirts and tight black pants trying to sell vials of fluorescent liquids. This was not a place Chad was comfortable in. He couldn't remember the last time he'd been in a similar environment. It could've been ten years or more.

There was nothing to worry about though, Kovacs had him covered. This was Kovacs's life. If it wasn't Thirsty Thursday at The Dirty Sombrero, it was something else somewhere else. If Carol could get away from his dad, she'd meet him here. If not, he'd meet someone else. It didn't matter to Kovacs. Some nights were worse than others, and if it was too bad, he might have to send Mandy some flowers—or buy her some jewelry. Now even that didn't matter, because he was free man. He and Chad would live it up, just like old times. He flagged down one of the waitresses with the vials.

"Hey, get me one of those for my buddy."

"No problem, Kovacs."

"Dude, I gotta work in the morning."

"Cut the shit, it's only 8 o'clock."

He didn't even get the shot down before a group of three women came over to see them. They were all mid-twentysomethings, all in the same club uniform of tight jeans and a halter top. For Chad, any of them would've been plenty attractive enough to make a great girlfriend, but before he could get used to their presence, Kovacs took he and Chad away from them and over to a semi-circular booth, conspicuously placed in one of the corners.

"Those girls were hot. How do you know them?"

"I've seen them around." He took a pull off his drink. "The one in the middle is kind of crazy. Larry at the dealership went out with her one night, and the next thing he knew she was texting him every five minutes. Total stage five cling-on. Don't worry, we'll see plenty more where they came from."

It didn't take long either. Everyone at The Dirty Sombrero wanted to be near Kovacs, and as the place became more crowded, the area around them grew. It was intoxicating for Chad to be associated with a cynosure like that. People looked at him as a person of importance too, because Kovacs chose him out of all the people whom he could potentially spend his time with in his life. Not only that, but a good chunk of the stories Kovacs entertained his audience with took place in college, and Chad was a part of them. Chad could not fathom how Kovacs told the perfect story that everyone around them loved, only to follow it up with an another equally perfect tale. Was it really this easy to be popular? Tell people about stuff he and Kovacs did in college? But there was something more. Kovacs wasn't simply telling people what Chad and he did, he was embellishing the best moments while glossing over the lowlights in a subtle way that Chad couldn't see. Kovacs had a knack for knowing exactly what the people around him thought was funny or interesting, and hitting those notes for all they were worth.

Take for instance, the Chinese Love Letters story. Chad considered it a funny moment in his life, but Kovacs turned it into something like an incident in an episode of a sitcom. Chad barely remembered it—and it happened to him—while Kovacs was able to relive it moment by moment, reminding Chad of details he'd long forgotten. And he knew Kovacs had told this story before, because someone at the table asked about it.

"Dude, Kovacs, I was telling my buddy that one about the Chinese Love Letters that happened to your buddy."

"Oh yeah. This is the buddy that it happened to."

"No shit?"

"Yep, that was me."

"Chinese Love Letters?"

"Oh Kovacs, you gotta tell us about the Chinese Love Letters."

"Oh man," he started a lot of his stories with something like "oh man," just to give that feel that this was a big one. "Chad was taking his Macro final. It was Macro wasn't it?"

"Yeah, freshman year."

"Right, and I'll never forget, because it was one of those days in May when it's really sunny out and everything is blossoming, and the grass is really green. You know the type." They all knew. Chad was wondering why he'd remember that. "So you're like starting the exam, mad hungover, because we were killing it the night before."

"Oh yeah, the test was like spinning around on the desk in front of me."

"Then he sees this Chinese chick—was this the one you banged later?"

"No, that was a different one, though this one was pretty hot too."

"Are you sure? I could've sworn it was this one."

"Dude, I would've known who I slept with. It wasn't her."

"Well, that doesn't mean anything. I don't remember half the chicks I slept with in college!"

The whole table except Chad erupted in laughter.

"Anyway, so Chad's looking over at this Chinese chick, and he sees her going through some papers."

"Yeah, these little sheets," Chad held his hands up and created a rectangle in the air to demonstrate something the size of about six inches by three inches. "And I'm getting nervous for her, you know. I'm looking down to the front to see where the TA is."

Somehow it felt natural for Chad to be as much the center of attention as Kovacs was telling this story. It helped that he was feeling the alcohol, but he really loved having all of these people so interested in what he was saying. It gave the story, Kovacs, even himself a whole new meaning.

"So the guy busts her, right?"

"Oh yeah, right behind her back, he grabs the papers."

"Then she has a temper tantrum."

Everyone was like "what?"

"Oh yeah, it was kind of embarrassing. She's telling him 'no no no!', and the guy is like 'you gotta pack up your stuff and get out of here.' I talked to someone that was sitting next to her after class, and he was saying how all the sheets—there were like three of them—were completely in Chinese."

"So Chad gets home after class and tells us the story, and we just thought it was the craziest thing, until…"

"…Until I look in the school newspaper a few days later, and find out it was all a big misunderstanding."

More whats from the crowd.

"Yeah, get this, the chick wasn't cheating, those were love letters from her boyfriend. He had stuffed them in her bag before Chad's exam, and she found them when she got there. They were just so touching, she couldn't stop reading them."

"What did they say?" One of the girls said.

"Man, I don't remember, it was like *Jerry McGuire* quotes or something, wasn't it?"

"Dude, you don't remember? This is the funniest part… besides, *Jerry McGuire* wasn't even out yet, was it?"

"I don't know. That was almost 15 years ago. How the hell am I supposed to remember that?"

The people at the table loved their interplay, and thought they were both funny, even if Chad was serious about not remembering and being exasperated that Kovacs was giving a hard time about it.

"Okay, the boyfriend wrote—get this—the lyrics to Michael Bolton's 'Said I Loved You… But I Lied'! Can you believe that?"

It was a small chuckle of disbelief at first, but then Kovacs launched into a racially insensitive impression of the Chinese boyfriend reciting the song while writing it out to his girlfriend. *Said I ruvved you but I ried…* The table was in stitches. Except for Chad. Replacing L's for R's wasn't something he found that amusing. And though he did now remember the story of the boyfriend's love letter being a Michael Bolton song, remembered reading about how the Macro professor brought the letters to the Asian Studies department, how they came back to him with their findings, and how it was decided to give the girl another chance, none of it added up to the gold Kovacs managed to mine, at least not to Chad. He looked around the room while people at the table brought up other Michael Bolton songs he could've communicated to her with. He saw someone standing off to the side at a tall table without any chairs at it, sipping her drink. It was Haley. He studied her for a second, trying to make sense of her in her surroundings. Even from a distance, he could tell she had on a little make-up, especially around her eyes. Her hair was roughly the same as in the office. She was wearing jeans like the rest of the women in the club, but instead of wearing her boots on the outside, she had them underneath the pant leg. Her top was much more conservative as well, a T-shirt instead of a halter top, but it was pretty tight and showed off her assets well. Chad watched as a guy here or there approached her, whom she politely talked to, then convinced to leave, or her friends that tried to get her to come out on the dance floor with them, which she also politely declined. She made eye contact with Chad. It took a fair amount of effort to extricate himself from the semi-circular booth. Haley was happy to see him.

"I saw you sitting over there with your friends when I came in."

"Really? Why didn't you say hi?"

"You looked like you were having a really great time. I didn't want to impose. You got quite the group up there."

"I only know Kovacs, the bigger guy in the middle that's the center of attention. We're old buddies. He's crashing at my place while he works out some issues with his wife."

Haley laughed at him.

"What?"

"You're drunk Chad."

"Maybe a little."

"What's Matt going to say when you come in hungover tomorrow?"

"Matt?"

"Our supervisor, Matt!"

"Oh, him." Chad in Accounting only thought of him as his supervisor, not by name, and Chad at The Dirty Sombrero on Thirsty Thursdays didn't think about him period. It never crossed his mind that Haley would have had any kind of friendly relationship with him to know him on a first name basis.

"So what brings you here?"

"My girlfriends dragged me out. They thought it might be good for me, and I thought they might be right, but I'm still not ready for this."

Chad looked over and saw Kovacs walking into a back room with Lars, Lisa's on-again/off-again boyfriend. How did Kovacs know him? Should he be asking that question based on what he'd seen tonight? Kovacs knew everyone. Then what were they doing back there?

"It's possible that neither of us belong in this place right now."

It was the kind of thing that Chad would have normally kept to himself, but the alcohol loosened his tongue, and allowed him to say what was on his mind with less reserve. Haley liked his assertiveness.

"How did you get here?"

"Kovacs and I took a cab. How about you?"

"I took my own car. I had a feeling I wouldn't want to stay too late. Would you like a lift home?"

"That sounds great. Let me grab my coat."

It was a lot nicer to be in Haley's car when they didn't have a daunting hike ahead of them. It still smelled clean and new, and the engine barely made any noise as they drove out of downtown, the beautiful city lights passing them on both sides, then trailing off in the distance.

"Sorry about the music... guilty pleasure..."

"Is that...?"

"Ashley Simpson, yep. I love all that stuff, Miley Cyrus, Taylor Swift..."

"You like Miley Cyrus?"

"I know, I'm a little old for that."

"It's not that, I just didn't see it as your type."

"As my type? And what, pray tell, is my type?"

"I don't know… you just don't… I don't know… you don't seem like the girlie girl type, you know?"

"I don't? What's that supposed to mean?"

She was smirking, but it didn't make Chad feel like he'd dug himself into any shallower a hole.

"You know, with the hiking… and like, you aren't obsessed with how you look… er.. I mean—"

"I don't care how I look? Thanks a lot."

"I don't mean like that… I mean… you know… you have a really pretty face… and—other than tonight, of course—it looks like you never have any make-up on. That's what I mean, I guess… you look pretty without trying…"

Haley was blushing. Chad was blushing too.

"That was really sweet of you, Chad. You made my night."

"Really?"

"Uh huh."

"Well, I'm just calling it like I see it… is that Kelly Clarkson?"

" 'Behind These Hazel Eyes', of course. I played this quite a bit on my drive back from LA."

"I bet."

They both laughed. They were in front of Chad's apartment.

"Well, I guess I'll see you tomorrow at work… if you're not too hungover."

"I should be fine."

"Thank you again for saying what you said. It meant a lot."

"It was no problem."

They embraced in the front seat of her car, and Chad felt the full force of those boobs he'd been eyeing in that T-shirt against his pectorals. They separated slightly and kissed. Then Haley pulled away.

"I'm sorry, I can't do this… it's too soon after the whole thing with Mariah… I just don't… I'm sorry…"

"No, it's totally okay. I still had a nice time. I'll see you at work tomorrow. Thanks for the ride."

"No problem. See you tomorrow, Chad."

"Bye Haley."

It wasn't totally okay for Chad that Haley wasn't ready to hook up with him, because he was beyond ready. We could make this novel much more transgressive and describe in detail what Chad did when he got back to his room to relieve some of the tension he'd built up in that moment with Haley, or rather, what he was almost unable to do due to the lack of feeling he had in that area due to how drunk he was, but we'll spare you those details. Let's just say he took care of some business, then fell asleep around midnight.

Haley, on the other hand, was sober, but high on the feeling she had from her ride with Chad back to his place. He had said she was pretty even without make-up. She looked at herself in her rearview mirror, and saw the eyeliner and mascara she'd applied before she went out. Chad said I look pretty without it. I look pretty without it. She had had this sinking suspicion that her ex chose her as his beard because she wasn't always so feminine, because she didn't wear hot outfits, or too much make-up. He used to tell her how beautiful she was, but she questioned that, questioned everything he ever told her, but especially what he told her about her looks, because he obviously didn't find her physically attractive anyway. And that night, at The Dirty Sombrero, she had put on eyeliner and mascara to make herself more attractive, but she still felt inadequate, not pretty. Now she felt the prettiest she'd ever felt, and Chad had made her feel that way. She couldn't wait to see him tomorrow morning... if he made it in that is.

Steve went out that night as well. He and Sara were celebrating the local prep school's decision to hire him as their next head lacrosse coach. It didn't pay a lot, but with his Army pension, what Sara made as an RN, and the potential to get a part time job or make extra money as a substitute, they'd manage. Plus, if he kept the job long enough, his kids could go there for free when they were older. He was so excited. He was an outside candidate for the job, with some other applicants with more coaching experience looking better suited; but the previous coach had left in disgrace after the team was involved in a major scandal involving players hiring strippers and sexual assaults. The Oak Grove Academy Knights were known across the country for their lacrosse team, sending players to top college programs like Syracuse and Johns Hopkins. Something that was such an enormous source of pride had become an embarrassment, and the athletic director and principal wanted someone who could turn things around, not on the field, but in the classroom and locker room. When they saw Steve and his professionally made ten-page proposal on how to instill discipline in the players; how he'd make grades and behavior a priority over winning; how his background at West Point as a student athlete and then as an officer in the Army during the Iraq War let them know how serious he was; and how all the other applicants, though maybe coming from a wealth of experience, never once mentioned how they'd breed a sense of character in their student athletes, they saw something in Steve they needed desperately. Maybe Steve wouldn't return them to winning form right away, but he'd make them better men. Plus, the athletic director was the lacrosse coach when Steve played at Quincy Adams, and he remembered his ferocity as a long stick middie when Steve's team beat the Knights Steve's senior year. The coach never forgot that, because he almost never lost to a public school, and took each defeat personally. He respected Steve, and saw this as an opportunity to give him a chance after what happened with his leg. He was almost as excited to hire Steve as Steve was at being hired.

Almost. Steve had been looking for meaning in his life for the past three years or so. He only did the culinary arts thing in an attempt to find a new career—it wasn't something he was all that interested in. Now he had a new purpose, and he couldn't wait to make the best of it.

They went to the same bar they had taken Chad to the night of Mr. Haley's funeral. His mother was watching the children. Sara could see in his eyes that he was much happier than he'd been since Mr. Haley first became ill months ago. She was hoping beyond hope that his mother would have the kids in bed and asleep before they got home...

"Dude, Steve, I can't believe you're coaching the Knights," Andy, his old friend whom he played lacrosse with in high school, said.

"I know. The athletic director was the coach back when we beat them."

Andy's wife rolled her eyes.

"What?" Sara said.

"He talks about that game all the time."

"What game?"

"Steve's never told you about when we beat the Knights of Oak Grove Academy?"

Sara looked at Steve. He shrugged his shoulders. Steve met Sara when they were in their early 20s. High school was something that wasn't exactly pertinent to either of them in their relationship, and though they might tell stories here and there in reference to something else around them, Steve wouldn't bring up something like the win over the Knights of Oak Grove Academy apropos of nothing, so Sara had never heard of it.

Andy called attention to the rest of the table: two other couples, Mark and his wife, and Colin and his girlfriend. They had played lacrosse with Steve in high school too. Andy let them know that Sara didn't know about their win over the Knights of Oak Grove Academy. What? Oh my God, how could she not know? Steve didn't know how she could not know. It just never came up, he guessed.

"See, here's the deal," Andy started, "no one beat Oak Grove. I mean, literally, they had undefeated seasons. Only some of the other private schools had a chance. Our school hadn't beat them since when?…"

"I don't think ever," Mark said.

"That's right, we'd never beaten the Knights."

"But we were close our junior year," Steve said. "We took 'em to overtime, and we'd never been that close before."

The guys laughed. The women were confused. Steve was too.

"What?"

"What? What do you mean 'what'?"

"I mean 'what'? What's so funny?"

"You. '*Oh, but we were close junior year.*'"

"Well, we were."

Andy pointed at him.

"Look at this guy. '*Oh, but we were close the year before.*' Remember when we said that right after the game? That at least we were close? What did you do?"

Steve smiled.

"That's what I thought." He turned to Sara. "Your husband here threw a fit after the game. We were happy that we were close, and he starts freakin' out, yelling at us about how close isn't good enough. I wanted to kicked their bleepin' asses! We're gonna get those F'ers next year, you better effin' believe it."

"No, not my Steve," Sara said sarcastically. She knew how intense he could be when he was invested in something. It made everyone at the table laugh.

"Anyway," Andy began again, "we didn't lose another game that season until the playoffs, when some Catholic school beat us in the second round. But we knew, with all the guys we had coming back, that we had a shot. We just needed to beat the damn Knights. They had this kid, DaQuan Foster…"

"He's still playing with the Long Island Lizards in the MLL," Colin said.

"No shit, huh? Figures. Anyway, this kid was the best attacking midfielder in the state. But we knew we had the best long stick middie in the state."

He put his arm around Steve.

"Cut it out."

"No you cut it out. Sara, your husband here shut this kid down. I mean shut... him... down. He didn't score once, didn't even get a shot on goal. Steve was probably closer to him that night than his girlfriend ever got. I mean the kid couldn't move. We saw that and... we just followed his lead..."

"I did shut him down pretty good, huh?"

"And he went on to be a professional?" Sara said.

"I guess so, huh Colin? I actually bumped into him when we made the Final Four at West Point. He was with Johns Hopkins in the other game. We lost so I never got to play against him."

"I'm sure he was glad about that," Andy said.

"Cut it out dude." Steve was enjoying the praise though.

"How come you never told me you were *this* good?"

"What are you talking about, honey? I said I was all-state, and that's how I got into West Point."

"Yeah, but the leader of the team. The hero of the big game. You must have been like the most popular kid in school."

All the guys laughed.

"Honey, I played lacrosse. This wasn't Oak Grove Academy. At Quincy Adams, if you didn't play football, basketball, or baseball, then you didn't matter as much. It was a bigger deal to Oak Grove that they lost, than it was to our school that we won."

"And now we're out celebrating you getting hired as their new coach."

On the ride home, Sara looked at her husband. She was thinking of when they first met. It was at a club downtown, in 2001, the summer after he had graduated from West Point and she from nursing school at DSU. She thought he was a good dancer, and she worked up the nerve to buy him a drink. He was so turned on that she was so forward, and they've been together ever since—except that they hadn't been, because in 2003 he was sent to Iraq, and for three years she either worried every day that he might be killed or hurt while he was there, or worried about when he would be sent back when he was home. And then he lost his leg and never went back.

She was so happy for him now. He was a good man and he'd been through a lot and he deserved a break, and that break had finally come. She wanted to talk to him about things. Ask him how he was feeling, bring up Mr. Haley, see if he was really okay. But there was another side of her that was so attracted to him at that moment, that she was afraid to bring anything up that might kill his mood.

"I hope the kids are asleep when we get home," she said.

He looked at her. This was not an "I've had a hard day and I hope the kids are asleep so I don't have to deal with them" comment, it was an "I hope we have some time alone" comment. On their way out of the bar, as he was holding the door for her and watched her walk through, he noticed how nice her ass looked in the new jeans she'd just bought at Kohl's. For a woman with two kids, she really wasn't fat, really hadn't let herself go at all. He had taken that aspect of her for granted lately, and tonight, while he felt a lot younger reliving high school moments with the guys, he was reminded of how hot she was, and now she was telling him I

55

hope the kids are in bed, and it made her even more attractive. He wanted to keep looking at her instead of watching the road as he drove.

When they got to the house and found out the kids were indeed in bed, they couldn't get his mother out fast enough. No, Chad hasn't called. No, we know he should've called. It's no big deal, really, mom. No *really*, mom, it's not a big deal I'll call him tomorrow okay thank you for watching the kids goodnight.

Mandy got into her car after work and blew into the Intoxilyzer 4100. Then she let the thing fall out of her mouth and cried. The court had ordered the Intoxilyzer 4100 installed after Kovacs was arrested for his second DUI. He was arrested in her car while his was being worked on because he crashed his driving in reverse really fast. His car was a Mustang convertible, he had the top down, and stuck his neck out like a giraffe with a silly look on his face, showing off for all his friends. Everyone thought he was hilarious, until he backed into the van of a carpet cleaner parked on the street in front of their neighbors'. She should've told him no when he asked to take her car a few nights later to hang out with his friends, told him it was his own fault, but he convinced her, like he always did, and look at her now, blowing into an Intoxilyzer 4100 in order to make her car run so she could drive home after work. Not only that, but she had to blow every fifteen minutes, otherwise the horn would beep uncontrollably until she parked it, and then after that she wouldn't be able to restart it. She'd suffered that indignity on her way to her parents' after she'd found out about Kovacs and his father's wife and she threw him out of the house. Her parents' was 20 minutes away, and after blowing once to start the car, she'd forgotten about it, and one mile from the house, in the neighborhood where everyone knew her, the car was beeping out of control. Her dad had to come get her.

Blowing into it now was another reminder of what Kovacs had put her through, yet how much she still loved him and how much she missed him. She had no idea where he was staying, didn't know that while she was crying, he was joking about strap-ons with a couple 15-year-olds at Chad's. Who knows if it would've mattered if she did know that. The Intoxilyzer 4100 beeped. It had been almost 15 minutes since she first blew. She broke down again. She had planned on going to her parents' again after work, but she couldn't make it twenty minutes in this car, with this damn Intoxilyzer 4100. She couldn't even leave the parking lot, she was that upset. So she sat there, after she called her mom, and waited to be picked up.

The number one question she had in her head wasn't 'why?', but 'how?' The why was easy, because he was Kovacs. Why does Kovacs do anything, right? But what she wanted to know was how, after everything she'd done for him, how could he betray her like that? How could he make her look like a moron in front of everybody? After everything he'd put her through, how could none of that mean anything to him? The problem was, as the Intoxilyzer 4100 beeped at her again, she knew the answer to that, and it was an answer she'd probably known for a long time and just didn't have the courage to face. Kovacs wasn't betraying her, he just didn't care as much as she did.

At 2 AM, while Mandy was crying in her childhood bed, and Steve and Sara were sleeping soundly, Chad was awakened from a deep, alcohol induced slumber by loud music and yelling in his living room. At first he thought it was a dream, but when it was accompanied by banging from the wall next door, he realized it was all real. He heard Kovacs' voice, plus two women. Jesus Christ, I better put a stop to this, he thought. He had fallen asleep with his light on, and when he walked over to the long mirror that doubled as the sliding door to his closet and saw his reflection with messy hair, bloodshot eyes, dressed in a white T-shirt and boxers, he figured he better do something about that first. There was more yelling and more banging. He better do it fast. He threw on the jeans from the night before, and his DSU hat.

Kovacs had the radio up loud, staggering around the room, telling the girls about the 90s Café.

"This is the best radio show ever. It's gonna be on in a minute, you'll love it."

The girls giggled.

"Kovacs, what the fuck is going on?"

"Oh, ladies, this is the guy I was telling you about. It's my roommate, Chad."

"I'm not your roommate, Kovacs. This is my apartment, and you need to turn this shit down and be quiet, or—"

"Oh, here it is!"

The N-N-N-Nineties Café.

Right after the bumper, the guitar intro to the Gin Blossoms' "Hey Jealousy" started in.

"See, see! He always starts with that one. This is the best radio show ever."

More banging followed by a muffled "I'm gonna call the fucking police!" Chad shut off the radio.

"Hey, what the fuck dude!"

"Everyone needs to leave now! It's 2 in the fucking morning, Kovacs. I could get kicked out of this building, man. We aren't fucking in college anymore."

Chad was feeling sick to his stomach, and had a pounding headache. It was only going to get worse, because Kovacs picked up a chair from his kitchen, and threw it through the glass coffee table. The women screamed and ran out of the apartment. Chad wanted to do the same thing. He grabbed Kovacs and told him to cut the shit, and Kovacs threw him aside, then sat on the couch and put his head in his hands, saying he was sorry and he was a fucking moron. Chad felt his cell phone in his pocket—he must've forgotten to take it out when he took his jeans off before he went to bed—, and called 9-1-1. Kovacs heard him talk to the dispatcher, telling her who he was, where he lived, and describing the scene he'd just witnessed, and he tried to take the phone from him. Luckily the neighbor had also called the cops, and they were already there, and found Kovacs and Chad struggling over the phone. They knew Kovacs well, and when they saw him on top of Chad, figured they'd have their hands full, so they went right for the pepper spray. It caught Chad in the eyes too, stinging him, and pushing him over that final edge to vomiting. A cop helped him into his bathroom to wash his eyes out, while two others dealt with Kovacs.

After Chad told him what happened, they went out to the hallway, where his neighbors were watching. There was a large, wet stain near the wall, and Chad found out Kovacs had relieved himself there before he and the girls entered his apartment. He was mortified. Only Miguel and Julía were sympathetic. Kovacs was swearing at him, calling him a traitor, and saying how Gwen was right to dump his ass. Then the cops took him away, and everyone went back to bed, and Chad was left with the realization that his place was trashed, there were no more

Thirsty Thursdays at The Dirty Sombrero, and that he had to be up for work in five hours. He threw up again, and then passed out on his bed with the lights on, wearing his jeans.

The next morning, as he went through his routine, the first thing he noticed was a shiner underneath his left eye. He must've gotten it in the scuffle with Kovacs. God Damn it! The one he'd gotten from Stacy's boyfriend had just gone away! His eyes were still bloodshot from the pepper spray, his head was pounding, and he had a gross feeling in his stomach, like he wanted to throw up but could avoid it. The shower was nice, but brushing his teeth made him gag. This was going to be a long day. He'd clean up the living room when he got home.

Haley had intended on giving him a hard time for his sorry state, but when she saw his black eye, she was concerned and wanted to know what happened. He gave her a Cliff's Notes version of everything. It made him feel good though to tell her the black eye wasn't a big deal when she touched near it and said he needed to do something about it, the way a boy in middle school flaunts his minor injuries to the girls as proof of his tough streak.

"So what are you going to do about him? Will he still be staying with you?"

"Oh hell no. I'm gonna pack his shit up when I get home and send it out tomorrow or something."

Chad in Accounting drank a lot of coffee and took a lot of ibuprofen, but he was fighting an uphill battle. Haley, out of pity, helped as much as she could, but in a way that only made it worse, because the less he had to do, the longer each minute agonizingly ticked away. He'd swear he'd look at the clock in the lower right-hand corner of his computer, and the numbers wouldn't move, the way 11:10 seems to last forever for someone wanting to make a wish at 11:11.

Then he got a text he wasn't expecting. Dave wanted to know if he'd be around later so he could pick up Kovacs's stuff. No. No, he couldn't see Dave right now, not the way he looked, not the way his apartment looked. He tried to think of a way out of it, but all the options sounded ridiculous and immature. He texted Dave back that that would be fine.

Now the rest of his day was filled with imaginary scenarios of Dave visiting and what he'd say, what they'd say to each other. Would he be cold, distant, unfriendly? Or would he be the bigger man? He hadn't seen him since the break-up, at least not in person. He'd seen plenty of Gwen's Facebook photos. He was Dave's friend on Facebook too. The best friend who stabbed him in the back and had an affair with his girlfriend of five years was his friend on Facebook.

Dave showed up around six to get Kovacs's things, which Chad had hastily stuffed in his backpack. He'd picked up the destroyed coffee table too, but the place still looked like a mess, especially by Chad's standards. He handed Dave the bag through the doorway, and instead of inviting him in, studied him. He had put on weight too, maybe a little more than Chad did. His hair was much more salt and pepper looking in person than it was on the Facebook photos. Dave made a few comments about how crazy it must've been last night, and how you gotta love Kovacs, but a guy's gotta grow up sometime, right? Chad offered a barely audible chuckle in assent. Then Dave asked how he'd been, as if the time they'd spent apart was due to one of them moving away to take a new job or something, and they were by chance now bumping into one another and catching up. He didn't do it on purpose, he was having as much trouble with the situation as Chad was, it's just that his awkwardness wasn't on account of the man across from him having had a pivotal role in the heartache he's endured over the past five years, it was on account of him being the betrayer, and it's difficult for the betrayer to win any sympathy from the one he betrayed. Chad said he was doing well, and didn't reciprocate the interest in how Dave was.

Who knows how much longer this scene would've gone on if Steve hadn't shown up, but his being there ended it immediately. Steve never forgave Dave for what he did to his brother, and when Dave asked him how he was doing he, he said:

"Don't talk to me like we're buds. You're lucky I have a wife and kids to think about, otherwise I'd drill you right now."

Dave exited after that, saying it was good seeing Chad. Steve shook his head and made his way inside the apartment. Chad explained everything to him, from Kovacs cheating on his wife with his step-mother, staying with him for a couple days, and then what happened last night and why Dave was there.

"That guy's a friggin' snake. I've always said that, even when you and him were buds. God I wish..."

It made Chad uncomfortable listening to Steve talk like that about Dave, because it just drove home to him that much more how much Dave got over on him, and how much he, Chad, was incapable of getting Dave back. He thought about Stacy's boyfriend too, and how scared he was in that confrontation, and felt even more inadequate to his younger brother, because he knew Steve never would've behaved like such a coward.

Steve filled Chad in on the details of his new job, and held up a six-pack he'd brought over to share with him.

"You sure you feel like having one now, though?"

"Yes, I *definitely* need one now."

They sat down on opposite sides of the couch after toasting to Steve's new job. Chad remembered all the times his mother wanted him to call his brother, and he felt a little guilty that Steve had made the trip over on his own. On the other hand, he seemed absolutely fine—Chad having no idea what Steve had been like before he got his job and the night spent with Sara—and figured his mom was overreacting as usual.

"So how you been since Mr. Haley passed?" Chad asked anyway.

"You know, I have good days and bad days. I mean, I'm not going to say I'm good, but I'm a lot better than I was."

Maybe his mother was right, maybe he should've called.

"How about you, how have you been?"

"You mean since Mr. Halley passed?"

"Yeah?"

"I've been good. I've been meaning to tell you, I saw Mrs. Haley that night of the funeral after I was with you guys at the bar. It was a trip."

"Why, why happened?"

"She was watching one of the MTV digital cable channels. She said it was Mr. Haley's favorite. There was like Disturbed and stuff playing in the background while we talked."

Steve laughed.

"He really liked that stuff, huh?"

"Oh yeah, Mr. Haley, he loved new music. I got him an iPod last year and showed him how to use it. He thought it was the greatest thing ever. He loved Tupac the most."

"Tupac?"

"I know, right? He never really got into why he liked the music he liked, just that he did."

"I can't believe I never knew that about him."

"He was a great man. He'll definitely be missed."

They sat in silence for a second and looked around the room. Steve spoke first.

"You know, I know the fact that I lost my leg makes you uneasy."

Chad tried to respond, but Steve stopped him.

"It's okay, it makes everyone uneasy. Even me."

Chad smiled and shook his head, realizing how silly he'd been to be uneasy about Steve missing his leg.

"Before it happened, I was in the cereal aisle, thinking about the generic cereals we used to get."

"Oh man, with the silly animals on the boxes? And what about the Ultimate Warrior cereal? Do you remember when you hid the box on me so I couldn't have any?"

"I didn't hide it, I just put it in a less conspicuous location."

"Yeah, under your bed!"

There was a commercial on TV of two Miller High Life deliverymen shaking a soldier's hand in an airport, making a point of saying that the soldier had his name on his military bag, not the name of an expensive designer label. Chad and Steve looked at each other:

"Sir, whose name is on your bag?" Chad said, mocking the commercial.

"Why, my name, LL Bean."

They laughed. It was a good end to the week for both of them.

Brick Steele, CPA

There was a celebration at work on Monday. Jodi, the slightly heavy, slightly homely receptionist had made it official on Facebook the night before: her boyfriend popped the question. All the women got her something, mostly flowers or gift certificates. Everyone crowded around to see the rock on her finger. Jodi's boyfriend worked at Home Depot, and that ring, even though he bought it at Jared's, and not one of the more upscale jewelry stores at the mall, set him back more than he could afford. Eventually he'd default on it, and the hit their credit took would hurt their chances of getting a loan to buy a house. But that wasn't anything anyone was thinking about then. This was a time of celebration.

Not for Chad in Accounting, though. Seeing Jodi be so happy reminded him of how unhappy he was. He hated seeing anyone have a successful relationship now, and anytime he heard of a relationship ending, it gave him a sense of satisfaction. Haley, having experienced her own heartbreak much more recently, was taking a different approach. She was right up there with the other women, saying how lucky Jodi was, and meaning it.

Chad in Accounting and his supervisor were left alone at their cubicles while Haley had some cake and chatted with the other women. He didn't think anything of it when his supervisor stood abruptly and ran to the bathroom. He didn't like his supervisor, and didn't care what he did. Had he known his supervisor was sitting in a stall crying, it wouldn't have made a difference, in fact would've made Chad in Accounting feel even more uncomfortable around him.

This wasn't a real let-it-all-out kind of cry his supervisor was having. It was one of those dysfunctionally masculine kinds of cries, where he's fighting every tear, every sniffle, every sob with everything he's got. He firmly believed that crying was a sign of weakness, and he was completely embarrassed by it. It angered and frustrated him that Jodi, dimwitted, overweight, ugly Jodi, got to have something he couldn't. Why? Knowing her, she probably voted No on Question 1 last week anyway. And why should she even have the right to vote on his rights? She sucked as a human being, I mean, just listen to her talk about stupid shit like *Sex in the City* and whatever stupid Matthew McConaughey/Kate Hudson Romantic Comedy that was in the theaters. It just made him seethe with anger. And heartbreak, because when the measure was on the ballot, it looked like it might succeed, that the state might finally let him and Adam be like every other couple, at least let him be like Jodi and her moron boyfriend…

Chad in Accounting's supervisor had a name, as Haley pointed out in the last chapter. What neither Haley nor Chad knew, though, was that Matthew was his middle name. His real first name was Brick. Brick Matthew Steele. The fourth of four children, but the only male, his father, knowing Brick would be their last child, wanted more than anything in the world to raise a famous quarterback. The first place to start was with the name, because everyone became what their name was, and Brick was a real quarterback name. His wife wanted to go with Matthew, but her husband looked so pitiful in making his case, she decided on a compromise: his middle name will be Matthew, and I'll call him Matthew, along with my side of the family, and you can call him Brick. She knew her parents didn't really like her husband, thinking him uncouth, and if they found out their son's real name was Brick, it would only make things worse. Brick would be his "nickname" to them.

As a two-year-old, the father was mortified to find his daughters dressing up Brick like one of their dolls. No, he needs to be Brick Steele, pro quarterback, not Brick Steele cross-dresser. Brick has no recollection of this, but when his sisters tell stories, it conjures up a well of resentment. He'd never have dressed like a chick if he'd had any choice.

Things didn't go as well as his father had planned as far as football either. He was shocked to see his son in 8th grade practice lining up as a safety on defense, and demanded to know what the story was.

"Well, Mr. Steele, sir," his coach said, "we tried him at quarterback, but I gotta tell you, the boy's a natural safety. You ever seen him hit anyone?"

They watched the practice. Brick flew all over the field, getting into every scrum, wanting a part of every tackle.

"The boy throws his body around like he's got a spare in the closet at home."

He looked at Mr. Steele after he made his comment. He was used to dealing with fathers who didn't understand why their sons weren't quarterbacks. He started the same way he always did.

"Mr. Steele, I understand how you feel about—"

"Hot damn, did you see that? He just upended that fast kid you got at running back. You get 'im Brick!"

He was so excited. The coach was excited too.

"You got yourself a fine son, Mr. Steele."

Unlocking the door to his apartment, Chad was approached by Anishka, a man from Sri Lanka who lived a few doors down and whom Chad always misidentified as being Indian. He had his cousin with him.

"Hello Chad, how are you?"

Chad wondered why he was being friendly, because he had treated Chad with a fair amount of disdain in all of their previous meetings.

"I'd like you to have my cousin stay with you for two weeks."

"What?"

Chad didn't disguise how shocked he was.

"Only two weeks. I'll pay."

"What? No. No, Anishka, I can't do that."

The cousin was telling Anishka that it was okay, they'd figure something else out, but Anishka was still pleading his case. Chad shook his head and entered his apartment.

He had to use a dining room chair as a table to put his bowl of fettuccine with alfredo sauce from a jar on. Frickin' Kovacs. He needed a new coffee table. Maybe tomorrow he'd go to

Goodwill or something. He could go to Ikea and get a new one too. What a pain in the ass. Frickin' Kovacs.

He didn't do anything over the weekend beyond some Red Box movies and playing video games. He'd broken down and bought *FIFA '10*, and was surprised he didn't see Miguel tonight, because he'd spent the whole weekend at Chad's apartment playing it. Julia must have made him stay home. He'll probably see him tomorrow. He couldn't wait to tell him about Anishka. In his head he imitated Anishka's deep, Indian accent. "Come on, only two weeks."

Tuesday morning, Brick was called into his boss's office.

"Hey, Matty, have a seat."

He hated being called Matty. Matt or Matthew or Mr. Steele, but not Matty.

"I just wanted to go over a few things. First off, how's Haley been working out for you?"

"Oh, she's great, Bert. Better than I could've hoped for actually."

"That's great... that's great..."

He trailed off and looked at some papers. Bert was a short, stout man, with dark balding hair and a pale, blotchy complexion, wearing a white dress shirt that hung off him a bit and a dark tie with a hastily tied knot that was coming loose already at 9:05am. This was in stark contrast to Brick with his closely cropped salt and pepper hair that had just enough on top that was pushed forward and up with pomade so it looked like a sculptor had crafted it out of marble; his healthy complexion that was due to a combination of a healthy diet and the right moisturizers, with only the slight crow's feet around the eye that made him seem not so much older as more established in life; and the dark gray tailored designer shirt that fit his tall, still well-maintained athletic torso perfectly, even in his 40s, and a darker gray tie with a full Windsor knot that looked as crisp and aggressive as the attitude Brick projected. At first glance, one would've thought they should've been on opposite sides of the desk, but Bert had something that Brick didn't: he could handle people; he knew when to use the carrot and the stick, and how to use each effectively to get the most out of his staff; whereas Brick had zero people skills, so Brick remained a supervisor while Bert was promoted to office manager.

"I guess I should just come right to the point."

Brick didn't like the sound of this.

"It's come to my attention that you and Chad don't always create the most... inviting... environment... if you know what I mean?"

"I don't."

Brick was scowling. His boss already found him kind of intimidating, which was why he didn't bring this issue up before, when Stacy was there, and no one enjoyed bringing things to Accounting. Before they hired Haley, the district HR coordinator came to him officially and told him something needed to be done, and he was dreading this meeting. Then they hired Haley, and she was so nice, it gave him a foot in the door and allowed him to sound more like Brick's buddy and less like he was confronting him.

But now Brick was scowling, and his resolve was dissolving.

"Until Haley came here, people said you guys were... ahh... um... well, let's just say you weren't very nice to people in the other departments who brought you work... work that's... let's be honest... a part of your jobs, right?"

Brick sighed.

"This isn't coming from me, it's coming from our district HR coordinator…"

There you go, Bert, let him know that your hands are tied, it's corporate that's putting the screws to ya, that he can't blame you. And Brick did take this seriously. It reminded him that his little world at work was only a small part of the much bigger picture. There were people above Bert who were meaner and less susceptible to his bullying—people that could potentially relieve him of his job.

"The thing is, Matt, I talked to Don, the district HR coordinator who brought these concerns to me, and I said this new hire Haley was infusing your department with a new positive energy, and that I thought it was rubbing off."

"Okay…"

"That's good, right? And he agreed with me… only, he wants to see this new positivity grow a little faster, if you know what I mean."

"I guess… I don't know… you mean you want me to smile more? Tell Jodi I think it's just grand she's engaged?…"

"Matt, this is serious."

"I'm being serious. I'm not Mr. Flowers and Tulips. I'm not good at faking it like most people… and to be honest, I don't like a lot of the people out there in that office…"

"Jesus Matt, you're not letting me help you."

"I did what you said before about getting more involved in stuff around the office. I joined that Jared kid's silly back-up quarterback fantasy league."

"See. How hard was that?"

"Bert, if there's nothing else…"

"I haven't finished making my point."

"I'll do my best to be Miss Congeniality from now on—"

"It's not that easy, Matt. See, Don thinks the introduction of Haley is a great place from which to move forward… a fresh start, if you will."

"Okay?"

"And in his mind, a great fresh start should include a kind of team building process."

"Oh no, none of that trust fall bullshit, Bert. Come on man, help me out here."

"It's not like that."

"Then how is it like?"

"Nothing extreme, just have everyone over on Sunday to watch some football."

"Oh God, Bert, you're killing me here. Adam and I had plans."

"I know it's short notice, but can't you change them?"

"I don't know Bert, this whole Marriage Bill getting defeated has hit us pretty hard…"

This set off alarm bells in Bert, just like Brick knew it would. Don had told Bert that the football party idea would be the best bet, because he didn't want to discipline Matt, and have him turn around and say he was discriminated against due to his sexuality. It wouldn't look good. Brick didn't know that part, he just knew any overt references to his sexuality usually disrupted Bert's equilibrium.

"I know, Matt. You know, we were all behind you. We wore the buttons, we let you go to the rallies, we let people off work early to make sure they got out and voted. But you gotta understand the situation we're in here."

Brick sighed again.

"This Sunday?"

"They want to get the ball rolling ASAP."

"Fine."

"All right, good. I'll e-mail you the details right now."

"Details?"

"Just some team building exercises."

"No way, Bert."

"Come on Matt. It's not a big deal."

"Bert, this is the weekend before Thanksgiving you're trying to pin us down for. I'll be lucky if Haley and Chad are free too. And now you want me to, on top of convincing them to give up their Sundays, hit them with these ridiculous teambuilding activities."

Bert was had there. He made a meek plea that Brick hadn't even seen them yet, but he was satisfied with the small victory that this was going to happen at all.

When Brick left his boss's office and returned to the set of cubicles he shared with Haley and Chad, Chad was hoping he was in big trouble. He didn't like his supervisor, and he knew his supervisor didn't like him either. The distressed look on his face told him this was going to be good.

"Guys, can you huddle around my desk for a sec?"

Oh man, Chad thought, he's leaving. He got the ax. Maybe they'll promote *me*. From Chad in Accounting to Chad the Supervisor.

"I just got done talking to Bert, and I guess the district HR coordinator feels like..."

Come on, out with it, out with it!

"...he feels like we need a teambuilding exercise, and they've decided I'm going to have you guys over to my place to watch some football this Sunday."

What?

Haley was excited.

"I've wanted to see your house, after you've told me so much about it. Is Adam going to be there?"

"I don't know, probably. I know you want to meet him."

"Oh my God, I hope so."

Brick liked Haley, and the idea of her coming over made him happy. Why hadn't he invited her sooner? He was busy with all those rallies, and she had that horrible thing with her niece, so he guessed it made sense. Chad on the other hand. He wasn't too fond of spending a Sunday with him.

"Okay, so Haley's in, how about you Chad?"

How about you, Chad? Please Chad, say you're busy, say you're, you're, you're just a wet blanket like you always are. Just say no, for Christ's sake.

"Yeah, I'm free."

"Okay, sounds good then."

Brick couldn't have known about Haley and Chad's moment after The Dirty Sombrero last Thursday night. Otherwise, he'd have been right in Chad not wanting to go, but an opportunity to be with Haley outside of work, even if it was at his dick supervisor's place, was worth it. If

Brick knew that Chad's only interest in going was to get with Haley, it would only have made him angrier.

They returned to their desks and their work. About ten minutes later, Jared with the Hyphenated Last Name in HR came by with a sheet of paper for Brick.

"Hey Matt, here's last week's fantasy results. Man, that Matt Moore pick might turn out to be a good one. Where did you come up with that?"

"Just lucky I guess."

Brick didn't like Jared. Not the way Chad didn't like him—more out of envy in Chad's case than dislike—but more because of what Jared represented to Brick. Brick's being gay made Jared uncomfortable, and he wouldn't have wanted anything to do with Brick under any other circumstances; but they were both former players on the DSU football team, though Brick was there about ten years before Jared; and then even more impressive to Jared was the fact that Brick was on the practice squad of the Phoenix Cardinals in 1992, and actually was called onto the game-day roster once and played some special teams and a few defensive snaps. To Brick it was as if Jared tolerated the gay part because the NFL part was such a big deal that he couldn't not tolerate it, and the fact that they both played football at DSU made Jared think they were equals and above everyone else in that office due to that fact. It was understanding this that made joining Jared's fugazi fantasy league all the more anathema, because Brick knew he was giving it a legitimacy, and with it Jared, in Jared's mind at least, which he didn't deserve.

"Oh, I forgot to tell you guys, the Sports Channel's *Lead Off* is going to interview me this Friday about the back-up QB fantasy league! I don't know, word must have gotten out about it or something."

"That's really cool, Jared," Haley said. Chad and Brick weren't as impressed or congratulatory.

"Just e-mail me any changes you might make this week, Matt, before the 1:00 games start."

"Sounds good."

Brick had not changed his team once since he created it at the beginning of the year. He drafted three Matts: Matt Leinart, Matt Flynn, and Matt Moore. They were curious picks to the other guys in the office who played in Jared's league, but Brick didn't understand the rules, and didn't want to understand them. He was only joining to make Bert happy, so he just picked three back-up quarterbacks named Matt and called it good.

"Why don't you have a team in the fantasy league?" Haley asked.

"Um... I don't know... it's not my thing," Chad said.

Really, Chad always wanted to be a part of the back-up QB Fantasy League, but he was waiting for Jared to invite him. He didn't know that Brick invited himself, or that all he, Chad in Accounting, had to do too was ask and he'd have been in too. He thought he wasn't cool enough or regarded highly enough, and that Jared's league represented an inner circle of guys he wasn't a member of. Finding out his supervisor was in it this season just rubbed salt in his wound.

Miguel visited Chad that night to play more *FIFA '10*. He brought over some fried sea bass and a rice dish Julía made. Chad told him about what happened the day before with Anishka.

"Do you know his story, man?"

"He came here from India, right?"

"Sri Lanka."

"Oh, okay…"

"Yeah, remember that huge tsunami that hit there about five years ago?"

"Uh huh."

"His wife and young son died in that."

"Oh wow, I didn't know that."

"Yeah, he's had a rough time. I don't know that you ever get over that. I couldn't imagine losing Julía and Richard like that, you know?"

"No, I know… I mean I don't *know* know, because I don't have a wife and kids, but I can imagine, you know?"

"Yeah… he's a really interesting guy, used to play cricket and stuff, and an amazing cook. Those Sri Lankans, man, they know their spices."

"You're not telling me anything, I can smell it sometimes."

"You've never had anything he's made?"

"Oh, hell no, the guy can't stand me."

"What are you talking about? I'm sure he understands you can't house his cousin for two weeks."

"No, I just mean in general. He doesn't like me."

"Why?"

"Who knows? Maybe he just doesn't like white people."

"No, I mean why do you think that, moron."

"What? I don't know, he just always seems angry at me… like, I mean, I didn't grow up with my dad, but he's like the kind of dad you can't do anything right for, that's the kind of angry he has for me. Does that make sense?"

"No."

"Whatever, I'm telling you the guy doesn't like me."

"There's no way. Listen, I'll talk to Julía, and we'll invite him over for dinner and you can come too. We'll do it this week sometime. Then you can get to know him. I swear he doesn't have an issue with you."

"What? No, I don't want to do that."

"Why not? Julía and I will be there. Come on, dude, you need a little culture in your life anyway."

"I watch international soccer with you. What was that Copa whatever thing we were watching back in May or June or whenever it was?"

"*Copa Libertadores*. It's like the Champions League of South America."

"Yes, that's it. We watched those on the Spanish Fox Soccer Channel, so I didn't even understand what the announcers were saying. I'd say that was a cultural experience. Plus watching your team get killed by the Brazilians, that was great too."

Miguel laughed.

"You know, that reminds me, you never gave me an answer on the indoor soccer league."

"Is Anishka doing it?"

"I'm serious. We got a pretty solid group of guys. It's not that competitive, it's just for fun."

"But I haven't played since intramurals in college."

"I don't even know what that means. Did you play 5-on-5 with a goalie?"

"Yeah."

"Then you're perfect. We just need a couple more guys to fill out the team in case some guys can't make it a week or something. It's really not that big of a deal."

Chad didn't know. When Miguel first brought it up, he was apprehensive. He was way out of shape, and really rusty. He couldn't remember the last time he even volleyed a soccer ball with himself.

"I got an idea, me and the some of the guys are gonna kick the ball around tomorrow night. We do it every Wednesday there's no Champion's League games on. Why don't you come with me. And then Thursday, me and Julía will set things up with Anishka for dinner. How does that sound?"

"I guess."

"Perfect—oh, dude, did you just see that?"

"You got owned."

"That's cheap. Ronaldinho's not that good anymore."

They were watching the video game's replay of AC Milan star Ronaldinho maneuvering around three of Miguel's Fiorentina defenders before putting the ball in the upper 90.

Tuesday nights at the London-Steele household consisted of *Real Housewives of Orange County*, or *New York*, or *New Jersey*—not *Atlanta*, though, Adam didn't like that one. Brick hated those shows, the same way Adam hated *Monday Night Football*, but neither chose on either night to watch TV in the bedroom. They might not have been looking forward to *Real Housewives* or football, but they were looking forward to seeing each other all day.

They lived in a beautiful house on the water, designed by Adam, who was a very successful architect. The inside was decorated with expensive art, sophisticated furniture, and state of the art appliances. It wasn't exactly Brick's style, but he left the decorating to Adam, and Brick handled the other aspects like fixing toilets that wouldn't stop running or changing the oil in their vehicles. When they were growing up, Brick's dad showed him and his sisters how to do all of that stuff, because he felt paying someone to do it was a waste of money, and even now that Adam and Brick had plenty of money to pay someone else to do those things, Brick still felt it was a waste of money.

"I don't know how you can watch this show? It's just a bunch of ignorant rich broads saying stupid things."

"That's *why* I watch it. It's better than that ESPN. I swear, if I hear another one of those morons say *at the end of the day...*"

Right then, in one of the interviews with the producers, a housewife said:

"At the end of the day, she's gotta look herself in the mirror..."

"HA!"

Adam let out a big, overly dramatic sigh, folded his arms, and shook his head. Before Brick could get too proud, Adam spoke.

"I forgot to remind you, tomorrow is *America's Top Model* night. The guys are coming here."

"Here? Is it our night again already?"

"Honey, it's been over a month."

"I just don't understand how you can handle listening to Tyra. *I'm smiling with my eyes*. Seriously? And that time she was patting herself on the back, like she was Rosa Parks, because she was the first black chick on the cover of *Sports Illustrated*."

"Please, tell me more. I thought you didn't pay attention."

Brick stared at him for a second, trying to keep from smiling.

"You know I hate you."

"Ugh! Why do you have to do to that thing Sunday? *I'm* supposed to have you on Sundays. Why can't you just be nicer to your co-workers?"

"You don't have to work with them."

"You're such a drama queen. Besides, I thought you said you liked that new girl, Haley."

"I do, but the rest are just tools. I found out from Haley that that Chad guy caught his girlfriend in bed with his best buddy, so that's why he walks around like blah all the time, even though it happened to him like five years ago or something. Then he used to make these awkward attempts to hit on Stacy, the chick that used to work in our department before she no-call no-showed; besides, she was no peach either. She always had some fake ailment that prevented her from doing her work. One time she said she was suffering from EBS—"

"*Irritable Bowel Syndrome*. I remember that one."

This wasn't the first time Adam had heard these complaints. Though Brick was exaggerating a little, Adam knew too that he felt lonely. He had no one to talk about football and stuff with, and though he loved the guys in he and Adam's social circle—and had grown closer to them after they all campaigned together in favor of Question 1—it would be nice if there were some straight guys or gay guys with similar interests to Brick that he could interact with. Adam understood how much a back-up QB fantasy league insulted Brick's sensibilities.

In high school, Brick was making it happen as a strong safety for his football team. He grew to be 6'3", 215 lbs., and an immense athlete. He could cover slower wide receivers, or move onto the line and help stop the run. His favorite thing to do though was blitz the quarterback. To just hit someone as hard as he could, use his body as a battering ram, it was the most amazing feeling. By his senior year, he became one of the defensive captains, and some mid-level Division I-AA schools were considering him for a scholarship, including Dodge State. For his father, his dream was finally coming to fruition—even if his son was hitting quarterbacks instead of being one.

Something wasn't fitting for Brick, though. He was gay. He knew it, probably from as far back as 8th grade. And he also knew that being gay and playing football didn't mix, so he pretended to be straight and date girls superficially. He lived in a small town about two hours inland, and there was no real gay night life or gay community to speak of, at least not out in the open.

Then he went to DSU in 1986. It wasn't quite what it is there now with Gay Pride week and open advocacy groups on campus, but it was a drastic difference from his small hometown. There were gay bars downtown, and once he discovered them, life changed for him. Yes, he was still in the closet, but now he had places to be open on the weekends and really explore his sexuality—really be that part of himself.

For four years, he lived these two lives: football Brick and gay Matt. His teammates and friends thought he was just a nice guy who went home every weekend to see his family and do his laundry; and his family thought he was just so busy with school and football that he barely came home to see them.

When DSU went to the Div I-AA playoffs in his senior year, he made some noise in a nationally televised game on ESPN against North Dakota State, and that led him to some invitations to undrafted try-outs with NFL teams. He didn't catch on that year, but the next year he got the invite to Phoenix and a spot on the practice squad, and week 14 he got the call up to the active team. His and his dad's dream was finally realized. His dad finally got to see his son in an NFL game.

The dual life took a toll on him though. He knew he couldn't be out and play professional football. We were still years away from John Amaechi coming out after retiring from the NBA, and this was 20 years before Michael Sam. If Brick really wanted a career in the NFL, he would have to work twice, maybe three times harder than he had been, because he wasn't quite as naturally gifted as the players he was competing with for a roster spot; and living this double life meant he had much less energy with which to do it.

He went back to training camp with the Cardinals the next year, and was cut before the second preseason game. From there, instead of going back to his hometown, he went back to the area around DSU, got a job as an accountant, and lived as an out gay man. It was liberating. He still hadn't told his family, but at the very least he wasn't hiding it from his coworkers and friends, or worried about bringing boyfriends home and someone finding out.

When he did finally come out to his family, in 1998, he could tell they were disappointed, especially his father; but also that that disappointment was tempered by the fact that Brick had played in an NFL football game. In a way it made it worse for him, especially with his father: he didn't accept that Brick was gay, he was just so proud that he had played in the NFL that he would overlook it. It angered Brick, the idea that being gay was something to be "overlooked," like he was telling his family he'd just been arrested for trying to sneak weed through the airport.

As he's lived his life in the 11 years since, he's met Adam and they've built their life together, and he's been very happy with that life. But then Question 1 was defeated, and with it their plans for a marriage next year, and the bitterness and estrangement came back to him, having to live the dual life he once had to live, not being fully accepted by society. Yet playing one game in the NFL was some kind of social capital that, didn't necessarily trump the way people viewed his being gay, but made people say "since you played in the NFL, I'll *overlook* the fact your gay." At times it made him seethe with anger, or like today with Jodi, made him break down and cry.

Chad wasn't sure what to bring. He'd never been to anything like this. Anishka decided he'd rather cook for Chad, Miguel, and Julía, which was a huge curve ball for Chad. At Miguel and Julía's, he'd bring a white or red wine, based on the dish she was serving, and he was set. Did Anishka even drink wine? Alcohol? What do you drink with curry? Chad had no idea that Anishka, looking at Chad as a bachelor living on his own, didn't expect him to bring anything. In fact, he assumed his mother cooked for him still, and when she didn't cook, he ate out. As

70

much as it would've been unfathomable for Anishka to think Chad had been cooking for himself at a young age because he came from a single-parent household with a working mother, it would have been equally unfathomable for Chad to think Anishka, or anyone else, would see him, an almost 33-year-old man who fully supported and took care of himself, as a boy that needed his mom to feed him. On the other hand, Chad's perception that Anishka's disdain for him was like a dad whose son couldn't do anything properly was pretty close to right. Though Anishka and Chad were about the same age—Anishka was 37—the fact the he had had a wife and son and Chad was a single bachelor made Anishka see view Chad in a patronizing light.

Miguel told him over the phone that beer, like Sam Adams, went best with the dishes Anishka would be cooking. Beer? Yes. Chad ran out to the store and bought a six-pack of Sam Adams Boston Lager.

Walking into Anishka's apartment was disorienting. The smells, the music, the decorations, it was foreign. The apartment itself was laid out a bit differently too. It opened into the living room like Chad's, but the kitchen was right behind it, separated by a wall with a large opening that allowed you to see into it, and then a hall to the left led to the bedrooms and bathroom. Miguel and Julía smiled and said hi from the couch that was against that wall that separated the kitchen and living room, while Anishka shook hands and told him how nice it was for him to come. As much as he was surprised by how cheerful Anishka was when he approached him on Monday about his cousin staying with him, he was surprised by how gracious a host Anishka was toward him now. He didn't know that Miguel, after broaching the subject of tonight's dinner, saw the disdain Chad spoke of on Anishka's face, and he took it upon himself to put in a good word. He wasn't entirely successful in dispelling all of Anishka's preconceived notions, but seeing Chad at his door with a six-pack of Sam Adams, something that would go perfect with the lamb dish he was cooking, demonstrated to him that Chad was more who Miguel said he was.

Chad took a seat in a chair on one side of the couch, and Anishka took a seat on the other. They started off with some drinks and talked. Miguel told them about Chad and him playing soccer the day before. Chad was expecting to hear about how poorly he'd done and how out of shape he was, but that wasn't where Miguel went.

"It looks like we're going to have a good team, huh Chad?"

Chad hadn't said for sure yet that he was even playing—what do you mean "we"?

"Yeah. Who was that one dude from Africa that was so good?"

"Martinson. Martinson Gagné. He's from Cameroon. I guess he's going to pharmacy school. Do they have one around here?"

"Yeah, there's a building in that office park behind the mall."

"He was telling me and Jorgé that his wife makes a mean jerk chicken. It might be too hot for even you, Anishka."

Anishka smiled. Chad was worried. He didn't like hot food.

"Speaking of Jorgé," Julía said, "how is María doing?"

"Good. She went in for an ultrasound last Friday, and everything's fine. He said they didn't want to know ahead of time what they're having. You remember Jorgé and María, right Anishka?"

He scowled and shook his head.

"We had them over that time you came by for dinner," Julía said. "Jorgé works with Miguel."

"Oh, yes, I remember him."

"Miguel said you looked pretty good yesterday, Chad."

"No, he and his friends were good. I could barely keep up."

"He's being modest. If you were just a little more aggressive you'd make a great defender. He wasn't falling for a lot of our fancy moves, and he gets rid of the ball up the field quickly. The guys were all saying you'd be perfect as one of our subs—or could even start if we needed you to."

Miguel was right about this. Chad was too self-conscious to see that he wasn't that rusty. In college and high school, he was used to being an attacking midfielder, a true number 8, and when he didn't have those skills yesterday, he was embarrassed. But he still knew where he should be positioned, still knew instinctively where to put the ball and where to look for it, he'd just lost a step, and like Miguel said, a level of aggression. So Chad, as usual, focused on the negative and what he couldn't do, and Miguel and the rest of the team were excited to have another solid defender they could count on.

When the meal was ready, they all sat at the table in the kitchen while Anishka served them. Everyone stared at Chad as he took his first bite. He'd never tasted anything so hot in his life. It was so spicy, the pain actually made him sick to his stomach. Miguel leaned in and whispered to him:

"You gotta eat it. It's a huge insult to come to a Sri Lankan's house and not eat his food."

Chad went for another bite, and they all broke out laughing.

"I have a special plate for you over here. We always make a batch that isn't as spicy for white people."

"No… no… it's okay…" He could barely talk. They laughed some more.

"It's okay. Anishka's food is a little spicy for Julía and me too."

Chad couldn't tell if the plate they gave him was spicy because he hadn't gotten over the bite of the other one, or if it was still hotter than he could handle, even when it was toned down for "white people." As they ate their food with ease, and he needed to drink after every bite, he felt the way he did when Miguel told him about Aconcagua the day after he went hiking with Haley. He was even blander than the blander dish Anishka had made for him, too bland, in fact, for what Anishka, Miguel, and Julía considered bland. He wondered if Haley could handle this spicy food.

After supper, Anishka served some *kavun*, along with some gourmet Peruvian coffee Julía's sister had brought over when she'd visited. Chad had had too much water and beer to drown out the spiciness of his food, and his back teeth were floating, so he excused himself as the group moved into the living room. On his way back, he saw some pictures on the wall in the hallway. One was of an amazingly beautiful woman with her arm around Anishka. The same woman was in a photo with Anishka and a young boy. That must be his family, Chad thought. God, she really is beautiful, like a total hottie. She could've been a model or a movie star, and Chad wouldn't have been any the wiser. He couldn't imagine even being with a woman that hot, let alone losing her in such a tragic way.

72

Over coffee and *kavun*, Chad told Anishka about himself. That he was an accountant, that his mother was a family law attorney, that his brother had been in the military, and now coached the local prep school in lacrosse. Anishka asked about a girlfriend.

"There's this girl Haley he went hiking with. She's a keeper. She speaks Spanish, and hiked Aconcagua."

Miguel patted Chad's knee with the back of his hand and raised his eyebrows a couple times.

"That's not really going anywhere. Her sister was the one whose infant daughter was killed recently by the father. She's still pretty upset."

Everyone was shocked that Haley's niece was the baby that had been killed, and they agreed that she wouldn't want to be in a relationship with someone new after a tragedy like that. Chad thought they were just saying that because it would sound insensitive to say what he was thinking, that it was only her niece and she shouldn't be making *that* big a deal of it—his libido talking. But they did have that opinion, because they grew up in cultures where the extended family meant more, and so Haley's situation, where she was living at home with her mom and helping her sister raise her niece, was common for a young woman, as opposed to as a result of her fiancé coming out of the closet and breaking her heart and her moving back home to get her life back together. They took for granted she'd have such a strong bond with her niece. Plus, their thought processes weren't controlled by their libidos.

They thanked Anishka for his hospitality, and he thanked them for coming by. Miguel made a comment to Chad in the hallway about it not being so bad, and Chad agreed, he genuinely had a good time. Between tonight's meal at Anishka's, and yesterday being the only American and native English speaker among the guys at Miguel's soccer practice, Chad was getting a sense of what Miguel meant by him experiencing new cultures. It was more than watching games on the Spanish Fox Soccer Channel. Maybe he would play on Miguel's team after all.

"Aren't you guys coming?"

Brick and Chad looked up from their computers. They let out some ums and ahhs, then Brick spoke:

"I would, but… it's Friday, and I want to get this done before—"

"Cut it out you two, Jared is about to be on TV."

Haley took each of their hands and led them from their seats. They put up a perfunctory passive resistance, but they knew her powers of positivity would always conquer their cynicism. The office was in the conference room watching Jared with the Hyphenated Last Name in HR's interview on the Sports Channel's *Lead Off.* Jared himself was at the local TV station, where his end of the interview was being conducted via satellite. *Lead Off* was a local morning sports show that discussed mostly the Boston sports teams, but also covered some national sports stories. As they stood in the back of the conference room, neither Chad or Brick knew they shared a common experience, neither knew that the other was thinking "this isn't a big deal, I've actually been on ESPN."

There was a big cheer when he first popped up on the screen. He was visibly nervous. He said "Well Lana" every time he answered one of host Lana Olafssen's questions. His blink rate was uncomfortably high. Off-screen, no one could see him playing with his fingers too.

"So Jared, where did you come up with this thing?"

"Well Lana, me and some buddies were watching that playoff game a few years ago when Tony Romo fumbled the snap when they were going for the game winning field goal, and we thought about making a fantasy league for back-up quarterbacks."

Some staffers had done a pre-interview, so Lana knew where this convoluted explanation was going.

"So you saw Tony Romo, and you thought you'd do a fantasy league that takes into consideration what back-up quarterbacks did for a team, including holding kicks, right?"

"Well Lana, I think you hit the nail on the head there."

"Okay... and what are the rules? How do you earn points?"

"Well Lana, we take into account a lot of factors, like whether he holds kicks, if he gets into a game or not, how much he's mentioned on TV..."

"And what would say, holding a kick be worth?"

"Well Lana, if it's a field goal, it's 3, and if it's an extra point, it's 1, and if he fumbles it, he loses 5 points."

"Wow, five points is a lot. Now do you do a draft like we do in regular fantasy football?"

"Yep."

A pause as Lana waits for him to elaborate.

"Um, you want to tell us how it works?"

They both laughed.

"Well Lana, it's three rounds, and everyone picks one quarterback a round."

"And who was picked first?"

"Michael Vick."

"And why is that, Jared?"

"Well Lana, we figured with the Wildcat and his reputation, he'd get on TV a lot and get opportunities in the game."

"But he doesn't hold kicks. Is that a bad thing?"

"Not really."

"And I read too that you were a back-up quarterback with Dodge State University while you were in college. Do you feel a kind of kinship to these back-up quarterbacks as well?"

"Um, not really."

Lana had no idea that she was striking a nerve here for Jared. He never liked to consider himself a back-up quarterback. Until she brought it up, he'd never even considered the connection between them and him.

"Okay, well it was nice having you Jared, good luck with your season, and thanks for coming on."

"Thank you, Lana."

And that was it. The show switched to a new topic. Everyone cheered. Everyone except for Chad and Brick. They had snuck back to their cubicles, not saying a word to each other. Haley noticed as the room was emptying out.

"Did you guys really skip out on that? Unbelievable."

Chad looked guilty. Brick was less interested.

"Being on the Sports Channel isn't that big of a deal."

"What do you mean? Even if it isn't, it was a big deal for Jared."

"I was on *Outside the Lines* once."

"On ESPN?"

"You were, Chad?"

Haley was stunned. Brick was surprised too. It was out of nowhere, like Ally Sheedy telling everyone in *The Breakfast Club* that she didn't do anything to get Saturday detention.

"Yeah, two years ago. They did a story about this girl MacKenzie, whose life I saved from my pervert neighbor a while back. When she was a senior in college, her volleyball team was in the national finals. The interview was on *Outside the Lines* and then some of it ran during the game."

"You saved a girl?"

"Yeah, like nine or ten years ago."

"Wow! Do you have the tape?"

"Uh huh."

"You'll have to bring it Sunday. I can't wait to see it! Why don't we watch that and maybe some of the tapes of Matt's football games?"

Haley was genuinely excited to see Chad's video of his ESPN interview and the tapes of Brick playing football, the way she was genuinely excited to see Jared on the Sports Channel today. For someone who worked on a TV show out in LA, one would've thought she'd have a more measured response, or maybe take the opportunity to remind them what her background in show business was; and for a lot of other people that definitely would've been the case, but not Haley. Plus, this story Chad had about saving a girl from a pervert was something she couldn't wait to hear.

Haley picked up Chad on Sunday. Neither really wanted to be there first without the other, but Chad wanted to much less than her, so when Haley asked if she'd like him to get her, he tried to be as nonchalant as possible, but responded with a "sure!"

"Wow, is this it?"

Your destination is approaching on your right in 200 hundred feet.

As they pulled up to the open gate leading into the driveway, they had a better view. Chad couldn't believe how nice it was. From a distance, it looked almost as if it sat on the ocean. There were three cars already there, his supervisor's Audi, a Land Rover, and a Maserati. Who had the Maserati?

"This is amazing Chad. I can't wait to use the hot tub. You remembered your suit, didn't you?"

"Yes, thanks for reminding me when you called."

They saw Brick in the doorway waving to them. Haley waved back, and they gathered their things out of her car and headed in his direction. Haley made some kind of heated nacho dip, and Chad brought a bottle of Pinot Noir that the guy at the liquor store recommended.

After introducing them to Adam, they got a quick tour. The living room area was a vast open space with a vaulted, exposed beam ceiling. The kitchen was state-of-the-art. The bathroom sink was made of marble. The bedrooms and office and other rooms were all beautiful, expensive linens on the beds, expensive carved woods made up the frames and furniture. And everything was in immaculate condition. They found out the Maserati wasn't a guest's, but rather the Sunday driving car Brick and Adam owned—the Sunday drive preempted this weekend, of course. Finally Brick took them to his office, which had his football memorabilia all over it. Chad had heard it discussed that his supervisor played in an NFL game, but seeing it was different: the framed jersey, helmet in a glass case, picture of himself on the field in his uniform. He wasn't so much impressed, as he tried to put it in the proper context: his gay tool of a supervisor was good enough at football that he played in one NFL game, and now he worked at the same soulless hellhole of a job that Chad did. And Haley too, accountant for *Love Shack*, now working in the same purgatory of cubicles in an office building. What was the point of it all?

They went back to the living room and did a get-to-know-you session. Haley told them what she did in LA, working on *Love Shack*. There was a momentary start-struckness, until she revealed that Sebastian had had his affair with *her* fiancé. They were still kind of star-struck. Then they turned to Chad. Same information he gave at Anishka's. His mother's vocation and last name rang a bell in Adam and Brick's heads. They asked if she was from a certain law firm. She was.

"Oh my God, that's *your* mom?"

"Chad, how come you never told me she's your mom?"

"I didn't think it was a big deal."

"How do you guys know his mother?"

It was a question Chad wanted to know too, but for some reason, instead of asking, he wanted to stay curious, or assumed his mother was a very prominent attorney that everyone knew, and he just wasn't in those circles.

"His mom is amazing," Adam said. "Our friend Sandy and her partner Janet had a baby— Janet was artificially inseminated. Anyway, for five years, they've raised this child together, she's in kindergarten, she calls both of them mom, and then Janet is diagnosed with breast cancer. She dies six months later."

"Oh, that's so sad," Haley said.

"Hang on cowgirl, not done. Janet's mother files for custody of the child, because Sandy's not a biological parent."

"No way, that's horrible!"

"It would've been a lot worse if Chad's mom hadn't represented Sandy in court. She was so kind and understanding, and she made the judge feel that too. It just sucks, because if they had been allowed to get married…"

He caught himself. The wound of the election was still very fresh for both he and Brick. Brick wasn't exactly paying attention though, he was looking at Chad, trying to figure out how his mom was his mom.

"I didn't know that. My mom's pretty cool about things like that, though."

"You should've seen her Chad, she was testifying in front of the state legislature on our behalf to get the marriage equality bill passed."

"Yep, that sounds like her."

Yes, but it doesn't sound like you, Chad. How could your mother be so vibrant, so assertive, so clever and intelligent, so not anything I associate with you. But the mere fact alone that a local LGBT advocate gave birth to and raised him gave Brick a whole new level of respect for Chad, even if Chad didn't know it.

They had some more hors d'oeuvres and chatted for a few more minutes, then decided it was time to check out those videos. Brick decided to show them his game in the Div I-AA playoffs his senior year against North Dakota State. A few years back Adam had had it put on DVD for him, and Brick had seen it so many times, he knew what points to fast forward to.

On one play, he sacked the quarterback on a safety blitz.

"And Carpenter is brought down by the safety, Brick Steele."

"Haha Jim, I don't know if you can have a better football name than that, Brick Steele."

Brick made Haley and Chad swear to secrecy on that one.

Chad's was on a VHS tape that his mother made when it first aired. When ESPN decided to run the NCAA volleyball championships on a Sunday against the NFL, they were looking for storylines they could develop around these athletes no one had ever heard of before. MacKenzie's seemed like gold, because it was compelling, plus they could use the material later in the week for an *Outside the Lines* segment. At first Chad wanted no part in it. The producer though, knew that without Chad, the whole thing wouldn't work—he imagined pictures of Chad flashing on the screen and the interviewer saying "Chad declined to be interviewed," and he cringed at the thought of his bosses seeing that. He had an idea that might work. He called Chad's mother for "background," and dropped the fact that Chad didn't want to be interviewed. That was all his mother needed to hear. She called Chad, told him he should be proud of what he did for MacKenzie, and then went into a thing about how the family was still reeling from Steve losing his leg, and how his being on TV could really be a good thing for everyone. Why was he being so selfish?

So Chad relented, and the interview was shot from the media center at DSU. It actually wasn't too bad after all, and he was glad his mother had talked him into it. Now though, the thought of playing it for his supervisor, a former NFL player; and Haley, who worked on *Love Shack*, made him apprehensive. What would they think of him?

Brick started the video for them. After a roundtable argument over the impact of steroids on Hall of Fame voting, which they fast forwarded past, the anchor introduced MacKenzie's story.

"This weekend, during the NCAA Women's Volleyball Championships, one of the players isn't merely thankful her team's gotten that far, she's lucky to even be alive for it. Here's her amazing story:"

They cut to a tall, slender girl with a white complexion and brown hair walking to a class with books in her arms, laughing with a classmate. The narrator told her story: all conference volleyball player, dean's list student studying marine biology, sorority sister. Then they cut to a picture of her as a 14-year-old. As the story unfolded, this girl chatting on the Internet, meeting this old man she thinks is 22, some of the explicit content in the chat, and Hestermann convincing her to see him, Haley, Adam, and Brick were stunned. Then the narrator went into the plans Hestermann made for her, while images of the van with blacked-out windows, chloroform, and the apartment he had 500 miles away all flashed on the screen. That's when Chad first appeared.

"I went to the store to get some toilet paper, actually."

He and the interviewer were smirking.

"Toilet paper?"

"Yep, we were out, none of my roommates were home, and I was upset, because Kovacs, one of my roommates, was supposed to get it."

The shot changed to the narrator stepping back in and telling them how if he hadn't gone out, he might not have bumped into MacKenzie on his way back.

"She said she was Hestermann's cousin, which sounded weird, because he was a lot older."

The narrator came back in and told them how he listened, and when he heard the scream, he went over. The version he gave was closer to the actual one than the one Kovacs told Amy and Brittney. Haley, Adam, and Brick could not believe what they were hearing. The Chad they knew, Chad in Accounting, wouldn't have stood by his door, and then actually gone across to see if the girl was all right, and stepping in when she wasn't. Hearing the doctor on-screen saying how the amount of chloroform Hestermann put on his rag would've probably killed MacKenzie didn't add much to their sentiment, nor seeing the mother breakdown when talking about that reality, nor the images of Chad with the family for events like graduations and birthdays and holidays, nor even how thankful they were that without Chad's intervention, none of those moments were possible. The point had already been made to them: how could the Chad who did that, who provided one family with so much hope and joy, be the Chad they knew, Chad in Accounting, who barely smiled, who bitched about climbing mountains, who didn't call when Haley was upset, who didn't care that Brick's life was on a ballot two weeks ago while his mom had testified on their behalf on the same bill. As much as they had a new respect for him, they were put off by how little this impacted him positively. Even in these on-TV interviews from two years ago, he was listless—not emotionless, there was emotion in there, but it was despair, defeat. How could he not be pumped reliving a moment like that, Brick thought. How could he not be happy every day that this girl's entire life, and everything's she's done with it, is a direct result of his actions, Haley thought. And while Adam saw some of this Debbie Downer Chad that Brick told him about in the man on-screen, or the man sitting next to him, the fact that he'd saved this girl's life, and the fact that he was his mother's son, made him think that Brick was exaggerating who Chad was, like he did everything about his job. Such a drama queen.

Chad couldn't remember the last time he saw a girl in a one-piece bathing suit that had a body nice enough to wear a bikini. Maybe it was Huey Lewis and the News' "If This is It" video, and that girl in the white bathing suit who has her sister tell him *"I'm not home..."*. But there was Haley, in the hot tub, in this sporty one-piece, bright green with black trim, looking amazing. He tried not to look at her chest too much, but the way it looked against the green and black, the colors meeting to bisect each boob, making them more prominent... dear lord, he was glad he went!

Haley was glad she went too. She had been developing feelings for Chad, and seeing how unhappy he was despite what they saw in the video of him, made her realize she wasn't ready to deal with someone like him, someone still depressed over a bad break-up five years later, when he had so much to be happy about. Subconsciously, Haley was someone who tried to stay positive no matter what, and if anyone had a reason to be depressed and listless, it was her, and though she never thought that, thought I have more right to wallow in my self-pity than you Chad, she did have trouble understanding how Chad could have let it eat him up so much.

78

What she didn't realize was, this self-pity had grown on Chad, he was so used to it, he didn't know anything else.

On the way home, Chad was hoping maybe he'd get a chance to kiss her again, and the anticipation put a serious look on his face.

"So that was a good time, huh?"

He realized he was making a serious face, and smiled, a little embarrassed.

"Yes, he has a really nice house."

"Tell me about it."

There was a trailing off of the conversation. Haley didn't want to engage in inane small talk, not now. She was going to make a stab at bringing Chad out of his doldrums. Apropos of nothing, she said:

"When was the last time you had fun, Chad?"

"What?"

"You heard me, when was the last time you had fun?"

"Um, that was fun, what we just did."

"I mean like… be silly… you know, totally let yourself go…"

He laughed.

"I don't know. I'm not really that kind of person."

"Everyone's that kind of person." She cranked up her stereo. It was Ashley Simpson again, "Pieces of Me." "Come on, Chad, sing it with me." She was yelling the lyrics. He laughed again, kind of uncomfortably.

"I don't think she actually sang it, did she?"

Haley turned it back down and laughed with him.

"See. Now you gotta sing it. What if we find something else? I have 80s on here."

"I don't really sing."

"Come on Chad, loosen up a little bit." She hit the search button until she found the 80s folder. "REO Speedwagon, this is perfect... seriously Chad?"

Come on Chad, sing. This chick digs you, you just need to sing this stupid song. You used to do karaoke all the time with the guys. Just do it, just sing…

She turned it off.

"I don't get it, Chad."

"I'm sorry, I'm just not a singer… I don't know what to tell you…"

"I mean like everything. Like, I saw you the other night with that friend of yours, and you looked pretty good up there at that table, you looked like you were having a good time. But it's like it's not something you can commit to. You're almost never happy at work—"

"Well, it's work. Work sucks."

"Yes, work sucks for everybody, but it's a lot nicer if you don't focus on that all the time."

"I know."

He wanted to tell her everything, that that job was a daily reminder that the job he loved, the job he wished he still had, was the job he had to quit after he and Gwen split. No, he didn't want to tell her that. He didn't know what he wanted to tell her, so he let her do the talking.

"I just don't get it. We watch this video about you saving a girl's life. A 14-year-old girl, and you saved her from some sick pervert, and look at all the things she's done because of you. Don't you think my sister would've liked someone to be there and save her daughter?..."

She started choking up, and Chad put his hand sheepishly on her arm, then let it fall off.

"I'm sorry, I never thought of it like that…"

"It's okay, I'm sorry I'm emotional. It's still kind of a soft subject."

They were at his apartment. He thanked her, and they said their goodbyes and see you tomorrow at works. Chad was kicking himself inside his apartment. You moron, why didn't you just sing?

The next three days at work before they were off for Thanksgiving were interesting ones for Chad in Accounting. Brick was very deferential to him, much more respectful than Chad was used to. Brick couldn't get the image of Chad's mom, both in court, and testifying in front of the state legislature, couldn't get how touched and inspired he was, no matter how much she didn't resemble Chad, out of his mind. Not only that, there was the ESPN video about his rescuing MacKenzie. He'd written off Chad in Accounting as a doughy toolbag, a complete waste of space, someone undeserving of his time, and after that Sunday, he couldn't reconcile that earlier impression with who he thought he was now.

Haley also treated Chad in Accounting differently. He was some kind of puzzle box, and if she could figure out how to unlock him, she knew she'd like what she found inside. She'd seen glimpses of what she thought was lurking within—at least she thought she did—and though the making him sing in the car strategy didn't bear fruit, she wasn't ready to give up yet. But did she have the energy emotionally to keep working at it?

For his part, Chad in Accounting, in his own mind, was still Chad in Accounting. Still trying to get through those three days doing as little work as possible, still looking at the clock on his computer every two seconds, still as miserable when he was within the confines of that workspace as he had been for five years. As far as his supervisor went, the guy was still a dork; and as far as Haley went, he was afraid he'd screwed things up with her by not singing, and was happy when he got to work on Monday and saw how happy she was to see him. He was still in.

Wednesday night, the night he couldn't wait for to get out of work, he spent playing *FIFA '10* and watching Champions League soccer with Miguel. Richard had to come over a couple times to get his father. He probably would've done the same thing on Thursday, considering the Fox Soccer Channel aired every Champions League Game on Tuesday and Wednesday, and Chad could've DVR'd and watched them all, or played *FIFA '10* when he ran out of games; but he had to go to his mother's for Thanksgiving. Steve, Sara and the two kids, went also. And there was some guy named Tom, about his mother's age, and his daughter, a woman a few years older than Chad.

Between the time he was with Gwen and the time since the break-up, his childhood home had gone through the changes any house does in that time: new carpets installed, furniture aged and then replaced, kitchens redone, etc. Because Chad hadn't been around for any of those things, the house became less his home and he felt less of a connection to it. The only room that hadn't really changed, the dining room where they were eating, was a place Chad and Steve seldom spent time in growing up, opting for eating their meals in front of the TV.

His mother had two announcements after the meal. First, she was to become a judge. Years of working as a family law attorney had brought her to this moment. There were congratulations and a toast. Second, she and Tom were getting married. Chad was somewhat nonplussed. Who was this Tom guy? How long had she known him? And why did everyone else seem to know each other, and to be less surprised?

Had Chad been a bigger part of his mother and brother's lives over the past five years, he would've known who Tom was. Tom was already a judge, but had been an injury attorney throughout much of the same time Chad's mother was practicing. He and his wife split about four years ago, and about three years ago, Tom and Chad's mother started seeing each other.

It was whatever as far as Chad was concerned. He was happy for his mom, and Tom seemed like a nice enough guy. He stayed for pie and chatted, then went back to his apartment with a bag full of leftovers. As he fumbled with his keys outside his door, Anishka walked by.

"Hello Chad, how are you?"

"Full, just came back from my mother's for Thanksgiving. How about you? Are you hungry? I have tons of leftovers?"

He didn't know what made him ask. Maybe it was from hearing everybody else over the past few hours saying "there's so much food here, eat." He also figured Anishka would decline, so he was surprised when Anishka came over and started going through the bag.

"It's turkey, gravy, stuffing, potatoes, and I think there's some apple pie. I can heat it all up. Like I said, I'm not really hungry, but I could probably snack."

Anishka was very hungry. He visited the house of another Sri Lankan family in the area—people his cousin found through other connections and was staying with—but they were serving fish. His wife, being from the coast, made the best fish he'd ever tasted, her fish dishes were his favorite things she cooked, and since she died, he couldn't bring himself to eat fish ever again. So he was very hungry, and the offer to eat a traditional American Thanksgiving dinner was too tempting to pass up.

They sat across from each other in the kitchen at Chad's dining room table.

"This is only my second time eating Thanksgiving dinner."

"Oh yeah?"

"Yes, the other time was when I first came here from Sri Lanka, and a local church minister had me over. It's very nice. Did your mother cook this?"

"As far as I know. My sister-in-law may have done some of it too."

They talked a bit about how each other's day was. Anishka mentioned the place his cousin was staying at, but not that he couldn't eat their fish. The mention of his cousin was awkward for Chad.

"I'm sorry I couldn't let him stay here. I just didn't know who he was, plus, all that crap with my buddy Kovacs staying here."

Anishka put his hands out and waved them in front of him as he swallowed his food so he could talk.

"Miguel explained that to me. I thought you were subletting a room in your apartment or you had a roommate, and when that whole debacle occurred with your friend in the hall, I assumed there was an opening."

They laughed. After a few more bites in silence, Anishka asked him about Haley.

"I can't believe Miguel brought her up to you that night. She's not really a big deal, we just work together."

"I bet she likes you. It's not good for someone your age to always be single."

Chad almost said "you're only a few years older than me", but caught himself, and was very thankful for that.

"I don't know. She and I went to my supervisor's place last Sunday…"

"And…"

"I don't know, it was weird, she was trying to get me to sing and stuff. She told me I needed to learn how to have fun."

"Maybe she's right."

Chad went into it all, what happened with MacKenzie and the ESPN video about it that Haley saw, and how Haley said that should've made him happier than it did. Then he told Anishka about finding Gwen in bed with Dave, and how much he'd loved Gwen and planned their future together, and to find out that…

…As he was speaking, he realized who he was saying this to, what Anishka had been through. Maybe Haley was right, maybe he should be happier. It could've been worse. He thought about the picture of Anishka's wife, how gorgeous she was, and how painful it must be to have lost her so tragically. He expected Anishka to have some kind of profound wisdom stemming from that traumatic event in his life, about how Chad was lucky, or needed to live each moment like it might be his last—or maybe some sage Eastern philosophy.

"You should be proud of saving that girl's life, Haley is right. Look at all of her successes as your successes."

"What do you mean?"

"Her life is a gift that was given to you in that moment you met her. All that she is would've been snuffed out by that man; and all that she became she became because of your intervention. How can that not make you happy every time you think of it?"

"I guess I just never really thought about it like that."

Adam cleaned up the remnants of their Thanksgiving dinner after everyone left, while Brick called his parents. He loved listening to Brick's local accent whenever he talked to people from back home. There were the perfunctory how is everything, good, how about you, yep, everything's fine. Are you still coming to visit for Christmas, I am, good, it'll be nice to see you, yes, it'll be nice to see you too.

He hung up the phone, and sat in the chair next to it, thinking about what Chad's mother had said in her testimony in front of the state legislature, the recent knowledge of finding out that she was Chad's mother bringing her words back into his mind:

The people against this bill talk of a slippery slope, that allowing marriage equality will start some slippery slope into all kinds of deviant behavior that's an abject insult to the men and women I'm testifying on behalf of here today. The real slippery slope is when we, as a nation that preaches freedom and equality, tell one segment of the population, tell two consenting adults, that they are less than. That their love is somehow not valid, somehow not real, somehow worthy of vilification. That's not the foundation this country is built on. The love of two consenting adults, whether it be a man and a woman, or two same sex partners, is always something to be celebrated, and to tell one group that their love, whether it's romantic love for their partner, or a nurturing love for their children, that we don't recognize that, that is the slippery slope, a slippery slope down a path to turning our backs on the foundations and principles that this country was built on.

In the auditorium that was holding the testimonies, the crowd was three-quarters in support of Question 1, in support of marriage equality, and they identified themselves by wearing red. That three-quarters erupted in applause after Chad's mother finished speaking. It sent chills down Brick's spine. Even thinking about it now energized him. How could anyone, after hearing that, not get what they were fighting for with Question 1? You really had to be heartless—not ignorant, heartless—to deny them their rights, as human beings, especially after hearing what Chad's mother said.

But, he thought to himself, Chad didn't even hear what his mother said. He didn't even know she was testifying, wrote it off as "my mom's always doing things like that." What? No one always does that. I bet Chad didn't even vote for us, didn't vote at all that day. How could he have a mother like that and turn out the way he did? Listless, apathetic, going through the motions, while his mother could inspire a whole auditorium, maybe even more than that.

Chad didn't vote that day, as Brick suspected. As far as writing off Adam and Brick's reaction to his mother's testimony, that wasn't exactly meant the way Brick took it. Chad knew his mother had these powers of persuasion. She was absent a lot, between school, passing the bar, and the law career after, but whenever he was around her, he understood her brilliance. He remembered a time he, Kovacs, and Dave were caught in high school smoking weed. While Dave and Kovacs' parents were upset with their respective sons, they all watched in amazement as Chad's mother verbally attacked the principal, asking them what proof they had? Kovacs ate the joint before the teacher who found them got too close. All they had to go on was the smell on their clothes, and a perception that the boys were high. That's it? You took me away from one of my clients because my son and his friends *smelled* like marijuana? Because you, in your infinite wisdom, *think* they're high? Well, they shouldn't have been outside the building anyway, they looked suspicious. Again, you called me down here, with my busy schedule, to tell me my son *looked suspicious?* The principal went through a serious of hems and haws, struggling to get a grip on what he'd assumed going in was such a sure thing. He had even threatened, before Chad's mom came, to call the cops. Now he was worried he was going to get into trouble for this, because he'd look like he was overreacting, and if he went through all of this, calling the parents, threatening to call the police, to end up with nothing... oh, and to watch those three boys laughing, to see the other parents moving from concern and embarrassment that their kids had done this, to being equally indignant that they too had been called away from work to attend to this, how did it all go wrong?

Chad was still grounded for two weeks. But mom, I thought you said?—you might be able to bullshit the principal, but you can't bullshit me. But you bullshitted the principal, not me. Me bullshit him? I got your ass out of there so that twerp couldn't damage your reputation or worse, get you into trouble with the law, and this is how you thank me? How about I make it three weeks?

As much as his mother might have been there to stand up for the LGBT crowd for Brick and Adam, she was there much more for Chad and Steve, even when she knew they were in the wrong. Chad didn't need Brick or Adam to tell him who his mother was, because, in Chad's mind, they were the ones who didn't really know what she meant to him. On the flip side, since he dated Gwen and then she broke up with him, he had barely been a part of his mother's life, didn't even know she had a serious boyfriend, so you could forgive Brick for thinking Chad didn't appreciate her the way he should.

When Anishka got in the door, he broke down and cried. It was too much, especially the fact that Chad's girlfriend cheated on him five years ago, the same five years since he'd lost Kalani and Sahan. If only it had been Kalani cheating on him, he'd still have both of them here today.

In school, Anishka had to learn English. His father wanted to him to be a doctor, and learning English was part of the deal. To Anishka, it was a symbol of White European oppression and colonization. Why should he have to learn their tongue?

In a class in high school though they were assigned *Midnight's House* by Kavith Asvadaya. Asvadaya's family had moved from Colombo to London before he was born, so he grew up speaking English better than Sinhalese. Though he was one of the greatest living English language writers in the world, and his *Midnight's House* was on a lot short lists of the best English-language novels of the last part of the 20th century, to that point Anishka had only read his novels translated into Sinhalese. Reading them in their first language, English, Anishka had a new appreciation for what Asvadaya was doing: he was taking this language of oppression— even if it was Asvadaya's native language—, and using it in a way that not only impressed the oppressors, but demonstrated a superior ability to use the language than most of them. Later Asvadaya gave a talk in Colombo that Anishka attended, and he was inspired further. He decided he no longer wanted to be a doctor. He would be a writer, in English.

Those were the days of the civil war though, and while being a writer sounded nice, having a stable, good paying job was necessary as well, so Anishka worked in advertising when he graduated, and got a position with a prestigious firm in Colombo—the idea being that he would work on his writing on the side and still eventually pursue his dream. That was where he met Kalani. She was a model in one of the ads. He impressed her with his poetry, though she had already had her eye on him too. They married in 1997, and had Sahan one year later.

Sahan's English school had off for Christmas in 2004, so they decided to stay with Kalani's family on the coast during that time. But Anishka was called back to work when an international soft drink company wanted a second pitch from them for their Sri Lankan ad campaign. So he stayed in Colombo, and Kalani and Sahan went to her family's. And then the tsunami happened.

That was it. One moment he had a family, the next… he wasn't sure. For five days he wasn't sure, until Kalani's cousin called and gave him the news. It would take another day for him to make it down there with all the road closures and destruction. When he did make it, there was no house left. He went to the spot where he thought Kalani's room was, where she and Sahan would have been staying, and he curled up in the fetal position and lay there. He wanted the sea to take him too. Three days later, having had no food or water, a group of volunteers led by an American church pastor found him, thinking he was a miracle survivor. He told them what happened back at the triage tent. The man who led the volunteers was from Chad's hometown, coming to Sri Lanka to help the moment he saw the devastation on TV.

Anishka asked the man if he knew someone in the US that could take him in. There was nothing left for him in Sri Lanka. He needed a fresh start. The pastor put him in touch with his brother who ran the Methodist church in the town next to Chad's. Within two days, Anishka had given their Colombo apartment to his brother, packed the few things he needed, and had his brother send the rest when he arrived in the US.

His plan was to write his first novel, to finally be a writer like Kavith Asvadaya. But in five years he hadn't really done any work on it. The book was to be about a man in Colombo who ran a small store and cared for the stray cats in the neighborhood, based loosely on a shopkeeper he remembered growing up. A week ago a friend from Colombo contacted him. He was with a new ad firm in New York, and they could use him there. Anishka was running out of money, so the thought was tempting; but now, after speaking to Chad, he felt he had to write that novel. How much better was he than Chad if he didn't?

He took his laptop off the desk near his kitchen, sat on the couch with a blanket and some tea, and wrote until 5am the next morning.

Interlude

Before Gwen, Chad really hadn't had any serious girlfriends. It wasn't that he didn't have women in his life that he'd form intimate relationships with, even develop feelings for, he'd just never had that aching love. The kind of love that almost hurts, but hurts in a good way. The kind of love that consumes all his thoughts. The kind of love where the object of that desire is the center of his world, where he can't imagine a world without her. The kind of love that becomes so much a part of him that it's almost routine.

In 6th grade there was Lucy. One day she was among a group of girls visiting Mara, who lived around the corner from Chad. They saw Chad, Dave, and Kovacs playing in the front yard, found out Chad's mother worked late, and suggested they all go inside and play Truth or Dare. Chad's dare was to spend 5 minutes alone with Lucy in the closet, which, unbeknownst to Chad, was Mara's idea because Lucy had confessed that she had a crush on Chad a week before. After five minutes of awkward making out, with teeth and tongues and hitting heads on walls, they decided they should be boyfriend and girlfriend. For two months they held hands in the park or at the mall, had occasional make-out sessions, and killed some time on the phone. Then, one day, Lucy approached Chad at school and said:

"I don't think we should be boyfriend and girlfriend anymore."

"Okay."

There was no heartache associated with this break up. As far as Chad was concerned, he had more fun at the mall with Dave and Kovacs anyway. I mean, when he brought her over to Tape World so he could buy *Dr. Feelgood* with his allowance, she had the gall to tell him she didn't like Mötley Crüe. He was better off without her.

In 8th grade there was Vanessa. All her friends had boyfriends, and she felt left out, so she cornered Chad in recess while he was waiting to get into the soccer game, and told him he was her boyfriend. She was kind of cute, short, a little overweight, but her boobs were coming in before most of the other girls in his grade, so he was good with that. They went to the Winter Semi-Formal together, which led to a lot of teasing from his mother, as she made sure his hair and outfit looked right. It was a rare moment of mothering she could indulge in, but the teasing made Chad self-conscious, and he almost didn't want to go. Then he saw Vanessa in her low-cut dress, and he changed his mind. A few weeks—and numerous afterschool make-out sessions at Chad's before his mom got home—later, Vanessa's parents found out what they were doing, and she was grounded. His longing for her breasts gradually waned as her sentence was carried out, and he was caught by one of her friends at a party making out with Julie Sludowski.

Freshman year was a whole new deal for Chad. Soccer wasn't a popular sport at Quincy Adams, so there was no JV, all the players were on the same team. That meant Chad, Dave, and Kovacs were brought into constant contact with seniors, and that meant senior parties. There were senior girls he'd hook up with that were totally drunk, that on Monday wouldn't give him the time of day. Kovacs almost got into a fight with a football player whose girl allegedly gave him a blow job at one such party.

Potential angry football players aside, this arrangement worked out well for Chad, Kovacs, and Dave for their first two years in high school. They could hang out together, egg houses, smoke weed, watch bad movies, and then, Friday or Saturday night, go to a senior party one of their teammates invited them to, hook up with a girl there, whether she be an older one from their school, or a girl from a neighboring town, and then repeat the process the next week.

Junior year, Kovacs and Dave each had steady girlfriends, which left Chad in the lurch. Part of the problem was, they were now the upper classmen whose classmates were throwing the parties, meaning these were girls they all knew, and though they weren't averse to getting drunk and hooking up, there was an awkwardness at school the next Monday that didn't exist before. Chad was also disillusioned that, with their respective girlfriends, Kovacs and Dave had lost their virginity, and Chad hadn't yet.

One night, when Dave and Kovacs were on a double date, Chad went to the mall to play *Mortal Kombat II*. There were some guys there from a neighboring town that the guys were used to playing with. They had some girls with them, and some beer in the car, and they were going to a party if Chad wanted to come.

Those guys drank 40s and smoked weed a lot more than Chad and his buddies did, and before he knew it, everything was a big blur. There was a girl who had been flirting with Chad from the moment he got there. She was thin and pale with bleach blond hair that was tied tightly back in a ponytail, and she had on dark red lipstick and black eyeliner that stood out in stark contrast from the paleness of her face. Though she wore a pair of Adidas track pants and a white tank top, she was cute enough that it looked flattering on her, at least to Chad. Later in the evening she took him into a vacant bedroom. All he really remembered was that her boobs reminded him of Vanessa's. The next morning, he woke up in that room with her lying next to him. There was a faint memory in his head of lying down, her unbuckling his pants, then asking if he had a condom. It was in his wallet, he fumbled around and got it, but his hands were too useless to take it out. She did that for him. He tried to focus, but there were three of her in front of him, undressing. He laid back down on the bed, and let her take over from there. Time stood still for him in his inebriated state, but for the girl, his penis, which didn't have the usual sensitivity, was frustrating. She wasn't used to being on top, wasn't at the highest fitness level, and expended a lot of energy getting him to ejaculate. Chad just had a series of disjoined images in his head of her bouncing up and down on him, and him grabbing for those boobs.

As he was waking up and collecting his thoughts, Drew, one of his *Mortal Kombat II* buddies, ran into the room.

"Dude, that's Harley McInnis's girl!"

Chad groaned. It didn't make any sense to him at that moment, but Harley McInnis was a famous local figure among them. He was a drug dealer, and in one case to scare some local competition away, he and a buddy smashed out the windows of the guy's car with baseball bats, while the guy and his friends were sitting in it. Among the other tales surrounding him, there was a rumor that a kid in a neighboring town hooked up with Harley's girlfriend, and Harley made his life so horrible after that the kid and his family had to move out of state. No one could verify that this happened, but no one had any reason to not believe it either.

Drew grabbed him by the shoulder to get him up, and he felt everything move its way into his esophagus, and he ran, vomit popping from the cracks of his mouth and around his hand, to the bathroom one door down. There was someone sleeping on the floor that he had to jump over, and he projectile vomited into the toilet. He cleaned up as best as he could and got dressed, as Drew attempted to hurry him along. He threw up again in a trashcan outside, before he caught a long and nauseating bus ride back to his neighborhood.

As what had happened had time to set in, Chad was terrified Harley would be coming for him, so terrified in fact that he was too afraid to even tell Dave and Kovacs what happened, meaning that, though he technically wasn't a virgin, to them he still was, which might as well have been as bad. Not only that, but the boobs thing made him associate his sexual experience with Vanessa, who was dating someone else in school. Chad had Chemistry with her, and depending on what she was wearing, the teen male animal lust in him could be overwhelming, to the point he even considered pleasuring himself in the school bathroom. He went from having a 95 for the first half of the year in Chemistry to an 80 the second half. One day, she had on one of those denim jumpers that were popular back then, and the top half was pushing against her breasts that were also pushing against her tight white turtleneck underneath. He couldn't stop staring, and without paying attention, put HCL into a test tube meant for water, and put the test tube over his Bunsen burner. Luckily Dave caught him, but his teacher was concerned enough to take him aside, seriously worried about his wellbeing.

"Is everything okay at home, Chad?" He said.

"Yes, Mr. Sandberg."

"Are you sure? Anything else that could be going on that you want to tell me about?"

Yes, I want to throw Vanessa across one of your lab tables and—

"I'm absolutely sure."

Senior year he officially lost his virginity on a class trip to Paris. Four years of French, of which he remembers very little, earned him a ten-day trip over April vacation, of which he also remembers very little. He, Dave, and Kovacs drank the entire time, were either drunk or hung over the entire time, and were considered off-limits by the chaperones of another school from Idaho that was traveling with them. Being labeled off-limits made them very appealing to the girls from that school, however, and one of those girls, Kelsey, took a shine to Chad. The third-to-last night in Paris, they had sex, and Kelsey didn't have a scary boyfriend back home, so Chad could tell Dave and Kovacs it had happened.

College was four years of serial dating with no one really memorable to report. He, Dave, and Kovacs pledged Tau Upsilon Lambda their freshman year, and from that point on, life was one big party, and they bedded as many women as they could, while engaging in as few serious relationships as they could. Out of the three of them, only Kovacs pretended he was in a serious relationship with someone, Mandy, but Dave and Chad knew that didn't mean much. Chad was proud of his "I don't want a girlfriend" lifestyle, and though there were some awkward moments when girls he'd slept with came to the fraternity house thinking he was her guy, only to see him with another girl, the system worked for him.

After college, though, when he, Kovacs, and Dave moved out of the fraternity house and into their own apartment, he found it was difficult to meet women. For four years, he had had a new crop of co-eds in each of his four classes every semester, not to mention, there were always people coming to party at the house. It was as simple as buddying up with a girl under the pretense of studying together, making eye contact first, then maybe asking for a writing utensil. By the time it started to go south, the semester would be over, and he could find a new girl in his next set of classes. At the house, it was even easier. A group of girls would show up, he and a group of his brothers would engage them in conversation, and the one that was most amenable to playing pool would be his. He'd let her win of course. Sometimes the girl would have sex with him that night, sometimes she didn't, and then the next night, another group would come, and he'd start the process over. Now he no longer had that crutch. He had to go on dates, which were very frustrating constructs. He had to make conversation, had to have interesting things to say. Not only that, but Kovacs would set him up on them, either because she was one of Mandy's friends, meaning there were a number of events that were off the table for conversation because Mandy wasn't supposed to know about them; or Chad was acting as Kovacs' wingman while he was out with another girl, meaning Chad couldn't mention Mandy at all, or any of the things he and her did together.

This was what his life was like for months after they graduated. He was hired in June of 1999, about three weeks after he finished college, at a tech firm operating out of a converted Baptist church downtown. The church had moved to a larger building on the outskirts of town when their congregation grew, and the tech firm, also growing out of its tiny offices during the 1990s tech boom, loved the idea of the church and its recreation areas. There was a basketball court, with a kitchen attached to it for dinner functions. They converted the prayer space into the work area, so all the cubicles, which were really more desks because they weren't closed off like cubicles, sat in a large, open room with a high ceiling that was much less stifling than the office and cubicles in a more traditional office space, like the one Chad in Accounting suffered through at the insurance corporation he worked at now.

It was in January of 2000 that Gwen started there, having just graduated herself from a double associate degree in graphic design and website programming. She was tall, but not too tall; thin, but not too thin; with long brown hair and blue eyes. The other endearing trait she had: she was single.

For Chad, Gwen was initially a small infatuation. He'd look across the converted prayer space and get lost in her looks for a second as she chewed on her pencil or played with her hair. Then there were his moments kicking the soccer ball around with some co-workers on the basketball court during break, where he'd hope she'd see him. She did, and one time remarked that he was good, did he play in college? In high school, then some intramurals for his fraternity. Ooh, that was a turn off for her, she hated frat guys, though she didn't tell Chad that.

He had made the connection though, and kept working away at her, hoping to win her over. She knew he liked her, but wasn't sure if she liked him. He didn't sound that interesting in his attempts to make small talk, and physically, he looked good, but not that good. From Chad's standpoint, his post college love life was becoming unbearable, and Gwen was slowly representing his only possibility for respite. More and more things she did were attractive to him. Her sense of humor, the way she walked, her outfits. She didn't have the large boobs Chad usually found attractive—a remnant from Vanessa in high school—she didn't like the shows on TV Chad liked (she didn't get *Seinfeld*—which should've been a warning sign right there), or the movies he was into, but it didn't matter. All that mattered was making her his girlfriend.

In March, his work had paid off, and he convinced her to come to a party they were throwing at his apartment. It was there she met Dave. *He* was what she wanted. He watched the TV shows she did, including *Dawson's Creek*, which Dave admitted to secretly watching on Monday nights while he went home to do his laundry. He was a better talker than Chad was, much more sure of himself. But she knew Chad liked her, and making a move on Dave would make for an awkward situation both at work, and here when she'd visit him. Dave didn't think like this, he was worried because Kovacs told him that would be a dick thing to do to steal a girl Chad was interested in. "Dude, you can't cock block your bro like that."

Who knows how it might have worked out if MacKenzie hadn't met Hestermann in a chat room. If Kovacs hadn't forgotten to buy TP and Chad not gone out to get it and come back at the exact moment MacKenzie was waiting for Hestermann to get back. If Hestermann hadn't left his door ajar. Gwen probably would've gone on writing Chad off, and probably wouldn't have thought about Dave again, and probably would've found another guy through one of her girlfriends; and Chad would've eventually gotten over her, and maybe would've found the girl he needed through a Kovacs and Mandy double date, or maybe he wouldn't and he'd have been single at 32 going on 33 just the same, only not as devastated.

But it did happen, all of it, and when Gwen heard about what Chad had done, what a hero he was, she was intrigued. She went on a date with him, and now the man who was unsure of himself and made bad small talk was confident and charismatic—even if Chad wasn't acting any different than he had when she wasn't attracted to him. One date turned into a relationship, and with it, Chad became completely and utterly Gwen's Chad. She was all he thought about. At work, he couldn't wait to see her, to talk to her, to know she was there. Then there were their nights out, the weekends together, and the knowledge that there would be more of them and that these feelings would grow stronger. This was before either had a cell phone, so time spent away for Chad was agonizing, wondering if she'd call, or e-mail, or something. He didn't eat well, had trouble sitting still, let his work slip. But he had her, and that was what was important.

As they grew closer and spent more time together, Chad wanted more, while Gwen was losing interest. The first six months or so was the building phase, adding on more days of the week to see each other, more weekends to spend together, until they were one. The second six months was the relationship phase. Getting used to being a couple, to being recognized as a couple, to regular sex, to seeing each other every night, either at her place or his. It was in this period that Chad was happiest, where he was getting back to regular eating habits, and sitting still more often. But this was the period when doubt crept into Gwen's mind. Chad said he hated *Dawson's Creek*, yet he would watch it so he could be with her. He often let her pick the movie they rented, the cuisine they ate, even what time they went to bed. She became bored.

The 18-month mark was the comfort period. Chad was accepting that he was Gwen's Chad, and he wanted to be Gwen's Chad, and only Gwen's Chad. The guys were talking about parting when their lease was up, and Chad thought this would be a perfect time for he and Gwen to move in together. Gwen was wondering if this was what she wanted. But like Chad, she had become comfortable too. She was used to his body, used to his lips, used to his voice on the phone, used to his idiosyncrasies. Even if they annoyed the hell out of her sometimes, she was used to them.

She had the built in excuse that her lease wasn't up for another six months to stall a potential move-in, so Chad got his own place—a small house he rented—which was essentially their place, since she stayed there a lot and left her apartment to her roommate. Things were only becoming worse for her though. Chad's comfort level made him that much more boring, and turned her off that much more. He was only romantic on Valentine's Day, and that was so canned with the chocolates and dinner at the Olive Garden that she barely had the enthusiasm to have sex with him after. She was ready to have The Talk, which she knew would devastate Chad, but she couldn't take it anymore.

MacKenzie was playing in a big volleyball game for her high school, though, and the family really wanted Chad to go, and Chad really wanted Gwen to accompany him. She suspected that he wouldn't actually go if she didn't (and she was right), and she knew how much it meant to MacKenzie's family to have Chad there, so she went. Seeing her play, seeing the family so happy and so proud of her, and Gwen being proud of Chad for what he did, all of it made the disillusionment in her body evaporate. Chad was a good guy, a really good guy, and she was lucky to have him.

It was like a fuel tank that she refilled. Eventually, it would drop back down to E. The problem was, during that time, as the disillusionment grew again, so did her comfortability in the relationship. She moved into his place when her lease was up. It only made things worse, as 24 hours a day without even the possibility of a space of her own—even just the idea that it existed for her had been a bigger deal to her than she understood—grated on her nerves. At the same time, as year 2 became year 3, there was that sense that she'd invested so much already, that to start over was too daunting a task. It was like she was at the grocery store, and she had picked her checkout line, and even if the other lines looked like they might be moving faster, she was afraid to move into one of them, because hers might start moving faster, and all the time she'd spent in that one would be for naught.

Call it capriciousness, not being truthful with Chad about her emotions, or what it really was, simply being confused, but while she was trying to figure it out, Chad went on being in love with her, loving everything about her, and loving that he was Gwen's Chad. And that love consumed him entirely. It made him afraid, afraid to try new things, afraid to go to new places, afraid to do anything except live his life with her. If she wanted to go on vacation, where do you want to go honey? Well, where do you want to go Chad? It doesn't matter. It frustrated her to no end that he deferred to her like that, but it really didn't matter to him. Anywhere he was with her made him happy. But it didn't make her happy.

Gwen's Chad was alienating himself from his friends and family too. His family thought she was controlling him, figuring there was no way he'd go so long without contacting them or that he'd always go to her family's house on holidays without her forcing his hand. Gwen had no idea they had that perception of her, because her perception of them was that they must be pretty awful if Chad neglects them and never talks about them like he does. Dave and Kovacs had a better understanding, seeing Gwen and Chad out on double dates and social gatherings. Chad was now dull and not the guy they had had so much fun with. Dave had also just broken up with his girlfriend, and as a single man, his eyes turned to Gwen. Gwen, confused and lonely, turned her eyes back to Dave.

Midway through year three, as Gwen's tank moved closer back to E, Gwen's Chad bought an engagement ring. There was no way for him to know that this wasn't a good idea. No way to know what Gwen was truly feeling, because he was so much in love with her, that nothing else mattered. The signs were there: Gwen was less willing to be affectionate, less willing to be physical, less engaging—sometimes she even slept on the couch. But Gwen's Chad was too far gone to see that, so he took her out to the Olive Garden, and popped the question that night when they got home. He knew something was wrong when, instead of crying and saying yes, she pulled him up from his knee, and had him take a seat with her on the couch.

The hardest part for her was how shocked Chad was at what she was telling him. I didn't know you were unhappy. What can I do to make it right? Anything, just say it, and I'll do it. She found herself saying things she'd always wanted to tell him, about how he needed to be an active part of the relationship, that he needed to make some decisions, and not always defer to her. That he needed to do something, be something, not just center his life around her. I will, he said, I'll be anything you want. That's not what I want...

She left that night and went for a drive. Then she did something, something her gut told her to do. Who knows how well a barometer her gut was for what was right and wrong at that moment, considering the mess of emotions running through her system, but she went with it anyway, and called Dave. He met her at the park, and when she hugged him, she was so overcome with emotions that she held him tight and sobbed on his shoulder.

For the next six months, Gwen lived with Chad, felt comfortable with Chad, while she carried on her first six months with Dave. It wasn't always easy to get away from Chad, especially since they worked at the same place, but she was able to use her demand that Chad become more of an independent person to give them more alone time. Dave's occupation as a realtor provided myriad neutral locations where they could surreptitiously carry out their trysts. There were many evenings in sleeping bags, lying there with him in the candle light, in an empty house that Dave had shown to prospective buyers earlier that day, when she knew she had to go back home to Chad, and the half of her that was bored fought with the half of her that was comfortable.

The tank was empty in June of 2004, when Chad was invited to MacKenzie's high school graduation. Much to Dave's chagrin, that filled the tank again, and Gwen told Dave that things between he and her had to cease. But her newfound affection for Chad dissipated almost as quickly as it came, because Gwen's Chad lapsed back into the old behavior that upset her so much. They went to Galveston, Texas to see her uncle, and they bickered the whole time, often instigated by Gwen. Any opportunity she had to pick a fight, she took it, whether it was packing and Chad asking her if she had this or that, or insisting on carrying her bags for her, or offering her food and drink he packed for the flight—everything annoyed her. She no longer saw the guy who saved MacKenzie's life, she saw the obsequious Gwen's Chad, unable to do anything but cater to her needs. Once they got home, she drove off and called Dave.

In October, Chad was supposed to be away for the weekend with Steve and Mr. Haley on a fishing trip. It wasn't exactly Chad's idea of a good time, but when Gwen heard about it she liked the idea of a weekend with the house to herself and Dave, so she talked him into going. Steve's wife went into labor on that Saturday though, and that cut the trip short. Chad would've called Gwen to let her know he was coming home early, but his phone was dead. It was probably for the best, though Chad could've lived his whole life as Gwen's Chad and been happy while she carried on an affair with Dave as long as he didn't know it. When he got home, and saw Dave's car parked outside, he still didn't think anything fishy. He must've come to see me and forgot I was away. Maybe he wanted one of my Playstation games.

He entered the house and didn't see them. He called out hello. He heard a commotion in the bedroom and walked toward it and opened the door. There was Dave, naked, gathering his clothes, while Gwen was in the bed, the covers up to her chin. It took a second to register, but unlike the surreal sensation he had from seeing Hestermann accosting MacKenzie, this was devastating. Gwen and Dave tried to say something, but there wasn't anything in front of Chad that words could assuage. Dave slipped out, and Gwen dressed.

She explained things to Chad the best she could, but it didn't make any sense. He didn't say a word, just sat there, in shock. Gwen kept imploring him, Chad, say something, please, say something. Then Gwen's phone rang. It was Chad's mother calling to tell them Sara had a girl. 7 pounds, 8 ounces, named Iris Jean after her two grandmothers. Gwen went to hand him the phone, but he wouldn't take it. His mom, thinking she was being controlling, demanded Chad talk to her, and Chad demanded back that he wouldn't. When push came to shove, though, he was still Gwen's Chad, so when Gwen told him to take it, he did. He was a shell communicating with his mother. He agreed that he'd go to the hospital that next day.

To Gwen's credit, she tried to make the post-break-up process as painless as possible. She kept Dave away, she got as much of her stuff out of the house as she could in as few trips as possible, and she offered to help with the bills so he wouldn't be stuck. She still cared for Chad, and seeing him so broken up, and knowing it was her who did it, was hard for her to stand, and she knew if it was hard for her, it was killing him.

After the first week of work following the revelation that Gwen and Dave were carrying on a relationship behind his back, after a week of pleading with her, trying to make the reality not real, Chad realized that he could no longer have a job in the same place as Gwen. From his employer's stand point, it was good riddance, because Chad wasn't a great employee, but Gwen was, and Chad was Gwen's Chad, and they felt like they were stuck with him if they wanted to keep her. The news of their split was exciting, it meant a possibility of extricating themselves from the albatross around their necks, and when he put in his notice, it was even more exciting. Despite their unfavorable opinion of him, they gave Chad's future employers rave reviews because they were so happy they'd finally be rid of him.

Chad's poor work rate was one of many examples of how much he'd let everything else in his life slip as he became more and more Gwen's Chad. In college he graduated Magnum Cum Laude, always managing his studies with his social life and partying, and he carried that ability to get things done with him to his job after he graduated. As Gwen's Chad though, that assiduous and effective work ethic was slowly pushed out by the need to continue being Gwen's Chad. He hadn't played soccer in years, barely saw any of his friends, who automatically sided with Dave in the break-up because they hadn't had much of a friendship with Chad since he'd become Gwen's Chad; and then there was his family. In his despair though, instead of turning back to these things he'd enjoyed prior to being Gwen's Chad, he continued to let those aspects of his life lie dormant.

And when he started at the insurance firm, first sat down at his cubicle, and first became Chad in Accounting, neither that work ethic nor any of the other things came back. He replaced the void left in Gwen's absence with a big old pile of blah. Blah became his identity, and even as he thought he was getting over not being Gwen's Chad, he was really just getting more and more used to the blah. Before he knew it, five years had gone by, five years that he didn't know anything about, five years that he couldn't think of anything he had done in his life, and in that five years, Gwen had married Dave and had two kids. Early in 2009, Gwen made a Facebook account—Chad had had one a year before that when some of his fraternity alums suggested it to the brotherhood in their newsletter—and Chad thought accepting her friend request would show her that he had moved on. Probably because she was still guilty for breaking his heart, she made herself believe that Chad really had moved on; but Chad's accepting her add request was more proof that the blah inside him had become too much a part of him. He would read into her status updates that maybe something was going wrong between her and Dave, that she'd come back to him and they'd go back to how things were. Then he was obsessed with getting a woman of his own so he could change his relationship status as a "that'll show you" gesture. While Gwen's five years had consisted of her becoming wife and mother, for Chad it was becoming Chad in Accounting.

What Chad didn't know, and it was best that he didn't know because it would've given him a false hope, was that Gwen wasn't happy with Dave. After their marriage and first child, Gwen saw things in Dave she didn't like. He was more socially conservative than she realized. He didn't like gay people, made chauvinistic jokes to his guy friends like "put your pussy away" or "do you need a tampon?" if they were "bitching" too much, and he cared more about money and flipping houses than he did books and art. When the housing crisis hit, and he lost money on a few properties, forcing them to rely more on her income and help from her parents, it created more tension between them. Part of her wanted to file for divorce, but part of her felt like something was wrong with *her*. Can I ever make a relationship work? I broke Chad's heart to be with Dave, and now I don't want him either. She was ready to suggest couple's counseling, which she knew Dave would be resistant to, but when she became pregnant with their second child, all bets were off. She was stuck with Dave, for better or worse, happy or unhappy, depressed or just postpartum stress, until death do they part. It took her this much effort to change checkout lines once, she couldn't change again, even if it didn't look like she'd make it to the register.

Dave had no idea how much calling people "retarded" grated on Gwen, but he knew she wasn't as happy as she had been. He chalked it up to the pregnancy and other "women problems", but it was still stressful on him. While Chad lost Dave and Kovacs in his split with Gwen, Dave lost Kovacs in his relationship with Gwen, because Gwen never liked Kovacs. Chad accepted her not liking Kovacs as a price he had to pay to be Gwen's Chad, so he limited his time spent with Kovacs from the moment they were officially dating. Kovacs and Dave, though, gradually grew apart as Kovacs became less and less willing to visit Dave and suffer Gwen's persnickety treatment of him. They kept in casual touch through social media like Facebook, but when Kovacs was kicked out by Mandy, he really felt like Chad was more of a friend to him than Dave, even if he hadn't spoken to him in a year. As strange as it sounds, Dave felt the same way about Chad when he picked up Kovacs' things. He sincerely expected he could sit down and talk to Chad about the problems he was having in his relationship—even if that relationship was with the woman that had been the center of Chad's world and Dave had taken that world away from him. Steve reminded Dave of who he was in Chad's life, and who he would probably always be.

MacKenzie gave Chad a gift when she bumped into him in the hallway almost ten years ago, but he couldn't see it because of Gwen. After talking to Anishka, Chad understood that the real gift wasn't a life with Gwen, but life itself. If Anishka, who lost a woman that was way hotter than Gwen, under much more tragic circumstances, told him MacKenzie's life should be showing him all the things in life that are worth enjoying, there was probably something in that. He thought about it, along with a host of other things, the weekend after Thanksgiving as he and Miguel played *FIFA '10* while Julía was Christmas shopping with friends. He thought about what Haley was telling him about taking life less seriously, despite her niece dying such a tragic death. He thought about Steve losing his leg and dealing with Mr. Haley's death, yet still being stronger than Chad who had only had his girlfriend cheat on him. He thought about his supervisor telling him about his mother and how great a woman she was. He thought about Kovacs, and how, though it ended poorly, it reminded him of who he once was: confident, fun, happy—that last one was the most important. And he also thought about being in his supervisor's house, about him having been in the NFL and Haley having worked for *Love Shack*, and now they both were in the same cubicles he was in.

Until Anishka showed him, he had no idea just how unhappy he was, and for how long. Five years, gone, without anything to show for it, except for a lot of money in the bank… yes, that was one advantage to living as a somnambulist for five years, he didn't spend anything. $40,000 a year with barely $25,000 in expenses. It was time to cash in the gift that MacKenzie had given him.

Lars and His Hedge Fund, Bianca and Her Bears

"I am one million percent sure Trey'narius is the father of my baby!"

"Well, let's hear it from him. Come on out, Trey'narius."

As he made his way down the runway, Trey'narius was greeted with a chorus of boos, along with some random beeping usually associated with a TV program censoring an expletive, though Chad couldn't figure out who in the audience would be swearing at Trey'narius and Maury bro-hugging. And who names their son Trey-narius? He had an idea when he saw a slightly older woman, whose hair Chad thought looked like the ribbon candy he saw on a holiday endcap at the drugstore the other day, on a flatscreen behind the action, presumably being filmed from backstage, yelling that the woman onstage was lying about her son's potential paternity. The other issue Chad had with *Maury*, after Trey'narius's name, out of all the elements of the show to have an issue with, was that none of Maury's guests understood how percentages worked. You can't be more than 100 percent sure of something, simply adding zeroes and commas to it doesn't make you any more sure.

"In the case of baby Kha'dasia, Trey'narius, you are NOT the father."

The stage exploded in emotion. Kha'dasia's mother was on the floor in tears, her face in her hands. Trey'narius danced around, proud of himself for knowing he wasn't the father of baby Kha'dasia. Maury was trying to patch things up, and before they went to commercial, the show was transported backstage, where Maury asked the mother if she had any idea who the dad might be, and through her tears, she nodded yes.

"Man, I should probably get up and do something," Chad said, to no one in particular. It was the Monday after Thanksgiving, but Chad had called in sick and was on his couch, watching *Maury*, eating the Lunch Combination #4 that Jade Empire had just delivered to him. I gotta play some *FIFA '10* before Miguel gets home from work and wants to play it too. He watched a commercial where two girls were working at a clothing store, and one remarked that Miss Perfect had just walked in. It turned out that Miss Perfect, instead of wasting her time at a traditional 4-year institution, had enrolled at the local for-profit college's medical assistant program, and now she was already working. Jesus, Chad thought, why don't they show all the parties and shit that girl at the 4-year school is going to. Dodge State should have their own commercial where a girl is getting her vitals taken by a medical assistant she knows. I'm here to get my shots, she tells the medical assistant, because I'm going to Africa on an internship through the anthropology department at DSU. Geez, the medical assistant would say, that's a lot cooler than spending 18 months at a for-profit training college.

Chad originally took the day off to get his résumé in order and look for new jobs. Though he had the money to live off of for months until he found something else, based on the way

96

today was going for him—lying on his couch in his sweats while eating Chinese and watching *Maury*, he figured it would be better if he had another job soon after he quit—although, if he didn't find anything as an accountant, there was always a career as a medical assistant, or what was this one now, massage therapy. There we go. He sat up and stretched. It was 12:30. He'd watch the rest of *Maury*, then go to Kinkos and run off some copies.

Coming out of Kinkos with a folder full of his résumé, he heard someone call his name.

"It is Chad right?"

It was Lars.

"Yes, it's Chad. Um… how are you?..."

"It's funny I bumped into you here, because I kind of need a favor."

"I don't even know you."

As if Chad didn't say that, he continued:

"Could you give me a lift to my place? Or hell, what are you doing today, maybe we could hit the mall and hang out."

Chad cocked an eyebrow. What else was he going to do today though, he could at least give the guy a ride home.

"Where do you live?"

"Winchester Estates. It's my folks' place actually."

Winchester Estates, the richest gated community in town. Chad had never been in there before. Why not, again, what was he going to do today?

As they entered Chad's car, Chad saw his reflection in his car window. He had on his State cap—backwards—State hoodie, track pants, and running sneakers. He didn't exactly look like Winchester Estates. Lars's button up shirt and designer jeans were much more appropriate. It didn't matter, he'll just drop him off and go.

As they merged onto the highway, they engaged in some small talk.

"So what were you doing at Kinkos?" Lars asked.

"Making copies of my résumé. I'm an accountant, looking for a new place to work."

"Really?"

"Yeah, why?"

"Well, my buddy and I just happen to be running a hedge fund, and we could use an administrator."

"Oh… I don't know…"

The whole thing sounded dubious.

"No no, it's legit. We have an office downtown, we have the investors. Your buddy Kovacs's dad was actually supposed to be one as a matter of fact."

"Oh yeah?"

"Well, not now, after what happened with the whole him fucking his dad's wife. It was Kovacs we had who convinced his dad to invest, and now the dad wants to pull it all out."

"Is that bad? Are you guys really leveraged?"

Lars wasn't expecting a question like that.

"Um… no, why do you ask?"

"No reason, just if you were really leveraged, losing Kovacs's dad's money could be like losing a lot more, you know?"

"Oh yeah, I know. This isn't some fly-by-night thing, my buddy Seijun is a really successful broker. We just started a few months ago, but we already have a good stable of investors. What are you getting paid right now?"

Chad furled his eyebrows at his perceived presumptuousness of Lars' inquiry, but decided it wasn't a big deal to answer it.

"40K."

"*40K?* We could probably do… 55…"

"Okay…"

"Let me take one of these:" he pulled a résumé out of the folder. "It can't hurt if I show it to Seijun, right?"

"No, it can't hurt, I guess."

At the gate to Winchester Estates, Chad was forced to show his license, his registration, and have his plate number taken down. It annoyed him to go through that, but that annoyance was soon forgotten when he saw all the beautiful houses. Jesus, I could get used to living here. They pulled up to Lars' parents' place, pristine and almost identical to its neighbors, next to a red, drop-top Mercedes sports car. When they got out, Chad got a closer look at it.

"It's nice huh?"

"I don't know if nice is the word. Divine, perhaps."

"It's my dad's, but he's letting me use it to make a good impression on our investors. $133 grr standard, but with all the shit added on, it was like $155. The thing goes 0 to 60 in less than five seconds."

"Jesus."

They went inside, where Lars offered Chad a drink, then asked the maid what she'd made for lunch. He spoke loudly and slowly, like he was talking to a child, then made a joke to Chad about how she was an illegal that couldn't speak English. He was wrong that she was an illegal immigrant, having lived in the US legally for over twenty years, after moving there from her native El Salvador; but he was right that she didn't speak English, at least not that well. That didn't mean she didn't understand it, she understood it almost perfectly, which Lars' mother knew, and used that to spy on her son when he was in her house. Chad took for granted what Lars was telling him, and didn't consider Miguel, or some of his new soccer teammates, would have been offended by Lars's comments.

"So what do you got going on man?" Lars said as they snacked on some turkey sandwiches.

"Nothing much. Why?"

"Well, I lost my license, and I was going to have Elsa take me to the mall, but shit man, why don't we go, and you can drive us in the Benz."

That car? Me, drive that?

Chad looked down and noticed his clothes.

"I'd have to go home and change first."

"Change? We'll get something at the mall. Do you have any money?"

"On me?"

"No, to buy new clothes with? We'll go to Neiman Marcus."

"Jesus, I'm more of an Abercrombie guy."

"Abercrombie? That's what gay guys wear to the club. Come on, let's get you something for for a straight guy—unless you are gay…"

"No no, I'm straight. Let's do it."

Lars told Elsa in as condescendingly a tone as possible that he would be taking the car for the night, that he was using it for work, and he'd call later. For the night? It made Chad uneasy to be leaving his car here, but that uneasiness was an afterthought the moment he sat in the driver's seat of the Benz. It accepted him, almost embraced him, like it was waiting for him all its life.

"You drive stick, right?"

"We just got here in my Jetta."

"That was a stick?"

"Yes."

"Wow, I didn't notice."

He put the car in reverse, and it lurched backwards when he released his foot off the brake. He wasn't used to this kind of power, but he could easily *get* used to it. Winchester Estates had too many posted speed limits—though no actual speed bumps due to the preponderance of sports cars among its residents—for Chad to really open it up there, but on the freeway, it was a different ball game. It just wanted to go 90, and go 90 like his Jetta liked to go 30.

"Nice, huh? Let me put something on."

He fished around with the MP3 player until the music started. Chad didn't know what he expected, but what he heard wasn't it. It was like 80s adult contempo.

Peter Cetera? "Restless Heart"? Chad had forgotten the song even existed, let alone remember the last time he'd heard it.

"This is the best part right here, check this out:"

He belted out the lyrics along with Peter Cetera's voice.

He turned it down a tick.

"God, I love that part, just the way he hits that note…"

"I guess man… yeah, it's Peter Cetera… I don't know…."

Chad didn't pay attention too much, he was enthralled in this car.

"You really like it, huh?"

"Oh yeah, this thing is amazing."

"We're going to use it as a tax write-off, you don't know how many investors have loved the car first, then us second."

"How would you use it as a tax write-off?"

"It's a fixed asset, right?"

"No, it's not an asset at all, you borrow it from your father. If he was charging you every time, yes, maybe, but taking it down to the mall isn't an expense."

"See, this is why we need you as our administrator."

"I'm sure your friend Seijun already told you borrowing your dad's car isn't a fixed asset."

"We're almost at the mall, let me change this over."

He switched folders in the middle of Climie Fisher's "Love Changes Everything", which was a little disappointing, because Chad kind of wanted to listen to that. He stopped on Flo Rida's "Right Round", and cranked it up.

"I know what you're thinking. I hate this jungle music too, but the women love it. It makes them think of their number one fantasy, getting fucked by big black men."

"What are you talking about?"

"You Americans are too PC to admit it, but you know it's true. I'm from Sweden, where all the women are white, and I'll tell you, all they want is to be dominated by a big, black man."

Chad shook his head.

"You shake your head, but you know it's the truth. Look at all the women outside the mall checking us out."

"I think it's more the car."

"Yeah, but the car doesn't make them wet like this jungle shit does."

They were looking though. And they were impressed. And the men were impressed too. Chad was happy Neiman Marcus was on the other side of the mall entrance they came in through, so they could drive around the parking lot and have more women stare at them.

"You know one chick who had had plenty of that black dick? Lisa."

Chad had forgotten about her, and his failures with her, and that Lars had had her.

"She had had so much of it, she was tired of it. The novelty wears off, you know. Damn, she was so good in the sack—I gotta hand it to you, man, I don't how you did it."

"Did what?"

"Had the self-control not to fuck her. She told me you two never did it. That was a good play my man, who knows how many black dicks have been inside her, it makes me feel dirty just to think about it... but she was so good in the sack..."

Chad didn't know how much more he could handle this conversation. Lars had a matter of fact way of saying things, like a special interest think tank's website, which made him sound like he knew what he was talking about; but what he said was so ludicrous it was impossible to take seriously, like a think tank claiming Obama's healthcare plan would exterminate old people. There was a part of Chad though that believed some of what Lars was saying, even if he didn't want to admit it. He thought white women would often go for a black man over a white one. He also never made the connection consciously that subconsciously his attitudes on the family he saw on *Maury* that day, like making fun of the name Trey'narius, made him a little more of Lars' mindset than he knew.

They went first to the denim section of Neiman Marcus, Lars pulling pairs off the shelf, opening them up, and holding them against Chad's waist.

"What do you think of these?"

"Christ, they're $200!"

"No shit dude, they're 7's."

"Sevens?"

"7 for All Mankind."

"What does that mean?"

"It means they're hot. What do you think?"

"I'll go try them on."

In the fitting room, he looked at himself from a few angles. God, these were nice. But nicer than the ones he got at Abercrombie for over $100 less? He saw Anishka in his head: her life is a gift. I'm getting them.

"Sweet," Lars said. "Let's get you some sneakers to go with them."

Chad felt great carrying his $200 jeans over to the shoe section. He should've been shopping at Neiman Marcus before this. Why did he always go to Abercrombie? And was Lars right that only gay men shopped there? In the sneaker section, he picked up a pair of Gucci hi-tops.

$500! He put them down slowly, trying not to reveal how shocked he was. He went to Cancun for Spring Break in college for less than that!

"What do you think of these?"

They were brown Cole Haans that looked similar to a pair of Pumas he'd seen at Journeys. Christ, how much are those? $150, not as bad, but:

"I saw a pair of Pumas that looked just like this for like $75 at Journeys."

"How old are you?"

"32. I'll be 33 in less than a month."

"And you get your sneakers at Journeys?"

"Is that bad?"

"Not if you're in high school."

"I don't get all my shoes there. I go to Dick's, Foot Locker, Macy's…"

"Well, now you get them here. What's your size?"

"11"

"Can we get these in an 11? Do you have the jeans? Go put those back on before she comes back."

Chad did as Lars said, and came back and tried on the sneakers with his jeans on. Lars was right, they looked great. But $350 for both? The gift, it's a gift, and it's not like you can't afford to splurge.

"Okay, let's get you some new socks and boxers, then we'll shoot over to H&M."

"H&M?"

"Yeah, we'll get your shirts there. They're cheaper, but still look nice. When a woman sees you, first she'll notice the labels on your jeans and shoes, because you won't have any on your shirt."

"Okay?"

"When she sees you rock H&M too, say when your shirt's lying on the floor after you two fuck and she reads the tag, she'll think you're stylish, not just a label shopper, plus she'll look at her own closet and think she's pretty cool too because she has some H&M stuff. You don't want to make her feel *too* inadequate."

It was more of Lars' foolish logic, but Chad liked the idea of spending less on something somewhere, especially since he spent another $100 on a pack of Burberry boxers. Lars relented on the socks, saying Chad's black Polo socks he bought at TJ Maxx were sufficient, but the total before tax was $450.

Outside of Neiman Marcus, in the mall itself, Chad was smacked in the face with holiday cheer. He hated this time of year, when the world was held hostage for a month as everyone sacrificed as much as they could on the altar of consumerism. The lame music, the frantic crowds, the quaint jewelry store commercials, it angered him, and he couldn't wait until it was all over and people went back to their normal lives.

At H&M, Lars picked out a dark purple, diamond checked sweater and a button-up, white and purple striped shirt to go underneath it. The two together weren't $50. Why didn't we go here to start with? It's a gift, a gift.

Chad was a new man in this new outfit. He still looked heavy, but he looked good, really good. Women were checking he and Lars out. Checking *him* out. Why was he shopping at Abercrombie for so long? In reality, women weren't checking him out any more than usual, nor did they check him out any less in his usual Abercrombie clothes; but in his mind, with the new confidence brought on by how he looked in his new clothes, he was getting the attention of the ladies.

"Listen to that song," Lars said.

"What song?"

"Playing above us. Wham!, 'Last Christmas'. I bet this song came out before most of these teenagers were born."

"Well, if they're teenagers, it would've come out before any of them were born."

Ignoring Chad, Lars stopped a group of high schoolers.

"Do you kids know what song this is? I'll give you C-note if you do."

He pulled out his money clip and peeled off a $100 bill. They listened.

"This is some old people's song."

"I bet my mom listens to it."

A girl held out her iPhone. She had an app that would give the title of any song after hearing a certain amount of it.

"Hey, that's cheating."

"You didn't say we couldn't use our phones."

Lars insisted they have supper at Elevens, a strip club on the edge of town—or "six-and-a-halves" as Chad and his friends used to call it. Chad didn't like the idea of a buffet at a strip club, but when Lars mentioned it was only $12.95, all you can eat, and featured prime rib, Chad was sold. He had just spent $500 on clothes after all.

"This is like the best deal in town man, Monday nights before the football game—only problem is the A-list talent doesn't get here until later too."

They were sitting at a table away from the main stages, watching the women, snacking on their food, and chatting.

"I haven't been here since college."

"You go to Dodge State?"

"Yeah. What about you?"

"Harvard."

"Wow."

"Well, I didn't graduate... that's where I met Seijun though. My dad wanted me to get an MBA... I mean, I needed the BA first, of course, but... my parents are pretty rich... really rich actually. My dad got a job as a higher up at APÖS, and they sent him over here as the vice president of US operations. He's even met Axel Päronträd. I borrowed money off them for my half of the start-up with the hedge fund."

"Wow."

Chad's first cellphone was an APÖS, back in 2001. At that time, Axel Päronträd was a hot, jet-setting European billionaire playboy, and while in 2009 he still had that image, APÖS was already seeing the first stings of the hit the new iPhone would give their bottom line—and ultimately kill the brand by the end of the next decade—meaning Lars's father's connection to Axel wasn't as impressive as it would have been back then; but it was still impressive.

"Yeah, that's why I had to dump Lisa."

"Why?"

"My mom thought she was uncouth, and I needed dad's money, so I couldn't afford to make her make him pull the plug."

"You boys doing all right here?"

"We're fine, Bianca."

"Who's your friend?"

"Bianca, this is Chad, Chad Bianca."

They shook hands. Bianca was in her mid-twenties, thin, about 5'5", with short, dark, dyed red hair, dark, red lipstick, and dark eyeliner and mascara around her dark eyes. Like the rest of the waitresses, she was in a black tank top and skirt with black boots. The tank top showed off all the tattoos on her arms and back, but the room was too poorly lit for Chad to really make out what any of the were. She wasn't bad looking though.

"All right everyone, let's welcome Peaches to the main stage!"

A tall blond in a long white dress and clear heels jumped on stage and immediately hit the pole, as the same Flo Rida song from Lars's car played overhead. Lars had his back to her, so he turned to see what she was doing. She flipped upside down on the pole, her dress collapsing over her, showing her body from the navel down—or up, rather.

"Ooh, damn, look at her."

"Peaches?"

She slid down the pole, then slid out of her dress, got on her knees in front of one of the men lining the stage, and licked one of the nipples on her bare chest. Chad wanted to know what other men would be at a strip club at 6PM on a Monday, eating prime rib and shrimp cocktails while a woman took off her G-string in front of them. And did these guys like this song? They looked like the kinds of guys who'd be at a bar at noon opening their mail, which was probably where they were at noon—or they were at home today watching *Maury* like he was.

"God, look at that, look at those moves, running her finger along her pussy, slapping her own ass, then thanking the guys for their ones."

"She's a stripper."

"Now this is what I call art. No, it's more than art. It's more direct…. That female body gently undulating up there onstage is a rare steak on a Wednesday morning, a glass of Johnny Walker black, a Camel unfiltered lit with a match from a book matches you got at a hotel, cupping the lit match in your hand as a biting fall wind whips past you and you duck your face behind the upturned collar of your wool pea coat in a feeble attempt to protect yourself from the cold…"

Chad finished off his Corona and shook his head. Who was this guy? And what am I doing out here with him, dressed in $500 worth of clothes he picked out, driving in his father's $150,000 car because he doesn't have a license. He felt a hand on his back.

"You want another?"

"What do you think Lars?"

"Huh?"

"Should I have another? When are we leaving, I don't want to be drunk."

"Have another. Maybe we'll stay for the game, I don't know."

"So another?"

"Yes, thank you."

The place wasn't too crowded yet, so Bianca had time to chat with Chad and Lars when she brought over their beers.

"So how do you know Lars?"

"He was seeing a girl in my building."

"That Lisa chick?"

She looked at Lars and he rolled his eyes, then she turned back to Chad and laughed. She found him attractive, going for clean cut guys like him. Chad liked that she found him attractive, hoping she might be the one to end his cold streak. He didn't exactly find all her tattoos attractive, but she had nice eyes and a nice body.

"So what do you do for work, Chad?"

"He's an accountant. He's going to work for us."

"Oh really?"

"No, not really."

"Lars, you're ridiculous. All right, I have to take care of another table. I'm off at 10, what are you guys up to?"

"Ten? That's a shitty schedule, you must not get any tips," Lars said.

"I make plenty on Fridays and Saturdays."

"I was thinking after this we'd hit the Blue Door downtown. You can meet us."

"That sounds good."

Chad didn't drink much more after that, and was sober enough to drive them downtown to the Blue Door at 9PM. He had never been there before, never even heard of it. As its name suggested, it was a blue door, next to an Irish pub. Without knowing it ahead of time, no one would think anything important was behind it, let alone a bar. On the other side of the door was a set of steep carpeted steps, which led up to an 80s themed lounge, with album sleeves and posters and framed photos of 80s musical acts and 80s movies all over the place. Howard Jones's "Things Can Only Get Better" played from the speakers above them. Lars led them to a booth in the corner.

"I love this place. What do you think?"

"Yeah, I guess."

"I'm like your age, 34, and you know, we were a little too young when this stuff was cool, you know? But our hot babysitters listened to this stuff, and they danced with guys who were cool and wore blazers with rolled up sleeves... anyway, what I'm saying is, you look at the women who are in their mid-40s in here, and it's like we finally got to hang out with the cool kids, you know? That chick could've been my hot babysitter."

He pointed to a tall, mid-fortysomething woman with long brown hair. She was dressed like the girls Chad saw at the Dirty Sombrero a few weeks ago, only her top was less revealing. Her friends were about the same, some shorter and fuller figured, some thinner. Chad looked around to see if the whole place was older people. One table had an older man with gray hair, dressed in a black blazer, black button up shirt, and black tie. He was sitting across from a woman, similarly aged, with bright red hair in a black dress. Another table had a woman in her thirties sitting by herself, reading *The Ginger Man*. Her hair was gross and stringy, almost as if she had dreadlocks. There was another booth with a group of young twentysomethings, the guys dressed almost like Chad, only with trendier haircuts and closer fitting clothes, and the girls distinguishing themselves from the cougars at the bar by showing off their much thinner figures in dresses with black leggings underneath, their limbs looking like pipe stem cleaners. Okay, Chad thought, at least it's not only old people here. Of course, the kids looked at all of them, including Chad, and thought they were all old, but they liked that, because they all thought the 80s were much cooler than the 2000s, between the John Hughes films and the music, and they saw these older people as cool older people who went to see the movies they thought were cool and bought the music they thought was cool when it was cool. Even though Chad and Lars would've been, as Lars said, too young to see those movies in the theater, or buy those records from the record store, the kids saw that they were older, and anyone older must have been old enough to remember all that stuff that happened before they were born.

A thin waiter with thick, black rimmed glasses came to their booth to take their order. He had an Irish accent.

"Oh, you've never been here before, right? You gotta try the Earl Grey Martini. We'll have two of those."

"Okay, two Earl Grey Martinis. Can I get you guys a menu, you going to want some food?"

"No, we're stuffed, we killed that buffet over at Elevens."

The waiter smirked and left to get their drinks.

"Man, I like that woman at the bar."

"Your old babysitter?"

"Umm, yes. I bet she knows her way around the bedroom. We just need to get some tight acid wash jeans on her and tease the hell out of that hair."

Chad didn't know if Lars was being serious about this. If he was or he wasn't, either one would've been equally believable as far as Chad could tell.

"Ooh, she just looked over here."

"Oh God, do we want that?"

"Are you going to tell me she's not hot?"

"I guess. She's in her forties though."

"Women are just getting started at that age. I bet she's a recent divorcée, if you know what I mean. Her hubby wasn't cutting it, or maybe he's on Viagara and found himself a new young woman too. She wants some young bucks like us."

The waiter dropped off their drinks and coasters with 80s pop stars on them. Lars' had Gary Numan. Chad didn't recognize his.

"Who is this?"

"You don't know Nik Kershaw?" The waiter said. Chad had thought he'd already walked away, and he was asking Lars this question.

"No, what did he sing?"

Lars and the waiter sang a few lines of "Wouldn't it Be Good". Chad still didn't know. Lars changed the subject.

"Shouldn't you be at that Irish place next door?"

"God, with all those tools? Stupid Americans think because some ancestor came here to avoid starvation in the fuckin' 1850s, that they can wear green and act obnoxious. Fuckin' morons. That place ain't Irish."

Chad and Lars laughed. After the waiter left, Lars leaned across the booth a little.

"There might be tools at that place, but in a couple hours, when all the girls are hammered, you can pick up some hotties. You just have to bide your time here first."

He left Chad at the table and went to the bathroom. Chad killed some time looking around the place, reading the album covers and movie posters on the wall. How did this all become retro? It didn't seem that long ago that he was in kindergarten, living on the base in Germany. When his parents divorced, and he moved over here, he found out that all of these movies and songs were popular in the US long before they were popular over there. At 8, though, he wasn't old enough for it to matter much, he was more of a novelty in third grade because he had lived in Germany, and the kids were excited to tell him about things like He-Man and Transformers. On second thought, it did kind of feel like that long ago, I mean, people all the time say "it doesn't feel that long" or that "time flies", but 8 years old really was 25 years ago. 28 might not have almost been five years ago, but 8 was 25.

On his way back from the bathroom, Lars started a conversation with his babysitter. Please, don't point over here, don't point over here. He pointed. He waved. The women giggled. No, don't you, don't you… he invited them to join him. What Chad couldn't hear over the Depeche Mode playing above him was Lars's pick up routine. He asked the woman if she had ever lived in Sweden. No, why? Well, you look like my babysitter I had growing up. Laughter. Are you from Sweden? I am, my father is the vice president of APÖS in the US. Oh wow. Yes, I'm here with my friend Chad, see him over there, hi Chad. More laughing. Why don't you girls join us.

Lars made sure his girl, Ursula, sat next to him, and then Chad was sandwiched between the three others. All of the women worked together at a local doctor's office. Medical assistants. Chad wondered if they'd "gone back to school." Ursula was 44 years old, and from closer in, she was attractive, like Lars said, with olive, Italian features, definitely mature, but not old. Of the other three, there was Aileen, sitting furthest from Chad, a slightly overweight 43-year-old married mother of two boys, out with the girls because her husband had the kids at a hockey game; then directly to Chad's right, Molly, also 43, and engaged to another doctor. She wasn't overweight like Aileen, but rather full figured, curvy. She was blond with blue eyes, and Chad was upset that she was engaged, because he thought she was kind of hot. And then there was Jacqueline, sitting between Chad and Lars to Chad's left, who looked similar to Ursula, only shorter and a little stouter. I know, people always say we look alike, like we could be sisters. She was married too. Within ten minutes of sitting down, Aileen had to go home and see her family.

"So how old are you boys?" Ursula asked. The women hadn't told Lars and Chad how old they were yet.

"I was born in 1975, and what did you say Chad, 1976?"

"Yeah, my birthday is in a little less than a month."

"1976? You guys are babies!"

"If we're babies, what does that make you ladies?"

"Oh my God! Chad, did your friend drive you here, because you know we're going to kill him, don't you?"

"Why?" Lars said. "When were you born?"

"Guess."

"No way, we're not doing that. I'll throw out a landmark, and you tell me if it's before or after. *Star Wars.*"

"Whatever, you guys were born before *that.*"

Ursula was enjoying her flirting with Lars. Molly made small talk with Chad while Jacqueline texted on her phone.

"So what do you do for a living, Chad?" Molly asked.

He told them where he worked and what he did.

"Oh wow, our office does work with them all the time…"

"You don't need to say it, I know they're a sucky insurance company. I'm putting in my notice tomorrow."

"And then what are you going to do?"

"I don't know. Lars over there wants me to work for his hedge fund as an administrator."

"Do you have money saved up?"

"Oh yeah, I could go some time without working and be all right."

"What does your girlfriend think?"

"Oh, I don't have one."

"That fucking asshole!" Jacqueline slammed her phone down.

"Is it Vic again?" Ursula asked.

"Who's Vic?"

"Jacky's hubby."

Molly looked concerned for about two seconds, then arched her eyebrows and went back to talking to Chad.

"It's okay to be single. I was single when I was your age too. Nowadays you can wait longer. You're young, live a little."

"Yeah, that's what I was thinking." Chad was trying to figure out how long ago it was that she was 32 going on 33.

"So if you're born in late December, that makes you what, a Capricorn?"

"Close, a Sagittarius. The 20th of December."

"Well, that makes you almost a Capricorn. You're probably more Capricorn than you are Sagittarius."

"You mean like on the cusp?"

"Yeah. People born close to one but in another are sometimes the other."

"Huh, I didn't know that. And what sign are you?"

"I'm a Virgo."

"When is that?"

"My birthday is September 1st."

"Oh, okay."

What Chad didn't know was Capricorns and Virgos were supposed to be compatible, and Molly wanted to believe that she was compatible with Chad. She wasn't considering hooking up with him, though she did find him attractive. She liked that he was a nice guy she could talk to, especially while her friend Ursula was putting the moves on Lars, and Jacky was fighting with her meathead husband; and instead of thinking their getting along so well could be just because it was, she needed to know there was a metaphysical reason for it. The fact that her future husband was a Leo was a bigger selling point to her than the fact that the two of them got along so well, or that he was so caring—the zodiac compatibility was what made it real for her. Chad enjoyed talking to her too, not because she was a Virgo—he had no idea what that meant—but just because she was nice and physically attractive. Usually a seating arrangement like this, where he was forced to turn his head to talk to one woman, while showing his bald spot to the other, would have been uncomfortable, but now he didn't even think about it.

"If you're wondering, it's September 1st, 1966."

"Really?"

"When did you think it was?"

"I don't know, mid 70s like me."

She smiled a "nice try" smile, but she was still happy he said it.

Bianca showed up a few minutes later. Had she been there before Lars brought the women over, Chad would've been happy to see her, but now that he was making a connection with Molly, he didn't want to interrupt that. Bianca went to the bar to get a drink and say hi to the bartender, whom she knew.

Chad noticed that the toe of Molly's boot was grazing his shin. He looked at her, and she smiled and looked away. Their moment was broken when Jacqueline had to get up to talk to her boyfriend on her phone outside. As she was sliding out of the booth, Chad noticed how nice Molly's butt looked in her light tan plaid skirt which went just above her knee, revealing her flesh until her camel-colored boots took over just below the knee. Her cream-colored turtleneck sweater showed off her nice chest. Then there were those crystal blue eyes and full pink lips, and the blond hair that stopped about an inch below her ear, just barely caressing her shoulders. Then there was that gaudy rock on her left ring finger, paid off with a doctor's salary. No, Bianca was a better play, but how would he make that happen without upsetting Molly, whom he liked talking to.

Jacky stormed past them, and they turned to go back into the booth, when they saw Lars and Ursula making out. Molly was exasperated.

"I'm glad you're here at least, Chad. I'd be all alone otherwise."

"Were they your ride?"

"Yes." She wanted to say she should've gotten a ride with Aileen, but she didn't feel that way anymore. She did need to go home though.

"I can pay for you to get a cab home if you need one."

"That's really sweet of you, Chad. I can pay for it myself, but you want to go downstairs and help me hail it?"

"Sure."

She threw on a brown leather coat and took his hand and led him down the steep steps. She stumbled a couple times in her heels, and he had to prop her up. Outside they stood for a second in awkward silence as Chad looked for a taxi.

"I might have to call for one for you."

"Aren't you cold out here with no coat on?"

"I'm fine." Though he was really wishing he had that hoodie that was sitting in Lars's car in the parking garage.

A cab came around the corner, and Chad waved his hand, getting it to stop.

"Oh yes, you did it!"

"I'm an old pro."

They stood facing each other.

"Well, it was nice meeting you Chad."

"Nice meeting you too."

They went for an awkward handshake, when Chad heard in his head again it's a gift, a gift. He put his hand under her chin and pulled her to him for a small kiss on the lips. She smiled, waved goodbye, and jumped into the taxi.

Yes, Anishka, her life is a gift to me. I'm a Capricorn, damn it! And that was a woman who's about to marry a doctor! And I didn't even give her my number so it didn't even matter anyway! And God it's fucking cold out here!

"Chad!"

Bianca charged over and gave him a huge bear hug. Lars had come down too with Ursula in his arms.

"We're going to Paddy O'Farrell's."

"Where's that? Not far I hope. It's freezing out here."

"It's right next store you dork!"

He looked at his watch, 10:45. It was still early. He did have to go to work tomorrow though. Now the fears about leaving his car at Lars's parents hit him again. If worst came to worst, he'd get a cab over there too. It worked for Molly. Jesus, though, that might run $40.

"I thought we didn't go over there until later."

Lars either didn't hear or didn't care, and didn't respond, locked in an embrace with Ursula, kissing in the cold.

"I think he has his mind on other things. Come on, you can buy me a drink."

She threaded her arm through his, and they followed Lars and Ursula into the bar. It was as their Irish waiter described it, plenty of "tools" yelling at the *Monday Night Football* game, laughing at the bad beer commercials, and making bad passes at the waitresses. There were some women here and there, but they were all among groups of these "tools", in some cases yelling about the games themselves. Lars got them a seat off to the side, vacant because it had the unique distinction of not offering a good view of the game, despite the myriad flatscreens littered around the establishment. A roar erupted from the tools after an interception was returned for a touchdown.

"Jesus," Bianca said. "What a bunch of douchebags, huh?"

"The game should be over soon."

"God. Don't tell me you're like that. Are you upset that you can't see the game?"

"No, I'll live. Plus, I have those 'douchebags' to tell me when something happens."

She laughed.

"You know what I hate the most? Fantasy football. You gotta be a *real* douchebag to do that. The whole thing is just so stupid. That's why I can't work at Elevens on Mondays... and frickin' Lars wants to come *here* early."

He lifted his head from Ursula and let out a "huh?", to which both Bianca and Chad told him it was nothing. Finally a waitress came over and took their orders. She was apologetic that it had taken her so long, but Bianca let her know that they were a sympathetic table. They

109

shared stories, the waitress said she couldn't imagine working at Elevens, that the guys must be worse, and Bianca assured her that she had no idea.

Bianca fingered the cuff of Chad's shirt peeking out under the cuff of his sweater.

"I like this. I like the preppy look in general. It's hot."

"I usually don't dress like this. Lars picked it out today."

He watched her sip her drink, with those dark, red, full lips. Watched her watching him. Watched her pupils dilate. She was attracted to him, but not the way Molly or Haley was attracted to him. Molly and Haley didn't know what they found attractive right away, and in their eyes there was a searching, an attempt to figure out what they were seeing; Bianca was much more aggressive, much more blunt. Her eyes told him I want you against my cervix, I want to do things to you that you won't be able to tell anyone about without blushing—that make you blush now just thinking about—I want to clear everything off this table in one violent motion and fuck you on top of it, while the douchebags behind us yell at their stupid football game, I want you to take me home…

…That reminded him, his car, he needed to get back to his car. It was almost 11:30, and by the time he got to it and got home it would be after midnight. He still had to go to work tomorrow, even if he was putting in his notice.

"Lars… Lars!"

He turned from Ursula, half-lucid.

"We gotta go back so I can get my car. I have to be up in the morning for work."

He didn't respond, and went back to making out with Ursula.

"Lars!..."

Bianca put her hand on Chad's arm.

"I can give you a ride. Where is it?"

"Winchester Estates. I parked it at Lars's parents'."

"Let's go."

Outside, she threaded her arm through his again, and leaned her head on his shoulder. She was wearing a long black coat, but her warmth radiated through it, which he needed in that icy late-November air without a coat of his own. When they got to her car, they stopped and looked at each other for a second, knowing what each wanted to do, and making sure the other wanted it too. He leaned in to kiss her, and she reciprocated tenfold, passionately cramming her tongue down his throat. He hadn't been kissed like that in a long time, and he wasn't ready for it, pushing her away at the same time he embraced her. As the kissing turned from bordering on violent to something more tender, Bianca became better aware of where she was, and she recognized how cold Chad was. Part of Chad was happy to be in the car with the heat on, but part of him would have risked frostbite or hypothermia to remain in that moment.

Bianca's 2003 Honda Civic did not move on the highway the way the Mercedes did. It made Chad anxious, like the world was in slo-motion.

"After we get your car, you wanna come back to my place?"

"Yeah, that sounds great."

Work in the morning no longer existed. In a sense his car no longer existed too. If Bianca had suggested they forget his car and go straight to her house, he would have been for it—almost.

There was a new security guard at the gate at Winchester Estates who didn't know who Chad was. Luckily they had his car information on file, and no record of it exiting the development, so he was allowed admittance. They wanted Bianca to fill out her information in order for her to be able to drive him inside.

"No fucking way, who the fuck are *you*?"

"Those are the rules ma'am."

"That's ridiculous. What is this, *1984*?"

"You don't fill this out, you don't come in."

"Fuck that."

The apprehension he had from the separation from his vehicle welled back up inside of him.

"Listen, take my license, and I'll go in after it on foot, how does that sound?"

"Are you sure?" Bianca said.

"Yes. Why don't I give you my number, and we'll go out sometime this week?"

"Okay."

He kissed her, waved goodbye, and then handed his license to the security guard. The air bit into him again, lashing his face and making his fingers numb. In the dark, every house looked identical, and it took him 20 minutes to find his car, wandering around with his keys, activating the alarm off and on until he heard it, blowing into his hands every few seconds to get some kind of feeling back. He wanted to sit in his car for a few minutes and let it warm up, but he didn't feel comfortable parked in Lars's parents' driveway, so he drove with his palms, looking through a slowly opening spot on his windshield that wasn't frosted over. Had the security gate not been down, he might have forgotten to pick up his license. The guard didn't think anything about his freezing red face or obstructed windshield, hardly disdaining to even wish Chad a good night as he handed the license to him.

"Jodi, how are you? I really like that sweater."

"Oh, *thank you* Chad."

"Is Bert in the office?"

"Yes, he should be free."

Chad was the happiest he'd been since he'd started at this job, and it was the day he was giving his two-week notice. Chad in Accounting would only exist for another 14 days—eleven when you factored in that it was already Tuesday, and his last day would be next Friday. Chad had the whole moment of breaking the news to Bert in his head, like he was imagining the performance of a play he had written; but Bert took the news a lot better than Chad was expecting, robbing him of some of the punch he was hoping his notice would have, forcing him to tear that play up.

Haley and Brick asked him if he was feeling better. He forgot that he'd called in sick the day before. It annoyed him to have to answer that, because he felt like it was further robbing him of the punch giving his notice should have had. When he finally made the announcement, again, he was disappointed by the reaction. Haley seemed almost happy to hear it, and his supervisor was indifferent.

Haley was happy to hear he was moving on, and that happiness wasn't tempered when she heard that he didn't have another place of employment lined up. For her, this change in Chad's life would be a welcomed positive step, long overdue. She was excited for him. As the day went on, Chad understood where she was coming from, and was back to being proud of himself. At about ten, Lars called.

"Hey, can you come down here? I showed Seijun your résumé, and he really wants to give you the job."

"Dude, I'm at work right now."

"Come down on your lunch break."

"I only get a half-hour. It'll take me 15 just to get downtown from here."

Lars sighed.

"Dude, what are you so worried about? Aren't you quitting that job anyway?"

"I put in my notice, that doesn't mean I don't need to—"

"Go ahead Chad, Haley and I can hold down the fort until you get back."

Chad wasn't paying attention to them, but Haley was listening to Chad's end of his conversation, and whispered to Brick to let Chad go.

At 11:59 he blew out of work and hopped in his car and headed downtown. Lars and Seijun occupied a wing on the fourteenth floor of a fifteen-story office building. Parts of it looked sleek and sophisticated, like the expensive ergonomically correct furniture or the flatscreens on the walls; but other parts looked unfinished, like those same walls that weren't completely painted, or the equipment on the floor or still in cardboard boxes. The secretary told him Lars and Seijun were waiting for him, and directed him to the office with the name Seijun Nashinoki on the frosted glass window of the door.

Lars was in a sharply tailored Helmut Lang suit, which looked nice, but nothing like Seijun's. The whole thing was clean and perfect, from the gray pinstriped coat and pants that couldn't fit any better, to the expertly knotted tie and matching pocket square, to the hair that was gelled and sculpted to his head without a follicle out of place, to the shoes that looked brand new, to the cuff links on his sleeves, to the manicured nails on his fingers, to the amount of shake and grab he gave when he took Chad's hand in greeting. Chad wondered, as he sat across from him in his Van Heusen blue shirt and royal blue tie—not expertly tied, the shirt hanging off of him, a half-size too big—if this had been a good idea. This Lars guy was ridiculous for bringing him down here.

"So what do you think?" Seijun said.

"You guys have a nice place."

"The money from our initial short sales should allow us to pay off most of the money Lars's parents put up, and we're only looking to grow from there."

"You guys do mostly short selling?"

"Seijun here has a diverse strategy. He's a genius."

"What Lars is saying is, I have a proven approach to investing that I've employed successfully for years. It's not a matter of if we'll make money, but how much. I'll show you a little more as you get settled in, especially since we'll need you to be the administrator."

"What exactly will you be hiring me for?"

"Basic back office functions. Making sure we're in compliance, tax issues, double checking my numbers, giving the investors the assurance that I'm not inflating the NAVs to boost my performance fee."

"Well, wouldn't I have an incentive to inflate the NAVs too, considering I don't get paid if you don't stay in business?"

"Yes, of course… I guess what I need most is someone to cover the nuts and bolts while I work my magic as a manager. How much time do you have right now? I could show you some of what I have in mind."

"Sure."

Seijun pulled out some printouts, showing transactions, etc. He had projections on his iBook, other printouts, tax forms, all things Chad understood, and all things Chad understood Seijun might not want to deal with if he had bigger fish to fry.

"Now, we have an office for you which we can take you to. It's not as big as this one or Lars's, but it's not bad. We can add a desk and an iBook and whatever else you need."

"An office?"

"Yeah, come on, let's go."

They walked two doors down the wing, away from the secretaries, to a slightly smaller version of Seijun's office, unfurnished with some cardboard boxes stacked inside.

"We should have this squared away by the end of the week. We'll get your name on the door. You'll have your own closet, maybe throw a couple extra suits in there. You never know when we plan an impromptu getaway to Vegas or the Caribbean, huh Lars?"

"Oh yeah, you'll learn quick to have an extra set of clothes and a suitcase packed."

"Wow. And you're going to pay me more than I'm making now?"

"Um… eventually…"

"Well, Lars said… that's okay, though, this is much better than where I'm at now… I mean, my own office…" Seijun's eyebrows were still furled. "…you can at least pay me 40K, right?"

"Um… Lars didn't go over this with you?"

"Over what?"

"Well, we can't actually pay you right now… we can pay you eventually when we take our 19 percent performance fee—you'll probably make more than 55K when all is said and done— Lars said you had money saved, that's why I figured you'd be perfect for this, you wouldn't mind working without pay initially…"

"That isn't what Lars said at all… I'll have to think about—"

"Lars, can you give us a moment?"

He nodded and left Chad and Seijun alone among the boxes.

"I'm sorry Lars mislead you. It's not like you'd be going a long time without money, only until the start of the next quarter, when we calculate our performance fees, we'll give you a prorated cut, one percent, which leaves Lars and I with a remainder of 18 percent. Does that make sense?"

"So my pay is contingent on the success of your investments… can I ask how much profit you plan to get on those short sales you were telling me about?"

"950K."

"Okay."

"Yes, so you do the math, 1 percent of that…"

"9,500."

"And that's just the start. As some of our other long-term investments come to fruition, we'll be bringing in bigger numbers."

"Well, at 9,500 a quarter, if that's what I'm looking at, I'm not doing *that* bad compared to my current situation... when would my first check come?"

"I imagine mid-January. It'll probably depend on you and how fast you can turn over the paperwork. That number would be cut by roughly two-thirds, of course, because you'd only be working with us for December, but we can throw in some extra because we'll need you to catch us up somewhat. And remember, that $950K is us just getting started."

"Can you give me a night to think about it?"

"Take the week, considering you wouldn't be able to start for two weeks until you're through at your current place of employment. By then, we'll have the office done-over, and maybe Lars and I can take you out to lunch. Tell you what, take the entire afternoon off at your current job on Friday. You, me, and Lars will grab lunch, see where things stand..."

"Okay, that sounds great."

Should he or shouldn't he? It dominated his thoughts on Tuesday and Wednesday. Based on what he had in the bank, and some investments of his own, he could live comfortably for a year, year-and-a-half. Probably wouldn't be good to have too many $500 shopping days, but otherwise he was all right. The thing that worried him was, what if Seijun lost money on the investments? He'd go three months with nothing. On the other hand, if he was right about earning double this quarter, that wouldn't be too bad. Based on the numbers Chad saw on the sheets, Seijun's estimate of 10 percent profit would net Chad more than he was making now. It was a gamble, and Chad wasn't a gambler. And then there was his own office. Imagine that, his name on the door. And he did have the money to live off of, and he could make even more than he made now if Seijun's investments were as good as he said.

He was happy on Wednesday evening to have his first soccer game to get his mind off things. They played at the Dodge State fitness complex, on an actual indoor soccer surface. It had been redone since he'd played on it last, over ten years ago, for his fraternity in the intramural league. They even had a small set of bleachers now. He invited Bianca to come watch. He hadn't seen her since Monday night, and though he was looking forward to it, he was afraid he wouldn't be any good at soccer and lose face with her. No, he wouldn't be afraid, he would just play. It was a gift, a gift.

Fifteen minutes in, one of their defenders, Walter, an Argentinean going to pharmacy school with Martinson, was gassed, and called for Chad to take over. This was it.

His first taste of action came when a short stocky player on the other team bumped him on his way up the field, and Chad held his ground. Martinson was playing back with him, and nodded. Ahead were Miguel, Jorgé, and Obi, a Nigerian guy that he didn't remember from the practice last week—another pharmacy student, it turned out. Things kind of went from there, with the occasional bump from the stocky guy trying to gain position, or a ball played too far that Chad cleared away or played back to the keeper, a tall, lanky Russian named Yuri, who worked with Miguel.

As the half was winding down, he noticed a lazy pass was made to the short stocky guy. Before he had a chance to over-think it, something happened to Chad. The 21-year-old Chad stepped in and took over for the 32-going-on-33-year-old Chad. With a burst of speed, he dashed into the passing lane, intercepting it and dribbling the ball alone up the field. All of the other players, including those on his own team, were moving in the opposite direction, not anticipating his steal. He had one defender to beat, and after a couple step-overs, he pushed the ball left, past the opposing lunging leg, then cut it back to the middle with the outside of his right foot, and continued toward the goal. Had the goalie not charged out to cut off the angle, there would've been time for the 32-going-on-33-year-old Chad to reassert his place and kick the 21-year-old Chad out, making him overthink things; but the goalie did charge, going low to block Chad's shot, and with no time to think, Chad chipped the ball over him, into the net.

There were howls and cheers from his teammates. He heard Bianca on the sidelines yell out his name. Miguel slapped him on the back.

"I thought you weren't very good, huh?"

Even his opponents were telling him what a good job he'd done. Jesus, where did that come from? he thought. Then he thought, I need a seat, I can barely breathe. Before the game was restarted, he signaled Walter back on. He needed to get into better shape, this was ridiculous. On the other hand, he really just did that! Wow.

Chad didn't play much more after that. He was a back-up, and the rest of the players were really good. Chad was content to sit and watch them, watch how natural they all were on the ball, how even their mistakes looked nice. South Americans, Mexicans, Africans, Europeans, they all understood the game in an intuitive way that Americans like Chad didn't have growing up with youth league soccer as an activity thrown in with basketball, baseball, football, track, wrestling… Chad could see younger versions of the team, like elementary school children, doing the same things their adult counterparts took for granted. It made him envious, but also proud that he had shown up so well and earned their respect. He hadn't been proud of himself in a long time.

He wanted to go home and take a shower, but Bianca said he could take one at her place. You don't want to go out? No, let's stay in and catch movie. Yes, Chad thought, this could be an all-around banner day. Bianca had a small apartment near downtown. It made Chad a little guilty that she'd driven so far out of her way the other night. Inside, it was clean, nothing fancy, but Chad noticed a few teddy bears on the couch. He didn't think anything of it. The bathroom had a bear theme as well, with cartoon bears on the shower curtains, and a porcelain cub holding her toothbrushes. All he could think about though was how close he was to getting laid. This was going to be good.

Bianca's movie was *Grizzly Man*, a Werner Herzog documentary about a man who lived among grizzly bears in Alaska, eventually getting himself and his girlfriend eaten by one. The whole thing was disturbing to Chad. Bears were scary, what kind of moron would want to live with them? He looked at Bianca, and wanted to make a move on her, but part of him didn't have the desire due to the movie they were watching; but he also noticed Bianca was really into the film, almost never looking at him, not giving any body language to suggest she wanted him to make a move.

When the movie ended, she asked Chad what he thought, and he said it was a trip.

"If you haven't noticed, I sorta have a thing for bears."

"I have picked up on a bear theme, yes."

"Yeah, I love them, ever since I was a little girl I've loved them."

"Hmm… well that's cool…"

"Yep."

He was sitting facing the TV, nodding, while she sat facing him in the lotus position, the shape of her knees forming underneath her long, dark brown skirt. She looked precocious with her thin fingers caressing her knees, wearing a burnt sienna tank top with spaghetti straps that left her bare from the chest up, and a long, white, flower-print scarf that was tied off on one side around her neck. Chad was thinking of something to say next, when she broke in:

"I want you to try something on."

"Try something on?..."

"Yeah, wait here."

Try something on? If it gets me laid I'll do it, I don't care, I'll do... wait, what's that?

"This is my bear costume."

"Bear costume?"

"Yeah, try it on."

It was a big brown suit, covered in fur, with a realistic bear head that went over his. The bear head had beady eyes and kinky fur that was a bit all over the place. It reminded Chad of Nick Nolte's mugshot. Also, it didn't smell great in there, and it was very stuffy. He could see Bianca intermittently as she moved in and out of the view through the eye holes. She was checking him out. At least she was liking it. He'd just do what he had to do, Bianca was hot, who cared if she was a little weird, she'd be great in the sack. She started undressing. Yes, yes! She turned down the lights and lit some candles. Yes! Chad didn't know what to do, though. He figured she'd want him to get out of the costume soon, and they could do it. Oh yes!

She ran her hands up and down his fur. She felt good, even if he was feeling her through the suit. He lifted his paw to do the same, but he was afraid he'd scratch her with the plastic claws. Then she started talking to him, calling him Mr. Bear. Chad didn't know what to do. Should he affect a bear voice? What exactly is a bear voice? Like a growl, maybe? What famous bears did he know? Yogi, Paddington, Smokey... Bianca, you can prevent forest fires?

She sat him down on the couch and curled up on him. Oh God, Chad thought, she's serious here. This has to be a joke. She knows Lars. Of course, that's it. That guy would make a great practical joker. She was licking around his bear nipples. Did this suit have nipples? Like that Batman suit George Clooney had. Bat-nipples, that was hilarious. This wasn't hilarious, though. She was calling him Mr. Bear, telling him she'd been bad, and what would he do? He wouldn't do anything in this suit, he could barely move in it. She took his paw and moved it down toward her crotch. This was too much for Chad, and he jumped up and pulled his head off.

"I'm sorry... I can't... I can't do this anymore... I'm sorry..."

Bianca was nonplussed.

"Oh... that's okay... um..."

She was naked, sitting on her couch, with Chad standing over her in a bear costume without the head on, his hair a mess, and his face moist. God, she was hot, she had a really nice body. Lots of tattoos though. He finally noticed that they were all kinds of bears or scene of bears doing things. He moved the head off the couch and sat back down next to her.

"I'm sorry," he started again.

"No, I'm sorry, I usually don't do this on a first date, I don't know what came over me... you just... you looked really hot in that costume... you still kind of do..."

"It's... it's hot in here... you know?..."

"Oh yeah, I bet... I... I didn't think of that... at least I... at least I didn't... at least I didn't go get the strap on, huh?"

"The stra—?... oh, you mean you..." he moved his right index finger back and forth, pointing from his crotch to her. "You... um, okay..."

"Yeah... I know... that's why I usually don't do it on the first date."

"Right... no... that makes sense..."

"I'm... I'm going to get dressed."

"Oh, yes, by all means... I think I'm going to... you know, work in the morning and stuff..."

"No, of course, that makes sense... maybe sometime later this week... we can... get together..."

"That sounds great... call me... we'll set something up."

As he turned to go after putting his pants back on, she stopped him:

"Promise you won't tell Lars or anyone about this?"

"Um, oh, yes, of course... it's our secret."

He got in his car, and in his sexual frustration dropped his keys as he put them into the ignition. He banged his palm on the steering wheel. Damn it! Damn it! What the hell was that? Really? Really, that happened? A fucking bear costume? What did I do, seriously, what did I do to deserve this? I mean really, a bear costume? And a strap-on! First Amy's asking me about one, now this chick wants me to strap one on and fuck her in a bear costume. Christ! There's no way any guy has ever done that for her before. No way. How would he have breathed in that suit?

Thursday, though, after a listless day at work, he thought about Bianca again. Could it be that bad, a bear costume? After they were done in the bear costume, they could have sex for real. He could deal with that. He called her, but got her voicemail. That's right, she has to work tonight. He told her that in the message, that he forgot she had to work, and they'd talk later.

After Chad was gone and the door was locked, Bianca, still naked, poured herself a large glass of their leftover wine and took a long sip. She was shaking. What the hell was she thinking?

As she brought her laptop over to the couch and started browsing, she knew the answer to that question. From the moment she met Chad on Monday with Lars, she could feel his desperation. Yes, she thought he was cute, but she knew right away he wasn't like the other guys Lars hung out with. He wasn't as confident or as smooth, he let Lars make all the decisions—even worried about drinking too much so he'd be okay to drive. Then when they made out in the parking lot, she got an even better sense of him: he was rusty, awkward, almost begging for it. He would've done anything for her—except leave his car at Winchester Estates—but even that told her, perhaps erroneously, that he was less of a chance taker and potentially more obsequious, that he would do anything she wanted. She thought he was perfect for what she needed.

And for the most part she was right, but even this was a bridge too far for Chad, and as Bianca was paging through some sites that catered to the kind of porn that depicted what she wanted Chad to do to her, myriad other thoughts zipped through her head: what if Chad told Lars? Why wouldn't he? Who wouldn't tell everyone they knew this story? Her reputation was ruined! Maybe Chad will blackmail her. He didn't have any proof though, and who would believe him? What if he calls her and demands things and threatens to tell everyone?

She didn't realize just how much this fetish was a part of her until she left Dan six months ago. He was a furry, and the bear was who he felt he was meant to be. When they first met, and he remarked on her tattoos, she thought maybe he was the same as her: someone who just really liked bears. Then a couple months into their relationship he showed her his suit. It was a little weird, but also a bit of a turn on. The sex in the bear suit followed soon after. For her it was their thing, something they did behind closed doors, no one else's business; but the fact that she not only accepted this side of him, but was into it too, normalized it for him in a way she didn't see coming. He became more bold, wanted to do things like wear the suit while he sat outside on the patio of their apartment, where the neighbors could see him. She tried making up a story about him working as a character for a company that does kids' birthday parties, and was mortified to find out from one of her neighbors that he had already told them he was a furry, and that she was into it.

The last straw came when they were getting ready to go to the mall, and he was in his suit, and wouldn't change out of it. They split up and he moved to Phoenix a couple weeks later to live with a commune of other furries. It was in her first relationship post-Dan, a month after he left, that she found out how bad things were for her. She and her new boyfriend had sex for the first time, and it felt horrible for her. He didn't seem to notice, he got what he wanted, so she lied about it being good for her too; but something had been rewired in her brain sexually. She thought maybe it would just take some time, but it never got better with her new boyfriend, and she found herself longing for him to leave so she could pleasure herself alone to websites that catered to what she wanted. But the sites were only so good, since she'd had the real thing.

That's when Chad came along. He exuded that combination of desperation and safety that, when combined with her own desperation, made her take a chance that left her humiliated— and worst of all, still sexually unfulfilled despite having been so close. She would have to settle again tonight.

Friday Chad left for the day after lunch, as he told Seijun he would, and went downtown, back to their fourteenth-story offices. As Seijun promised, Chad's was finished, and it was better than he had imagined. His name was on the door, the inside didn't have any cardboard boxes, instead it was clean, had a polished wooden desk in the center, adorned with various office accoutrements, like pens, staplers—and an iBook. What?

"Yeah, we got you an iBook. Do you have an iPhone too?"

"No, just this old Blackberry."

"Okay, we'll have to get you an iPhone. We can do that today. We like to sync everything up, use the same platform for all of our work."

"Yeah, that makes sense."

He stood up from behind his desk—*his desk!*—and walked around the rest of his office—*his office!* There was a closet, with wooden hangers already in it. There was a mini-fridge, stocked with Sam Adams. Look behind the books in the bookcase. He did. A bottle of Hennessey. Seijun got that trick from *Eat Drink Man Woman*, which made no sense to Chad, but he liked it.

Seijun and Lars took him around the rest of their wing of the fourteenth floor. He'd have access to their bathroom, which was clean, had faux marble sinks, faux mahogany walls, and brass handles. Plus, they had Charmin. There was a game room, which had a PS3, Wii, and Xbox 360; a Hi-Def flatscreen; digital cable; leather couches. Then they had a workout room, with a weight bench, elliptical, and treadmill, not to mention another flatscreen with digital cable. He could watch the Fox Soccer Channel while getting himself back in shape for soccer. This certainly was no dreary cubicle. Who cared if he wasn't sure if he'd get paid or not?

They went to a sushi restaurant downtown, a few blocks away from the building. Chad had never had sushi before, finding the concept unappetizing. Also, the menu was out of Chad's price range.

"Don't worry, Lars and I have this."

"I've never had sushi before."

"Always a first time for everything. We'll just get a couple boats and call it good."

"Don't forget the sake."

When the food came, Chad liked some pieces, and some were too much for him. Sea urchin especially. He had no idea how Lars and Seijun could eat that. He also didn't like the sake at first either, but as he drank more, it tasted better.

"Hey, so did you end up seeing that Bianca chick?"

"Yeah, I went to her apartment a couple nights ago to watch a movie."

Seijun raised his eyebrows, and Lars slapped him the back.

"Thatta boy!"

Chad wanted to tell him no, they didn't do anything, but he let it go and gave them a wry smile.

"All right, so I know you're a little tipsy, but what do you think? Could you get used to working with us?"

Chad emptied his container of sake into the matching tiny cup, trying to get all the drips out.

"I think I could get used to this, yes."

And he pounded it down like a shot.

Lars's Bromance and Krystel's Dolphins

Haley and Chad went out for lunch on Chad's final day as Chad in Accounting. There was no office party, no cake, no going away presents. In his five years at that branch of that insurance corporation, he had only made one connection with any of his co-workers, and that was Haley, who only started a few months before, so no one else was all that concerned that he was leaving, just as they weren't all that concerned when Stacey no-called no-showed. If anything, they were hoping Chad's replacement would be as pleasant as Haley, and then, who knows, maybe they could get rid of Matt and bring someone nice in in his place too...

"So are you excited to be starting at your new job? I bet you must be."

"I've been going over there for a couple hours each night after work, so it'll be nice to finally be going there full time, as a full employee."

"I bet. I'll miss having you in the cubicle next to me, but it was good for you to get a fresh start."

"Yeah, I think so."

They sat in virtual silence for a few moments, picking at the nachos in front of them, and occasionally making comments about how messy this one was or how that one had too many jalapenos on it. Haley broke the monotony.

"Guess what?"

"What?"

"My friend hooked me up with some hiking buddies of his, and we're all going to do the Governors Range on New Year's."

Chad had no idea what she was talking about, but he replied with an "Oh wow, that's great" just the same. Haley wouldn't let him off that easy though.

"You don't even know what I'm talking about, do you?"

He smiled.

"Was it that obvious?"

"Yes Chad, it was that obvious." She smiled back. "The Governors Range is 8 peaks, all named after former governors. You already did the biggest, Birnbaum, which is in the middle. Then there's Mt. James, Mt. Henry, Mt. McInnis, Mt. Lewis, Mt. Roberts, Mt. Raymond, and Mt. Alphonse. It's like 23 miles to go through all of them."

"At once? You do them all at once?"

She laughed at his astonishment.

"Yes, of course. I've never done them in the winter before though. It's like a three-day trip. I've heard, because the weather can get really sticky up there, it's a good test of how ready you are to do Denali."

"Wow, and you're doing that on New Year's?"

"If the weather holds, hopefully."

Fuck that.

When he got home he barely had a chance to settle in before Lars showed up.

"Hey big boy, how was your last day at your old job?"

"I'm glad it's over. You want a beer?"

"Yes."

Lars followed him over to the refrigerator, where Chad handed him a Sam Adams, then got one for himself, and opened both with a souvenir bottle opener magnet from Nashville that was stuck on the door. His mother had gotten him that magnet when she went to a family law conference there three years ago.

"What, did you take a cab over here?"

"No, I drove the Benz."

"Oh sweet, did you get your license back?"

"Hell no. I just drove very carefully."

He winked, and Chad shook his head. The beer tasted very good, better than any beer had tasted in five years. He felt like a weight had been lifted off of him. He was finally free of a burden he didn't even know he was carrying.

"Tonight, you and me are doing karaoke at the Green Dragon. It's the best, scorpion bowls, pu pu platters, and tons of hot chicks."

"Dude, I hate karaoke." Or do I? Chad thought. Chad in Accounting hated karaoke, but the Chad before him loved karaoke with Dave and Kovacs.

"Don't worry about it, you and me will do a duet. It's just to make the girls see that we can have a good time, and aren't afraid of putting ourselves out there and commanding the room. They love that kind of shit. Charisma is the name of the game."

Chad was convinced. Lars took him to his room to pick out an outfit.

"Jesus, where did you get these clothes?"

"What are you talking about? You don't like them?"

"It's all Abercrombie and shit. Haven't you bought anything since our trip to Neiman Marcus?"

"Should I have?"

"I'm going to pretend I didn't hear that. Where are the jeans we picked out the other day?"

"Hanging over on the chair, like you said."

"Exactly, let them air out instead of washing them too much. Let's do those and the shoes we bought, then we just need another shirt."

"What about one of these Abercrombie ones?"

"No way."

"What about what you said about how the shirt should always be cheaper?"

"What?"

"You know, when we went to H&M, you said the shirt should be cheaper, to make the girl feel better or something."

"What about this sweater? What is it, Nautica?"

"Yeah, my mom bought it for me for Christmas last year. I barely wear it."

Lars held it up to his nose and inhaled.

"Wear this over one of the Abercrombie shirts, and then I'll give you a hit of my Jean-Paul Gautier in the car."

"What?"

"My cologne."

As Chad was dressing, Lars went through the rest of his wardrobe.

"Is this all you have for suits?"

"Yeah, is that a problem?"

"This one isn't bad."

It was dark blue with pinstripes.

"I got it at Target for $350."

"You got this at *Target?*"

"Yep."

"Wow, that's sick." He hung it back in the closet. "Monday we'll have to take you downtown and get a couple suits cut. But I want you to wear this one in and see if Seijun guesses that you got it at Target."

"Wow, Seijun, yeah, *he* can dress. I've never seen anyone with style like him."

That comment hurt Lars a little, because he always assumed he and Seijun were equally stylish. Undeterred, he proceeded as if he hadn't thought anything of it.

"You know what his secret is?"

"No, what?"

"Hong Kong."

"Hong Kong?"

Chad was expecting something like *GQ* or a secret style book he didn't know about. Hong Kong didn't make sense as an answer to a question like "do you know the secret to Seijun's style?" It would have been like someone responding "Miami" to a question on how a person could grow such great tomatoes.

"Oh yeah. He did the math out once, and discovered that he could get the best designer suits cheaper in Hong Kong, even after the expense of airfare and hotels and everything, than he could in New York—even cheaper still if he gets more than one made in a trip."

As Chad was contemplating the concept of one flying to Hong Kong for designer suits, there was a knock at the door. They both went to the living room to see who it was. Lars didn't know what to think of the teenage girls he heard giggling on the other side. Chad said, almost whispering:

"It's Amy, a girl from down the hall. She and her friend probably want to show me something they have cooked up for a YouTube video."

He opened the door, and there they were, Amy dressed like Wonder Woman, and Brittney like a female version of Captain America. Both outfits were very tight and very revealing, with big red boots and long red gloves, Amy in the traditional Wonder Woman red top with gold trim and blue bottom with white stars, while Brittney had on a blue bikini top with a white star on each, and then a red and white stripped bottom. She also had a red mask over her eyes. There was something disquieting about their appearance to Chad. There were mature female elements that made them attractive, like the boots and the gloves and the bikinis; but at the same time, they had very young frames—very thin and not fully developed, which made Chad uneasy with the fact that he found the other aspects attractive. They giggled even more as Chad and Lars took them in upon opening the door.

"What are you girls up to now?"

"Another request."

"I should've known."

They giggled again.

"It's not that bad. Nothing about strap-ons. They just want us to dress up like super heroes and wrestle."

"Okay…" Chad could not believe this. He turned his head, and noticed Lars. "oh, geez, I almost forgot, Lars, this is Amy, from down the hall, and this Brittney, her BFF."

More giggling as they shook Lars's hand. Unlike Chad, who felt odd about finding the girls attractive, Lars had no problem with this at all. He figured they were probably between 14 and 16, which wasn't that bad, right? And strap-ons. He didn't know why she said that, but it had to be hot.

"So what do you want us to do? I'm not filming this, so don't even ask."

"We just wanted you to see us do it, so you can tell us if we look like dorks or not."

"Whether you look like dorks or not isn't the issue, it's the fact that some weirdo dude is requesting on YouTube for you girls to dress up like Wonder Woman and wrestle. Doesn't that strike you as odd?"

They giggled again.

"A little, but it sounded like fun. Come on, you and your friend just take a seat and watch us."

They did as they were told, but as Chad watched the girls in their superhero outfits, the tangle of boots and gloves and flesh prone and struggling on the floor in front of him, his sensibilities were only hurt that much more. It felt like seeing a five-year-old in a pageant, made-up to look like a woman, in an adult dress and with adult hair and adult eyelashes, a shuffling of signals that were meant to denote a small child and signals that were meant to denote a mature woman, leaving him with a sensation that something wasn't right, an innocence lost, so to speak.

The girls felt uncomfortable with this one too. Maybe they were embarrassed in front of Chad and his friend, or maybe what Chad said about the request being from a weirdo sunk in a little more, or maybe it was just that neither really had the aggression required for something like wrestling. Whatever it was, after only a few minutes, as if sharing one brain, the girls stood together and declared that they agreed with Chad, that it was a little weird. Chad offered them some Vitamin Waters from the fridge, which they took, then went to the living room to catch their breath on Chad's recliner, Brittney sitting on the seat portion, while Amy was on the right arm, facing Chad and Lars, with her legs crossed, swinging them coquettishly as they hung down over the side.

"So what are you boys up to tonight?"

"Lars wants to go to the Green Dragon."

"Oh geez, my mom used to go there. She dated a bartender or something."

"Did she do karaoke?"

"Oh God, probably. Probably sang some Cher song or something while she was drunk."

The girls giggled. Chad looked over at Lars, and he was daydreaming, only snapping out of it a bit when he heard the girls. Then Chad noticed, or thought he noticed, as Lars let out a fake laugh to act like he'd been a part of the conversation, something that gave him pause: Lars was checking out Amy. Like *checking out* checking out. No way, he has to be daydreaming, it's just a coincidence. You're being overly protective, Chad, not every guy is a perv, plus, the girls do look kind of hot—ugh, cut it out dude, they're 15! Chad stood and went to them.

"All right girls, we should probably get moving, plus I'm sure you want to get changed, I bet you're cold in those outfits."

He helped them to their feet.

"What do you mean?" Lars said. "We still have a couple hours, they can hang out a little more."

"No, Britt's mom is coming in a little while, and she'd probably shit her pants if she saw us looking like this."

They giggled again and then let themselves out, wishing Chad and Lars a good night.

"Wow, I'd like to hit that."

"Dude, they're only 15!"

Lars read in Chad that he didn't find that funny, so he covered his tracks to keep Chad from thinking him a degenerate.

"*15?* Wow, I thought they were at least 18 or 19. That's crazy."

It had the desired effect: Chad felt better about Lars, thinking that he was just unaware of how young Amy and Brittney were, and not a perv after all.

The Green Dragon was pretty full for Karaoke Fridays. It was held in a big lounge off the main dining room that looked more like a tiki bar and less like a Chinese restaurant. On Saturdays, the same space was used to spotlight local stand-up comedians. An older woman showed them to their table and took their drink orders, each getting a beer to start with.

"All right, this isn't looking so bad, huh?"

Chad looked around and saw quite a few good looking women, not all of whom were in groups that included men. This had potential. He still had a lingering sexualized feeling from seeing Amy and Brittney dressed up like superheroines that made him uneasy, and he wanted to drink that feeling away and replace it with feelings for women more his age.

"Oh lord, is that 'You're so Vain' that woman is singing?" Chad said.

Lars let out a howl to the woman in her early 50s belting out the Carly Simon. She was starting to wander the crowd, really feeling it.

"Jesus, Lars, don't encourage her. She might come over here!"

"Would that be so bad?"

"Yes!"

She was wearing a shirt that was a little too small for her, and her ample mid-drift was making its way out. She had on big glasses and long, stringy hair. Chad did his best to not make eye contact with her.

"We need to get our song in before it gets too late."

"What? I need to drink a little more first."

"No, pretty soon it'll be too late. We need to get ours in before the line gets too long. I'll go up and put it in."

"Wait, what are we doing?"

" 'Almost Paradise'."

"What? Dude, that's gay!"

"Don't worry, I'll do the Ann Wilson parts. It'll be great. I'll be right back."

Left alone, Chad looked around the room. He didn't recognize anyone. There were a lot of really hot women though. Lars knew what he was doing at least as far as picking out the location. As long as I don't make a total ass out of myself doing karaoke. He noticed Lars talking to two girls. One was short with brown hair, the other taller, with blond hair and brown streaks. He thought the shorter one was cuter, but it was obvious Lars already had his hooks into her. The tall one was more intriguing. She had on a zebra-print skirt, black halter top, and white go-go boots. Even from a distance, though, he could tell that her face was a bit beaten, pale, with a few spots of acne or the scars remaining from previous breakouts. She stood there, with her arms folded, over her boobs, swaying and twisting and pretending to be involved in Lars and her friend's conversation. Lars pointed over in his direction, and all three of them waved.

Lars, unbeknownst to Chad, had used his classic European city pick-up line. He asked the girl, Marissa, if she had ever been to (this time it was) Paris. No, why do you ask? Lars knew before he even approached her that Marissa had never been to Paris. He had listened to the uncouth manner she and her friend, Krystel, spoke to one another, and he deduced that she'd make for a good fuck that night, as long as Chad was willing to be a good wingman and fall on the grenade—Krystel. As he suspected, the girl was turned on by his worldliness, and even more turned on by the fact that he, someone who had been to Paris, would mistake her for someone he knew there. He didn't hesitate to drop that his buddy Chad had been to Paris too. He didn't know Chad had actually been, he assumed erroneously that he hadn't, but he wanted to make sure his wingman looked as worldly as he did. A very important detail.

When they returned to the table, Lars and Marissa were sitting close to each other, kitty corner on one side, while Chad and Krystel were a little more centrally located in their seats, across from one another. The moment the waitress came over, Lars ordered a scorpion bowl for he and Marissa to share, and without asking first, one for Chad and Krystel to share too.

"Chad, I told the girls we're taking them to Paris with us the next time we go."

"Oh, that sounds good, since I don't remember much of my first time."

Lars, though nonplussed, went with it, not giving away in his face that any of this was a surprise. The girls wanted to know what he was talking about.

"My French class went senior year. Me and my buddies were so wasted the whole time, though, we barely remember any of it."

Everyone laughed. Lars was astounded. The dropping of the Paris line was a test to see how well Chad as a wingman could think on his feet, but now to find out he knew French? The wingman possibilities...

"*Chad, les femmes ont l'IQ d'une pomme de terre.*"

"Huh, what did you say, something about a potato? I barely remember any French, I haven't used it since high school."

"You don't speak French, do you Marissa?"

125

"No."

"Growing up in Sweden, we learn a lot of languages. French, English, German... when your native language is spoken by only 7 million people or so, you need to learn something else to get ahead."

"I bet."

Chad checked out of that conversation so he could get to know Krystel better. She didn't seem too enthused to be there though. She wasn't making much eye contact, and was looking at her phone constantly.

"So do you go to school?"

"Huh?"

"Do you go to school?"

"Um, no, not right now, but I will be soon."

"Oh yeah, where? Doing what?"

"Harvard Law."

"Harvard Law?"

"Uh huh. I know it's tough to get into, but my dad said if I really wanted it, he'd make it happen. He's really rich."

A group of four co-eds were screaming out the lyrics to "Love Shack". Chad asked the next question, even though he already knew the answer.

"Where did you go for undergrad?"

"Huh?"

"Undergrad. Where did you go to college?"

"Um, I haven't yet... it's a long story—"

"Yeah, but you can't go to law school, much less Harvard Law, without an undergrad degree of some sort first. Like my mom has a degree in psych. Then you have to take the LSAT. I assume you haven't done that yet either."

"Um, no... but my dad said if it's what I want, he'll make it happen."

"Yeah, but he can't unless you have an undergrad degree. I mean, your dad could be Bill Clinton, and Harvard Law still won't admit you into their program unless you have a four-year degree first."

The waitress and a bus boy brought the scorpion bowls and pu pu platter. Lars and Marissa immediately jumped into their drink, while Krystel was less sure. She didn't like the idea of sharing her germs with Chad. Some kind of germaphobe thing she'd concocted in her head, just like the Harvard law. Chad could care less. He didn't know what to make of this girl, whether to find her attractive or repulsive, but her having any issue with sharing his germs wasn't anything he'd be insulted about.

"So your dad went to Harvard?" Chad started again.

"I think so. He went to something like that."

How do you not know your parents' educational history?

"You don't know?"

"I don't know, he told me once, I forget... what about your mom, did she go to Harvard?"

"No, she and my father both went to Dodge State, just like I did."

"Oh, is your dad a lawyer too."

"My mom's actually not a lawyer anymore, she's a judge, and no, my father is a retired Lt. Colonel in the Army. He was stationed in Germany when we were growing up, but he's since moved back here with my step-mother and half-siblings."

"Germany, wow, that must've been scary."

"Scary?"

"Yeah, isn't that near Iraq and those places?"

"Um… no, it's in Europe… right next to France and stuff."

"Really? So it's not like a Third World country?"

"What? Germany? A Third World Country? Who told you that?"

"I don't know, no one, I just thought…"

Chad had never considered this before. Was this a common misconception by less educated people, that Germany was a Third World country? If it was, though, how was this the first time he'd heard of it? And the Harvard Law thing on top of that. What was going on in this girl's head?

He drifted over into Lars's conversation with Marissa.

"Do you like Obama?"

"Uh huh."

"Because he's black."

"No."

"But it helps, right, that he's black."

She smiled and picked a piece off her chicken finger.

"Maybe."

"Maybe? What do you think of health care?"

She shrugged her shoulders and chewed her food.

"Do you think everyone should have it?"

She smiled, shrugged her shoulders again, and nodded.

"When was the last time you had sex with a black man?"

Without missing a beat she examined her chicken finger and picked another piece off and put it in her mouth.

"A couple years maybe."

"How about a Swedish man?"

She laughed.

"You'd be my first."

"I like that. Do you prefer black men or white men?"

She shrugged her shoulders again, picked at her food, and smiled at him.

"I bet it's black men."

This questioning went on, sometimes sexual, sometimes innocuous or a total non sequitur. And the entire time, she smiled or laughed, and picked at the food from the pu pu platter. She was cuter than Chad's girl. She was short, with a dark complexion and dark hair, and blue eyes. She had on a tight T-shirt and tight blue jeans with black boots over them. Chad looked back to Krystel, whose complexion was a paler olive, which made her acne and acne scars stand out. Her hair was a bad dye job, a mix of blond and brown, set off in a poof kind of high on her head. Her legs, or what Chad could see of them when they appeared from around the table, were very raw. She had on boots too, but her zebra-print skirt was pretty short, and showed her limbs, which were a pale olive like her face, with shaving razor marks and a bruise or two. The rawness struck him, though. He looked back to her eyes, big and brown, softer than he remembered from when she first sat down. Chad tried to picture her in a Harvard lecture hall, and felt sorry for her.

He was relieved that they left before he had to sing. It turned out Lars never even put their song in, because he encountered Marissa before he had a chance to. From the Green Dragon they went over to Lars and Chad's offices, taking a cab because Chad had had too much of Krystel's half of the scorpion bowl. Lars brought everyone to the rec room, with the flatscreen and all the video game consoles. There was a stereo in there as well, which Chad hadn't seen before, and Lars put on some music. Flo Rida again. He pulled Marissa to him and they danced. Then they started making out. Krystel wasn't impressed, so Chad offered to show her his office.

He loved that he had an office, with his name on it, and his stuff in it. Krystel was impressed too. She thought Chad and Lars were equal partners in whatever kind of business they ran, which must've earned him quite a bit of money if they could have offices like this with all this stuff in it. Chad offered her a beer, but she declined. She took a Red Bull instead.

"Boy, this is pretty nice here."

She was wandering around, inspecting, putting dollar values on everything. Chad noticed a Tramp Stamp on her lower back, right under where her halter top was tied, two dolphins arranged like a circle. He asked her about them, breaking the rhythm of her perusal.

"Yeah, dolphins are my favorite animals. You know, they're the only animals who have sex just for pleasure?"

She looked as though she was hoping to impress him with this nugget of trivia. Chad misinterpreted it as an opening, and replied:

"Well, dolphins and humans, of course, are the only animals that have sex for pleasure."

"What are you talking about?"

Chad was in the process of moving toward her. He had decided, perhaps due to the amount of alcohol in his system, or to the length of time it had been since he'd last had intercourse, that Krystel was plenty attractive enough, and he'd like to have sex with her right on his desk—*his* desk, he still loved saying that—and to find out her remark about dolphins and sexual pleasure wasn't the invitation he expected it to be, angered him, but he kept his cool, holding onto a slim hope that maybe this was still going to happen.

"What do you mean what am I talking about? You said dolphins were the only animals who have sex for pleasure, and I said yes, aside from humans."

"Humans?"

"Yes, humans have sex for pleasure too, obviously."

"Yeah, but they aren't animals."

"What do you mean? Humans are animals."

"No they aren't, they're people."

Chad looked at her, and her expression told him that she was sure she'd gotten him here. Oh, he thought he was so smart with his you need a degree to go to Harvard, well I got him this time, fancy office and all. Chad didn't know what to say. Here was a grown woman in front of him, in her mid-twenties, without the knowledge—basic knowledge to Chad's mind—that human beings were members of the animal kingdom. He wanted to call Steve and have him ask his 5-year-old daughter if she knew that humans were animals.

"People is just another way of saying humans. Human beings—you and me—are members of the animal kingdom. We're mammals, actually, just like dolphins."

"Mammals?"

"Yes, warm-blooded animals that give birth to their young, not hatch them from eggs. We also have hair on us."

"Dolphins don't have hair."

"Yes they do, but it's like really tiny, like kids do on their arms."

"Are you sure about all this? I don't think you're right."

Chad didn't know what to say, because he'd never had to defend these ideas before. Humans were animals. Humans and dolphins were mammals. Germany was a rich, developed, and stable country like the United States. One cannot go to any law school, let alone Harvard Law, without a four-year degree first—okay, that one wasn't a universally known fact, considering Special Agent Johnny Utah, FBI, went to law school on a football scholarship in *Point Break*. He was sobering up now, and though he still wanted to have sex with Krystel, he could see how he was a lot further from making that happen than he thought.

"I thought God made us different from the animals."

"Humans are different from the rest of the animal kingdom because we can think and talk and build all of this stuff we have here. Whether you believe in God or not, though, it doesn't matter who created us, we're animals. Dogs have a better sense of smell than us, that doesn't make them not animals, does it? We just think more."

Chad was proud of himself. That was a great analogy, the one about the dogs. Krystel heard something else in his comments that caught her attention.

"You don't believe in God?"

"Um, I don't know, I've never really thought about it... I'm not really religious if that's what you're asking. How about you, do you go to church?"

"I used to not, but I started going ever since I was in prison."

She dropped it in a very matter-of-fact manner. This wasn't from someone who has had this on her mind awhile, looking for the perfect spot to drop the bomb. She said it as if she said "I got this halter top at TJ Maxx." Chad finished his beer and went into his minifridge for another. He decided he'd ape her matter-of-fact manner and not show how stunned he was.

"You did time?"

"Yeah, I'm on parole, I just got out after two years. My baby's father got busted for selling drugs out of our house."

Second bombshell, baby's father, and second bombshell A., he sold drugs out of their house. A bombshell and a sub-bombshell, always the best kind. But for Chad, none of these were exactly bombshells, because he was beyond being surprised by anything Krystel said. He didn't know what he considered her as, potential mate, crazy girl he was taking care of while his buddy fucked her friend. He was fascinated by her.

"Yeah, it was crazy, the SWAT team raided the house. We were watching TV, and they just crashed down the doors. My boyfriend was like 'Krystel, just stay on the floor.' "

"And where was the baby?"

"Upstairs asleep. She's with my mother now. I have to reapply for custody of her."

"And you got two years? You must've been selling drugs too."

"No, I swear I didn't. It was a whole bunch of bullshit... I don't know..."

Chad tried to imagine the scene. The idea that there were real SWAT teams and they really raided houses, that it wasn't just something on TV, was astounding. He didn't know which was more astounding, that someone could not know that humans were animals, or that someone could be raided by a SWAT team, but here both were embodied in Krystel. He moved closer to her.

"It must've sucked to spend two years in jail like that."

"Yeah. I got into a lot of fights. But I'm a survivor, I'll make out all right in the end. I have dreams you know. You might think I can't go to Harvard Law, but my dad says if I want it he'll make it happen."

Harvard Law again. Now Chad felt bad about giving her a hard time about it. Who was this dad that promised things he couldn't deliver on? Where did she get this idea in her head about Harvard Law anyway? And was it Chad's place to keep telling her how untenable it was? He put his hand on her back and rubbed it. She didn't tell him not to. Her skin was softer and warmer than he expected. She was softer and warmer than he expected. Was this right, though? Did he even like this girl? When was the last time he got laid though?

Marissa burst in, livid.

"Krystel, we're leaving!"

"What? Now?"

"Is everything all right?"

"Yes, except your friend Lars is an asshole! C'mon Krystel, let's go."

"Oh, okay."

They turned toward the door, before Chad stopped them. He offered to get them a cab, but they declined. Then he and Krystel exchanged numbers. He wasn't sure why he did that, and was even less sure when she spelled her name out for him—"Krystel", it looked like one of those odd spellings for names the people on *Maury* gave their children. He walked them to the hallway, then locked the door and found Lars in the rec room, almost passed out on a couch, with Savage Garden's "Truly Madly Deeply" playing on the stereo.

"The girl was on the rag."

"What?"

"Riding the crimson wave, baby. There's a saying in Göteborg: 'when the red tide comes in, the fisherman doesn't eat.'"

"Sorry man, that sucks."

"No, it's the breaks. You gotta roll with the punches. Come, sit with me."

Chad did, and Lars took his hand. It felt really odd with the Savage Garden playing in the background.

"You did a great job tonight as my wingman. I mean that, I appreciated that shit. That Krystel was a major grenade, and you not only kept her company, but you brought her into the other room. She didn't come in once and complain that she wanted to go home. You're a good man, Chad."

"Uh... okay... it really wasn't a big—"

"With Seijun being married, I'm kind of out on my own, you know... the Green Dragon, you can't do that flying solo, you know... but he's settled down... his wife's cool shit though...

documentary film maker... did something on prostitutes in India or some shit... won a bunch of awards..."

He was getting really close to Chad, his hand tightening. Then he closed his eyes and started singing along to the Savage Garden.

"God, that guy has such an amazing voice..."

"All right man, I think maybe we should get going... I'm gonna, I'm gonna..."

It took a few tries to get his hand free. Then he stood quickly, before Lars could reassert his hold. Lars kept his hand out, where it was, as if he couldn't comprehend that Chad would want to extricate himself from the moment he thought they were having.

"Um... okay, Chad man, you get going... I'm gonna stay here... you all right to drive?"

"No, we took a cab here, remember?"

"Oh yeah... okay... have a good one..."

"You okay to stay here yourself?"

"Oh yeah, I do it all the time. I'll see you on Monday... big first day..."

"Big first day..."

As Chad had told Krystel, his parents both attended Dodge State, and that's where they first met. His mom was a psych major whose parents were funding her education, while his dad was a PoliSci major, paying for school through ROTC. He had a strong, domineering personality, and was turned on by the fact that she challenged him and seldom let him have the upper hand. She was turned on by how smart and direct he was—plus how hot he looked without his shirt on. When they graduated, he was stationed in Germany, which was exciting for Chad's mother at first, because she loved the idea of living in Europe.

What she didn't love the idea of was being a housewife. She didn't study her ass off to get a 4.0 to be a housewife. She became increasingly disillusioned with the inanity of life on base, and that disillusionment manifested itself in an animosity toward her husband.

His father felt this disillusionment, and countered with his own. He spent much of the day having the people under him obey his orders, and to come home and find a wife that undermined him was frustrating. Chad remembers this period in his young life as being very chaotic, and before Gwen, he always associated his father with the bad guy, and his mother with the savior. He'd be playing with his toys, and his father would scold him for making too much noise, or not cleaning up after himself, and his mother would immediately jump to Chad's defense, which would eventually lead to an argument between his parents.

Chad looks back on that time now and sees in his mother things he saw in Gwen: the constant picking fights, the mentally checking out, the growing lack of affection—things with Gwen that he was too naïve at the time, or too in denial of at the time, to place the kind of stock in he should have. Did his father do the same thing? Was he in denial? Did he think like Chad did, what did I do wrong, what could I have fixed? At 8, when his mother announced that he and Steve were moving back to her hometown with her, and that she and his father were splitting up, Chad was excited. No more of this overbearing presence that made him afraid to play with his toys or eat and make a mess. No more worrying that anything he did would get him reprimanded. And America seemed like such a great place, instead of being Americans in Germany, they'd be Americans in America, which just made more sense. n high school, when his mother confessed that his parents' marriage ended after she was caught having an affair, it still didn't diminish his mother's position in his eyes, nor make him more sympathetic to his father.

Chad's father put in for a transfer to the US after the split so he could be near his sons, which he was granted a year later. In that year, though, he met Mika, a German woman, and fell in love with her. Now he didn't want to go back. Now he was fine with sending part of his monthly wages to Chad's mother until his boys turned 18, and starting over with Mika. He rescinded his transfer request, and over the next twenty years, rose to the rank of Lt. Colonel, having a distinguished career as a US military representative in an Eastern Europe transitioning from Cold War adversary to US ally.

The move to America felt like a Godsend to Chad. New friends, a new neighborhood, neighbors like Mr. Haley to show him how to play catch. He didn't know how much of a struggle it was for his mother initially. She was the bad guy, not his father as Chad thought. Her parents were embarrassed and did little to help her beyond offering a house her father had bought from his brother after he moved to San Diego. They had been renting it out, and continued to rent it out to Chad's mother, until she earned enough money as a lawyer to buy it from them. The whole thing was a shock to Chad's mother, because her parents had always been supportive, but the idea that their daughter would throw away a life with an Army officer who had a good chance of promotion to have a fling with a staff sergeant was appalling, and they didn't want to humor her any more than they had to. It upset his mother that her children were ostracized by her parents along with her, but for Chad and Steve, not knowing who their grandparents were anyway, they never thought anything of it—plus, they had Mr. and Mrs. Haley.

Things changed for Chad as far as his father went after he caught Gwen in bed with Dave. Now his mother, who had always been his hero, was the bad guy, and his father, though not necessarily the good guy, was at least a more sympathetic figure. He intended to reconnect with him after he retired from the Army and moved home with Mika a few years later, but one lunch date turned him off to that. He was the same overbearing man he had been—perhaps worse. He was rude to the waitress, and made disparaging comments about feminists that Chad took to be shots at his mother. Instead of finding a source of support and sympathy in his father, he felt worse after their meeting, because he realized that his mother was right to have dumped him, that he couldn't imagine having spent his entire life living with this man, and he wondered if *he* was that bad, if Gwen was right in cheating on him too.

On Wednesday Chad called Miguel from his office and told him he had too much work to do to be able to make the soccer game that night. He considered having the secretary make the call for him, because he could do that, but he thought that might be a bit much. Just the fact that he was calling from *his* office was enough. It was getting on for 6 o'clock. Everyone else, Seijun, Lars, and the receptionists, had left almost two hours ago. He wanted to get a few solid hours of work in with no one bothering him. Monday they spent the day shopping for more clothes: three suits that together set him back $4500, then a few more outfits at Neiman Marcus and Saks that set him back another $1500. $6000 in one day on clothes, out of his own pocket. He could afford it now, but if more money wasn't coming in—let's just say that'll have to be the last $6000 shopping day for the time being. The suit he was wearing cost more than all his old clothes, including the suits, combined. It was more than a month's rent at his apartment. But he stood and looked at himself in his mirror. It was really sweet. Olive with pinstripes, three pieces, of which the coat was draped over the chair on the other side of the desk, leaving him in the vest, pants, and white shirt. Man, he looked good. He'd lost five pounds since he started using the elliptical last week too. And then there was his new haircut, more closely cropped to his head, making his bald spot less conspicuous.

He sat back down and took a sip from his beer. Much of the work Seijun needed from him right now was easy enough, inputting these numbers into this new spreadsheet, double-checking this set of figures to make sure Seijun had calculated them right, and, most importantly, filling out various IRS forms Seijun had fallen behind on. The serenity of it all, in his office, while *PTI* played on a small flatscreen next to him, sipping on a beer. This was no Chad in Accounting scenario, no cubicle with his toolbag supervisor, or the dumb broads who talked about the last episode of *The Bachelor* like it carried the weight of a G8 summit meeting, or Jared with the Hyphenated Last Name in HR and his Back-Up Quarterback Fantasy League. If Jared could see him now... or Haley...

The catharsis was broken by a call on his new iPhone. It was Krystel. She wanted to go out to dinner. He looked at his watch. He had agreed to meet Lars and Seijun at Seijun's wife's friend's art exhibit opening at 9. Krystel suggested TGI Friday's at 7. He thought about going home and taking a shower, but he realized he could take one here, and he also had a fresh outfit in his closet. Life was good.

When he got to TGI Friday's, Krystel was already there at a booth near the bar. He didn't recognize her until she stood and called his name though. She was wearing these black rimmed glasses, and her hair was down, though kind of frizzy and not straight against her head, and instead of a halter top, she had on a red sweater with a white button-up shirt underneath, that was tight against her chest somewhat, but was otherwise unremarkable. It was when she stood and stepped outside the booth to get his attention that he saw the full extent of her outfit: a short, red and black plaid skirt, fishnet stockings, and black boots that came up past her knee. It was as if she were a stripper going to a bachelor party, playing the part of a sexy version of the 80s teen movie nerd. Oh, thank you God, Chad thought. Across the room, they heard the sounds of the waitstaff banging something loud and singing happy birthday to someone. It reminded Chad that his own was this Sunday—and that he'd told his mom he'd go to her place this Saturday to celebrate with his family. He made mention of the fact—the Sunday birthday, not the celebrating on Saturday—to Krystel, thinking she might joke about the waitstaff doing that routine to him too, but she barely acknowledged it, and went into her own diatribe about how horrible her day was, between her parole officer giving her a hard time, to her job giving her a hard time, to Marissa being a bitch.

"What do you do for work?"

"I work at a bunny factory."

"A bunny factory?"

"Yeah, you know, stuffed bunnies, for little kids."

She said it in a way that was like "what are you, a moron?"

"I know," Chad said, "but why here, in the US? Don't they make those things in China, where the labor is cheaper?"

"Oh, yeah, that...." Another Chad curve ball. Why would he ask a question like that? "They said something when we started about how they wanted to make bunnies here in the US, give people here jobs. I guess they give a lot of work to girls like me coming out of prison, because I'm not the only one on parole who works there."

"Ah ha, I see..."

Chad took a sip off the beer Krystel had ordered for him before he got there, and looked at the menu. He didn't know what he wanted, all the food was either greasy and gross, or heart healthy, bland, and gross. It was like going to Applebee's with Haley. He settled on quesadillas before the waitress came back, while Krystel ordered some enormous salad with an exotic name. Her phone buzzed.

"It's Marissa again, God!"

"What's up? Is something wrong?"

"No..." then she went on another diatribe about Marissa, all the things she does that annoy Krystel, but all the things about her that Krystel likes. Chad wasn't really paying attention. "Alone" by Heart was playing above them, and he found himself getting into it. Lars had him listening to all kinds of 80s music now. Every time he bobbed his head to the music, Krystel thought he was nodding to what she was saying, which made her go on longer. After the song was finished, he found a break in her conversation, and interjected:

"It's good to have a best friend like her."

It was sarcastic, but Krystel didn't pick up on that.

"Oh, Marissa, she isn't my best friend."

"She isn't?"

"Oh God no." Come on, Chad, how can you be so dumb, of course Marissa isn't Krystel's best friend. "Taylor's my best friend."

"Oh, Taylor, oh, okay. How come you don't seem to hang out with her as much as Marissa then?"

"She was killed by a serial killer a few years ago."

It was that same matter-of-fact tone she used to tell him she'd been incarcerated. At least in that instance he could understand her not wanting to make a big deal about something so embarrassing, but a friend murdered, and to be equally unemotional, set Chad back a bit.

"Oh man, that's horrible. I'm so sorry."

Chad didn't expect her to go on about it, let alone tell him what she did, again, in that same matter-off-fact tone.

"Yeah, we were coming home from a quick trip to the video store, when Taylor saw this really hot guy hitchhiking."

"Wait, you were there?"

"Uh huh. Yeah, she sees this guy, and she's like pull over. I was freaking out, because I knew if Antonio found out I had some random guy in the car, he'd shit his pants."

"Antonio?"

"Yeah, my baby's father. I was like six months pregnant at the time."

"Oh God."

"So anyway, Taylor begs me to pick the guy up, so I do. She's always been boycrazy, always sleeping around with guys she barely knew. So he's giving us directions, and we're driving and driving and I start noticing there are fewer and fewer houses, and I'm starting to freak out,

134

because I told Antonio we'd only be going to the video store, and now it was like really late, so I ask the guy how much further, and he says only a little more, and I'm like dude, that's what you said 15 minutes ago, then Taylor starts calling me a bitch for giving him a hard time, and now I'm getting pissed, and the guy's like both of you girls shut up and he pulls a gun out of his backpack."

Chad was riveted, drinking his beer, not touching his quesadillas. And it was in this tone, that was a combination of the matter-of-fact way she said she'd been to prison, and the whining woe-is-me diatribe with which she complained about her job and Marissa, that made the whole thing all the more surreal.

"So he has us park in this secluded area, and he pulls out these zip-tie thingies and ties me to the steering wheel and tells me if I move or make any noise my friend is fucking dead. So I was like really scared, you know."

"Yeah, no doubt."

"And I can kind of hear what's going on outside, but I can't really see it, and then he comes back and gets me and I see Taylor lying face down in the grass passed out. So he lays me on the grass, and starts to take off my shirt and sees that I'm pregnant, and he freaks out and was all like I'm so sorry I didn't know you were pregnant and he just runs off. So I get up, and I go over to Taylor, and she's not moving. So I carry her into the car and take her to the hospital, and that's when I find out she's dead. I guess he strangled her."

"Wow, that's crazy. I can't believe that. Did they ever catch the guy?"

"I don't think so."

"Well, I imagine you'd know if they caught him, you'd probably be asked to testify or something."

"I'm just glad I wasn't killed too, you know."

"Yeah, you were lucky you were pregnant I guess."

"Yeah, it just wouldn't have been fair if I was killed too because Taylor is a whore."

It took a second for what she said to sink in before he could muster a "what?"

"You know, because we wouldn't have even been in that situation if she didn't want to pick up some random dude. I didn't want to pick him up, I knew Antonio would kill me, but she was all about picking up guys. It was her fault she got killed, but if I was killed too it would've sucked. God, I always forget they make these salads too big. I can't finish this. You want some?"

Chad shook his head. Who was this girl in front of him, looking at her phone again, complaining again that it was Marissa? Who was this girl that thought her dad, whoever he is, could get her into Harvard Law? Who was this girl who had had her house stormed by a SWAT team and had almost been killed by a serial killer? No, he didn't want to eat some of her salad.

"So, you're probably wondering why I called you."

He wasn't actually, he thought this was a date between them, but he agreed with her anyway.

"It's not like some kind of date or anything. I wanted to ask you about the whole Harvard Law thing."

"I thought your dad had that all figured out."

"I know… but if I can look like I've done some research or something, he'll believe me that I'm really serious."

"Right… I mean…"

"You know, I'm a lot smarter than I look. I dressed like this tonight to show you that. I think you thought I was dumb last time after I said humans weren't animals—I looked that up on Wikipedia, you were right about that one—"

"Wait, this outfit... oh... okay, I see..."

"Yeah, I look a lot smarter, don't I?"

Chad didn't know what to say. He didn't need to say anything, because Krystel was certain she was right, that she looked infinitely smarter than she did the night Chad first saw her, it was more of a rhetorical "don't I?" All Chad could think of was those knee high boots and fishnet stockings on those legs, under the table, crossed, no more than a foot in front of him. Should he tell this girl what she wants to hear? What does she want to hear though?

"Um... have you taken any college courses at all?"

"I got my GED in prison."

"I mean, you look really... nice... tonight... but an outfit isn't enough to get you into law school if you don't have the credentials. I mean, you could go to college in a dirty, purple cat sweatshirt and matching sweatpants..."

"But the clothes help."

Chad considered having her stand and spin around so he could see the entirety of her sexy outfit again, under the dissimulation that he was judging it on how "smart" it looked, but then he remembered the serial killer story she had just told, and he became more tender in his approach.

"Krystel, what exactly is it you want from me? How do you want me to help you?"

"I don't know, you said your mom is a lawyer—"

"Judge now, actually."

"Right, but she went to law school and stuff... like, I don't know..."

"I don't know either. She had a psych degree from Dodge State."

"So I need to get a psyche degree?"

She had a small notebook and a pen that she'd taken out of her purse, and she started writing what he told him.

"How do you spell 'psych'?"

"You don't *have* to have a psych degree."

"I don't?"

"No, you just need a four-year degree of any kind. Hell, one of my fraternity brothers had a theater degree, and he's a lawyer now—though he's still trying to make it in LA as an actor..."

"A theater degree?"

"It's not just about the major, it's about all the gen ed classes you take with it."

"Gen ed? What's that?"

"General education, like science and math and English. Like, even for my business degree in accounting, I had to take two lab sciences, so I took this lower level physics, and geology. And I had to take English 101 and a business writing course. See how all that stuff adds up, so you have a certain knowledge base going into law school? I mean, I could apply to law school at DSU right now if I wanted to, I'd just need the LSAT."

"What's that?"

"Didn't your dad tell you about any of this?"

She looked away and her eyes welled up with tears. Now Chad felt really bad.

136

"I don't know, probably... I just don't know any of this stuff..."

"Don't get upset, Krystel, I'm just trying to figure out what's going here, you know? I mean, where did you get this idea from that you were going to go to Harvard Law? And I guess my other question is, why would your dad tell you he'd get you in there without asking you the same questions I am?"

"I don't know, I talked to him on the phone a while ago and told him I wanted to go to Harvard Law, and he said if that's what I wanted, he'd make it happen."

"And that's it?"

"Uh huh."

Her eyes had dried up some and she was drinking from her water with a straw. She put her glasses back on and went back to her matter-of-fact exterior.

"You didn't answer my first question."

"Yes I did."

"No you didn't. I want to know why you have this desire to go to Harvard Law."

"Oh, that question... I don't want to tell you, you'll just laugh at me..."

"I won't, I promise."

"Really, you promise?"

"Yes, I swear I won't laugh."

"Okay... I saw *Legally Blonde* in prison, and one of the girls said I reminded her of Elle."

"What?"

"I knew you'd think it was stupid..."

She was tearing up again, and Chad didn't want that to happen, so he took her by the arm.

"I don't think it's stupid, it's just... it's the movies, it's not real life. They make things up, you know... I mean, have you seen *Point Break*? In that movie, Keanu Reeves's character goes to law school on a football scholarship."

"Yeah, so?..."

"*So?* Didn't we just go over this? You have to get a four-year degree first. But it's Hollywood, they don't care what the real rules are, they make them up for the movies."

"So you're saying I can't go to Harvard Law?..."

"I... I didn't say that. I have no idea who your father is, I don't know if maybe he has a lot of pull, because maybe he does and he can get you in; but even he can't get you in if you don't at least have some prerequisites, and a four-year degree is one of those. Besides, if you really want to be a lawyer, there's nothing wrong with going to a less prestigious school than that. With your GED you could probably go to the continuing education system at Dodge State, take night courses, maybe enroll full time at the main school after a year or two, and then go from there."

"My parole officer said I should do something like that too."

"Yeah, see, she could probably help you out with everything."

"Yeah..."

"Is something wrong?"

"I don't know, it just seems like a lot more work that I was expecting... are you sure all this is right?"

"I'm absolutely positive. I'm also absolutely positive that you are plenty capable of making it all happen."

"Really?"

"Yep."

Her enormous smile vanished as quickly as it came, back into her matter-of-fact veneer.

"It's my clothes. I knew they'd make me look smarter.

Chad was too enamored with Krystel now to end the night without her, so he invited her with him to the art exhibit. There was a part of him that thought she might look ridiculous, especially in her outfit, but it was that same outfit that she looked so hot in that was the deciding factor in him wanting her company. The whole thing really touched him, though, from the matter-of-fact way she described being arrested and almost murdered by a serial killer, to how vulnerable she looked when he cracked that exterior interrogating her about her desire to attend Harvard Law School. Then there was the outfit. Thank you God!

Chad was curious to go to this. He'd heard that the exhibit had caused quite a stir, especially in the local GOP community. The title of it was "Good Women", and was comprised of a series of displays, with clothing store mannequins acting out various scenes, attempting to deconstruct popular images of women. In front of each was a written description by the artist, explaining her inspiration, and what she was going for. The first scene Chad and Krystel came across had a mannequin dressed like a high school cheerleader, tied to a stake, with red and orange pieces of cellophane cut to look like flames at her feet.

"God, what is that?"

Chad went to the description.

"It says she got the idea from a soap opera, where two girls were kidnapped, taken to a high school, dressed like cheerleaders, and tied to the stake, where they would've been burned to death, had a heroic cop on the show not rescued them just in time. 'The cheerleader is a loaded image of femininity in American society. I liked the idea of setting it on fire, burning it up, and hoping a new femininity, much less limiting, could emerge from its ashes. Plus, the cheerleader is the image of the ideal girl, and I want to show that even the ideal woman, if viewed as threat to men, is as likely as any other woman to be burned at the stake.' Hmm, I don't know, what do you think?"

"I think it's really weird. Let's keep going."

The next one had a pregnant woman on a gurney with her feet in stirrups. She was wearing only a Johnny, naked from the waist down with her legs open. Two other mannequins were standing next to her, both male, one in a lab coat with a clip board, the other in a suit with a GOP button on his lapel. In the woman's genderless crotch, in a small hole near where her vagina would have been, an American flag had been stuck.

"This one's pretty obvious, huh?"

"No, what's going on?"

"It's saying the government wants to control women's bodies, wants to decide what they should do with them."

"Oh… why does she have a flag coming out of her… you know?"

"It represents her as a woman, her vagina. Like, it's saying, women should decide what goes in and comes out, like with abortion."

"That's not right, if it was about abortion, the flag would be in her belly."

138

"No… I mean… it makes more sense down there, doesn't it?"

"Why? If she was having an abortion, wouldn't they just take it out of her belly?"

"No, they'd go in through… I mean… I don't know what you're saying exactly…"

"I'm saying, everyone knows babies come out through the mother's belly, so why would they—"

Chad frowned. He was confused.

"Wait, what?"

"What?"

"What did you say about babies being born?"

She hesitated, thinking this might be like the humans are animals conversation, but here, she was certain she could win this argument, if there was one.

"I said babies are born through the mother's stomach, why?"

"Didn't you have a baby?"

"Yes, and the doctor cut it out of my stomach, like they always do."

"You know that that's only in certain cases they do that, that usually it comes out of… you know…"

He pointed at her crotch, and the way she held her legs together under her skirt to try and cover herself up as he referenced that area, made her even hotter to him, even if she was saying babies aren't born through a woman's vagina.

"What's your problem? Cut it out. I thought you were a nice guy, not a perv."

He looked around, and people were looking at them. He couldn't tell if it was Krystel's smart outfit, or if they could overhear the conversation.

"I'm not trying to be a perv. I'm telling you the truth. "

She saw in his eyes that he was serious, not just just trying to be gross.

"Who told you that babies come out of… out of there?"

"Who told me? We learned it in school. We saw a video of it happening in school. Didn't you take sex ed in high school?"

"I dropped out of high school… you don't understand… the hole is so small… and a baby is… it's pretty big… you can't fit a baby through there. It has to be cut out by a doctor."

"Then what did women do before there were doctors?"

"What do you mean? There's always been doctors."

"Um… well what about your period? What do you think that is?"

"It's not the size of a baby coming out, it's just blood and stuff."

Chad was stumped. He was playing a game he didn't know the rules to. He thought he knew the rules, but here was Krystel in her sexy stripper librarian outfit, letting him know that the rules as he understood them did not exist.

"This is kinda boring. Can you just take me back to my car?"

He saw Lars, Seijun, his wife, and the artist chatting across the room from him. He knew at the very least he'd have to explain why he wasn't staying.

"Sure, I can take you back, but I need to say hi to my friends first. Is it okay if I just go over there quickly, say we can't stay, and then we'll go?"

He saw Lars waving him over, and he put up a finger.

"Okay, I'll go to the bathroom and meet you at the front."

Chad watched her beautiful body in her "smart" outfit walk through the exhibit and past a massive sculpture made of used auto parts, watched her legs move in those boots and those fishnets and that skirt, in a way that was both self-assured and awkward all at once, and he knew he was falling for her. What would everyone think if he brought her home? How would he explain her to his friends and family?

He left her to go see Lars, Seijun, Seijun's wife, and the artist. Seijun's wife was named Noriko, and as stylish as Seijun was, she was equally impeccable though not as flashy a dresser in her turtleneck and flared, flowing dress pants. The artist's name was Justine, and she was white with brown dreadlocks and wore a rustic peasant dress. She gave Chad a hardy handshake, making him think she was a lesbian, until she pointed out her husband chatting with some other people on the other side of the room.

"So what did you think?"

"Well, we only made it as far as the pregnant woman on the hospital bed, but I really liked what I saw. I think Krystel may have had something at dinner that didn't agree with her, so we're going to have to split early."

Everyone let out groans that that was too bad and they were sorry. As he saw her emerge from around the corner, he bid them all a good night, and rushed over to meet her. He tried to put his hand on her back, but she didn't reciprocate as they walked out together.

Back at the car, she demanded he show her on his iPhone that women gave birth to babies through their vaginas. He looked it up on Wikipedia.

"Here it is:—"

She snatched the phone from him before he could continue and read it for herself.

"It doesn't say anything about a baby coming out of there."

"Let me see it... yes it does, right here, 'from a woman's uterus.' "

"What does that mean?"

"Click on the link to it. What does it say?"

She mouthed the words, trying to make sense of scientific terms that she'd never heard before. Then she got to the word vagina and trailed off. Chad took the phone back from her.

"Are you all right?"

"I'm not stupid you know. I'm... I'm not stupid..."

"No one said you were—"

"You think I'm stupid. Don't you? You were laughing at me with all your friends back there. I saw you."

"I told them you weren't feeling well. If they were laughing it had nothing to do with you."

"You're lying, I saw you laughing... you really didn't tell them?"

"No, I mean it."

Chad didn't know if he entirely understood either, but he felt something for this girl. She sounded so pitiful, sobbing, with her face in her hands, yet she looked so hot in her short skirt and fishnets and black boots that went up past her knee. He wanted to protect her and console her, and at the same time make love to her. When they pulled into the TGI Friday's parking lot, he didn't know which car was hers, so he parked far from the restaurant and pulled her to him and put his arms around her as she cried. At first she reciprocated, but then she pulled herself away. Chad's touch reminded her that her emotional outburst had been taking place the whole time in front of him, not in some liminal space where only she knew she was crying.

"I'm sorry, I'm a total mess huh? You must be like 'what did I do to end up with such a crazy crying bitch?'."

"No, it's okay… it's…"

Krystel was fixing herself up in the mirror underneath the sun-visor, making her best attempt to restore her matter-of-fact exterior, and though failing in actuality, succeeding in her own mind. Chad felt himself losing her, and couldn't tell her what he wanted to tell her. The same old Chad afraid to take a chance. Then Anishka's words came back to him, it's a gift, a gift.

"Krystel, I think you're a very beautiful woman."

She stopped what she was doing and looked at him.

"What?"

"You heard me, I think you're amazing. I want to be with you—or at least see you again after tonight. I don't think you're dumb. You might not know a lot of things that the average person does, but you're not dumb. You pick things up rather quickly actually."

"My teacher in prison told me that too…"

"And you look so hot in that outfit."

"Really?… Like hot because I look smart?…"

"Um… sure… but hot like sexy hot too, like that skirt, and those boots, and those fishnets… you know what I mean?"

Their eyes met for a second, before she turned away.

"I don't know, you're not really my type. I like guys with lots of tattoos and stuff."

"Yeah, but those guys can't get you to where you want to go in life. What do you want Krystel, to be raided by SWAT teams, or to go to law school?"

"I don't even know if I want to go to law school anymore after tonight…"

"That's fine, you can do whatever you want, and I can help you."

"Yeah, help me if I look like this. Marissa was right, I do look like a whore."

"What are you talking about? Oh Krystel…"

She was crying again, but she wouldn't let Chad touch her.

"Before I left tonight, Marissa told me my outfit didn't make me look smart, it made me look like a whore."

"That's not true… like from here up, you look very smart… and then from here down… you don't look like a whore so much as you look really sexy."

Chad thought he'd put his foot in his mouth, only to have her stop crying and turn to him.

"You mean it?"

"Yes, I mean it."

He went to reach over and kiss her, but she gathered up her purse and opened the door.

"I have to run, my parole officer will get pissed if I'm out too late."

"Let me drive you to your car at least."

"No no, it's just over there. Maybe I'll call you next week sometime, okay? Bye… and thank you for putting up with me tonight."

She slammed the door and walked off.

"But I want to take you back to my place and have tons of crazy sex…." Chad said, quietly, as he watched her saunter across the parking lot, to a bright red tuned out Honda Civic. She turned it on, and he heard the engine, and the massive stereo pumping out a massive bass line.

141

As she sped by, and he saw the lit undercarriage and the spoiler, he thought, of course that would be her car.

When he went to work on Friday, he noticed the guys were wearing casual clothes. Casual Fridays, of course, how did he not know?

"Guess what?" Seijun said.

"Casual Fridays, I know, I forgot."

"No moron, pack your bags, we're going to Vegas for the weekend to celebrate your birthday."

"What? You're not serious."

"We are," Lars said. "Our plane leaves in three hours."

"Jesus, you are serious."

The guys laughed.

"Oh my God, I need to go home and pack something... and change, I need to change too."

"Well, do it quick. Our limo will be here in 45 minutes."

He couldn't believe it. Vegas! He blazed out of there, into his car, drove home as quickly as he could without breaking the law, and ran into his building. He saw Miguel coming out of his apartment.

"Miguel, you're never going to believe it. The guys at work are taking me to Vegas for the weekend to celebrate my birthday! I gotta run and pack quick. Our limo leaves for the airport in like 30 minutes!"

"Oh, wow, Vegas?... um, so then... okay... that sounds great man, have a great time."

He grabbed his smaller suitcase, and threw all of his Neiman Marcus clothes in it, took the nicer of his three suits from his closet, and then ran into the bathroom, shoved all his toiletries into a Ziploc bag, and gave himself a quick once over. Shit, he was still in a suit! He changed into one of his Neiman Marcus outfits so he'd look more like the guys, checked to make sure everything was off in his apartment, then dashed out the door. He made the limo with 10 minutes to spare.

While the guys slept on the plane, Chad was too excited to do anything other than stare out the window and think. And they were flying business class! He'd never flown anything other than coach before. He tried to imagine what Vegas would be like in his head, but nothing could prepare him for what he saw as the limo from the airport drove them to their hotel at the Palms. The beautiful buildings, resorts, fountains—it looked like it was all built somewhere else and dropped there by enormous cranes. And the excess money and luxury around him, Chad never read Veblen, wasn't familiar with the term Conspicuous Consumption, but it was what he was looking at, and he'd never seen so much of it in one place. As Seijun and Lars took him to their suite, with its a hot tub and bar and flatscreen plasmas, Chad thought, through his disbelief, that this was the good life, this was the world that had been denied to him for so long, and he was finally here, able to enjoy it.

"One of our clients actually owns this thing," Seijun said. "He gave us the keys when I mentioned you to him and that this weekend was your birthday. It's his little gift to you."

Seijun and Lars were in agreement that it was way too early to do anything other than rest and get the flight out of their systems. All three guys hit the hot tub, snacked on some room service, and took naps. Around 7 Seijun wanted to do something.

"Why don't we hit the tables?" Lars said.

"You know I can't go near those. They'll kick me out."

"It's just the blackjack, not everything else."

"I don't want to give them a reason to ruin our weekend. We're here for Chad, not us."

"Why won't they let you near the tables?"

"Seijun was caught counting cards."

"Counting cards? Wow, how much did you make?"

"Enough that they decided to shut me down. Did I tell you I went to Tahoe a couple years after that and the casinos *there* had me on their books too? Yeah, so if we do anything, we'll play the horses."

"Dude, there are no women at the horses."

"Then you guys hit the tables, and after you pick up some women, you can come back and find me. How does that sound? Did you get a hold of your buddy?"

"Yeah, he texted me while we were on the plane. He said he'll be up here around 10 or 11. He should be bringing three or four guys with him."

"Guys?" Chad said.

"Yeah, USC football players."

"Lars's friend is an agent. He gives kids all kinds of benefits to get them to sign before they turn pro."

"Yeah, you can't tell anyone who you saw up here tonight, but word on the street is he's got Johnny Dawkins."

"What, Heisman Trophy candidate Johnny Dawkins?"

"They just better not cause any problems. If they break shit, you're paying for it Lars."

The guys got ready around seven, as they planned, Lars and Chad wearing almost exactly the same thing: striped button-up shirts, black blazers, and designer jeans; while Seijun looked much better, at least in Chad's eyes, in a simple wrinkled linen dress shirt and khakis. He was beginning to see that, as cool as Lars might be, Seijun was a completely different animal. He kind of preferred to join Seijun playing the horses, but the way Seijun put it, that Lars and Chad would do their thing and meet up with him later, Chad took it as something that was predetermined, as if Seijun wouldn't have wanted Chad there.

The main casino was bigger and more chaotic than Chad expected. People were yelling, walking fast, walking slow, security men looking serious, waitresses looking exasperated, rich people looking smug, poor people looking poor. He was glad he looked rich. The slot machines reminded him of the arcades he used to play in, made him pine for *Mortal Kombat*. He thought about throwing some cash in one, but Lars insisted that the craps table was the thing to do.

Chad had no idea what craps was, how to play it, or how he'd make money from it. He let Lars decide what to do, but he got a little worried when Lars lost $100 of Chad's money right away.

"Dude, I can't afford to lose money like that!"

"Don't worry man, we've got you covered."

"Got me covered? I just lost $100. At this rate my birthday will end up *costing* me money."

"It's only the first game. These things even out. Give it time, and we'll win it back. I feel good about this table."

"All right. I've got to go to the bathroom anyway. I'll come back and see how you're doing."

He didn't know exactly where the bathroom was, but he didn't feel like asking anyone, so he wandered through a maze of slot machines, until he came across a small bar area where guys were watching some basketball games. Wow, the Lakers are playing a home game this early on a Friday night. Then he remembered that he was in the Pacific time zone. When he came out of the bathroom, he realized he was lost. He had no idea how he ended up in his current location, or how to get back to Lars. He took a seat at the bar and ordered a Bud Light.

Lars would probably wonder where he was. He fingered the chips in his blazer pocket. The thought of giving them to Lars so he could lose them all didn't sit well with him. It was his birthday, and it had already cost him over $100. Then he thought of Anishka. It's a gift, it's a gift. He called the bartender over.

"Do you know where they do the horse racing?"

"The race book?"

"Yeah, sure."

The bartender pulled out a small, brochure-size map, and marked off three locations with his pencil. Chad took it and found Seijun at the first one after about five minutes of walking.

"Hey, what's going on? Where's Lars?"

"I got lost going to the bathroom, and I figured I'd just shoot over here and see what you were doing. Plus, Lars already lost $100 of mine, and by that rate I'll be broke by tomorrow. I needed to stop the bleeding."

Seijun laughed. He asked Chad if he'd ever bet on horses before, and when Chad said no, Seijun handed him a sheet with a bunch of information on it.

"This is the next race. It posts in about 25 minutes, so you have until then if you want to put in your bet. I usually do more exotic things, like tri's and exactas, but you can just do a simple across the board."

"What's that?"

"You put money down for it to win, place, and show, so it's like three bets in one. Your best bet, though, if you're going across the board, is to pick something in the 10-1 range, otherwise, you'll barely win your money back if it does anything."

Chad had no idea what he was talking about. He looked at the sheet in front of him:

1. The Human Fund	25-1
2. Hello Newman	2-1
3. Rochelle Rochelle	11-1
4. I Love the Drake	5-1
5. The Roommate Switch	9-1
6. Poppy's a Little Bit Sloppy	50-1
7. Witch-ay Woman	15-1
8. Den of Iniquity	3-1
9. The Velvet Fog	16-1
10. Jimmy's Sweet on You	7-1

"I think I like this one."

"Number 5? 'The Roommate Switch' huh? What do you want to put on it?"

"I don't know, what's a good number?"

"Well, the lowest is two bucks, but remember that everything you bet is multiplied by three."

"Multiplied by three?"

"Across the board. You're covering if the horse comes in first, second, or third."

"Oh, I see, so I get paid whether it comes in first, second, or third? That's what across the board means?"

"Yeah. Or you can just bet it to win."

"No, across the board. I'll put… $4, how's that? So $12."

"Sounds great."

Chad gave Seijun the money, then watched him go to the booth to put in their bets. He looked around him. There weren't very many people their age there, mostly men his father's age and older. They smoked cigars or cigarettes, some had sport coats, some had track suits, some had V-neck T's with a gold chain—those guys were usually overweight and short. The only women were usually around the same ages, in cocktail dresses or tighter jeans than they probably should've been wearing. Very few of them actually played any horses, they usually accompanied their men who were betting. Seijun returned and gave Chad his ticket. When post time came, their race was put on an enormous screen on the wall in front of them. Chad looked at all the smaller screens around it, and the boards of information about various races around those. At the top of each was a place name he didn't know, Evangeline, Santa Anita, Pimlico.

"All right, so you're in on the 5. I have the 1 over the 2,3,7, and the 4 over the 1,7,9."

"Okay."

Chad watched the big screen as the horses were loaded into their stalls. Then the camera angle switched so it was on the other side, and the stalls burst open.

"And they're off!"

Chad watched his number 5 start out near the back. God damn it!

"Hello Newman in the lead followed by I Love the Drake Witch-ay Woman and Poppy's a Little Bit Sloppy…"

His number 5 started to make a move. He heard grumblings around him, a person yelling here or there.

"As they reach the turn it's Hello Newman followed by Rochelle Rochelle I Love the Drake Witch-ay Woman and Jimmy's Sweet on You…"

The five was catching up. Oh, come on five, come on five.

"…the home stretch it's The Roommate Switch charging hard, Hello Newman Rochelle Rochelle The Roommate Switch Hello Newman Hello Newman The Roommate Switch!"

"Go Five! Go Five! Go Five!"

"And it's The Roommate Switch followed by Hello Newman Rochelle Rochelle and Jimmy's Sweet on You."

"Holy shit I won!"

Seijun gave him a high five. He wanted to go get his money, but Seijun explained that he had to wait until it was official. Chad tried to do the math out on what a $4 across the board bet would be at 9-1, but then he realized that he had no idea what any of that meant. Then

145

three numbers popped up on the board under Evangeline: 7.62, 5.21, 3.44. Chad went to run up and cash in his winnings, when Seijun stopped him again:

"Don't you want to take a look at the next race first?"

Chad's iPhone buzzed. It was Lars texting, wondering where he was. Chad called and explained what had happened, with him getting lost, and finding Seijun. Lars wanted him to come back to the craps tables, that he'd found some women, but Chad was fine where he was. He'd just won back almost all the money Lars had lost for him.

Over the next couple hours, he would bet on four more races, and though he didn't win another, he did have a place and a show, which meant he didn't lose as much. He enjoyed having Seijun explain the ins and outs, not only of horse racing, but Vegas in general. Where to go for cheap food, how to get a room comped, what shows to see—which, by the way, the guys had tickets to see a boxing match tomorrow night. Chad wasn't sure, if he ever came back to Vegas without Seijun, he'd be able to do all the things Seijun suggested.

Around 9, Lars showed up with about five women, one of whom was a bride to be. She rushed over and gave Chad a kiss on the cheek and wished him a happy birthday. They didn't want to join the guys for a bite to eat though, and Seijun insisted that he was hungry, and Chad thought he could eat too, so the two parties separated, with a plan that they would meet at one of the clubs later on. The guys left the casino to go eat at a place Seijun knew in another part of Vegas. It was a strip club. It reminded Chad of the first night he hung out with Lars. He didn't talk much, listening to Seijun and Lars trade stories. Things they did at Harvard together, things they did at Harvard separately, things they'd done in Vegas together, things they'd done in Vegas separately.

Chad felt like he was being included into an exclusive club, but at the same time he felt slightly left out. These two had a long history, the way Chad, Dave, and Kovacs did, and Chad missed that part of his life. As Seijun and Lars traded stories, Chad daydreamed, and thought about his time with Gwen. Did he alienate Dave and Kovacs? Then he thought about Dave and Gwen cheating on him. He'd never have that friendship back. Maybe he could start something new with these guys, but it wouldn't be the same, either for him, or for them.

After a quick wardrobe change and freshening up of their look, the boys went down to the clubs, where they found the bachelorette party, among many other groups of women. They were everywhere, men and women, coupling, separating, re-coupling with new partners. Chad's birthday made a perfect ice breaker for Lars, and he used it with group of women after group of women. Chad loved being the center of attention, even though he technically wasn't, it was Lars. One girl out of the bachelorette party had taken a shine to Chad. Her name was Tiffany, and she had rich, ebony-toned skin. Chad wasn't sure he'd met a woman before who was that black. She had short black hair that came just past her ears, and was wearing a shiny silver strapless dress that she constantly had to adjust to make sure it covered her boobs. Her body was fit, but not too muscular, and she had a very direct way of communicating. Everything about her exuded power to Chad.

The downside to her was that she was engaged to someone back home, and she made it clear she didn't plan on cheating with anyone. She would leave Chad alone for periods of time, then come back to him after he'd talked to other women and tell him what she thought of them. That one was cute, that one wasn't, he could do better than her. Part of Chad wanted her to leave him alone because she wasn't available to him, but part of him found her very attractive. She was like a statue in a dress, but her skin felt like velvet. As she sat next to him at the bar, sipping her Sex on the Beach, adjusting the top of her dress, or crossing her legs and fixing the strap on the heel of her shoe, he had trouble focusing on anyone else. Then one of the other girls in the bachelorette party would ask her to go to the bathroom with her, she'd leave, and Chad would talk to another girl that Lars introduced him to. After a few minutes, that girl would leave, and Tiffany would come back.

"I think she liked you. You should go for it."

The alcohol and Anishka's words spoke to him.

"I think you like me too. I'd like to go for you."

"I'm off limits honey."

Her eyes looking back at him over her glass as she sipped her drink told him otherwise. What happens in Vegas stays in Vegas, right? What Chad didn't know was that Tiffany wasn't engaged. She just said that so she'd have a reason to keep sketchy guys she wasn't interested in from bothering her all night. Saying "no" either wasn't enough, or would make her seem like a "bitch" to guys that figured if she was single in Vegas she should accept every guy's advance. Chad she was iffy on, which was why she gave him the same line that she was engaged, so she could find out what she thought about him. Her hunch was that he wasn't used to being around black women, and to him she was probably an exotic novelty. She was right about the first part, but not the second part—Chad just thought she was hot, and she was giving him the time of day. Anyway, it was whatever for Tiffany. She decided he was cute enough, and safe enough—perhaps most important—so she told him with her eyes that her being engaged didn't matter, that she was game. She found that as much as saying she was engaged could give men a legitimate "no" that didn't risk insulting guys who thought she owed them something because they hit on her, that saying she would cheat on her fake fiancé didn't bother any guys whom she'd told that lie to earlier in the evening; and Chad was no exception.

He moved closer to her and rubbed his hand on her knee that was crossed over on the other. She put it down so both legs were together, took his hand by the wrist, then in one quick motion, put her other hand behind his head, pulled him to her, and they kissed. As quickly as she did that, they were making out. Chad forgot he was at the bar, in front of a lot of people. He didn't really care either. Everything about this felt amazing. Krystel and Haley and Gwen were miles away, in another world. Then she stopped and pushed him back slightly.

"Oh my God, I can't believe I did that! If my boyfriend finds out...! Who gives a shit, right?"

She bit down on her lower burgundy painted lip, and her eyes lit up. Chad was about to respond by kissing her again, but Lars came by.

"The party's moving upstairs. My buddy has a VIP suite—even bigger than ours—and he invited us all up there. I guess Johnny saw some campus reporter and didn't want what he was up to to appear on some blog or something. You know how that shit ends up on ESPN."

"What is he talking about?"

"His friend is an agent who wants to represent Johnny Dawkins."

"Johnny Dawkins? In this hotel?"

"Yeah, you wanna go up? Round up your girlfriends."

Seijun had found a guitar, and was showing off his musical skills, singing BBMak's "Back Here" with his best possible boy band voice. The party going on around them was pretty crazy, but Seijun, Chad, Tiffany, and a couple other girls from her group, had found some sanctuary in a small living room area. The girls were next to Seijun on a sofa, while Tiffany sat on Chad's lap in a chair with her arm around his neck. The girls were howling and started singing along with him in a loud, obnoxious voice.

Tiffany and Chad were laughing, kissing each other. Everything about her felt perfect. He didn't know how much he could stand it, but he couldn't convince her to leave her friends— even if he could tell she wanted to.

Then the fourth girl in the group came in with dire news about the bachelorette. She was off somewhere crying, saying her impending marriage was a mistake. The fourth girl had confiscated the bachelorette's cellphone so she couldn't call her future husband and tell him they were through, but she was going to need her friends' help if they were going to keep this situation from becoming worse. Chad hoped that meant that against all odds she would be staying with him and abandoning her friends, but he was wrong. She got up, kissed him again, put her finger to his lips and asked if he'd be around tomorrow.

"Go to the club. I'll be looking for you."

And that was it, she was gone, and Chad had a vicious attack of blue balls. Seijun read the situation and got the two of them a scotch and soda.

"Tough break man. That Tiffany girl was pretty hot. Too bad she was stuck with her friends."

"Seems like the story of my life lately."

Seijun looked at his watch.

"It's just after 3. I know the perfect place to grab a bite to eat. Let's go."

"What, now?"

"Of course. You're in Vegas, man. We'll sleep all day tomorrow."

They took a cab to a much cheaper casino on the outskirts of the strip, which had a dimly lit lounge with a buffet. It looked like an Elk's Lodge or something. There was a band performing Peter Gabriel's "In Your Eyes" on a small stage set off on the far side of the room from where they came in, four members, with a female lead singer and male musicians. Chad thought she had an amazing voice.

Chad decided to forgo the buffet in favor of an order of fries, but Seijun told him they made a great Reuben sandwich that he just had to try, so Chad ordered that—with a side of fries. He wasn't really hungry for a sandwich.

"I try to come out here every time I go to Vegas, and I always get the Reuben. I love a good Reuben."

He lit a cigarette and offered one to Chad, but he declined. The song wrapped up, and the band had a quick conference.

"I wonder if Lilith saw me come in."

"The lead singer? You know her?"

"Oh yeah. If she saw me, they'll play a certain song that she knows I love. Let's see."

Lilith and the lead guitarist each sat on stools, the lead guitarist with an electric guitar in his hands, and her holding a tambourine.

"This one is for an old friend I just saw walk in."

148

When Chad heard the opening guitar, his heart sank. It was Mazzy Star's "Fade Into You", which was a beautiful song, but it had been forever tainted in his mind. It was Gwen's favorite. As Lilith started the opening lyrics, Chad was transported to one night, a New Year's Eve, when Gwen had had too much to drink. She was hysterical, throwing up and crying, telling Chad she thought she was going to die. This was somewhere in the middle of their relationship, when things were going really well—though from Chad's perspective, he thought things were always going well until he caught her in bed with Dave and found out they weren't. After vomiting, Chad took her into her bedroom and found her Mazzy Star CD, hoping the song would calm her down. It did, but when it ended, she wanted to hear it again. For the better part of an hour, sitting up in her bed with her head resting awkwardly on his stomach, he hit the repeat button on the remote, playing the song over and over, until she settled down and fell asleep. The next morning, a morning Chad thought would never come, Gwen couldn't remember a thing that happened that night. She was too hungover then for him to tell her what he did for her, and after that he felt like it didn't matter anymore, so she never knew how much he took care of her that night.

When the song was finished, Lilith visited them at their table, where she had a cigarette with Seijun. She looked like a taller version of Bianca with longer hair and fewer tattoos. She was in a long, low-cut, claret dress, which, when combined with her voice and the dignified way she held her cigarette, exuded an elegance Chad wasn't expecting. Or maybe he was, because he was getting used to expecting the unexpected lately. As she and Seijun caught up, Chad daydreamed, thinking of Bianca and her bear suit. She hadn't returned his calls, and though part of him thought that was a good thing after what happened, another looked at Lilith in front of him, who reminded him of Bianca, and he thought about how he'd just struck out with Tiffany when he seemed so close, and that part of him longed for Bianca, would've worn the bear suit for her if she'd been there right now, wished he'd just played ball and worn the bear suit a couple weeks ago, because he wouldn't be so sexually frustrated watching Lilith's elegant fingers put her cigarette to her elegant lips, take a drag, and exhale with an elegant laugh after Seijun said something she found funny.

After her cigarette, she went back to the stage, where she and the band performed "Nothing Compares 2 U", and Seijun and Chad were left alone again.

"Wow, so you used to come to Vegas a lot."

"Yeah, it was a good place to make cash. I'd get a cheap flight, then work a free room, free food, and count cards. After a while though, they caught on. Plus, now that I'm with Noriko, I prefer to stay home or travel with her than do this kind of thing. I don't need to party like I used to."

"Yeah, that makes sense."

"We needed this night though. It's good to have an outing like this. It's a good teambuilding experience."

Chad contrasted this teambuilding with the trip to his supervisor's with Haley. What would Haley think if she could see him now? What would any of them think? Wow, Seijun was right, this Reuben was good.

"I wish you'd had a chance to get to talk to Noriko the other night. That's too bad about your friend."

Chad thought about getting into more about Krystel, but he decided against it. He let Seijun tell him about Noriko instead.

"We met in Boston. She was going to film school at BU. She had dreadlocks at the time, like her friend Justine had at the art opening... Blur was playing at the Middle East... this was before they became big with that 'Song 2' song. It was her eyes that attracted me to her... I mean, look at me, dreadlocks isn't exactly my type, right?... but she looked—outside of the dreads—like the Japanese movie stars from the old Kurosawa and Ôzu movies my parents used to watch... she actually said the same thing to me when I first approached her, that I looked like an actor from one of her parents' old movies... it's funny, because we had so little in common, me a Harvard business major trying to make his way into exclusive clubs and forming important business relations, and her a granola eating film major with dreadlocks... but the number one thing we had in common was a shared experience, you know what I mean?... we both grew up Japanese-American... I could tell her about my mother calling, and she'd know what I was saying without me needing to explain all the cultural baggage that comes along with that... we were like each other's home away from home, you know?..."

"Let me have one of your cigarettes."

"Oh, yeah, sure man, here. You need a light too?"

"Please."

Chad set his alarm on his phone for 7AM. He figured he would be so tired that early that he would sound sick enough when he called his mother to cancel on the family get-together, and he was right. She even offered to go to the store for him, but he said Miguel and Julía already offered. He then apologized for not being able to make it after she went to the trouble for him—a little icing on the cake to drive home just how sick he was and just how much he wished he could've been there. He went back to sleep until 5PM, when he and the guys went out to eat before getting ready for the fight.

When he checked his phone he noticed he had a text from Haley. He couldn't wait to respond to it that he was in Vegas. But then he read it:

"Hey Chad, hope you feel better ☹"

Hope I feel better? How did she know I was sick? Who knows, but he was in too much of a hurry to get into a big texting thing, so he just responded with a quick "thx ☺"

The whole thing was soon forgotten. Everything was forgotten while he was in Vegas. Everywhere he went he felt like a VIP with Seijun and Lars. They were smooth, confident, and totally knowledgeable of the ins and outs of the city. Often Chad had no idea where they were in relation to where they had just been, had no idea what to say to any of the staff at the places they went, what to tip, how to act. He followed their leads and hoped he could fool everyone into thinking he was on the same level of his friends.

Over the past 24 hours, since the plane trip, he was becoming less enamored with Lars—if he was ever that enamored anyway—and was trying more to emulate Seijun. I mean, look at all these juiceheads and jackasses at the fight, in their busy T-shirts or gaudy button-ups with huge collars, they were total tools. But then he looked at himself and Lars, and saw that he was only slightly better, in their white dress shirts and black blazers—Lars called it the "Marcello Mastroianni look," whatever that meant. Seijun was in the vest and pants of a heather gray

150

three-piece suit, no blazer, and a light pink dress shirt, tie, and garters on his biceps that he guessed held the shirt in place. It looked like something out of the 1930s. He was another level of cool, something that Chad would probably never attain, but the mere fact that Seijun had taken a shine to him, thought he was good enough to hang out with, made Chad as happy as he'd been since he'd been with Gwen.

After the fight, they made their way down to the club, where Chad found Tiffany, looking as beautiful as she did last night. He tapped her on the shoulder, felt that velvet skin, and she turned and embraced him, hard, pressing her boobs to him. This was going to be a good night, he just knew it.

"Oh my God! I'm so glad you're here! There's this sketchy guy who's been bugging me. See him over there?" She pointed to a juicehead in a tight T-shirt with Armani Exchange logos all over it. "I told him I was engaged. You're going to have to be my boyfriend tonight, okay?"

"That's fine with me."

He had his hands on her waist, and he moved them down her lower back, to her butt, and yanked her toward him. She let out a quick scream, then jumped up, crossing her legs around his torso. Their foreheads met as he held her, and they kissed. This wasn't the first kiss of last night, the kiss of ice breaking and sudden passion, this was a kiss of familiarity, between two people who were used to kissing each other, and had waited 24 long hours to be able to do it again. Chad could feel her butt and legs in his hands and arms, feel her navy jersey dress and her velvet skin, and he wanted more. Feeling wasn't enough, he couldn't touch her enough to fulfill his needs.

"You know, we have a hot tub in our suite."

"Oh yeah?"

"Yes, and as you can see, my friends are both down here in the club."

"What if I told you I had a feeling you might say that, and I brought my bikini with me just in case."

"You did?"

She took one arm away from the back of his neck, and let the tiny purse on it slide down to her hand, where she shook it to show Chad she had her bathing suit in there. In there? How big could her bikini be if it fit in there? He didn't want to wait to find out. He let her down and took her by the arm towards the club's entrance. She stopped him so she could tell her friends what she was doing, then let him lead her by the hand, trying to keep up in her heels and not let him drag her, but not wanting to let go of his hand.

Chad was a little disappointed that she went into the bathroom to change into her suit, and also a little disappointed that it wasn't as revealing as he expected, just a simple red string bikini. But her rich ebony body looked so perfect in it it didn't matter, all that mattered was that she was getting into the hot tub with him. While she was changing, he had a moment to look at himself in a large wall mirror and see that those five pounds he'd lost didn't amount to as much as he'd thought as far as his waist went. He made sure he was in the hot tub before she could see his spare tire.

"God you look amazing."

"Jesus I hope so, I work hard on this body! But thank you anyway, that was very sweet. Oh God, that water feels amazing, oh wow... now before you do anything, I want to make one thing clear: my hair does not get wet. Do you understand?"

Chad was so worried her "let's make one thing clear" was her setting boundaries about how far they'd go sexually, that the hair caveat was no problem. All he wanted was to get that body in his hands again, get those lips pressed against his, taste that tongue. This was finally happening. After over two years, he was going to get laid, and this chick was hot. She whispered in his ear:

"Do you have protection?"

"Yes, in my wallet. It's in my pants."

He jumped out of the tub, not self-conscious now of his spare tire around his waist. He was soaking wet, dripping water all over everything, including his expensive jeans, and the money and business cards in his wallet, until he found his condoms. He tried to open one, but he couldn't get a grip with his wet hands. He looked back and saw Tiffany coming, slow, measured paces, her dripping skin shining in the faint traces of angled, horizontal light that broke through the half-opened blinds of their otherwise dark suite, her eyes wide and focused, like a tiger he thought, looking directly at him. The anticipation of what they were about to do was overwhelming. She, in her beauty and power, made it overwhelming. God, two years, he thought, what if I go too quick? No, that's why you rubbed one out in the shower this morning, right? Don't be a putz, don't ruin this! She took the hand that held the condom, still in its wrapper.

"You need some help with this?"

"You need some help with this?" It sounded silly now. So did all his apprehension before the act, now that they had done it and she was lying on his chest, sleeping, and he was wide awake, with a pain in his groin, wanting a cigarette. It didn't matter that he was rusty, that he didn't last as long the first time. She did all the work, and she was happy to go again and again as long as he could get it up. She was getting something out of her system, using Chad's loins as her medium, and he was fine with that. The problem was, their moment was destined to end, and Chad wanted it to go on forever. He wanted to stay in Vegas forever, and do this forever, and never go home and back to the life he knew, even if his life back there now included a new job at a place he really loved. Tiffany's phone rang at 5AM. He watched her naked body slip into that navy jersey dress, balance on one foot and then the other as she yanked on her shoes, then reached behind her as she fixed their straps. He wanted her to be his girl, to watch her get dressed in the morning after they had sex the night before, every morning and every night, for the next 100 years. But Tiffany wouldn't even give him her number—he didn't even know if Tiffany was her real name—she just kissed him, told him she had a blast, and wished him a good life. Last night suddenly didn't matter as much anymore, because he knew it was over, that he'd never have it again, and he was back to being alone. 5AM: it was officially his 33rd birthday.

They had to leave themselves a few hours later to catch their flight home. Lars made some jokes about Chad having Jungle Fever, which annoyed him, but not more than he was annoyed that he couldn't be back in Vegas with Tiffany for another night. His mom had called too, saying she needed to see him on Monday, maybe they could get lunch. What, no mention about how he was feeling? No happy birthday even?

Tired and jetlagged, the car dropped him off at his building, and he went into his apartment, dumped his bags on the floor, and slumped himself on the couch. Wow, he did have a blast though, huh? The best birthday ever. There was a knock at the door. Jesus, who the hell is that now? He yelled come in. It was Miguel.

"Hey man, how was your trip?"

God, he wasn't in the mood for this.

"You know what they say, what happens in Vegas stays in Vegas."

"Oh yeah, I know. The problem is, I didn't know you didn't tell your mother you were going."

"Why?"

"Because she called me, I assumed to tell me the party was off, and I, not thinking you wouldn't have told her, said 'don't worry, I know, the party's off. How exciting is that, his job taking him to Vegas?' And then she was like 'what?'"

"Why would she be calling to tell you my party was off?"

"Well, it was supposed to be a surprise. Your brother Steve asked me, and I helped him find that Haley girl through your old job, and Anishka and some of the guys from the team were going to come. Next time you're going to use me for a lie, give me a heads up first. I would've covered for you and said you were sick if I'd only known."

Chad started laughing. He couldn't stop.

It wasn't the affair with his company's staff sergeant that felt like the biggest betrayal to Chad's father, it was the admission from Chad's mother that, behind his back, she had taken the LSAT at a German university away from the base, she had applied to law school at Dodge State, and had made arrangements with her parents to move into her uncle's house. In his mind, he had done everything for her, everything for their family, and it wasn't enough.

He thought about fighting her when she said she was taking the boys with her, but she called his bluff, asked him how he planned on taking care of them without her, asked how he took care of them now *with* her, and he knew, even if he didn't want to admit it, that he had been a father to his children when it was convenient for him, and without his wife there, it wouldn't ever be convenient. He'd change that though. He'd put in for a transfer and move back to the States and be a father to his kids.

But as the year went by, and the kids weren't there to remind him that they existed as more than just a voice on the phone—a voice from Chad and Steve that he could tell didn't really want to talk to him—he grew less interested. It was easy to forget them when he didn't need to care for them. He didn't know how much Chad's mother was struggling, and he didn't care, didn't have to. Still, there was this far off concept of a transfer and the need to go back and reestablish that connection.

Then he met Mika, a waitress at a bar he and the other officers frequented. She had a typically German directness, and she accepted Chad's father's directness as the natural order of things. Unlike Chad's mother, who grew to resent the tone his father often took with her, Mika would've respected him less if he wasn't like that.

This coincided with continued success in the army. He was now a Captain, commanding units in joint NATO operations, and tagging along for bigger meetings among superiors. The transfer was going to hurt his career, force him start at the bottom at a new base in the States, which was something he increasingly didn't want to do, but felt he had to do—there was something about his wife leaving with the kids like that that made him want to go back there and become a part of their lives again, as if leaving them alone would mean she won. But here was Mika, offering him a chance to start over in Germany while his career could stay on the same trajectory. He rescinded his transfer request.

Chad was happy to hear this news. The specter of his father coming back had always loomed over them, this idea that he might step in and stop or fight with his mother over all the leaving his toys on the floor or eating McDonald's that Chad had grown accustomed to in the States. Then, when word came that his father met a woman and was marrying her there, he and Steve were both relieved and then alarmed at the prospect of having to go back over there for the wedding—something that didn't happen when there was a dispute between the parents over who should pay the plane fare.

Over time, Chad and Steve grew to understand their father as merely a concept. When people asked, they'd tell people their parents split, and their dad is in the Army, stationed in Germany. Beyond that, he didn't matter. By the same token, Chad's father's new life in Germany replaced his previous one. He had two children, a son who grew up and went to college in the United States for forestry, and never came back once he discovered the National Parks; and a daughter who married a black man and moved to Amsterdam because her parents didn't approve of him. When Mika's mother passed away, Chad's father thought it was as good a time as any to retire from the Army, and he and Mika moved back to the States.

After the initial meeting with his father, Chad contacted him again, to see about joining the Army. He was still depressed after finding Gwen in bed with Dave—it had been almost two years at this point—and seeing all the attention and respect Steve was getting for his status as an Iraq War veteran made him even worse. He wanted to be a part of what Steve was a part of, he wanted people coming up to him and thanking him for his service, wanted to be respected. That would show Gwen, when everyone was telling him how great he was. His father, upon hearing his interest over the phone, was excited. The fact that Steve had gone to West Point and fought in Iraq and his father couldn't claim any credit for it was a source of frustration for him, so to be able to make up for that with Chad was perfect.

His enthusiasm drove home to Chad how much was involved with something he had taken on on a whim: boot camp, commitments, deferring to superiors. Even if he could join the officer's corps as an accountant, he'd still have to learn basic fighting techniques, still have to give his life over to the Army, and, most importantly, he'd still have to be motivated, which he hadn't been in any phase of his life since Gwen left him. Eventually it became too much, but he didn't have the heart to tell his father, so he started avoiding him. Chad's father took this lack of commitment in his son as further evidence of the kind of man his ex-wife's lax methods in raising him had produced. He ignored the fact that of his other two children, one married a black man and raised their "half-breed" children in Amsterdam—something that shouldn't have been a source of shame, but was extremely embarrassing to him and Mika—, and the other preferred to spend the winter in Yellowstone Park than visit his parents on Christmas.

Chad was now 33 years old, but he wasn't any less apprehensive about meeting his mother for lunch. Maybe apprehensive wasn't the word, because he wasn't afraid of being scolded by her, rather, he just wasn't in the mood for it. He worked out explanations in his head, but really there wasn't much he could say. He had behaved like tool to his family, even if he had had a great weekend for his birthday.

Lars came by to see him in his office.

"Hey dude, I know you gotta deal with your mother today, so I thought I'd bring you these:"

It was a pair of squared-off, dark rimmed glasses.

"They'll make you look much smarter and more sophisticated. You'd be surprised how much of a difference they make, they work like a charm with my mother."

"Thanks man, but I don't need glasses. I have perfect 20/20 vision."

"No no, they're just glass, see?"

Chad put them on and looked at himself in the mirror. He imagined himself sitting across from his mother, her asking why he was wearing glasses. Would he lie about his eye sight? She'd probably see right through that. Then he imagined himself telling her they were just glass, just an accessory. He shuddered at the thought of telling her that. But Lars looked excited at the prospect of Chad utilizing these glasses, and in the process, helping Chad out of what he thought would be a sticky situation for him.

"Thanks man, these should definitely help."

"Definitely." He put his arm around Chad. "You're a good guy Chad. Too bad we didn't get to spend too much time together in Vegas, but that happens sometimes. Maybe we'll hit the Green Dragon again this Friday."

His mother was already at the restaurant when Chad arrived. She had her reading glasses on and had been interrupted from scanning the lunch menu by someone she knew coming over to her to say hi—someone who seemed important based on the suit he was wearing and the way he carried himself. Chad couldn't remember when she started needing reading glasses, but to him the rest of her looked the same for as long as he could remember, Chad never noticing that the crow's feet and other wrinkles had become more pronounced, or that the gray hair she dyed brown was also thinning out a bit. The change he did see though, was that being a judge, and no longer just a lawyer, suited her. Watching her cordially yet effectively return the man in the suit's greeting while letting him know without telling him that it was time for him to leave her; or with a unique blend of command and politeness asking the waiter if a dish could be prepared differently from how it was described on the menu, the waiter subconsciously knowing that she's not really asking him, but also knowing that the cook is going to prepare the meal the way she wants it if she decides that's what she wants to order; this and everything else his mother was made more sense with her as a judge than as anything else, as if she had always been this and it was the world that was catching up to *her* by finally promoting her to the bench.

His mother barely recognized Chad, not having seen him since before Seijun and Lars's make-over. This put a whole different spin on the occasion. This was *her* son, in that expensive suit and that crisp, stylish haircut? Where was the dull, depressed, dissociated Chad she'd gotten used to over the past five years? She stood and hugged him, wishing him happy birthday.

"Wow, you look great honey."

155

"Yeah, it's this new job. I spent a little on some new clothes, plus, I'm working out every day. They have a fitness room and everything."

"Yeah, I can see it. And you're making good money?"

"Well… I'm not making any money right away, but when the quarter ends I'll get a percentage of what the fund brings in. But I have a lot of money saved up, so it's good for now."

She was so excited to see him looking so good, she didn't even think about the fact that he was working at his job for free, and spending his savings on an expensive suit.

"So I talked to Miguel," he said, wanting to cut right to the chase. This had the effect of reminding her, in spite of how well her son looked, that she had planned a big birthday for him last Saturday, and he had not only cancelled on her, but had lied about what he was doing.

"I wish you'd just told us you were going to Vegas with your friends. We would've been okay with that."

"I didn't find out until right before we left."

"And when was that?"

"Friday when I got to work."

"So you had a good 24 hours before you actually called that you could've called. I mean, you called me three hours before, forcing us to scramble to tell everyone that everything was cancelled. Steve's kids were all excited to help you open presents, and they'd never been to a surprise party before, it was going to be so much fun."

"How was I supposed to know you were going to have a surprise party?"

"That's not the point Chad, why would it ever be right to lie to us in order to get out of a birthday party we were having for *you*?"

"I don't know…"

"Seriously Chad, what is your problem with us? With your family?"

Whoa, Chad wasn't expecting *this* line of questioning. *Problem with my family?*

"What? I don't have a problem with my family."

"Yes you do. Ever since you started seeing Gwen. It's not just me. You can't call your brother when I ask, you couldn't bother to visit Mr. Haley until it was almost too late, I call you and 90 percent of the time it just goes to voice mail…"

All of the things she was saying were true, but Chad didn't see how they added up to the whole she was accusing him of. There was an individual explanation for each example she gave, but they all sounded silly as he tried to bring them to his lips in his defense.

"And we all thought, after you and Gwen split, that maybe that would change, but it hasn't—in fact, it's gotten worse. It's not like we live far away. I mean, you come over on Thanksgiving, and I find out you don't even know the man I'm about to marry. How do you think that made me feel?"

Chad was speechless. He had never considered that any of his actions had had these kinds of consequences. How was he to know that Steve's kids were disappointed because Chad cancelled on his surprise party? How was he to know the weekends that he didn't have the energy to leave his apartment after Gwen left him were being interpreted by his mother as a snub?

"Chad, do you resent me for cheating on your father?"

"What? No, of course not. Where is all this coming from? I don't have a problem with you, or Steve, or his kids, or Mr. and Mrs. Haley. You're reading into things that aren't there."

"Are you sure? You really don't harbor any feelings of resentment toward me, especially after what happened with you and Gwen? I know you were seeing your father for a bit a few years ago, I wasn't sure if maybe…"

"Maybe what?"

"Maybe he was telling you things, making you more sympathetic, or maybe you already were more sympathetic to him considering…"

"No, it wasn't like that at all… I was jealous of Steve, because everyone was treating him like a hero, and I thought dad could help me maybe…"

"Join the Army?"

"I don't know, yeah I guess… it was a crazy idea… I mean, I could barely do 30 sit-ups, let alone handle the Army…"

"That's actually very ironic."

"Yes I know, me in the Army…"

"No, that you went to your father because you were jealous of your brother for being a war hero. Your father was actually very jealous of Steve too."

"He was?"

"Oh yeah. Back in college, he felt like he was missing out, because he was in ROTC while the Vietnam War was going on, and by the time we graduated, things were pretty much done over there. I don't think he ever got over that. He did some stuff during the first Gulf War and Kosovo, but by then he was so high up he wasn't going to be shot at. Then moving back here and learning about Steve… that was too much. I think Steve represented everything your father stood for but wasn't able to ever be, if that makes any sense."

"Wow, I never knew that."

"Yep… but why would *you* of all people feel jealous of your bother? You saved a girl's life from a pedophile. I'm lucky to have two sons who are heroes."

"Cut it out mom, it's not the same thing."

Chad felt like she was patronizing him, and he didn't like it. His mother was genuine in her sentiment though, and wanted to prove her case further.

"Hey, you never know what that guy could've had in that room. He could've had a gun. That was very dangerous and very brave, and I'm just as proud of you as I am of him."

Though the things she was saying made sense, at the same time it made Chad's sense that she was just trying to make him feel better worse.

"You know, you look great. I'm glad to see you looking so good, like you're finally getting over that Gwen—"

"God mom, I don't need this."

"Need what?"

"This. You, here, saying I neglect the family, telling me I'm as much of a hero as Steve was, and now going on about Gwen. Yes, I was hurt by Gwen. Is that what you want to hear? Yes, seeing her in bed with Dave sucked, really bad. And yes, maybe I haven't quite gotten over it yet…"

He couldn't believe he'd said it. He felt tears welling up in his eyes. He couldn't let his mom see him cry though, and he certainly wasn't going to cry in this restaurant. Maybe it was the lingering fatigue from the weekend in Vegas that caused all of this to come out after his mother's prodding. For five years he knew he hadn't gotten over Gwen, but never said it to anyone. He hadn't gotten over Gwen. It took on a different hue when it wasn't something that only existed in his mind, when it was out there, in the ether, and he could see his mom reacting to it. His mom noticed all of this, and she reached across and took his hand. She quickly removed it though, when their waiter came to the table to refill their water glasses and ask if they needed anything. He realized when he got there that he wasn't wanted, and extricated himself from their situation with as little awkwardness as he could.

"I'm sorry honey. I know you went through a lot with Gwen. I guess I never understood just how much. I didn't mean to give you such a hard time…. You look really good now though. It looks like things are getting better for you. That's *good*. Listen, maybe when you come over on Friday, we can celebrate your birthday then. We can even pretend it's a surprise party to make your niece and nephew happy."

"Friday?"

"Yes, Friday Chad, it's Christmas."

Oh my God, Chad thought, how did I forget Christmas?

"You didn't forget Christmas, did you?"

"No—no no, not at all, it was just… you know, with all this stuff here going on with us…" She sighed.

"Leave it to you to forget Christmas, Chad."

Chad didn't hear from Krystel until a week after New year's. It was actually through Bianca, whom he literally bumped into at a New Year's Eve party he went to with Lars at the Dirty Sombrero, that Krystel entered his life again.

After talking for a few minutes, Bianca and Chad agreed that maybe they needed a night without the prospect of sex to get to know one another, and planned a date at Applebee's for the next Wednesday, Bianca's night off. Chad also had a soccer game that night, the first one for him in weeks, and it was pretty rough. A good portion of the team couldn't make it, meaning there weren't any subs. Chad, thinking his time on the elliptical made him prepared for this situation, found out that a few weeks of semi-regular cardio does not a 70-minute indoor soccer game make. Not to mention Miguel had him play out on the right wing, which he used to play in school, but hadn't done at all on this team. He kept losing his man on defense, and not hitting the crosses right on offense. The team lost, and he felt like a large part of it was his fault, even though Miguel blamed it on the people who couldn't make it.

That left him lethargic for his date with Bianca. It didn't matter, they didn't have much in common anyway, and found their time together to be pretty dull—plus, a woman from Chad's past had reentered his life, and she was all he could think about; more on her next chapter. For Bianca's part, she was more there to feel Chad out, see if he'd said anything to anyone. The embarrassment over what had happened, plus the fact that she felt that he perhaps had something on her, had already made her lose any potential romantic interest in Chad, even if he didn't know that. It didn't take long in their conversation for her to confirm that he hadn't told anyone about the bear suit, and she was mentally looking to end the night as soon as possible.

An interesting thing occurred though, while they were sitting in their Applebee's booth, picking at their nachos and struggling to make a conversation that Bianca didn't want to have. Marissa and another girl recognized Bianca, and came over to say hi.

"Chad, this is Marissa and Taylor. I went to high school with them."

"I know *him*. You were the nice one. Your friend Lars was a total ass."

"Hahaha, she met Lars?" Bianca said.

"Yeah, we were at the Golden Dragon."

"What, *you* know him?"

"Lars? Yeah, he comes to Elevens a lot."

The fact that Marissa was hanging out with a girl named Taylor wasn't lost on Chad, so he asked Marissa where Krystel was. There was a lot of eye rolling among the three girls. Chad decided to just come out with it. He told the story Krystel told, about the serial killer and her friend Taylor's murder. They all laughed. Chad wasn't sure if he should laugh too.

"So that never happened?"

"She fucked my boyfriend Antonio, so she hates *my* guts."

"Her baby's father?"

"Her what?"

They laughed again. This time Marissa talked.

"She's never had any kids."

"Did she and Antonio get their house raided by a SWAT team?"

More laughing. Chad couldn't believe this—or rather, he really could believe this. It seemed to fit Krystel even more than it would have had her stories been true. There was no SWAT team, no prison time, no baby she needed to regain custody of, no serial killer. Chad couldn't figure out if this made her more or less attractive to him. It was probably lingering images of her in her smart outfit.

Chad listened as Taylor and Marissa told story after story about what a horrible person Krystel was. Bianca didn't really know them that well, but from time to time she'd chime in with an anecdote. Krystel was a liar and a thief. Chad found out that the night they went out and Marissa kept texting, Krystel had stolen Marissa's necklace, and was confronting her about it. She'd learned her lesson, which was why she was hanging out with Taylor now.

Taylor had much worse to say about Krystel. Beyond the pattern of lying and stealing, there was also the matter of her having sex with Taylor's boyfriend, Antonio, whom Taylor was still with, and whom she also had had a child with. Chad telling her that Krystel told him that they were boyfriend and girlfriend and had a child infuriated her even more. Who does that bitch think she is? And then telling Chad she was killed by a serial killer because *she* was a slut? It was time to round up the girls and find her, this bitch needed to be taught a lesson.

"What about her father?" Chad said.

"Her father?"

"Yeah, she kept telling me she was going to go to Harvard Law, and that her father would make it happen."

This one they didn't find so funny.

"Her father is dead actually," Taylor said. "He killed himself when Krystel was young, just before he was supposed to go to trial for some fraud thing or something."

159

Chad didn't know what to say at this point. The girls were still upset though about the other things Chad told her, and they left in a huff, ready to confront her.

"Jesus Chad, it looks like you got yourself in the middle of something."

"God, I didn't mean to. I should probably warn Krystel."

"No, don't. I grew up with these girls—well not Krystel, Marissa and Taylor met her a few years ago. Anyway, they're always at each other about something, and then a week later they're best friends as if nothing ever happened. You don't need to get involved with all that."

Krystel wouldn't let him off that easy though, showing up at his office the next day. Chad was thoroughly embarrassed, seeing her in his doorway, dressed in a short black skirt and black boots and a black and blue striped halter top, confronting him about what he told Taylor.

"Why were you talking shit about me?"

"Jesus Christ Krystel, come in here and shut the door. You can't just show up here like this, this is my job."

She did as he asked, but was still indignant, standing in front of his desk, scowling with her arms folded.

"I don't give a fuck if this is your job or what, if you got something to say to me you need to say it to my face."

"What are you talking about? You told me Taylor was murdered by a serial killer."

"No I didn't. Why would I do that? She's alive."

"I have no idea why you'd do that, but you did it."

"No I didn't."

"The girls also told me your father is no longer with us."

"Hey, you better leave my father out of your mouth!"

She was getting increasingly belligerent, and all Chad could think of was Seijun seeing him with Krystel, looking and sounding like Krystel, and how that would reflect poorly on Chad. He didn't want that so desperately, that he lost some of the tact he might have had in handling a situation like Krystel's—not to mention that, again, that new woman in Chad's life was dominating his thoughts, and he was annoyed that Krystel was interrupting those thoughts.

"Listen, you can't be here doing this. I don't know if you've noticed, but you don't fit in this environment, and if my boss sees you, it'll make me look bad."

Some of the steam went out of her.

"What do you mean?"

"Look at you, you look trashy, you look ridiculous. And you're swearing at me about some wannabe ghetto bullshit about me talking trash about you because I was surprised a friend you said was dead was alive in front of me at Applebee's last night. This is ludicrous. We're not on *Maury*, this is the real world, and I don't have time for crap like this."

"Oh…"

Chad had again thrown Krystel a curve ball. Chad got the sense from the look on her face that she had mapped out this confrontation in her mind, and didn't see it going any differently than confrontations in the past. But Chad had made her feel self-conscious. He reminded her again that there was a world above her own, a world with Harvard Law and babies born through women's vaginas and humans as animals; and he reminded her that she was

160

substandard in that world, that that world looked down on her, laughed at her maybe. Were the people he worked with laughing at her right now? Her face went red. She tried one last perfunctory threat about how she better not hear about him talking shit about her anymore, but it was barely audible, and she was on the verge of tears. Before they could come, she bolted out of his office.

Seeing her like that, vulnerable, like she was before in her smart outfit, made Chad almost wish she could come back. He wanted to stop her, tell her he wanted to help, that he felt sorry about her losing her father. But he knew he dodged a bullet, that that scene could've been a lot worse. He'd never know the extent of what she'd told him was true or false, and why she told him so many lies, or even who she really was, but maybe some things were better off not knowing.

About four months later, while Chad was at a convenience store to get a six-pack, he passed a stack of that day's edition of the local newspaper without seeing it, and went to the counter to make his purchase. On the cover of the newspaper that he didn't see, was the picture of a young woman in a column on the right hand side. Her name was Noël Devón, an art student at Silverman-Moore, and the small headline above her picture read "Silverman-Moore Student Faces Expulsion for Art Project." Two patrons, one a man and one a woman, locals who frequented the store a lot and were waiting behind him to get their lottery tickets taken care of, remarked on the story.

"Did you see this? Yeah, they said this girl pretended to be someone else for three years for her art project."

"I saw that! Yeah, they said she would just say or do whatever random shit came into her head to see how people reacted. Like she said she was on a date and told the guy her friend got killed by a serial killer. It was some fucked up shit."

"Kids today are crazy!"

Chad stopped and turned to look at what they were talking about. He could see the picture in the newspaper. The young woman had short, dark hair, that was kind of spikey on top, like a feminine version of a masculine haircut. But then there were the eyes, he thought he recognized them, but he couldn't be sure…

"Can we help you buddy?"

This was a small town convenience store away from downtown, and Chad was neither recognized by the locals nor looked the part of their usual patrons. Instead of picking up a copy of the paper, or even trying to join their conversation, he apologized and, feeling self-conscious, got out of there as quickly as he could.

Vanessa, the Right Bus

Growing up, Christmas was full of fond memories. Chad's mother was always either on vacation from her job or school would be on break—or a combination of the two when she working as a paralegal while going to law school. She bought he and Steve tons of toys, took them out to eat at fun places, did all kinds of exciting activities with them. They'd make day trips to the aquarium or to see basketball and hockey games. It was like his Christmas day would last an entire week, as his mother made up for the lack of time she spent with her boys throughout the rest of the year.

Christmas in 2009 was his best one since those days as a child. After his mother reminded him that it was only a few days away, he went out that evening to Neiman Marcus and bought two $500 gift certificates each for Lars and Seijun, and when he couldn't think of anything else for his mother, he bought her one too. The woman waiting on him helped him pick out Hermès scarves for his receptionists, and luckily, the woman also had children, and told him the names of a few things Steve's kids might want.

For some reason, walking through the mall with his Neiman Marcus bags full of gifts, he didn't feel as antagonistic toward the holiday as he usually did. Yes, the kids were still loud and annoying, and yes, this was perhaps the 500th time he'd heard Mariah Carey's "All I Want for Christmas is You", and yes, this was all so commercialized, but it didn't all seem so God awful. He stopped at a sports memorabilia shop, seeing if maybe, by a slim chance, they had a soccer jersey for the team Miguel liked. Instead he saw, on clearance, a box of Major League Lacrosse trading cards. That might be cool to give to Steve Jr. But the soccer jersey for Miguel gave him an idea: he knew of a soccer specialty shop downtown. In the past he never went downtown between Thanksgiving and Christmas, but now that he worked down there—at a job he liked— the frantic shopping crowds and congested streets didn't frustrate him as much. He parked in his office's garage, and wandered around, first stopping at the soccer shop to get Miguel his jersey, then the hiking shop to get a gift certificate for Haley, and then he bought Steve and Sara a gift certificate to an Italian restaurant so they could have a night out together.

In all he spent another $3000 on gifts for everyone, but it was worth it, more for him than it was for the people receiving them. Instead of worrying about the money he spent, he did something he'd never done before: sat in a window seat at a café and watched the people outside as he drank his coffee. People were making him happy again. The couples, the kids, the elderly, the workers, the college students, the hipsters, the muscleheads, they were all okay with him. It felt good to be happy.

His mother was right, over the past five years he had become too disconnected from the people closest to him, and this was his first foot back in their direction. And it wasn't just the gifts, on Christmas he did his part in his mother's surprise party plan, and later played the Wii with everyone. The old Chad, Chad in Accounting, would've just been wanting to get this day over with so he could go home and watch TV; but now he lost track of time, was disappointed when Steve and Sara had to take the kids home, and looked forward to seeing them again, even offered to watch the kids when they used the gift certificate he gave them.

New Year's was more of a mixed bag compared to Christmas, but still more fun than he could remember a New Year's being. He and Lars started out at the Dirty Sombrero, which had an expensive cover charge that Lars had paid ahead of time. Something about the whole thing didn't feel as cool as it should've though, especially after Vegas. The jackasses and muscleheads combined with the girls in the same old tight jeans and halter tops were worn out to him. He saw Jared with the Hyphenated Last Name from HR, and could tell he was impressed with Chad's new look. Back when Chad was Chad in Accounting, this kind of approval would've meant the world to him, and right after leaving that insurance firm all he would've wanted was this moment, for Jared to see him now; but tonight, it just made him feel like he was too similar to Jared, almost as much of a jackass as he was.

Things picked up though, in the second part of Lars's New Year's celebration: an 80s themed party at the Blue Door. They even packed preppy clothes to change into after they left the Dirty Sombrero: pastel polos, khakis, loafers, and sweaters tied across their shoulders. This was more Chad's style. "Private Eyes" was playing instead of that Flo-Rida and whatever else the kids listened to—did he just think that, "what the kids listen to"?

It was there he bumped into Molly.

"I saw you when you came in. I tried calling to you but it's too loud in here. Love your outfit."

"Yeah, I love yours too."

She was dressed in a black leather skirt and top, with black nylons and ankle-high black boots. Her hair was frizzier and she had on tons of make-up.

"I was saying to Ursula when we were getting ready, how ironic it is that we look at pictures of ourselves from the 80s, and we're so embarrassed, yet we're going through all the trouble tonight so we can look like that again!"

She took his hand to take him further away from the bar, to an area that was less hectic so they could talk. He felt the engagement ring on her finger, and thought she was taking him to meet her doctor boyfriend, so he was surprised to find them off in a corner, alone together. Til Tuesday's "Voices Carry" was playing above them.

"Is your boyfriend here tonight?"

"My fiancé? No, he went hiking, of all things."

"In the Governor's Range?"

"Yes… sorry, are you a hiker? No offense, it's just not my thing. The last thing I want to be doing on New Year's Eve is freezing in a tent on a mountain, but that's just me."

"No no, I'm with you there, it's not my thing either; no, my friend was telling me she was doing that too. She wants to do some big one in Alaska."

"Mt. McKinley—or Denali, the *real* hikers call it Denali. Oh yes, she must be on the same trip as Dave is—Dave's my fiancé's name, I don't remember if I told you. Yes, he loves hiking, and Denali is his big dream, and after that, Everest. I went with him up Birnbaum a couple years ago, like after we'd only been dating a few months. What a disaster."

164

"Oh, don't I know it. I just did Birnbaum back in October with that friend. I don't think I've ever been so stiff!"

She looked at him and bit her bottom lip.

"Ever?..."

The symmetry of the situation, that he was going to have sex with a woman who was engaged to a man named Dave, wasn't lost on Chad. At the Blue Door though, it didn't matter, as they were slow dancing to "Heaven" by Bryan Adams, or she was sitting on his lap, playing with his hair, and they were making out. Later though, back at her place, in their bed, with all the pictures of Molly and Dave surrounding them, it felt worse. The sex they had was awkward. Unlike Tiffany, who did all the work and made it a non-issue that Chad was so rusty, Molly was hoping he'd take the lead, and his rhythm was a little off as he still hadn't quite hit the elliptical enough to have the cardio to sustain his end. Molly, used to her hiker and his fitness level, wasn't expecting this. Then she went on top, but didn't quite feel up to it either; but by then they both were committed to making this happen, so they soldiered on, slept, and had an awkward goodbye in the morning.

Chad was alarmed to find himself tagged by Lars on Facebook in a ton of pictures from New Year's of him and Molly. He called him and explained the situation, that Haley knew her fiancé and might see these pictures, and Lars, considering they weren't pictures of him anyway, was happy to take them down. Chad liked looking at the rest of them though, and he reposted the best ones onto his own wall so everyone could see how great he looked.

A couple hours later he saw a notification in his inbox that Vanessa had commented. Vanessa? High School Vanessa? He didn't even remember having her as a friend. She commented on multiple photos, usually nothing more than an LOL or LMAO, but there were also a couple "you guys look great" or "you clean up well Chad"s that piqued his interest. He responded below with a thank you and a how have you been, expecting nothing more than something perfunctory in return.

What he got was a message telling him what she'd been up to the past 15 years since high school. She had an 11-year-old daughter, worked in a daycare, and she was single. Chad went through her photo albums. She was a little bigger, but not much, and those boobs were as prodigious as ever. Her daughter was a little olive-skinned thing with black hair that fell over her face. A lot of the pictures were of her playing soccer in the local youth league. When Chad replied, filling her in with a very white-washed Cliff's Notes version of his life, he remarked on Vanessa's daughter's interest in soccer.

They traded a couple more messages before Chad asked if she was free on Friday. He didn't want to wait until Friday, but he'd made plans with Bianca on New Year's for Wednesday, and Haley wanted to see him on Thursday. The high school lust for Vanessa had come back. Part of it was the unfulfilled night with Molly, but then there were all of Vanessa's pictures on Facebook. One album was of her at a bachelorette party, in a low-cut tight black dress that he couldn't stop looking at. Then there was a Halloween one, where she went as a cowgirl in a tight button-up shirt with the top couple buttons undone.

And that lust infected his thoughts the way it did back then. The soccer game on Wednesday when he was forced to play out of position, the whole time he was out with Bianca, it was Vanessa's Facebook photos, even when Marissa and Taylor were telling him about how much of what Krystel had told him was untrue, all he could see was that cowgirl or bachelorette party. Then the next day, when Krystel stormed in on him, he was on Facebook looking at those photos again, and that was why he was so short with Krystel for barging in on him.

Haley recognized something wasn't right with him when she saw him on Thursday for lunch at Applebee's, but accepted his explanation that he was just tired from catching up work that had fallen behind during the holidays. She gave him her gift, an Aztec brown-colored shirt with the silhouette of a moose in a tannish color with the words "Moore's Location" written above it and "Pop. 302" written below it in the same tannish color.

"I got it at a gift shop at a town near where we staged our other car. The 'Moore' is the same 'Moore' that Silverman-Moore got its name from, but I thought you might like it anyway."

"No, this is really cool, thank you!"

He gave her a card with the gift certificate in it, and was glad after she told him how happy she was that he gave her that, that she then told him about her hike, less because he was interested, and more because he didn't feel like holding up his end of the conversation with Vanessa's boobs on his brain.

"It was great. One of the nights there were winds that were like 90 MPH."

"Wow!"

"Yeah, I thought the tent was going to blow away with us in it! It was a great experience, and the guys all agreed that I'll be able to hold up my end when we go out to Denali."

The hikers all call it Denali... he'd forgotten about the connection between Haley and Molly's fiancé, and now it made him uncomfortable.

"They were saying too that because I'm a woman, and because I'm doing it for a cause—for Mariah—that we should be able to get more money from sponsors and whatnot. One of the guys works for North Face's corporate offices, and he thinks he'll be able to get some of our gear comped."

"Wow, that's great. It must be so exciting."

"It is, I can't wait."

She took a sip from her drink, then became excited and grabbed his arm.

"Oh, you'll appreciate this. So Dave, one of the guys we were hiking with—he's a doctor— apparently while he was with us over New Year's, his wife had sex with another man."

Chad coughed on his nachos and went for his his water.

"You okay?"

He's was able to muster that he was fine, that he'd just eaten a jalapeno and swallowed it wrong. He took a big sip, bypassing the straw, wiped his eyes, and told her to continue her story.

"Well, here's the crazy thing, she confronted him after he got out of the shower when he got home after the hike, when all he wanted to do was just lie down and relax. She tells him she can't go through with their marriage, that they don't have enough in common, and that she's found someone else, a Capricorn, and they're more compatible."

"What?"

"I know, how horrible. Who does that?"

"Wow. Well, are they going to work it out?"

166

"What is there to work out? She wants to leave him. He's pretty broken up about it. I thought maybe you and I could hang out with him one night, since we both know what he's going through."

What! Jesus Chad, what the hell have you gotten yourself into? He thought it strange that Molly remembered when his birthday was when they were at the Blue Door, but women seem to be better with dates than men, so he didn't place too much stock in it; besides, their sex was so bad that night, he thought he'd blown it. He was a Capricorn? Did that really mean more than bad sex? What should he do, should he call her? Tell her the truth, tell her about Vanessa, tell her he isn't even really a Capricorn?

"Hello, Earth to Chad, do you want more another water?"

"Oh, sorry... yes, and maybe we should get the check too."

A few months before, he and Miguel were watching a soccer game on TV, and the announcer said that "goals in the Serie A are like city buses: you wait all day for one, and then two or three come in quick succession." Now it was women who were the city buses, after going over two years without one, he had Haley, Molly, and Vanessa, all potential girlfriends, but none actual girlfriends yet, and he wasn't sure which one he wanted. All night Thursday and all day Friday he thought about this, how Haley sounded more interested in him while they were out for lunch, how Molly looked like she was going to dump her boyfriend for him, but he always went back to Vanessa and those Facebook photos. If she looked half as good tonight his choice would be easy.

She looked better than half as good. Maybe not bachelorette party good, but close enough. She had on a tight black dress with a tight green cardigan sweater that covered her arms and closed right underneath her breasts, and black tights and black boots that blended seamlessly on her legs. Her hair was chestnut-colored, a little darker than he remembered, and it was back off her face in a short ponytail, revealing all the features he remembered: the dark eyes, the pronounced but not too pronounced nose, and that small mouth with big lips, which she'd painted a dark burgundy. The way that whole face lit up when she saw him on the other side of her door, the enthusiasm with which she hugged him, pressed those boobs against his chest, gave him pause, made the air struggle to make it up his esophagus and through his mouth.

"Oh my God, how are you?"

"I'm good," he croaked, then cleared his throat and repeated it, which made them both laugh. They were apart, but still in each other's arms, examining, looking for signs of age but finding more familiarity.

"Wow, you look great, Chad."

"So do you Vanessa."

"You're a bad liar. I need to lose like 20 pounds."

"No, you don't. You really look great."

She blushed, looked away, then looked back and saw that Chad was serious. Chad was too turned on by her for dissimulation. It made them both feel like high schoolers again. Instead of inviting him in, she bounded through the door and took him by the arm.

"Come on, we don't want to be late for our reservation."

Chad took her to the same Italian restaurant he'd bought the gift certificate to for Steve and Sara.

"Wow, this place looks nice. I've always wanted to go here."

"Yeah, me too, and Olive Garden is always so packed on Fridays, plus this stuff is probably better than that anyway."

"Oh I know... I'm just so happy to see you again. How long has it been? Since graduation?"

"I think so... time flies, doesn't it?"

"What can I get you two to drink?"

"What do you like for wine, Vanessa?"

"Geez, I don't know. Pinot, something like that. Do they have that?"

"Let's try this Chianti. It should be close."

"That sounds great. And can I get a Diet Coke too?"

"Yep. And for you, sir?"

"Just a water with lemon."

Vanessa put her elbows on the table and rested her chin on her hands, staring across at Chad. Usually a man spending this much money on a first date would be expecting something from her at the end of the night, and usually this would be the point that she'd see the writing on the wall and draft excuses in her head while the guy bragged about his job or what toys he had or the places he'd traveled to; but all of those past guys were fugazi. Chad looked like the real deal, ordering wine, dressed in 7 for all Mankind jeans, and not speaking in constant double negatives or using "fucking" as his go to adjective. It made her nervous though, because she did use double negatives, and she did swear a little more than she should, and they didn't make 7's in her size, and she barely knew how to order wine. She was afraid that she was the one who was fugazi, and that whatever he saw in her he'd discover wasn't there, and he'd be drafting his own excuses to get rid of her at the end of the night.

Chad enjoyed her staring at him. They hadn't even ordered their food yet, but Chad felt like he'd gotten on the right bus. He thought it might freak her out to tell her that though, so he restarted the conversation.

"So did you go to the reunion?"

"I did. You didn't hear what happened?"

"What happened? No, what happened?"

"Oh geez, I figured everyone in our class knew."

"I don't talk to anyone in our class anymore."

"Not even Dave and Kovacs?"

"...That's a long story. Why don't you tell me what happened first, then we'll get to Dave and Kovacs."

Their wine came, and they put in their food orders. After they'd each had a glass poured, Vanessa started her story.

"You remember Toby, right?"

"Oh yeah, didn't he become rich with some Internet start-up?"

She rolled her eyes.

"Yes. Anyway, he always had a thing for me in high school. I barely knew about it, because he was such a geek, and he never said anything really—plus, I had my own issues with guys, you know?"

168

"You mean you and Bobby? I used to see him at Dodge State, he was on the football team. I don't know what he's doing now."

"And I don't care either, he was an ass... Anyway, back to the reunion. Toby shows up in a limo, and proposes to me, *in front of everybody!*" Chad's mouth popped open. "I know, right? I was so embarrassed! And he wouldn't leave me alone either. He's all telling me how he'd take care of me and Edie, how no one cares about me like he does, and I'm like close to losing it, you know? I kind of freaked out on him, and some of the other girls took me to the bathroom—with a margarita, which was good—and I stayed there until he left. I guess it was Kovacs who finally got him to leave. They said he literally carried him out. Kovacs was always a good guy, huh?"

"Yeah, that's Kovacs for you... I had no idea Toby was so obsessed with you. I mean, I'm not saying it's hard to fathom, because you were hot in high school."

"Cut it out! You're making me blush! I wasn't that hot, geez."

"You were that hot..." He was about to tell her, without even thinking about it, how much he was obsessed with her too, how much he lusted after her in Chemistry.

"And...?"

"And what?"

"You were going to say something after that. 'You were that hot' and...?"

"Um, no... I was just going to say how... in Chemistry... I remember you looked pretty hot... and I thought Bobby was a lucky guy to have you."

She cocked her head to one side.

"Aww, that's so sweet of you to say. Why didn't you tell me that back then?"

"Because you were with Bobby."

"Not right away I wasn't. I only made him be my partner in class so I wouldn't have to be Toby's. We didn't start dating until after Christmas."

"You didn't want to be Toby's partner? I can see that. He was pretty creepy."

"Oh my God! He was always trying to do all my work for me, and I was like leave me alone, I'll do it! God... you know he gave me this big letter at the end of our senior year, and listed off all these times I broke his heart and whatever, like how he'd give me a Valentine's card or flowers or something and then find them in the trash—shit I don't even remember. He went into this big thing about how at our winter formal sophomore year, I told him I'd dance with him, then went to the bathroom and never came out, while he waited for two hours. First off, what kind of moron waits two hours for someone? I mean, if he's so fucking smart—oops, sorry—if he's so frickin' smart, you think he'd get the hint. And the other thing is, I remember that night, and he was the last thing I was worried about. Parker Pruitt and I had just broken up, and he was there with Lucy—God I hated her. I caught them making out, and all I wanted to do was get the hell out of there, so I went to the bathroom with some friends and left after that. I don't even remember Toby asking me, I was so upset."

"*You* dated *Parker Pruitt?*"

"*What?* He was cute... whatever..."

She smiled and took a sip of her wine. She was feeling it a little bit, but it was a nervous affectation to go back to her drink. She couldn't see that Chad was drinking almost as much as she was, and was thinking he needed to slow down too if he wanted to drive her home.

"If it makes you feel any better, Toby didn't wait for two hours for you."

"Oh yeah?"

"Yeah, I remember that night too, and Kovacs gave him a massive wedgie and he ran out after that. I don't know how long it was after he asked you to dance, but it couldn't have been two hours."

Vanessa let out a really loud laugh, then caught herself and chuckled a little more softly.

"That's so awesome. I love Kovacs."

"Oh yeah, that Kovacs, he's a one of a kind," wanting to change the subject off of Kovacs he continued: "have you heard from Toby?"

"Once since the reunion, a couple days later. He sent me this long letter essentially about how he'd worship me, how he'd always be there and always tell me I'm beautiful and all this gross crap. He sounded more obsessed with me than anything; it felt like a bad Romantic Comedy, only I wasn't having it."

"So what did you do?"

"Nothing, and luckily, that was the last of it. I don't know if he'll be at the reunion this summer. I hope not. Ugh, love without consent is disgusting..."

"What?"

"Love without consent is disgusting. It's not fair to the person being loved to have someone obsessing over them that doesn't even know it, and has their own life and problems and stuff... I don't know, does that make sense?..."

"Yes. 'Love without consent is disgusting', I'll drink to that."

Chad had always felt guilty about his role in that winter formal wedgie. He and Dave were called in to distract Toby while Kovacs snuck up behind him. Toby's face turned bright red and his eyes teared up. Chad saw him there, in his dress shirt that was a few sizes too large, his hair that was slicked down over the left side and curled in the back, staring at the doorway, drinking his drink, leaning against a pole. When Dave and Chad approached him, he kept looking around them to see the door, but was genuinely excited that they were talking to him, only to find out it was only a ruse, as Kovacs grabbed him by his tighty-whities, lifting him until the band broke, then pulling the band around Toby's neck, yelling "Now it's a necklace! Now it's a necklace!" Discovering the other end of that incident, that Toby had been obsessed with Vanessa when she didn't want him, and that he tried to marry her almost five years ago, which would've meant that Chad wouldn't be here right now, sitting across from Vanessa and those boobs and that cute laugh and those sexy lips, made him less guilty and more proud, as if Toby got what he deserved.

Their food came, and after a few bites, Vanessa restarted the conversation:

"So what's the deal with you and Kovacs and Dave? What's this long story? You guys were like inseparable in high school."

"Well, I guess it's not that long of a story. I met this girl Gwen when I got out of college. We dated for like four years, and she was the love of my life. Then one day I came home and found her in bed with Dave."

"What?... Oh my God! She wasn't... the one he was with at..."

"Oh yeah, they're married with two kids."

"Oh my God Chad, I'm so sorry."

"It's all right, it was five years ago, I'm over it now."

"Jesus... well, if it makes you feel any better, you look a lot better than he does. It's her loss... I'm sorry, was that a bad thing to say?"

"No, of course not."

With boobs like those, nothing you could ever say would be bad. It was because of those boobs that he could finally, for the first time in over five years, say truthfully "I'm over it now." With those boobs resting across from him, Gwen was a million miles away and a million years ago.

While Vanessa was in the bathroom, Chad checked his phone. Seijun had texted to invite him to Noriko's friend's art exhibit for its last night. As they gathered their things and he paid the bill, he mentioned it to her, and she was so excited that he hadn't been drafting his escape plan in his head, that she said she'd love to go.

"It's that female empowerment thing with the mannequins, right? It was on the news the other day. I really wanted to see that.... You know, I saw some movie from the 80s on TV the other day that had Samantha from *Sex and the City* and she was like a mannequin or something. It was really odd."

"You mean *Mannequin*?"

They were walking out to his car.

"I guess."

"No, that's what it is, *Mannequin*. It was kind of a big deal. Kim Cattrall, Andrew McCarthy. It had the big song by Starship, remember that? *Nothin's gonna stop us noooow...*"

"Oh yeah, I know that song, I used to love that when I was growing up."

"You don't remember the video?"

"I didn't have cable, my parents were too strict."

"Was that why we used to hang out at my house all the time?"

"Well, that... and because your mom worked late..."

She gave him the smile that let him know that she wanted what he wanted. She didn't know he wanted it, had no idea what Chad was thinking, because when he saw that smile, his body shut down for a second. He was wishing he hadn't suggested going to the art exhibit, wishing they could just go back to his place and he could get his hands on those boobs and everything else; but luckily for him he didn't suggest that, because Vanessa, not knowing he wanted what she wanted, would've thought he was drafting his escape plan, that her smile had been too much and turned him off.

At the exhibit, they walked close together, arm-in-arm, bumping and touching one another constantly, joking about the various scenes depicted by the mannequins. It was a completely different experience from when he took Krystel there a month or so before. With Krystel he and her were almost standoffish, while he and Vanessa felt like old friends—except none of Chad's old friends made him lose his mind the way Vanessa could with her boobs, and now the promise that he'd get to have them at the end of the night.

"I kind of like the cheerleader tied to the stake. Remember when I was a cheerleader?"

"Oh yeah, that's right, you were a cheerleader."

"Um hmm." She crossed her wrists over her head and leaned against the wall. "Would you have saved me back then?"

Oh God, Chad thought. What do I say to that?

"Yes!... I mean, yes, of course I'd save you..."

You moron! "Yes!"? Jesus, what's wrong with you? But she's giggling and taking you by the arm again. God, how much more can I take?

The cheerleading thing might have been the last straw. Visions of pep rallies and Vanessa bouncing up and down, and those boobs in that cheerleader sweater bouncing up and down, and time standing still for Chad, as his teenage body writhed in an inner sea of chaos, while his face stared at her with a blank expression, making Dave and Kovacs think he's baked and holding out on them by not sharing. He was falling into that zone again, a place he hadn't been since high school. He barely remarked in his head that Vanessa took for granted that babies came from a mother's uterus as they passed that exhibit, barely remembered Krystel and her smart outfit.

"What's this one here?"

Vanessa took him by the hand over to a female mannequin dressed like a cowboy kissing a female mannequin dressed like a housewife from the 60s. The description talked about Paula Cole's "Where Have All the Cowboys Gone", and whether or not a woman's identity was tied to the identity of what the ideal man is.

"You know, I dated a woman once."

"You did?"

He spotted Seijun and everyone else and led Vanessa in their direction.

"Yeah, way back when I was in my mid-20s. Edie was barely a toddler then. Her dad was nowhere around, and I was fed up with guys, and I was working as a waitress in this restaurant, and one of the cooks was this lesbian chick."

"Oh, was she one of those butch kinds?"

She giggled.

"Yes, though she wasn't like really fat or with a buzzcut or anything. She had all these cool toys—um, I don't mean like *toys* toys, but like she had a motorcycle and a boat and jet skis and a house on the lake—anyway..."

"Anyway..."

Chad liked this banter about her lesbian relationship, because it was easy for him to keep up with in his diminished mental state.

"Anyway, she was like really controlling, like always trying to tell me what to do, how to live my life, even how to raise my daughter. I was like fuck that, you're worse than most guys I know, you know?"

"I've heard that about lesbians, that they can be very controlling."

"Cut it out, not all lesbians, just her... besides, I'm not a lesbian anyway, I like guys too much..."

"That's good, it's a lot nicer having you on our team."

He introduced her to Seijun, Noriko, Justine, and Justine's husband, and then mentally checked out as Vanessa talked to them about her time in high school as a cheerleader and how interesting the scene of the cheerleader being burned at the stake was. He couldn't stop looking her up and down, from her boots and her legs, to her butt and her back and her boobs and her neck and that cute mouth with that cute giggle and those dark eyes and chestnut colored hair pinned back against her head. Seijun, Noriko, and Justine, remembering Chad had a different girl with him the last time, took his demeanor as a sign that this was a first date, and he wasn't impressed with Vanessa, that he just wanted to get the date over and done with. Vanessa wasn't sure what to make of Chad now either. Was he embarrassed to be with her in front these people? Was she not smart or sophisticated enough? They were having such a good time too, why was he so despondent now? Maybe Chad *was* too good to be true.

But then he went back to wanting her hand and walking close to her as they went out to the car. He was still kind of quiet, but it was cold and windy out, so they couldn't really carry on a conversation anyway. Chad was ready to cash in that smile from earlier at the nearest ticket window, and that's all he was thinking about. He had no idea how he had been read by Vanessa five minutes before.

"So, what should we do now? You wanna watch a movie or something?"

"Watch a movie?"

"Or something, I don't know. Do you have to be up in the morning?"

Ten minutes ago he's embarrassed to be seen with me, and now he wants a nightcap? Who does he think I am? On the other hand, I was kind of banking on that nightcap too…. All right, let's see what he does if I suggest going to his house.

"Um no, I don't have to be up early. You wanna go to your place though? Mine's a mess. I didn't get a chance to clean too much this week. Plus yours is closer."

"Yeah sure, that's fine."

Okay, so he doesn't have a girlfriend he's keeping me from. Does he think I'm an easy lay though? Not good enough to be his girlfriend, but good enough to fuck? Do I care? Yes, I care, I don't want to be used…

"So, did you have a good time with me tonight, Chad?"

"Yeah, I had a great time. How about you? Did you have a good time?"

"I did, it's been really fun… do you think your boss liked me?"

"Of course. You're very outgoing. You were able to just jump right in there and talk to them, which is something he likes."

"You weren't embarrassed about me?"

"Embarrassed?"

Jesus Christ, he didn't want to be having *this* conversation now. He wanted to be back at his place, having lots of sex with Vanessa. He didn't have the brain capacity to blow sunshine up her ass.

"Yeah, you were just kind of acting weird when we went over to see all of them. I don't know…"

"I don't know either. I don't know what you're talking about."

"You sure? I mean, it's okay if you were, I just want you to be honest before we…"

Chad had no clue where any of this was coming from. Women made zero sense to him, and apparently Vanessa was no exception. He was the happiest he'd been in a long time with her tonight, and she's sitting next to him in the car telling him how she thinks he's embarrassed by her? That's it, "happiest I've been in a while", I'll say that, and hopefully end this conversation.

"Vanessa, I'm the happiest with you tonight that I've been in a long time."

"You mean that?"

"Yes, I wouldn't say it if I didn't mean it."

"Okay, good."

He looked over and saw in her face that she believed him. Thank God. Then he looked down and saw the seatbelt across her breasts, making them even more pronounced. Please God don't make me have to work anymore for these. I need them now, and everything else. I'm tired of working.

"Jesus Chad, look out!"

He swerved the car, just missing a guy who pulled out in front of him.

There were noises coming from Chad's apartment as they approached. The TV was on. Did he forget to turn it off? He's never done that before.

"Is your roommate home?"

"I don't have a roommate."

Vanessa looked worried. Chad put his finger to his lips and motioned her to stand away from the door. It wasn't locked, so he opened it slowly and peered in. Amy was asleep on his couch, wearing a red dress, watching *Teen Mom* on MTV. Chad let Vanessa know everything was all right.

"Amy, what are you doing here?"

She saw Vanessa and jumped up and gathered her shoes lying on the floor beneath her. She hadn't planned on him bringing a girl home, and wanted to leave as fast as she could.

"Um, my mom had some dude over, and I just didn't want to be there. I know you keep the spare at Miguel's, so I had Dick get it for me for a sec. I'm really sorry, I shouldn't have done that."

"It's all right. Is it okay to go back? You can stay if you need to."

It hurt his soul to tell her that, knowing if she took him up on his offer he wouldn't get to have Vanessa. He turned to Vanessa, who was so hot standing there with the concerned look on her face.

"No no, I bet he's gone now, or they're done doing what they're doing. I'll leave you two alone. Bye, and nice meeting you."

She walked out the door, and Chad raced behind her to make sure she was all right, and she assured him he didn't need to worry.

"Wow, I wasn't expecting that."

"Who is she?"

"Amy, a girl from down the hall. Her mom is kind of neglectful of her, but she's a really nice girl. Usually my friend Miguel, who lives right across from me with his wife and son, take care of her, or she stays at her friend Brittney's. This is the first time she's ever done this though."

A smile formed on Vanessa's lips.

"I think she likes you."

"What? I don't know, she's 15. She probably thinks I'm an old man."

"15-year-olds always have crushes on older guys. I know I had my share. At 15, you don't consider that 30-year-olds who date teenagers are creepy. I think it's kind of cute. It looks like she even dressed up for you, with all the make-up she had on, and that red dress."

"Oh that doesn't mean anything, she and her friend are always dressing up to make YouTube videos."

Vanessa was still smiling, and she shook her head.

"So, I imagine that kind of killed the mood, huh?"

Please, please say it didn't, please...

174

She put her hands behind her back, making her chest stand out even more, almost thrusting itself in his direction like a 3D movie.

"No, not at all."

Yes yes yes!

He reached down and took her by the face with his hands and kissed her. She reciprocated by grabbing him passionately by the neck, returning his kisses, and lifting herself off the ground to meet his face. He part carried part walked with her into his bedroom, where they took off their clothes and each other's while trying to maintain their level of intimacy. There she was, with no shirt on, those boobs two perfect spheres in her black bra. Maybe she was a little chunkier than the girls he'd been with, but he wanted those curves right then more than he'd wanted anything else. But then she unhooked that bra, and those boobs he'd lusted after the entire night—and a good portion of his high school years—fell out, looking more like sagging water balloons than the perfect spheres that had been held in place by Victoria's Secret just moments before. He almost asked her to but it back on. She pushed him on the bed and turned out the light in his room, so all he had was his sense of touch, and his hands told him that they were the same boobs, and that the rest of her was the same rest of her.

The next morning he woke up to her lying on his chest. She looked so peaceful, sleeping, breathing out of her cute little mouth, her chestnut hair partially covering her eyes. He brushed it away and kissed her on the forehead, which caused her to stir, look up at him, smile, and fall back to sleep, looking more peaceful than before.

After another hour he extricated himself out from under her, threw on a pair of gym shorts and a T-shirt, and started making them breakfast. About fifteen minutes later, he heard movement in his room, then Vanessa making a stop at his bathroom. She joined him in the kitchen with her hair back in a ponytail, wearing one of his Abercrombie button-up shirts, through which he could see her black bra and panties.

"Ooh, whatcha making?"

"Pancakes, you want some? I made coffee too."

"Wow, I'm not used to this. Usually I have to do all the cooking."

"Well, when I spend the night at your place, you can cook me breakfast, how's that?"

"Deal." She took a sip from her coffee. "I hope you don't mind, I borrowed one of your shirts."

"No, not at all. It looks better on you than it does on me."

Chad couldn't believe how hot she looked, leaning against his counter, drinking her coffee in his shirt, which barely covered her legs above the thigh, and had the top three buttons undone, showing off her cleavage. This had to be what people talked about, about finding the one you were meant to be with. He had forced it with Gwen, he saw that now, because he tried to convince himself she made him feel like this, but she never did. Or was he trying to convince himself now? Had he just been single so long he was desperate? But she really did look hot. Gwen never wore his shirts, never had those boobs, never felt that nice lying on him—in fact, she made him uncomfortable when she was lying on him, but he always though that's just how that was. Now he knew that was wrong, that a girl could lie on you and and make you feel even more comfortable than sleeping alone. But he couldn't screw this up, couldn't get too involved too soon like he did with Gwen. He needed to take it slow.

Vanessa came up behind him as he tended the pancakes, put her arms around him, and rested her head between his shoulder blades. Even though she knew she looked hot in his shirt, she thought her face was a mess. She considered getting her make-up from her purse after she woke up, but when she smelled the coffee in the kitchen, she decided she'd rather him see her looking like a crack head than delay her caffeine fix. But he surprised her. He looked at her leaning against his counter, drinking her coffee, in his shirt, and it was obvious that he wasn't embarrassed to be with her. She couldn't remember a guy looking at her like that the morning after. The night before, yes, but never the morning after. She couldn't remember anything other than her daughter ever making her put down her first cup of coffee in the morning before she was done with it either, but that's what she did, after he turned back to the stove, and she put down her coffee and walked over and put her arms around him.

A few weeks later, on another Saturday morning, while lying in Vanessa's bed with her on top of him, he received a text message. It was from Dave. What could this be? He hoped it wasn't some patronizing message about how happy he was that Chad was seeing someone—he and Vanessa had made their budding relationship official on Facebook a couple days before. For so long his sole purpose in changing his relationship status on Facebook had been so Gwen could see it, and it was ironic that when he finally had the opportunity, Gwen was so far from his thoughts that it didn't matter anymore, all that mattered was Vanessa. He opened the text:

"Hey man, kovacs died in a car crash last night. Call me."

What? Kovacs, dead? It wasn't official in a text, so he called.

"Yeah man, Mandy called me about twenty minutes ago. He was coming home from a bar or something, supposedly drunk, and he hit a tree."

"Oh God."

"Yeah, I guess it was quite a mess. They think he was going like 75 in a 30. He wasn't even supposed to be driving, he'd lost his license… I know this is a lot to take early in the morning like this…"

"No no, I'm glad you contacted me. I imagine they don't know when the funeral is yet."

"No, I guess he has to have a toxicology report done and whatnot. I don't know if that shit takes time or what. I'm sure Mandy will let us know. She wants us to be pallbearers."

"Okay."

"Okay… I'm going to let you go, I'll talk to you later."

"All right man, later."

"Who was that?"

"Dave… he just told me Kovacs died in a car accident last night…"

Vanessa jumped up to her knees on the bed, which caused the blanket to fall off her, showing her nude body.

"Oh my God, Chad, I'm so sorry."

She put her arms around him, leaning to down because he was sitting with his back against the headrest. Her bare breasts were pressed into his face. Other than the brief spell when he was living with him recently, Kovacs had been out of his life for too long for the sting of his sudden death to be real yet. What was real was Vanessa and her boobs, her flesh against his body. She didn't know that, in her mind Kovacs and Dave meant to Chad what they meant to

176

him in high school, and she wanted to be there for him. Chad could've enjoyed her kind of sympathy all day, but he heard her sniffling above him. He rose to his knees too, the blanket still covering the lower half of his body somehow, and held her at arm's length. She looked away under his gaze, wiping the tears from her eyes.

"I'm sorry, I just know how much he meant to you."

"No, it's okay…"

He pulled her to him and guided her down with him so they were lying together again, her naked body over top of him and the blankets, crying on his chest until she fell back to sleep. It made Chad feel a little guilty. Shouldn't he be as heartbroken? At one time Kovacs was one of his best friends. He sat there for an hour, trying to make himself feel sad while Vanessa slept on him, making him feel great, and as a result, guiltier.

The funeral was that Thursday, and all the days leading up to it were phone calls and emails and Facebook messages, offering condolences, or from mutual friends and fellow fraternity brothers from college seeing if he wanted to talk. All of it made him awkward, because he couldn't feel this loss enough, at least enough to equal the amount of support he was getting from everyone. That awkwardness translated into taciturnity, which everyone read as him being upset and not wanting to talk about it.

Vanessa now understood how he felt though. Earlier in the week she treated him delicately like everyone else, afraid how his mood would be, and not sure if his enthusiasm to still see her was a front to hide his sorrow; but when he invited her and Edie to watch him play in his soccer team's championship game, and she sat in the small section of bleachers before the game started while Chad and his team played with Edie and showed her some soccer moves, and saw how genuinely happy he was to be doing that, it all clicked. She hadn't listened enough during their first date, when Chad told her that Dave slept with his longtime girlfriend, and that was why he wasn't at the reunion. Dave and Kovacs had turned their backs on Chad, they had all grown apart, they weren't the Three Musketeers—or Three Stooges—they were in high school. After dating him for three weeks, she finally saw Chad as a 33-year-old man, not the 13-year-old whose house she used to go over to after school so she could make out with him because his mother wasn't home.

She would be turning 33 too next week, but Chad had made her feel more like she was in high school again. For so long she had only been excited about life vicariously through Edie, and now when she had something of her own to be excited about, she was selfishly hoping this Kovacs situation wouldn't put a damper on that. Chad reminded her though, as he was showing Edie how to volley the soccer ball, that they weren't in high school anymore, they were two adults who met again on Facebook as if it were a dating site, and the one thing they had in common was that they knew each other as kids. She really didn't know him as well as she thought, and she realized that he didn't know her as well as she thought either. Or maybe they knew each other better now after almost fifteen years of living two separate lives without knowing one another. Maybe he didn't want this Kovacs thing to put a damper on what they were building either. As long as he never stopped looking at her the way he did when she was in his kitchen in his shirt.

When Chad got there the next day, Vanessa was still getting ready.

"I'm sorry, I'm kind of a mess today. You look nice."

"Thank you. You do too. I like that dress."

It wasn't quite the black dress from the bachelorette party pictures, a little more modest, but it still hugged her curves the way so many of her clothes did, which drove him wild.

"I just want to look good, because I have a feeling a lot of people from high school will be there."

She was standing with her face close to the mirror, applying eyeliner. It was one of the many things about being in a relationship that Chad missed—watching a woman get ready—that he didn't know how much he missed until he was with Vanessa. The fact that he had a woman—his woman—to take to something like this was another. Someone's hand to hold, someone to be attached to, to belong to, a pair to be a part of.

Vanessa stopped for a second and turned to him. He was looking at her like that again. She looked at her phone. 9:30.

"What time do we have to be there?"

"The service starts at 11. I should be there a little before that."

"So we have like an hour? That's plenty of time."

"For what?... oh, yes, we have time for that..."

They didn't quite make it on time, but fortunately his mother and Steve were there in one of the back pews, and he and Vanessa were able to sneak in next to them. He saw Gwen and Dave closer to the front, in another pew, with some of his fraternity brothers and their significant others.

Mandy gave a short word on Kovacs, referred to him as Jeremy mostly, talking about what a bright, charismatic person he was. This was the one moment when it struck Chad that this was real, Kovacs had really died. It was as if someone as larger than life as Kovacs couldn't ever really be killed by anything, but here he was in a casket, the same person who stayed at Chad's apartment only a few months before and took him to the Dirty Sombrero and told everyone stories about college and high school, who came home and made too much noise at 2AM, played some silly radio show called *The Nineties Café*, and smashed Chad's coffee table after getting into a fight with him. All of these memories were too much all at once. He wanted to be alone, away from this scene, away from his mother and brother and Gwen and Dave and Mandy talking about all the great things Kovacs did in a tone that was more reprimanding than memorializing, as if she was scolding him for dying like this and leaving her alone; and most of all, he wanted to be away from Vanessa. Her presence next to him made him uncomfortable as he was overcome with this wave of emotion. But then he looked down and saw her legs crossed next to him, remembered watching her put those black tights on those legs after they had sex. Were those the same tights she had me use to tie her to her bedpost last weekend? Now she was as real as the realness of Kovacs's death, and he let her take his hand as the urge to cry left him.

Carrying the body out to the hearse with Dave and the other pallbearers reminded Chad of the Guns N' Roses video for "November Rain". What was the name of that model who was dating Axl Rose at the time? Man, they disappeared off the face of the planet quick, didn't they? Used to be everything was Guns N' Roses, and then—Jesus, he almost slipped going down the stairs of the church. No more thinking about Guns N' Roses and Axl Rose until the casket is in the hearse.

After the body was safely inside, the funeral procession moved to the cemetery, where Chad had to help carry the body to Kovacs's final resting place. Then there was the final ceremony and the body was lowered and everyone headed back to their cars. Mandy caught up with him.

"I want to thank you for coming Chad. I know what happened between you and Kovacs a few months ago, and I wanted to apologize. It was a hard time for all of us, and I'm glad you at least let him turn to you."

"You don't have to apologize."

"You were always a good friend to him, and I know he always thought that, no matter what he said."

All of this made Chad uncomfortable, but he had Vanessa there squeezing his hand. That's what he wanted, to be back in bed with Vanessa, not here with Mandy telling him how much Kovacs liked him now that he was dead.

"Anyway, Kovacs drew up a will a few years ago. You've been named in it. Tomorrow his lawyer is going to play the tape he made. Here's his card, he's right downtown if you'd like to go."

"Um yeah, okay, that sounds good. What time?"

"At noon. Do you think you could get off from work?"

"Yeah, that's fine."

"Okay, I'll see you then."

She gave him a big hug with a lot of emotion in it. It was like she had a lot of things to tell him, a lot of things she wanted him to feel, and that hug was the only way to convey the message so he'd understand, and it took that hug to remind Chad that he and her had, through Kovacs, enough history that he did understand. As he and Vanessa walked back to the car to drive back to the church, he thought about when Mandy first met Kovacs. It was a beach themed party at the house, and Kovacs was walking around in a grass skirt and a coconut bra. Chad didn't think anything of it when Kovacs and Mandy were talking, all the guys earmarked a girl that they hoped would be theirs for the night; but Mandy saw something in Kovacs she wanted, it wasn't just his wild side, she wanted to tame that wild side, and it became her obsession to succeed. Kovacs loved that she cared enough to want to tame him, and part of him wanted to be tamed; but another part loved disappointing her more, and maybe she loved being disappointed more than succeeding too. Whatever it was, Chad and Dave and the rest of the brothers, while they knew Kovacs was falling for Mandy and they thought she was good for him, they also knew what Kovacs did when she wasn't around, and they thought they were keeping that info from her not only to protect Kovacs from getting in trouble, but protecting her from getting hurt too. And Chad felt in that hug that she was telling him she knew all along. Kovacs had disappointed her one last time by dying.

Back at the church rectory, everyone from the funeral was milling around, catching up with one another, and offering condolences to the family. Chad left Vanessa with his mother and Steve while he went to get some food from the buffet table. It was there that Gwen appeared beside him, as if she materialized from out of nowhere. It startled him, and he almost dropped the plate of cheese and crackers he'd put together for him and Vanessa.

"Hey Chad, longtime no see, huh?"

"Um, yeah, it's been a bit. You look good."

"You always were a bad liar."

And he was lying. Gwen looked like she'd aged ten or fifteen years since he last saw her. He didn't remember her looking this bad in her Facebook photos. She had bags under her eyes, and crow's feet in the corners. Her hair was stringy and it looked like it had been dyed.

"It's been a rough year, what with the housing market being slow and whatnot. Dave lost a lot of money trying to flip a few houses, and now we're trying to get back to even—but you don't want to hear about my problems, how are you doing? You look good."

"Thank you. I've put on some weight since the last time we saw each other, but I'm trying to hit the elliptical, you know how that goes."

"Ha ha, oh yeah. Is that Vanessa with you? I remember her from the reunion, poor girl with that toolbag giving her a hard time about marrying him. Me and Kovacs usually didn't see eye-to-eye, but I was glad he took care of that dork..."

"Yeah, Vanessa told me about that. She and I have been seeing each other for a few weeks now."

"I saw that on Facebook. That's good Chad, I'm happy for you."

"Thank you."

Chad didn't know that while he was at the buffet table talking to Gwen, his mother was telling Vanessa all about how in love he had been with Gwen, and how heartbroken he had been for the five years or so after the break up. She thought she was doing a good thing, by telling Vanessa how much better she was for Chad and how much he seemed to be over Gwen now that she was in the picture. It had the opposite effect, and she let Chad know when they were back in the car heading to her place.

"So, I had an interesting conversation with your mom while you were up getting food."

"Oh yeah?"

"Yeah... she said you weren't really over Gwen yet."

He sighed. Why does my mother hate me?

"So, is it true?"

"No, of course it's not true."

"It's okay if it is Chad, you and her had like five years, you and me only have three weeks."

"It'll be four tomorrow."

"You've been keeping track? That's sweet... you really are a nice guy Chad, you know that? And Edie likes you too, and she almost never likes the guys I date... I just... I don't want her to get attached if you're still in love with someone else, you know?"

He sighed again.

"It's not like that. My mother doesn't know what she's talking about. I don't know why she said anything."

Out of the corner of his eye he saw Vanessa reaching down and adjusting her tights.

"God, these things keep falling down. I think I'm losing weight, or maybe we stretched them out tying me up, huh?"

She slapped him on the arm. How could she do this to him, adjust her tights and talk about the things they do in bed, when he's trying to drive? And she thinks I still have a thing for Gwen? Gwen almost never wore skirts or dresses, and when she did she didn't wear tights or nylons underneath. She also never did the things in bed Vanessa did, or had Chad do the things Vanessa did. Oh man, now she's lifting up her dress and adjusting her tights above her thigh.

"You know, I bet you wouldn't think I'm as hot as you do now if I lost weight. I was thinking about this you know, I think you're a chubby chaser."

"A what?"

"You heard me. You dig fat chicks."

"Cut it out, you're not fat."

"I'm not thin either. I bet you'd like me even better if I put on another ten or twenty pounds, huh?"

He shook his head and smiled. He didn't want her to put on any more weight, but he knew he didn't want to get into *that* conversation.

"You know I thought about that when I saw Gwen. I thought, she's too skinny for Chad, you have nothing to worry about Vanessa. Besides, you know the way he looks at you... but then your mom started talking about how hung up on her you were, which made me worry, so I watched you, looking for any sign in your body language... oh, look, he's leaning away from her, that's good, but oh no, he laughed at something she said... it's stupid, I know, it's just, I haven't been this happy with someone in a long time, and Edie likes you too, which is very rare, and I don't know, I guess I get nervous and I look for any excuse to worry..."

"I haven't been this happy in a long time either—you know, it's hard for me to concentrate on driving when you do that."

She had pushed the seat back and put her leg on the dash, pulling her tights up some more.

"What? They're bunching up on me. If it wasn't so cold out I'd take them off completely."

Chad laughed, more at himself for being so ridiculous, which made Vanessa laugh too. She took his hand and kissed it, then held it against her face as she curled up in her seat without her seatbelt on.

"Did you want to stay for supper tonight?"

"Yeah, that sounds good."

"Good. And maybe you can help Edie with her math homework too. I'm horrible at math."

Chad was right in thinking Kovacs would've wanted to write Chad out of his will after what happened between them, but he didn't consider that Kovacs didn't plan on dying only a few months later. That night in jail he said to himself that fucking bastard, first thing I'm doing when I get home is writing him out of my will. But the will was done on a video made with his digital camera, and he never felt like reshooting it. He'd get to it eventually he figured.

In a small conference room at the lawyer's office building, there were two groups of chairs, divided by an aisle down the middle, with four rows of four on each side, and Chad sat in the back right corner near the window. He saw Dave and Gwen across the aisle from him. He wished Vanessa could be there too.

Right away, the video started bad. Kovacs sat in front of them wearing a smoking jacket and holding a bottle of Johnny Walker Blue.

"Ted told me, because of all the shit I've got now, I better do one of these things, but it probably won't matter. I bet I'll have reshot this so many times over the next fifty years as me and Mandy have a bunch of kids and grandkids that this video won't ever see the light of day."

Mandy broke down crying. Chad looked over and saw Gwen crying too, her head rested on Dave's chest. Despite the recent romance with Vanessa, and the renewed interest in his family, Chad still had that disconnected element in his personality that made this sad, cruel irony more a burden to him than something to affect his own emotions or rouse his sympathies. Maybe if Vanessa had been there next to him, and upset too, and he had someone to experience those emotions through, it would have been different; but by himself, he was uncomfortable and fought a strong urge to pull out his phone to see what time it was.

Things went a little more smoothly from there, though Kovacs would occasionally bring up all the kids they were going to have. "I give the house to Mandy—though obviously when we have kids, one of them will get it...." There was a further tension there that Chad didn't recognize, between Kovacs's father and wife, Carol, whom Kovacs had an affair with, and Kovacs's mother, who resented the presence of Carol there after what happened. Mandy resented her presence there too, but she also resented Kovacs's mother, because she thought his mother enabled Kovacs's wild behavior; the mother in turn thought the same thing of Mandy. Then Mandy's family resented Kovacs and his family for what they put their daughter through. Only two days before she had finally been able to get the Intoxilyzer 4100 removed from her car, and in the interim had been borrowing her mother's. It was one of many burdens they had had to endure while Mandy was with Kovacs, and they felt now that watching him make an ass out of himself on this video would be the last one.

About ten minutes in Kovacs got to what he was leaving Dave and Chad.

"I leave all of my sports memorabilia to Dave. That includes all the cards and signed balls and jerseys. It's all in my man cave, ready for you to take. Chad, I leave you my arcade games. Remember when we were growing up and we said we'd like to get some arcade games when we had the money? Well I did. I got your favorite, *Mortal Kombat*, and my favorite, *Galaga*. They're in the man cave too."

Kovacs had been drinking from his Johnny Walker Blue throughout the video, and the alcohol was affecting him. The mindset he'd had earlier on, that no one would ever see this, that he'd have to make a new one later in life, had evaporated, and now it was turning into a confessional.

"You know, I gotta say, what you guys did—letting a girl come between you like that—was wrong. Bros before hoes man, that's the way it should be. We were all good friends before Gwen got in the picture, then Chad man, you just disappeared, and what you did Dave was even worse, you can't sleep with your friend's woman! We were like the Three Musketeers, and you guys ended that over some girl."

Chad could feel Dave looking at him, feel Gwen looking at them both, and he wanted to run. He didn't come here to be lectured by a dead man. And the video only grew worse from there. Confessions to Mandy about how he wished he could be a better husband, how bad he felt every time he hurt her; tearful admonishments to his parents for their acrimonious divorce, which he was stuck in the middle of; then ramblings about people in his life at the time of the taping that no one there knew. Everyone was relieved when it finally ended.

Chad said a quick goodbye to Mandy, took a receipt from Kovacs's lawyer which he was to take to a nearby storage facility to pick up the games, and left without saying anything to Gwen and Dave. What was he going to do with two arcade games? Did his mother's garage have room? Maybe Steve would want them? Why would anyone want them? God, that whole thing was a mess.

His mood lifted a little bit though back at his office, when Lars came in.

"Oh dude, that's so sweet. *Galaga*? Bring it over here, we can put it in the rec room. *Mortal Kombat* might be too violent, but I bet you could sell that on eBay or Craigslist."

"Really, you think we could put that up here?"

"I'll ask Seijun, but I bet he'd love it."

"Okay, sweet."

"Hey, I wanted to ask you, have you talked to Molly lately?"

"Oh God no. I heard from Haley that she dumped her boyfriend."

"Oh yeah, Ursula texted me the other day. She thinks you're like her soul mate or something, like you have a cosmic connection. She wanted me to give her your number for her."

"Jesus Christ. I should probably take care of this."

Lars laughed.

"What did you two do that night?"

"Dude, it wasn't even like that, the sex was horrible—on both of our ends, I'm ashamed to say. I figured she wanted as little to do with me as I did with her. But then I'm out to lunch with Haley a couple days later, and Haley's telling me how she dumped her boyfriend. It's fucking ridiculous. I don't want anything to do with her now that I'm with Vanessa."

Chad's phone beeped.

"What's that?"

"An email. Christ, Gwen sent me a message on Facebook!"

Lars found this amusing in a very Kovacs's bros before hoes kind of way.

"What did she say?"

"Sweet fucking Christ, she wants to see me too. Vanessa was already jealous of me talking to her at Kovacs's funeral over some stupid stuff my mother said."

"Dude, you need a night out away from all these bitches. Let's hit the buffet at Elevens tonight."

"I can't, I have plans with Vanessa."

"Fuck her man, we'll get some hotter chicks tonight."

"I don't want any other chicks, I want her. Dude, she's It man, The One."

"Whaaaaa? No, cut it out, you barely know her."

"I know her enough."

"Dude, she has a kid and stuff, you don't want that shit. Plus, you can do so much better."

"Man, I don't know…"

"Come on dude, let's do it, we'll go right from here."

"No, I gotta see her tonight. Maybe tomorrow, how's that?"

"So let me get this straight, you fucked this chick the same week you fucked me, and she's in love with you and dumped her fiancé for you, and you didn't think it was a big deal to tell me?"

"It's not like that, I never thought I'd see her again."

"Did you think you'd never see me again after we had sex?"

"It's not the same thing, she and I had really bad sex, you and me didn't."

"So if I sucked in bed, you would've ran out on me too?"

"No… I mean… it was like she and I felt like we didn't fit… something about it didn't work, it felt like a mistake… and she was engaged to a doctor, I figured, she'd just forget about me and go back to him. Does that make sense? I haven't even heard from her."

"Because she doesn't have your number!... Tell me what you wanted again from Empire II."

"The General Tso's meal with fried rice and chicken wings."

"What fucking number is it, I don't see it!"

"It's like L6, right, let me see."

"There is no L6! You're talking about the lunch menu."

"Oh, whoops. You want me to just order, since you don't like to call anyway?"

"Would you? I'm just getting an D3, and extra crab rangoons. I'm going to have a seat on the couch and start on this wine."

After he put in their order, he poured himself a beer and joined her on the couch. Vanessa had a house in a residential neighborhood a few towns over from Chad. She preferred to live in the town Chad lived in, because it was closer to downtown and the mall and everything, but on her salary at the daycare and the small amount of child support she got from Edie's father after they finally tracked him down a few years ago, she could only afford to buy a house in this town. It meant longer drives, but it also meant Edie could live in a house, not an apartment. They had been there for two years, and the change in Edie was remarkable. She could practice soccer in their backyard, and Vanessa could sit on their patio and read a book and watch her. She could do her homework or sleep in peace without banging from upstairs or yelling from next door. Vanessa thought the biggest thing though was that Edie knew with this house that they weren't moving again anytime soon.

Vanessa was lying down, so Chad put her feet over him and started rubbing them.

"Oh God, that feels great. I've been on my feet all day, between the kids at work, and getting my own ready to go see her dad. I probably should go upstairs and change for you. I didn't get a chance to before you came over."

"I wouldn't worry about it."

"It's nice to just relax here with you and a glass of wine."

"Yeah, I was thinking the same thing. It was kind of a crazy day for me too."

"Oh yeah, that's right, how did that thing go? What did you get from Kovacs?"

"Two arcade games, *Mortal Kombat* and *Galaga*."

"What? That Kovacs.... What're you going to do with them?"

"Lars wants the *Galaga* one for the rec room in our office, and I may put the *Mortal Kombat* on eBay or Craigslist."

"Ooh, I bet you could get a lot for that. Where are they, at his house?"

"Some storage place somewhere. I have the ticket in my wallet. If I don't get them out of there in a month or something, I'll have to pay to keep them there."

"That's dumb. You can always keep them here if it comes to that, I think we have room in the garage."

"Hopefully it won't… man, the whole thing was a mess. Kovacs was drunk, as usual, and he said all these things about how this wasn't the final will, and how he'd be changing it after he and Mandy had all these kids and grandkids."

"Oh my God Chad, that's horrible. That's so sad."

"Yeah…"

He trailed off and massaged her feet. Naked feet grossed him out, but she had on black tights under her jeans, which made them more of a turn-on. He could've sat there and rubbed them and listened to her moan in relaxation all night, but he knew he had to break this moment with another piece of news she probably didn't want to hear.

"Gwen sent me a message on Facebook after. She wants to see me."

She pulled her feet away and underneath her and sat up.

"Why?"

"She didn't say."

"What did you tell her?"

"I haven't responded. I wanted to tell you first."

"You want my permission?"

"I don't know… no, I just didn't want it to be a secret."

"Like the chick with the doctor?"

He sighed.

"The chick with the doctor wasn't… never mind, no, it's because of what happened yesterday. I figured I'd tell you now, so if it came out later, you wouldn't think I was keeping it from you, I don't know."

"Well, do you want to see her?"

"No."

"Then why didn't you just tell her that? Why haven't you responded yet? You do want to see her. God Chad…"

Tears welled up in her eyes. Why, why did this always have to happen to him? He goes two and a half years without a sniff of a girlfriend, and even the one he had before that was barely anything. Now he's with a girl he really wants to be with, finally, and all these other chicks are coming back and making his life hell! He wanted to punch something.

"You know, all day I was waiting to see you. My day sucked today, but I thought, Chad's coming over, it'll be good then…"

"What do you think I was thinking! I'm sitting in this awkward room with my dead friend on a video tape getting wasted and telling his wife how many kids they were going to have! Where do you think I wanted to be? Here, with you!"

She stopped crying and looked at him. He was scary, staring straight ahead, his face crimson. She didn't know what to do. She didn't know he was capable of such anger. He had been so laid back in the previous four weeks. She couldn't know the years of futility that had built up inside him, couldn't see him in that cubicle thinking of bad Kanye West jokes to impress a co-worker that wanted nothing to do with him, couldn't see him standing outside the bedroom door of a drunk woman who peed in her purse, couldn't see the bear suit or the girl who thought babies came out of mother's stomachs, couldn't see Chad all alone looking longingly on Facebook as Gwen posted another pic of her and Dave and their new baby. All she could see was the new Chad, the one who'd lost five pounds and wore nicer clothes and worked in an office for a guy who let them put arcade games and workout equipment in their rec room— worked in an office that had a rec room for God's sake! To her, all these women coming up now sounded like women that he'd want more than her, or women that he fucked just like her, that made her less special, reminded her that as much as she thought she had, she really only had three weeks—or four weeks, as Chad reminded her.

She reached out and touched him, afraid he might lash out, but he didn't, he wanted her to touch him. She uncoiled herself from her end of the couch and put her arms around him from behind, resting her chin on his shoulder.

The doorbell rang.

"Oh shit, that must be the food."

"Do you need any money?"

"Um... no, I think I have enough." She looked through her purse. "Do you have any ones for tip?"

"Yeah, give me a second and I'll see."

Dinner and the wine and movie after lightened the mood. Neither brought up Molly or Gwen again, and any remaining tension evaporated during the sex. Chad thought about a lot of things that next morning as Vanessa was lying on him. Was Lars right, could he do better than her? She was overweight, and she did have a kid. Did he want that responsibility? He was just gaining some form of relevance in the world again, did he want to cash it in now with her? What about Tiffany in Vegas? How easy had that been? What about Gwen wanting to see him? She had two kids too, and they were Dave's kids, and they were younger. And he was just telling himself that he and Gwen didn't fit like he and Vanessa did. No one made him feel the way Vanessa did. But was that true, or had he been irrelevant so long he forgot what everything felt like? Why was he listening to Lars though? Lars was full of shit half the time. Lars couldn't appreciate this, just lying here with her on him, her flesh, her mouth, her breath. Chad didn't need anything else, did he?

Vanessa was thinking too, with her eyes closed, pretending to be asleep. She was falling too hard for Chad, and needed to back off, or at least let him sort all this out with these other chicks. She told him so when they both got up.

"There isn't anything to sort out... I... I..."

He sighed.

"I really like you Chad, it's just... I'm going to be 33 next week, I have an 11-year-old daughter to think about... I mean I think about you when you're not around, and I don't want to be wondering who you're thinking about."

He went from ten minutes before wondering if he wanted to settle down with Vanessa, to wondering what he could do to fix this and convince Vanessa that he wanted to be with her, and only her.

"Listen, we've only been dating for three weeks—"

"Today makes four."

She smiled. Maybe I'm making a mistake, she thought.

Oh, she smiled, please God, let me back in, let me back in. I need this. I need this.

Why does he have to look at me like that? Why does he have to make me feel younger? And why does he have to, just when I start to let myself fall for him, give me reasons to question everything? Why do guys have to suck so bad? And this one doesn't even suck and he still sucks.

"What can I do to fix this? I want to be with you Vanessa. Things were going so well, until—"

"Until your ex came back into the picture and some other chick that was engaged to a doctor who you had bad sex with."

"I told you, they don't matter. Molly was a mistake, and Gwen and I are through. I wish my mom hadn't said anything."

"No, I'm glad she did… look, let's just give it a few days. Maybe the rest of the weekend, and we'll talk Monday. Maybe we just need a little space. You go out with your buddies tonight, I'll go out with my girlfriends, and we'll see how we feel, okay?"

"All right."

Chad wasn't happy with the situation, but he wanted to make the best of it, so he called Lars, who was more than happy to take him out for the night. To Lars's mind, women were all the same, and you as a guy couldn't do anything about it. Fuck 'em—literally. Chad didn't agree with Lars, he wanted to be spending the evening with Vanessa, not at Elevens eating buffalo wings while Peaches entertained them on the main stage.

Lars knew a couple of the dancers that night that had early shifts, and they accompanied he and Chad to the Blue Door. As Chad feared, Molly was there. She rushed up and gave him a big hug. She knew right away that something was wrong when Chad didn't reciprocate it.

"Maybe we should go talk," he said.

Something dropped inside of her, even though she expected this to happen. She didn't have Chad's number after New Year's, and had been coming to The Blue Door religiously since then, hoping he'd be there, but he had never come, and she kind of knew, even if she was holding out hope. They went to the same corner they had on New Year's, New Order's "Bizarre Love Triangle" playing overhead, which Chad recognized, but couldn't remember the name of it or who sang it.

"So how've you been? I've been trying to get a hold of you since New Year's?"

"Um, I'm good, really good, um… I've met someone."

"You've met someone? What? What about?…"

"What do you mean what about?… You're engaged to a doctor."

"I ended it with him to be with you."

"You what?"

He feigned surprise, and she was upset enough that she didn't suspect his insincerity.

"Why would you do that? I mean, wasn't that… you know, what we did… kind of awkward? I mean, I'm not saying you, but I wasn't very good… I just figured…"

He thought self-degradation would win the day for him, remind her how bad he was in bed and make her not want to be with him.

"Of course we were bad in bed at first, that's always how it is with a Virgo/Capricorn love match?"

The song changed to "Drive" by the Cars.

"A what? What are you talking about? I'm a Sagittarius."

"No, you're on the cusp, you're closer to being a Capricorn."

"What does that even mean? Listen, you're a really cool chick, Molly, but Vanessa and I, we've known each other since high school, and this just kind of happened, but I really want to be with her."

"How can you say that? You and I are meant to be together. What is this Vanessa's sign anyway?"

"I don't know, her birthday is Wednesday, what is that, the tenth? February 10th, what sign is that?"

She paused. Oh God, had she thrown everything away on a guy who wasn't meant to be with her? He was a Sagittarius after all, and Vanessa was an Aquarius, they were a perfect love match. Molly had turned him into something he was not, a Capricorn. She pushed him back and ran out of the place, hoping to catch her now ex before he went to sleep.

Holy shit, Chad thought, she thought because we were bad in bed, we were made for each other. He shook his head and found Lars with the two strippers. All he wanted now was to go home and tell Vanessa all about this craziness. Then he had a moment of perspicacity: what if he talked to Gwen too and sorted things out. He could get her behind him the way he did Molly, free himself up completely for Vanessa. He used his phone to log onto Facebook and reply to her message, asking her if brunch on Sunday would work. Then he was so happy, he joined Lars and the two strippers on the dance floor for "Rhythm of the Night".

"I love Gloria Estefan," his girl said in his ear.

"This isn't Gloria Estefan, it's Debarge!"

Chad agreed to fulfill his wingman duties and accompany Lars and the girls back to the office rec room. This time he'd barely had anything to drink, so he was good to drive. Perhaps if he'd been more intoxicated, he wouldn't have thought what happened next to be odd at all.

Lars turned on the stereo, Chad assuming it was more Flo-Rida or something. The opening wasn't that at all though, it was more the 80s adult contempo he liked to play when it was just he and Chad in the Mercedes.

"This song is amazing. 'Look Away,' it's Chicago post-Peter Cetera."

The girls looked at each other, arched their eyebrows, then giggled. They looked at Chad to see if he was as into this as Lars, or if he thought this was as weird as they did.

What was Lars doing? Was this some kind of joke?

He had a fist up, closed his eyes at parts, lip synched at others. This had to be some kind of joke? This wasn't a cool retro 80s song, and even if it were, the girls weren't impressed. He hit the one he was with on the arm to get her ready for the chorus.

She tried to feel it with him, if only out of fear of not knowing how he'd react if she didn't. Throughout the second verse he talked about the song like it was the greatest thing ever, like he was a writer at *Rolling Stone* explaining the virtue of Bob Dylan's "Blowin' in the Wind". The girls pretended to be impressed, again, afraid that the man in front of them was unstable and capable of anything. After the second chorus, there was a short electric guitar bridge, and Lars did some air guitar, before telling everyone to really listen to this part, the finale, when the band really got into it. Chad wanted to run. He shouldn't have cared what these strippers thought of him, but he wanted them to know somehow that he didn't approve of this craziness.

As the song faded out, the Flo-Rida song Chad was becoming very familiar with faded in. It flipped a switch in the girls, as if on instinct, and they stood together and danced with one another. Lars sat down on the couch, while Chad stayed where he was off to the side, leaning on the arm of a chair. The girls were hot, in an any girl/exotic dancer kind of way, wearing short dresses and heels with tons of hair and tons of make-up. They made out, caressed each other's bodies, moved in a sultry, seductive manner, as if each was trying to turn on the other, and not Lars and Chad.

Chad was fine with that. He wanted to be back with Vanessa. What was she doing right now? Who was she with? It was midnight and he hadn't heard from her. Should he text her? What would that tell her, that he couldn't go one night without her when she specifically asked for one night. No, he couldn't do that. Oh no, the girls are splitting up. Lars's is going over to him, Chad's is moving in his direction. And then it happened, his phone buzzed. Yes!

"Hope ure having a good night ☺. I miss you ☹, and I'm kinda drunk, lol!!!"

Chad's girl was there, about to straddle him, when he held up his finger.

"I'm sorry, I gotta... my girlfriend's texting me..."

"Oh... I'm... okay..."

Chad stepped out of the room and replied:

"Night's okay, have a funny story to tell you, and I miss you too Vanessa, hope your having a goodnight too."

Two seconds later his phone rang.

"Oh my God, I'm such a moron, I'm so drunk... my friends took me to the Green Dragon to watch some stand-up. This one guy was so hilarious. I wish you could've seen him. He did this whole thing about browsing at the buffet line, and wanting to kill the people in front of him."

"Holy shit, that's John Pinette! You saw John Pinette?"

"Yeah, that's his name, you know him?"

"Yes! I love him! I had no idea he was in the area, I would've gone."

"Ugh, I should've called you if I'd have known... are you drunk too?"

"No, I'm DD for Lars. We have some people over at the rec room in the office."

"Yeah, I can hear the music playing. It sounds like fun. I won't keep you, I just thought since you texted me back so fast that maybe you were already home..."

"No, but I could leave now if you wanted, it's not a big—"

"No no, I don't want you to do that... maybe tomorrow night you could come over and watch the Super Bowl with me and Edie—unless you already had plans..."

"No no, not at all, I don't already have plans. That sounds good."

She let out a sigh.

"Okay good. I'll see you then. Sweet dreams Chad."

"Good night Vanessa."

There was a hurt in his loins. This was the first weekend night since their first date that he would be spending alone, and hearing her voice sound so soft and drunk and adorable made him hurt even more. He sat in the hallway, his back against the wall, staring at the words "Call Ended" on his phone. His girl came out after a few minutes.

"Hey, everything all right?"

"Yeah, it's good."

"Um, you don't have to stay... I can catch a cab back to Elevens to get my car."

"I can give you a ride."

"No, don't worry about it, I'll be fine... you know, I won't tell your girlfriend if you want... I mean, it's no big deal to me..."

"Thank you, but no, I'm good. It was nice meeting you...?"

"Destiny."

"Destiny, I'm Chad by the way."

It was Super Bowl Sunday, and the thought of Dave and all his lunkhead friends coming over to get drunk and yell obscenities and ignorant sexist, racist, homophobic remarks at the screen made Gwen sick to her stomach. She had already planned to take the kids to her parents to be away from it all, but the mere thought was still enough to affect her. She remembered the years in the past, the obnoxiousness, the loud laughing at bad light beer commercials where guys were hit in the balls by monkeys… had she always hated Dave's friends? Some of them were Chad's fraternity brothers, and she had thought when they were dating that Chad didn't see them that often because he was so obsessed with her, but maybe he knew something about them that she didn't.

This wouldn't be that same boisterous event that was anathema to Gwen, with Kovacs passing away recently. Maybe Kovacs and Dave didn't see each other as much as they used to, what with Gwen and Dave having kids and their financial troubles, but the Super Bowl was like a holiday for them, and they had been watching them together, every one, since grade school. Dave wasn't looking forward to his party any more than Gwen was. He sat on the couch watching *SportsCenter*, listening but not listening to them discuss New Orleans' long road back from the devastation of Katrina, trying to gin up excitement for a game that was making him feel a hurt he was too stubborn and too vain to admit he was feeling.

But Gwen couldn't see that in him. She saw herself making herself up in the mirror, not believing that it was Chad of all people she was making herself up for, not believing that she was nervous to see him, embarrassed at her crow's feet and dark circles under her eyes, putting on a skirt, trying to make her small breasts look perkier and fuller in her black low-cut top, seeing Vanessa in her head and wanting Chad to see the things in Gwen that he saw in Vanessa. She expected Dave to say something, ask her why she was going through so much trouble to run out to the grocery store—a skirt no less, she never wore skirts!—but he just sat there, watching *SportsCenter*, not at all concerned with what she was doing. I'm leaving him, she thought, no matter what happens at brunch with Chad. He obviously doesn't love me anymore, and I don't love him.

Chad was just as concerned about his appearance as he readied himself to see Gwen, and he was just as nervous, but he was mad at himself and mad at her for all this stress. Why did she do this now? For five years she tortured him, left him a shell of himself, and now, as he was finally rebuilding, she jumped back in and threatened to make it all fall apart again.

You asked for this though. You sent her a message on Facebook last night saying you wanted to see her.

It's because I want to know. I want to know if she ever loved me, why she stayed with me so long if she didn't, why she did what she did with Dave, why she asked to see me again recently. I want to know if all the things I feel about Vanessa are right. I want to be able to go to Vanessa and say "see, I'm here for you, I want to be with you."

Had he not bumped into Molly, and had she not told him that it was how bad in bed he was that made her want him so bad she dumped her doctor fiancé for him, he wouldn't be stressed out picking out an outfit imagining what he was going to say to Gwen right now; but it was that moment, when Molly told him that Capricorns and Virgos are supposed to have bad sex, that he thought of Gwen, and after thinking about her and wondering why she threw in her lot with him for so long, he remembered her Facebook message asking to speak with him, and on a whim decided to return her message and agree to meet for brunch to find out the answer. Now he was regretting it, because he didn't want to see her. He was afraid his mother was right, afraid he still loved her, afraid she still had the hold on him she'd had ever since they first started dating.

And of course, she would wear a skirt. She almost never wore a skirt or a dress for him when they were together, said she hated them, but here she was coming to his table in a black skirt with black nylons—and he didn't remember her boobs being so big.

Gwen was overcome with emotion. She couldn't help crying. Chad was sitting before her, the man she always hoped he would be, the man he was always supposed to be, the man that saved a 14-year-old girl's life from a sexual predator; but as they hugged hello, she felt the same timid, apprehensive arms around her. What was she doing here? This was a bad idea.

"What's the matter?"

She recovered herself, dried her eyes and fixed her face in her compact.

"I'm sorry, I shouldn't have come, it's just…" She sighed, then laughed. Chad smiled, not sure what to make of this.

"What's so funny?"

"I don't know, life I guess. I don't know… I don't know why I asked to see you…"

"Can I get you two something to drink?"

The waiter, having seen how emotional Gwen was, went to Chad first for his order, hoping Chad might order for both of them and he wouldn't have to talk to the crying chick. Chad asked for a mimosa, and Gwen let the waiter off easy by saying quickly that she'd have the same. It was the first time Chad could remember her ordering the same thing he did. She almost always had something different from him, and would get annoyed if he ordered the same thing she did. Part of it made him angry, because he thought of how hard she had been on him when they were dating, but the other part made him curious, to see what this new Gwen who deferred to him would do.

"I guess I should just get it out: I'm leaving Dave."

"What? Why?"

For five long years, since he first caught her in bed with Dave, he dreamed of her telling him that sentence. Now it was a complication, the last thing he needed. Why couldn't she and Dave leave him alone and let him move on with his life?

Gwen went into a long rant over a few mimosas and part of her vegetarian eggs Benedict. Everything, from her falling out of love with Dave, to the ignorant things he says, to him not being affectionate with her anymore, to the financial troubles and how he sat around the house all day doing nothing while she had to deal with the kids and paying the bills. Chad was still of split-mind about all of this: part of him resented her for the way she treated him, and saw similarities in this with what she must've been saying to Dave about him back when they were together; but the other part wanted to know why she was emptying all of this information out to him.

Gwen didn't know why she was telling him all of this either. It frustrated her to look at Chad across the table and know that she couldn't have him like that, that with her he would always shrivel up into the half person he was with her. Already he was letting her have her way in their conversation, as if they'd never broken up.

There was a break in their conversation where she considered all this, and she decided to lay all her cards on the table.

"I'm going to be honest with you Chad, um… I guess seeing you like this, seeing how good you look now, it made me think… I don't know, that maybe we could, um… but I understand now that that's not possible, you know… like, for whatever reason, I don't know, you can't be this guy when you're around me… I don't know what it is, but…"

"Wait, you want to be with me again?"

"No, I… I don't know, I thought maybe I did, but…"

But what God damn it! Jesus Christ, just spit it out!

"All right, I have a question, since you're having so much trouble figuring out what you want to say. Did you ever love me?"

She went from playing with her eggs Benedict to looking at him, with wide, searching eyes. He had never talked to her like that before. Where was this backbone when they were dating?

"Yes, of course I loved you… I loved you…"

"But…?"

"Chad, we went over this back then, your whole identity was wrapped up in being my boyfriend, in being Gwen's Chad. If we got back together this you that you are now would only devolve back into Gwen's Chad again. I can feel it, I felt it when you hugged me."

"What do you want then? What is this me that I am now?" He stumbled as he said it, trying to repeat what she said while replacing the correct pronouns.

"The guy who saved that girl's life. I'm finally looking at the guy who went into that room when he heard a girl scream and saved her from a pedophile. You carry yourself with more confidence now. You look better, you sound better—but that guy doesn't exist when he's with me. For whatever reason—it's like *Superman II*, I'm Lois Lane, and when you're with me, you go to that big chamber in the iceberg and lose all your powers to make yourself Clark Kent. It sucks, because I want Superman, but I can't have him."

Superman huh?

"Then what does that make Dave?"

"Lex Luthor, I don't know… no, he's not that bad… he is that bad, isn't he?"

"You're asking the guy whose girlfriend he stole."

They laughed.

"I wish now I hadn't let myself be stolen… I thought I wanted to be stolen, but I really just needed a fresh start… we needed a fresh start."

"So that's what it was, me saving MacKenzie?"

"Uh huh."

"Everybody makes such a big deal out of that—you're sitting there calling me Superman for Christ's sake."

"Chad, you were a hero. That girl and that family owe everything to you making a choice that you weren't going to just sit in your room and pretend you didn't hear anything. Think of all the milestones in her life you and I went to, her graduation, her volleyball games; all the pictures they sent us of things like proms, awards ceremonies, holidays. Every one of those made me love you again, and then I'd lose that person and you'd go back to being Gwen's Chad."

"I was never that person, Gwen, can't you understand? Can't anyone understand?... if you were only there, you'd see that I was no hero... I didn't punch the guy like Kovacs said... all I did was walk in... and the door was—"

"Chad, none of that matters! Ugh! Can't *you* understand? Stop being so God damn modest for two seconds? Do you think that girl or her family care that all you did was open the door and that Hestermann guy saw you and freaked out? Their daughter would've *died* if you hadn't done that. Dead. D-E-A-D. And I looked at you and thought 'how brave he was, to hear a girl scream and go over there, having no idea what was going on, and save that girl's life'..."

"And I disappointed you."

She sighed.

"I used to think so... but I see now that that wasn't it. I'm no good for you. We were no good for each other. Look at what happened to us after the fact: I married a guy I didn't really love, and you spent almost five years letting yourself go—don't think I didn't see the way you looked in your Facebook pictures before the past few months. What happened to you anyway? It was that Vanessa girl, right? She got out of you what I couldn't."

"No, it was before her. She and I have only been dating for a month. It was actually..."

Anishka, the gift. He laughed.

"What?"

He told her about Anishka, his tragic story, their Thanksgiving leftovers meal, and what he told her about MacKenzie.

"See?"

"But that's different. He wanted me to stop feeling sorry for myself and live life, because otherwise I'd be letting her down. So I quit my job at that insurance firm, and bumped into this guy Lars, who got me the job at the hedge fund. He and my boss Seijun were the ones who changed my look and the elliptical they have there has allowed me to work out."

She shook her head.

"What?"

"I should probably get going. It was really good seeing you again though. Do you think Vanessa would mind if you and me talked every once in a while?"

"She and I have a lot to talk about ourselves... I don't know, give it a little time, she's still a little jealous of you after seeing us together at the funeral."

"I understand."

Chad watched the Super Bowl with Vanessa and her daughter. He couldn't remember the last time he'd watched the Super Bowl, and though he hated all the bad commercials and the silly spectacle everyone made of the game, when New Orleans went for an onside kick to start the second half, he was all in. He'd never had so much fun watching a football game that didn't involve Dodge State.

He had so much he wanted to say to Vanessa, but he waited for the game to end and Edie to go to bed before he told her. He brought the tape of MacKenzie's story from *Outside the Lines* to show her too. When their moment came though, Vanessa started.

193

"I'm sorry I was a pain yesterday, I was—"

"No no, you had every right to be… I mean, I might think the same thing in your position."

"I know, but—"

"Listen, before you go any further, I want to get some things off my chest. First, I saw that Molly chick last night at The Blue Door."

"Oh God, do I want to hear this?"

"Yes, it's pretty funny."

"Okay…?"

"She thought she and I were meant to be together because we were so bad in bed."

"What?"

"She said it's because Capricorns and Virgos are never good in bed together."

"But you're a Sagittarius. I don't get it."

"Exactly, and you're an… Aquarius?"

"Very good."

"And when she found out, she ran off, because she found out she made a big mistake. It was crazy. But it got me thinking…"

"Got you thinking what?"

"Got me thinking, 'if that chick liked me because we were bad in bed, which makes no sense, why did Gwen like me?' So I messaged her back, and we met today for brunch."

Now Vanessa was getting nervous. Why would he do this now though, after we just had such a great night watching the Super Bowl? He didn't look like he had something bad to tell me though, though she could remember guys in the past who realized they were in love with their exes coming to her with excited expressions telling her how happy they were, and how much they wouldn't have figured out how much they loved their ex if they hadn't dated her. She couldn't handle another one of those.

"Chad, if you're getting back together with her, just tell me and cut all the bullshit."

"It's not like that at all. I'm trying to show you that I'm over her."

"Oh… *oh*, okay… you don't have to do that—"

"No, I need to show you something. Do you have a VCR?"

She did, down in the finished basement that acted as a rec room. They brought it up and into the living room and hooked it up. She had no idea what he was about to show her, and really didn't want to be going through all this. Then they had to wait for it to rewind, because Chad hadn't done that since watching the tape with Brick and Haley.

But then it started.

"Were you on TV Chad?"

"Yeah, I will be in a second."

She was all excited. What could Chad be doing on ESPN? Then she heard the story, about MacKenzie playing volleyball in college, being in the national championship, then the fact that she was almost killed at 14. What the hell was Chad showing her? Who was this girl? She just listened though and didn't say anything. It scared her though, having a daughter of her own, listening to MacKenzie describing meeting Hestermann online, thinking he's 22, then sneaking away to meet him. Just as she was about to tell Chad she couldn't watch this because of Edie, there he was, telling the interviewer how he had to go out to get toilet paper. Wow, he looked so defeated, so unhappy, so not the guy she knew next to her. But the story he was telling the interviewer, how he bumped into MacKenzie out in the hallway, how suspicious that was, how he listened, and acted when he heard screaming, and finally, how that action saved her life.

"Oh my God Chad, that's amazing."

She was crying. She had a daughter of her own, and she hoped that if anything bad ever happened to her, God forbid, someone like Chad would be there to help her, and here was Chad, sitting next to her. Chad put his arms around her and held her head to his chest.

"Are you okay?"

"Yes, it's just… you don't know until you have a daughter of your own… maybe you will with Edie, but…" she lifted her head and dried her eyes with her sleeve. "Thank you for showing me that. It meant a lot."

"See, Gwen told me today that she only fell in love with me because I saved Mackenzie. She wanted me to be Superman, and I couldn't live up to that… I don't know, but we both know that we're better off without each other, that's what we figured out today."

"Superman, huh? Ha ha, that's funny. I've always liked Clark Kent better anyway…"

"Really? You know, Lars has some glasses I can wear that are just glass."

"Ooh, that sounds hot."

After leaving Chad at The Blue Door, Molly went straight home to see her Dave and tell him everything, tell him it had all been a mistake. When she got there though, she found him with Haley looking at photo albums of hiking trips. They were sitting really close together on the couch, and they didn't separate when they saw her.

"What are you doing here?" Dave said.

"Who is *she*?"

"This is my friend Haley. We did the Governor's Range together on New Year's."

"Chad's friend Haley?"

"Um yeah, how do you know Chad?"

"You know *Chad*?" Dave said.

"Yeah, we worked together before he quit a couple months ago. He's the guy I was telling you about whose girlfriend cheated on him. How do you two know him?"

"He's the Capricorn." Dave said.

"Chad? No way, you have the wrong guy, he'd never do that…" Or would he. How could he? Especially him after what he's been through. Hmm, she really liked Dave though, they had so much in common. Maybe he was a little older than her—okay, 15 years older—but it's not like she wanted to marry him, just spend time with him and talk about hiking and stuff. Plus, who cared if he was 15 years older, he was still really hot.

Molly made her plea, that it *was* her and Dave that were really cosmically meant to be together, that she was wrong about Chad, he wasn't really a Capricorn, he was a Sagittarius and his new girlfriend was an Aquarius. Dave had heard enough. He humored her obsession with astrology when they were together, because he didn't know how much it clouded her mind, but seeing how prodigious it really was was embarrassing in front of Haley. She was probably wondering what I could've seen in this crazy woman to begin with. He told Molly he thought it would be better if she left, and after a lot of begging on her part, she finally relented. Haley was about to leave too, but Dave asked if she could stay.

195

Haley wanted to text Chad, or call him and scold him for breaking up Dave and Molly's relationship, but she was happy with Dave, and deep down was happy Chad had slept with Molly, though it made her feel guilty to admit it. She would sit on this, see how things went, then mention it to Chad later. That little bastard.

The day after the Super Bowl Lars arranged for a moving company to transport the *Galaga* machine from the storage facility to the office rec room. Chad had to admire Lars's efficiency in such matters. He had money and he knew what he could get done with it if he used it properly. Both he and Seijun each had a history of playing *Galaga*, and a rivalry soon followed as the two got in a few games and knocked off the rust. Chad was afraid to join in it was so competitive.

Throughout that week his relationship with Vanessa grew. There was the birthday, where he met all her friends and family and she told him they all liked him; and then that Friday she and Edie went out to dinner with him and Steve and Steve's family, which was also a success. His next plan was to take her and Edie out with Miguel and Julía and Richard, but that would have to wait until Vanessa and Edie came back from Florida for Edie's February vacation. They had made the plans months before Vanessa and Chad started dating, and though they considered altering them so Chad could come along, he needed to stay behind and work. So Chad spent that Friday night with her after going out to dinner, then drove her and Edie to the airport.

Now it was the Friday after, and he had spent seven long days without her, sleeping alone at his apartment. It was harder than he thought it was going to be, and as he watched Seijun and Lars's heated *Galaga* competition, he wondered how much work he really would've missed had he gone along. Secretly he rooted for Seijun, but outwardly he wanted to remain neutral, especially considering he'd agreed to join Lars out that night to get his mind off of missing Vanessa.

Seijun and Lars reminded him of himself and Dave when they used to play *Mortal Kombat* and *Street Fighter II* in high school. They always joked that the only reason Kovacs ever played *Galaga* was because he sucked so bad at *Mortal Kombat*, which Kovacs never admitted, but was true. Dave was hyper-competitive at everything, whereas Chad often didn't care one way or the other; but Chad had a knack for fighting games, had an innate ability to figure out which characters worked best against others, what things they did well and what their weaknesses were, and could discern the patterns in his opponent's attacks and anticipate what their next move would be and counter it appropriately. It irked Dave that he couldn't beat Chad on a consistent basis, no matter how hard he tried.

Mortal Kombat II was so popular that the local arcade had a big tournament, which Chad won, the prize being $200 worth of tokens that could only be used at the arcade—as good as gold as far as he was concerned. Dave was eliminated in the first round, and instead of staying to see how Chad did, stormed out and caught the bus home. Kovacs stayed, even though he hated *Mortal Kombat*, and cheered Chad on and talked trash to the other spectators about how good his boy was and how he'd beat everyone.

Chad thought about all that as Seijun rolled the score over and Lars fell to the ground dramatically. Was Dave ever a friend to him? It seemed like such a given—pre-Gwen obviously—but now he wasn't so sure. He tried to think of one good thing Dave ever did for him, one good moment they ever had together. Paris, they had Paris. That was an amazing time... no, I'm crazy, Dave and I were great friends in high school, weren't we? Now Kovacs was dead, and Kovacs was the one who stayed while he won the *Mortal Kombat II* tournament. Now after five years and two kids and all the heartache it caused Chad, Gwen was leaving Dave. Now Chad didn't even want Gwen, even if he could have her, because he had Vanessa. She would've stayed to watch him play in the *Mortal Kombat II* tournament.

Lars was excited to go out with Chad again, though Chad wasn't so sure. The thought of staying in and thinking about Vanessa all night sounded worse though. After their last night out, Chad asked Lars what the whole deal was with the Chicago song, and Lars explained that he loved messing with strippers.

"Did you see how quickly they went from not knowing what to think to dancing in front of me the moment I turned that Jungle Music back on?"

And it was at Elevens that they started, having supper at the buffet and checking out a few strippers. Then they went to the Dirty Sombrero, met a few girls Lars knew, who took them to a party near Dodge State with a bunch of kids that were about ten years younger than he and Lars. Chad didn't want to be there. He was seriously involved with a woman with an 11-year-old daughter, beer pong and binge drinking didn't have the excitement it once had. He wanted to leave, but Lars convinced him to stay and accompany the girls with him to Vito's, a much seedier strip club in a dirtier part of town. Chad didn't like this idea, but he agreed under the condition that he'd stay for one drink and leave after, and that Lars would get a ride home with the girls.

When they got there though, Chad regretted that decision. It was dirty, with all kinds of bikers and thugs and creepy looking characters, and they all looked at Chad and his crew like they either wanted to fight them or laugh at them. How could Lars be enjoying this? Why would he want to be here? Doesn't he know how stupid they all looked? But Lars had some romantic notion about it, like the depravity was something to be celebrated, like those poverty tourists who travel to Third World countries and take pictures of starving kids on the streets. If this were a zoo, there weren't any cages, and to Chad's mind these wild animals bite. He saw the men leering at the girls they had with them, wondering what he would do if one of them made a threatening move. He couldn't do anything to protect these girls in this place. Those bikers would eat him alive. But Lars and the girls were so sure this was where they wanted to be. Besides, the music was the same. Flo-Rida was pretty universal at the strip club it seemed, no matter where it was. One drink Chad, you promised.

They took a seat around one of the stages, near the only group of similarly attired patrons. There were two guys, one about Chad's age, and the other a little older. The older one had a rubber mask of a political figure set back on his head, as if he'd been wearing it on his face, but took it off for a second to get some air. They had four Thai women with them in shiny dresses and black pleather boots.

The sense of finding a familiar face in a strange location that these two similarly attired men brought faded after the one with the mask pulled it down and pointed to Lars.

"Who let that fucking Swede in here? I fucking hate Swedes! Matty, get Guido over and tell him to remove that man!"

"Cut the shit, dude, you're scaring the ladies."

"Hey, what's your fucking friend's problem?" Lars said.

Oh Jesus, Chad thought, please don't do this! But instead of telling Lars to stop, he sat there helplessly.

There weren't any girls dancing at their stage, so no one stood in the masked man's way as he leaped up and darted across to Lars. Before any of them knew what was happening, Chad had been knocked to the floor and the man had Lars from behind in a rear naked choke hold.

"You bastard fucking Swede! I know you voted for Nixon! I'm fucking Hubert Humphrey damn it! You ruined my life!"

Matty walked over and wedged his hands in between the man's arm and Lars's neck.

"All right Mads, that's enough. I can't fucking take you anywhere."

Once Mads released Lars, Matty went over to Chad, who was resting back on his elbows on the floor. He helped him up and dusted him off.

"Hi, I'm Matty."

"Um, I'm Chad."

"I know."

"You know? Have we met?"

"This music kind of sucks, huh? Flo-Rida? What the hell is that anyway? Let's try this:" he snapped his fingers, and the song over the speakers changed to Ashley Simpson's "Pieces of Me." Chad looked around, but no one else in the strip club missed a beat, as if the song had never changed. "You've heard that one enough though, huh? How about this?" He snapped his fingers again, and the song changed to OMD's "If You leave." "I've always loved this one."

"How did you do that? Is this some kind of joke? I think it's time my friends and I—"

"Your friends are fine. Why don't you come back with me to the VIP room?"

"Um, I don't..."

"Please, I want to make up for my friend Mads's abhorrent behavior. It'll be fine, Vanessa will never find out."

A wave of apprehension went through Chad's body. Who is this guy? How does he know me? Did I meet him at Vanessa's birthday party? He does look kind of like one of her friends' husbands. Now he was embarrassed that he didn't remember. This guy seemed like a weirdo, but he'd see what was going on in the VIP room for a second just to make sure he didn't insult one of Vanessa's friends.

Matty led him around the corner through a swinging door into a brightly lit room. There weren't any strippers in there, just a group of people at a table playing cards, and some others sitting on some leather couches having drinks. One of them was the guy who accosted Lars. How did he get in here?

"Who, Mads? He's always in here. You mean when he was out... oh right, that would seem odd, wouldn't it?"

What the hell is going on? That guy read my mind! No way, this isn't happening. Lars must've put something in my drink. I'll fucking kill that bastard!

"No, it wasn't Lars, no one put something in your drink."

"How the fuck do you know what I'm thinking?"

"I am what you're thinking. Watch:"

he snapped his fingers again, and Chad heard the words 'he snapped his fingers again' come through a large speaker mounted on the wall. What the hell is going on? he thought...

"Jesus, that's my..."

Then he tried to stop thinking, afraid of his thoughts coming through the loud speaker so everyone could hear them.

"Watch, I can do this too:"

Er schnippte mit den Fingern. Was ist das? Deutsch? Ich kann nicht Deutsch. Wie macht er das? Was passiert! He snapped his fingers aga—

"Okay, enough of that. Here, let me have a look at you."

Matty took Chad by the shoulders and looked him up and down. Chad turned away to the people playing cards. There were two white guys, one of them bald, and a black woman sitting on the lap of the other. He noticed after a moment that the guys were twins.

"I wasn't sure how you'd turn out you know. I kind of put you through the ringer a bit, didn't I? The girl peeing in her purse, the bear suit, the one who thought babies were born through a mother's stomach—which never really happened, but the 'people aren't animals' thing maybe did."

"Wait, how do you know all this, are you… God?…"

"Ha! He wishes," said one of the guys on the couch, sitting next to Mads. Chad noticed that Matty was sitting with them, yet standing in front of Chad at the same time. *Why would God be in the form of a late-twenty-something guy? I thought God was supposed to be in my image or something—or at least an old guy.*

"You are in my image, sort of."

Chad looked down and saw his left arm connected at the wrist to Matty's right, and he was pulled closer, so that his shoulder met Matty's, melding together like Siamese twins.

"Sometimes I have to remind myself where you begin and I end. See, everyone else here, the people playing cards, the people drinking at the back, they all once looked like me—look at those guys over there."

Chad turned back to the card table and saw a black man with the others. He had an "M" tattooed over his right eye. There was also an Asian dressed like a detective from an old movie. In a corner behind the table, there was a blond woman in daisy dukes and a tight white T-shirt with large sunglasses next to a short, white guy in a dark Hawaiian shirt with a mustache and aviators. Then he looked to the couches, and saw a guy about Matty's age, sitting with his legs crossed, reading *King Lear*. Standing next to that was Matty again, only older, in between an overweight man in his 40s, and a kid who looked like a 90s teen pop idol. Finally, there were two teenagers, a boy and girl, fraternal twins, with dark hair and dark eyes, both looking at him, the boy filming him with a digital camera.

Then he saw an image of himself break away from his merger with Matty and join the people on the couch. He hadn't even noticed that he himself was no longer connected.

"Is this heaven? Am I dead?"

"No, you're still alive. Hopefully you'll live forever actually… anyway, this is getting a little too indulgent."

"As if it weren't already," one of the twins at the table, the bald one, said.

"You're right, and you've still got some work to do before you come back here—or I've still got some work to do—but anyway, here:"

He snapped his fingers, and in an instant, Chad woke in his bed. What a weird dream.

Amy's Adventure

Wow, I do look a lot older, Amy thought as she studied herself in the long mirror in her mother's room. Her mother didn't come home the night before, and Amy hoped to be gone before she got back. She looked just like a business woman, with her hair up and tight against her head, wearing a black suit with white pinstripes and black nylons and leather pumps. Her face was covered in foundation with a lot of mascara and eyeliner and dark red lipstick—though not too much, she didn't want to "look like a slut." She spun and danced and thought about all the fun she was about to have.

Back in her room she made sure everything was packed. She had her bikini, her red dress she wore when she went to the winter formal with Brittney, and her Wonder Woman costume. He said he'd buy her anything else she needed, but she had to bring that Wonder Woman costume no matter what. It all fit in a Chanel bag he bought her just for the occasion. As she looked around for her iPod, she saw the book Chad had given her for Christmas. *The Beginner's Guide to Directing Movies*. She thought about that night she wanted to surprise him, how she thought his buying her a gift for Christmas meant he felt the same for her that she felt for him. She wore that red dress she wore when she went to the winter formal, she put on her make-up, had Brittney help her with her hair, then got Richard to give her Chad's key. Richard thought she looked so hot he would've done anything for her. But then Chad came home with that other woman, and now he was in love with her—that's what Dick said, said his father told him and his mother that at supper one night. Dick was saying it so Amy would get over Chad and consider dating him, but she didn't want Dick, she wanted Chad, and Chad only thought of her like his little sister or niece or something.

Not all guys thought of her that way though. Some guys Chad's age saw how mature she was for her age, and now she was going to see one and spend an amazing week with him at his family's cabin in the mountains. Eat your heart out Chad.

As she rushed out to catch her cab to the train station, she passed Chad in the hallway.

"Hi Amy, how are you?"

"I'm great Chad, how are you?"

"I'm good… I'm not even going to ask."

She giggled. I spent all this time making myself look like this, and all he thinks is I'm going to make another YouTube video with Brittney. I'll show him. He'll be so jealous. Oh my God, I can't wait to ride on the train! I hope I look all right. I'll have to call Brittney and tell her. I hope she's not mad that I'm ditching her like this. I hope she doesn't tell on me. No, she'd never do that.

Amy was right, Chad didn't think anything of it when he passed her in the hallway. Monday was his last day without Vanessa. She and Edie would be flying in this evening, and he'd be leaving right after work to pick her up. That was all he thought about. One week without her was torture, and he knew from his Friday out with Lars and the disaster that that was he was

200

done partying like a twenty-year-old. He hadn't heard from Lars since that night, and was hoping to talk to him that day at work, find out exactly what happened. He didn't even notice Amy hopping into a cab instead of waiting for the bus or Brittney's mom. He didn't even notice that it was a little late in the morning to be going to school.

He wouldn't get his chance to talk to Lars, because Lars wasn't at the office. Seijun said he'd called in sick, and that was it.

"It's not like we need him here much anyway. He's usually just bugging us when we're trying to do our work."

Seijun told Chad this as he got in another game of *Galaga* in the rec room. Chad was able to obtain a basic idea of what Seijun wanted done that day in between levels, and then he went into his office and tried to concentrate.

The fund had had larger than expected gains in the last quarter, and Seijun was doubling down, leveraging them even more for potentially bigger returns. Chad received his first pay check, roughly $9000 for about 6 weeks-worth of work, which meant he'd be making more than he did at the insurance firm if those numbers continued—and based on Seijun's projections, they could be much more prodigious. At that moment, it didn't matter though, all that mattered was picking Vanessa up from the airport and biding his time until Edie went to bed. Vanessa's texts told him that she was feeling the same way.

"miss u so much ☹" "u better be staying over tonight!!! lol" "can't wait to see u ☺" "just so u kno, ure not getting any sleep tonight. lol!"

Finally enough hours had passed from the present to the past, and it was time to leave work and get Vanessa and Edie. He didn't know that Vanessa had spent ten minutes in the airport bathroom, making herself up so she'd be pretty for Chad after their flight, annoying poor Edie who had to stand there at the mirror, wondering why her mother was going to such fuss. She made herself up, made sure her sweater was unbuttoned over her tank top, and made sure he felt her chest as she hugged him hello. Chad thought she was even prettier than he remembered. A week was a long time.

The whole ride home Chad and Vanessa held hands and looked at each other and thought about all the things they wanted to do to each other, while Edie told Chad everything about their trip from the backseat. Then they had pizza, and Edie fell asleep on the couch as they looked at some pictures. Chad carried her up to bed, tucked her in, and saw Vanessa standing behind him in the doorway.

"You don't know how long I've been waiting for this."

You've been waiting?

Wednesday evening, while he was eating supper with Vanessa and Edie, he had a call from Miguel. He figured it was about some soccer game he wanted to watch or seeing if Chad minded if he played *FIFA* while Chad wasn't there.

"Hey man, are you at Vanessa's? You need to come over here."

"Why, what about?"

Miguel sounded graver than Chad ever remembered him being.

"I think you just need to come over here and we'll explain then."

When he got there, he saw Miguel, Julía, and Amy's mother in the hallway talking to a police detective. They called Chad over when they saw him. The detective was a big man of Irish descent with gray hair and icy blue eyes. After a quick introduction he cut right to the chase.

"When was the last time you saw Amy?"

His "saw" sounded like it had an "r" on the end of it in his local accent.

Chad almost said yesterday, and then realized he hadn't been home since Monday morning.

"It was Monday morning. I was leaving for work as she was going to school."

"What time do you leave for work?"

"About 9ish, like quarter of I'd say."

"You didn't think it was odd she was leaving so late for school?"

Jesus, no, he didn't, did he?

"You know, now that you mention it—I should have, it was just my girlfriend and her daughter were flying home from Florida that same day, and that was kind of on my mind."

The detective wrote some notes in a little pad.

"Did you notice anything else odd about her, what she was wearing, her demeanor, anything like that?"

"Um, well, she was dressed up like a businesswoman—"

"To go to school?"

"Well, the thing with Amy is, she and her friend Brittney are always making videos on YouTube—Miguel and Julía know what I'm talking about—but they're always up to something, and I just thought maybe it was a school project or something like that."

The detective's pupils dilated.

"YouTube videos, huh? Does she use the computer a lot?"

Her mother had no real idea, but Chad, Miguel, and Julía were all in agreement.

"Do you know if she used any other sites or met or came into contact with anyone over the internet."

Oh my God, Chad thought, this was serious. Amy was really missing, and this cop really thought something bad might have happened to her.

"What is this about?"

"Amy has been missing since Monday. The school received a call on their answering machine Sunday night from a woman saying she was Amy's mother and that Amy would be out of town for the week because her grandmother passed away. After not coming home for two nights, Amy's mother called Brittney's mother, who was already suspicious when her daughter hadn't hung out with Amy, considering the two were inseparable. After questioning Brittney, they found out she ran off with some guy named Lars."

Chad went numb for a second, then leaned against the wall and slid down, until he was resting on the carpet. The detective went over to him.

"Is everything okay, Chad?"

"No, no it isn't. Lars is my co-worker... I... he met Amy here, at my apartment..."

Amy's mother shot over to him.

"What was my daughter doing at your place!"

Julía restrained her and pulled her away, but she was livid. The detective took Chad and Miguel into Chad's apartment to question him further. Chad went into everything, about Amy and Brittney's YouTube videos, the creepy requests, how Chad warned her about that because of his own experience with MacKenzie and Hestermann, and how she and Brittney came over one time in their superhero costumes. He told the officer about Lars's comments, and how he told Chad he didn't know how young the girls were. From there, he never heard Lars mention her again. He got the detective a bunch of pictures of Lars off his Facebook account, and gave him Lars's address in Winchester Estates.

Outside, the detective explained to a more stoic Amy's mom what the situation was, that they were going to put out an APB for Lars, put his pictures on the news, and see if anyone knows where they could be. They'd let her know when they heard something.

The detective left, and Amy's mother broke down in Julía's arms. While Chad was in his apartment with Miguel and the cop, Julía scolded her, telling her what a good guy Chad was, how nice he had been to encourage Amy's love of movie making, and that she had no right to blame Chad for this. She let Amy's mother know all the times they had had Amy over for supper, let Amy spend the night when *she* had men over. Then, in her moment of anger, she leveled the blow she immediately wished she had back: she said "maybe if you'd been a better mother to her none of this would've happened!"

Amy's mother's first instinct was to protest. Who was this woman to tell her what kind of parent she was? But then she realized that *this woman* was the one who was taking Amy in when she thought Amy was at Brittney's or out chasing guys or whatever. This woman, and Chad, the guy across the hall, whose friend is the guy that took her daughter God knows where. *Her* daughter, the one this woman just told her she probably didn't even deserve to have.

She went back into her apartment, sick to her stomach. She thought about her poor girl, in the hands of some guy who knows where doing who knows what. My daughter wants to direct movies? How did I not know that? She could be the next Steven Spielberg or something, wow! If she's not dead. No, no, nonononono, she's not dead! If Chad knew that guy and he worked with him, then he must not be a killer, right? But what is he doing with her then? Oh God, don't think about it!

She sat near the window sill, and saw her Exposé CD next to her. What was this doing out? Was Amy listening to it? She popped it into the stereo. She knew what song she wanted.

She started crying again. The song brought on more pain than just the fear of what happened to her missing daughter. When she was first pregnant with Amy, she was scared and excited at the same time. She loved the father so much, he was rich, smart, athletic, sexy, great in bed. He was the perfect guy. She met him while waiting tables at a bar downtown. They were the same age, but she went to Quincy Adams—about 5 years before Chad—and he went to Oak Grove. To him, she was some cute chick he slept with on the side, but not anything serious. The first thing he did when Amy's mother told him she was pregnant with his baby was ask: "are you sure?" then "how much do you need to get it taken care of?" Taken care of? Weren't they going to get married? Live in a nice house? Didn't he love her?

No, he wanted to be done with her, and for nine months she sat in her room in her mom's house and thought about him, listening to Exposé's "I'll Never Get Over You Getting Over Me", hoping that he'd come around, hoping he was just scared but he'd really come around and love her. Then when she had the baby she called him and a woman answered the phone. It was his fiancée. Now she didn't want Amy. She thought Amy would win him back, and when it didn't, Amy didn't matter.

Amy's mother's mother did a lot to help her in the early years, including securing a substantial amount of child support from the father. It's that child support that pays for an apartment in Chad's building, floats them by when Amy's mother is between jobs, and keeps Amy's mom in booze and men. It also reminds Amy's mother how much her heart was broken, like a scab pulled off once a month for fifteen years, reopening the wound. The check, and Amy's eyes. She had to have *his* eyes, and she had to see them in her every day.

As she listened to the song, the song that she used to put on repeat for hours on end, she understood what all of this must've meant to Amy. It wasn't Amy's fault she had his eyes, and Amy didn't deserve it when she looked at her mother in the way he did for her mother to go out and get drunk and bring some guy home.

She was looking out the window as the maintenance guys were across the quad replacing the outdoor lights on another building. Their apartment was a two-bedroom like Chad's that opened into the living room the same way, but the kitchen was smaller, part of it separated from the living room with a wall that had a large opening. There was clutter everywhere, stacks of books, fake flowers, clothes, old catalogs; blankets and robes all over the couch and recliner. Amy was really the only one who cleaned, and she only understood "clean" as everything being moved from off the floor.

She went to the computer that was right behind her as she faced the window, against that wall that separated the kitchen and living Room. She turned it on and went to YouTube. She was horrible with these things, but luckily Amy's account was still logged in. There were all her videos. What is this, "I Wish the Phone Would Ring"? Oh my God, that's my daughter on here! She looks so cute! Why didn't she show me that she did this?... but Amy's mother knew the answer to that, and started crying again.

Then she paged down through the comments on her page. "Show some titsssssss!" "U should make out!" "Get nakidddddddd!!!!!" Jesus Christ, she's only 15! Who are these perverts? Most of them sounded like they were from another country and stuff, but it was scary. And the only person who was looking out for Amy and telling her she needed to report these guys was the guy living across the hall that she just blew up at. Certainly Amy's mother wasn't looking out for her. Julia was right, so right. Please God, protect my daughter. I promise I'll be a better mom to her, I promise. I'll go to AA and stop sleeping with all kinds of guys and stuff. Just don't let her get hurt, please!

"Chad, it wasn't your fault. Why don't you just come back here and we can talk. Please."

"How did I not notice that she was going to school at 9? And Lars, damn it! That fucking bastard. I introduced her to him."

"You didn't introduce her, she went over to your apartment."

"What if something happens to her? I'll never forgive myself."

"It's all over the news, they'll find her soon. Come on, please come home."

He had planned on holding firm to the stance that he'd stay at his apartment for the night, that he needed to be alone, that he was embarrassed and upset with himself, and most importantly that he could be closer to Miguel and Julia in case any new news came. But she used the word "home" to describe her dwelling to him. It wasn't "my place" or "my house" it was "home" with the "our" implied in front of it, in fact, it was more familiar because it omitted the "our." Couples that had been together for a long time didn't say "I'll see you at *our* house," they just called it "home," and Vanessa just called it "home."

"All right, I'll tell Miguel and see you in a few minutes."

The detective tracked down Lars's mother, and she knew right away where Lars was. Elsa had heard Lars make the plans to go to their house in the mountains with Amy over the phone. Lars didn't think anything of it, assuming Elsa didn't speak English. She told his mother, who put that knowledge in her pocket. It wouldn't be any harm, no one else was using it, why not let Lars have it for a week. But then the police called. A fifteen-year-old girl? Oh God. She called their lawyer. Don't say anything else and wait until he's arrested. It might not be as bad as it looked.

Lars never really erased from his mind the image of Amy dressed like Wonder Woman, sitting on the arm of Chad's recliner. 15? Come on. And was 15 that bad? The age of consent is 16, right? And couldn't he even marry her in some states? He didn't want to marry her though, just date her, see her dressed like Wonder Woman, have sex with her.

Is that bad, have sex with a 15-year-old? Chad seemed to think so, but Lars noticed Chad had all kinds of hang-ups. Look at him, he could get tons of women, and he settles for the first fat chick with a kid that comes around and sucks his dick. He didn't know how to live life. These rules were invented by stuck-up dudes that were jealous of guys like me that knew how take life by the balls and get the most out of it. And it's not like she isn't into this too.

A few days after meeting them at Chad's, Lars bumped into the girls at the mall. They chatted. Lars told Amy how cute she looked dressed like Wonder Woman. She giggled. She liked him, that was for sure. Then he got to thinking. She must be on Facebook. He looked on Chad's. Not there. Damn, all he had a was a first name. And a high school. She must go to Forest Hills right around the corner. There she is. I'll send her an add request.

And it just went from there. Chats, messages—nothing out in the open though. Amy, for her part, kept up her end in the hopes it would get her closer to Chad. Maybe Lars would put in a good word for her. Chad buying her a Christmas present gave her the impression that it was working. So she went for her move... and was thoroughly embarrassed. That night she was on the computer at 2AM, and found Lars on there, and they chatted. She poured out her heart, and he took mental notes, using them later to win her over, show her that he was the guy for her—though not telling her about the other women he was sleeping with during the same period.

Conversations became more sexual in nature. Amy had never had a boyfriend before, and she thought everything Lars told her about people and relationships was the gospel truth. Amy was falling in love with Lars, and she wanted to see him. She had him over to her place a couple times when her mom wasn't home, but Lars found it hard to sneak in and out of the building without looking conspicuous. He was her first kiss. He told her she was beautiful. He also had her dress up in the Wonder Woman costume. She wasn't ready to go the way yet though. Lars thought she should be by now, and he suggested a trip to his parents' house in the mountains to make her more comfortable.

For Lars's part, Amy was one of many potential female conquests. He liked talking to her because she was a girl and hot and obviously liked him, which stroked his ego. But this cockteasing with the Wonder Woman costume was too much. He needed to hit that. It was like a mechanism had gone off in him, from the moment her saw her at Chad's, and that mechanism drove him beyond normal rational thinking and accountability. He convinced himself that none of this was truly wrong, just wrong in the eyes of some arbitrary rules system laid out by some stuffed shirted morons.

Those same stuff shirted morons had his license, and while he was willing to take a 15-year-old girl to a house in the mountains, doing it with a suspended license was too much of a risk—plus, his mother wouldn't let him have the Mercedes that long. But how would he get Amy on the train with him? They'd want her ID, find out she's only 15, and the gig is up. How would they get her past that? When in doubt, play your CARD: Class, Age, Race, Descent. No one questions you if you look like a rich white businessperson, right? So we make Amy look older, richer, and more powerful. She actually had the business suit from a previous YouTube video, and Lars had her take it downtown for tailoring; and she also knew how to do her hair and make-up. As expected, the agent didn't think twice when she took her ticket—and Amy is a really good actor.

Amy was nervous, but she was so excited. All she wanted to do was jump into Lars's arms and watch the city turn into the country and mountains from the window. She wanted to text Brittney all day too. Then they got to the house, and Lars changed. He wanted her to drink, wanted her to do coke with him. She didn't do drugs, and didn't like alcohol after seeing what her mom was like. He wouldn't let her watch *Gossip Girls*. They went in the hot tub, and he was pawing all over her. She kissed him. She liked kissing him, but then he touched her down there! She screamed and jumped out and ran into the bathroom and locked the door.

Lars was shocked. This was a 15-year-old girl for God's sake, how could he be getting shot down by her? He went to the bathroom door to convince her to give him what he wanted. This is what couples do Amy, look at your mom. He was right about that, Amy thought. If you loved me you'd do this. Well, if you loved me you'd wait until I was ready. Lars didn't expect that. Come on, normal women are ready by now, if you loved me you'd be ready by now. If *you* loved me you'd wait forever for me to be ready. I want you to take me home. I can't take you home, there aren't any more trains until tomorrow. Then I want to go home tomorrow. And what, you're going to stay in the bathroom until then? If I have to. He knocked loudly. Come on, cut the shit! This is ridiculous! You're acting like a little girl! It scared her. What if he knocked down the door? She sat huddled in the bathtub until the knocking stopped. She heard him doing something, banging things around, muttering to himself, then the front door opened and slammed. He was gone.

She waited fifteen minutes, then crept into the living room. She wanted to call Brittney, but she had no service. She considered packing her things and leaving, running to the nearest house and asking for help. Lars turned out to be a jerk. She was so stupid for falling for him. Now she was crying, freezing in her bikini, kneeling on the kitchen floor. Then she thought she was acting even stupider for crying about it. This is a pretty nice place, and if Lars wasn't here, she'd take advantage of it. First thing's first though: she grabbed the biggest knife out of the drawer, just in case Lars came home drunk and wanted to try something. Then she fished out a menu to a local pizza place in another drawer, and found some cash in Lars's bedroom. She went into another room, which was Lars's parents' room, but she didn't know that. She found his mother's red silk pajamas, and while they were a bit big on her, they were warmer and more comfortable than the bikini. She locked herself in that room when the pizza was delivered and turned on the TV. Now this was the life: mushroom and pepperoni pizza, diet Pepsi, and *Gossip Girls*. Then tomorrow she'll go back to the train station and go home.

She was awoken in the middle of the night to Lars coming back with another woman. They had sex in the bedroom next to her. It was like being at home. She barely slept, then got up and dressed around 5, and had a cab pick her up at 6, sneaking outside without her heels on in the freezing, snowy ground, so she wouldn't wake up Lars and his girl. She had to wear the suit again, because the only other clothes she had were the bikini, the dress, and the Wonder Woman costume. The train station was open that early, but the next train home wasn't until 9. The area around the station was more built up than the remote location of the house, and she spotted a Dunkin' Donuts across the street. She ran as well as she could on the frozen road in her heels, in the dark because the sun hadn't come up yet, the wind biting her legs and unprotected face.

She forgot too that she didn't look like a 15-year-old in her suit and made-up face. She was hoping someone would see her and want to help, but no one had any reason to think anything was wrong with her. She took a seat in the corner with her OJ and bagel sandwich, and looked at the paper. That's when Dirk and his ski buddies came in and sat at the table across from her.

Dirk was so hot, hot in a very teen X-Games kind of way. She made eyes at him, and Dirk, thinking she was probably older than him and more sophisticated than him, couldn't believe it. He took a chance and asked her for the sports section, and she smiled and was very amenable in obliging. Wow, she did like him.

"I'm Dirk, by the way."

"I'm Amy, nice to meet you."

"What're you, in town on business?"

"Business…?… oh yeah, because… yeah, business. Yeah, it was some big real estate thing, it finished last night, so I was going to take the train back in a few hours."

"Oh that's rad, like tons of money an' stuff?"

"Yeah, one of those cottages over there in the woods."

"Oh, that the rich yuppies own. Sweet."

She giggled. Do women who sell multimillion dollar properties giggle? Dirk thought. Maybe all women giggle when they meet a guy they like.

"So what do you do Dirk?"

"Oh, me and my buddies over there go to DSU. I'm a business major, actually. Gonna like take over my dad's construction company when I'm older an' stuff."

"Oh, wow, that's really cool."

"Yeah?"

"Yeah…"

She made eyes at him and giggled, wanting to play with her hair but couldn't because it was up. Dirk couldn't believe this.

"What?" He said.

"What do you mean 'what'?"

"Like you're all like smiling and staring at me and stuff... I mean I like it, don't get me wrong, but..."

She giggled.

"So, like, you know, do you have a boyfriend?"

"A boyfriend?" She giggled again. "We just broke up... so to speak... why, do you have a girlfriend?"

"Um, no, not at all."

"That's cool... I mean... you know..."

As much as Dirk couldn't believe this 25-year-old businesschick who sold multimillion-dollar properties could be into him, Amy couldn't believe this totally hot snowboarder that was in college could be asking her, a sophomore in high school, if *she* had a girlfriend.

"Hey, listen, me and my buddies are going to hit Goose Eye today, do some snowboarding. We're staying at Austin's, my buddy over there's parents' place, just outside of town. It's really nice, and some other people are coming up from State tonight, it should be a pretty sweet party. I don't know if..."

Oh my God, Goose Eye Mountain! This cute guy was inviting her to Goose Eye Mountain? She'd always wanted to go there! It's like only the coolest ski resort in the state. Except, how would that work when she had no ski clothes?...

"I'd love to... the only problem is, I only have this... and my bikini..."

"We'll save the bikini for the hot tub later.... The rest of your gear we can rent. It's no problem."

Ugh! What about money? She took enough of Lars's money to get the cab, and had enough left over to get the bagel and OJ. She didn't want to take more than that because she felt he owed her the cab money after what happened, but anything more would be stealing. But now this cute guy was asking her to go to Goose Eye Mountain with him!

"Um... I don't really have enough money though either."

He was puzzled by this one. A real estate agent who sells multimillion dollar cottages can't afford a lift ticket and to rent some gear? Amy could tell her ruse was fading, Dirk was seeing cracks. She needed to think of something quick.

"I only have a business credit card, you know, a company thing. I wasn't expecting to be here to ski, so I just brought that and figured I'd put everything on my expense account. I can't very well put snowboard stuff on it, can I?"

"Oh, geez, I totally didn't think of that, you're right. Don't worry about it then, I'll cover you."

And that was her Tuesday, Dirk teaching her to snowboard, dinner with the guys and some of their girlfriends—one of whom let her borrow an outfit, though it was still a bit big on her. All the girls remarked on how small and thin she was, and how jealous they were. They were pleasantly surprised too that she wasn't stuck up. Wow, it was hard to believe she was older than them, but the guys swore she had to be at least 25 from how she looked earlier. A 25-year-old real estate agent who watched *Teen Mom*? Really cool. They wanted make-up tips from her too.

The party was amazing. She'd never been to anything so great. She still didn't have service, otherwise she would've called Brittney to tell her how much fun she was having, and how much she missed her and wished she was up there with her to experience it. Had she had service, she would have seen the texts she missed from Brittney telling her that their moms knew the truth.

She didn't drink at all, but unlike Lars, no one was upset after she said why. But their understanding made her want to try some beer. God, it's so disgusting, why do people drink this? Then there was Dirk. He was so amazing. So strong and comforting when he was teaching her to snowboard, so patient and calm, and so Goddamn hot!

And Dirk couldn't believe this hot chick in the business suit could be here with him, ready to hook up. Man though, what do you do with a girl that's this high class? She doesn't even drink. The girls all seem to like her. God, look at her in that bikini. Let me lean in and see what happens.

Oh no, he's going to kiss me. Don't act like a dork Amy, don't act like a dork! Yes! After the initial kiss she moved in and pulled him from behind his head to her and kissed him more aggressively. Dirk read this and reciprocated. Oh God, he's so good, and so nice. I need to tell him the truth… no Amy, you need to have fun… what's one night, and then you can leave him and never see him again. I can't have sex with him one night though, he'll know I'm a virgin, won't he? Should my first time be a one-night-stand? God he feels so nice! Yes, let's go to the bedroom.

This was it, she decided. Dirk was as good a guy as any to be her first time. 15 wasn't too young, and he was 19, which wasn't too old, right? Yes, she wanted this, she was ready… and so was Dirk—maybe a little too ready. Amy had never seen anything like that before, and she let out a screaming "oh my God!" Dirk put his hand over her mouth.

"Shhhh… oh man, I swear this has never happened before, I swear… oh man, oh God, oh fuck."

Amy giggled. She put her hand on his shoulder.

"Hey man, it's okay, it happens to all the guys"—does it?— "don't sweat it." Ugh, did she just say "don't sweat it"?

"Really? I mean, has it happened to other guys you've been with?"

"Yeah, sure. Listen, if you want, you can tell your friends and stuff that we did it. I don't mind. It's not like I know all these people, right? And after tomorrow we'll all be strangers anyway."

"We will?... I mean, yeah, of course, we will, you're right…"

She was sitting up in the bed in the lotus position. Dirk laid down beside her, and she joined him, curling herself into his arms. She didn't want her first time to be a one-night stand anyway.

The next morning the girls offered to give her a ride home, since they were going that way. Did she mind stopping at the outlet malls though? No, of course not. She didn't have any money though—business card, remember? Oh yeah, when do you have to be to work again anyway? Thursday. I got two days off after finalizing that great deal. Man, she was getting really good at lying. It was just like acting, only easier. It was like these people wanted to believe she was someone, and all she had to do was give it to them. She couldn't believe she was helping late teens/early twentysomethings with their make-up. But they loved how she did it, she *just* had to show them how she got her eyes like that.

It was Wednesday night, as she was eating at TGI Friday's with the State girls near the outlet malls, about an hour from home and an hour from the mountains, when the cops busted into Lars's parents' house, finding neither Lars nor Amy, but finding evidence that Lars was staying

209

there, and probably had taken he and Amy out. There was a town-wide APB, but Lars did their work for them, coming home later that night with a different girl. The cops thought she was Amy, and they swarmed in, separating the two, pinning Lars to the ground and not believing his girl that she wasn't Amy, even thinking her license was a fake ID.

"You morons, that's not her, she left Monday night."

"What the fuck are they talking about Lars? Who is Amy? I'm not fucking 15 you morons. Do I look 15? Jesus Christ!"

By the time they sorted that out and arrested Lars, Amy had seen the texts from Brittney, and apprehensively walked into her apartment, hoping her mom wouldn't be there. Her mom was there, and tackled her she was so excited. Amy didn't know what to say, her mom inundated her with apologies and diatribes about her YouTube page and praise about her YouTube videos and more apologies and how worried she was and everything. It was overwhelming, and at first Amy was too stunned to react, but she slowly understood that her mom was worried, and had also somehow for some reason found her YouTube page and liked her videos, but not the creepy guys making requests. Did her mom just say she was proud of her? Amy had to cry too. After their moment, Amy's mom went next door and told Miguel that she was home, and then called the detective, who told her that Lars had been arrested.

That night, Dirk and all his friends saw Amy's picture on the news. Holy shit! 15! Now Dirk was stuck between a rock and a hard place, because he wanted his friends to know the truth, that he didn't have sex with a 15-year-old, but the truth kinda sucked too. The girls, other than Dirk sleeping with her, thought it was pretty cool that a 15-year-old could be so worldly, and kind of wanted to hang out with her again.

Chad got the call from Miguel that night telling him that Amy was all right. The next day he got the rest of the details from the TV. Lars had been released on bond, his official story was that Amy wanted to run away from home, and nothing happened between them. Amy told the police what actually happened, which led to the even bigger story of how she fooled a bunch of college kids and an entire ski resort town into thinking she was a high-end real estate agent. In fact, everyone in town who saw her couldn't believe she was the same girl that went missing on TV.

The first thing Chad heard when he made it to work that next morning was someone playing the guitar. It was Seijun, with the door shut in his office. The secretaries informed him that investors had been contacting him left and right, wanting to take their money out. Jesus, we're so leveraged right now we'll lose everything. He went to the door and listened. Seijun wasn't just playing, he was singing, Brittney Spears's "Lucky," in a raspy, Blues singer voice.

Chad slowly opened the door. There was Seijun with his guitar sitting in the lotus position on his desk, wearing a white V-neck undershirt and navy blue nurse's scrub pants, barefoot. His hair was messy and over his eyes, and he hadn't shaved.

"Seijun?"

He nodded but kept singing.

"Jesus man, what the hell is wrong with you? Are you fucking singing Brittney Spears?"

"We're done Chad. You've seen the numbers, we're leveraged to the hilt. Lars man, he fucked us…"

He transitioned into Brittney's "Sometimes."

"Dude, have you been drinking?"

He nodded again without missing a beat.

Chad ran over and put his hands on the guitar.

"Jesus Christ dude, pull yourself together."

"Why? All of it, everything I worked for— we worked for—done because Lars wanted to fuck some 15-year-old."

Chad grabbed him by the V-neck.

"I know that fucking 15-year-old. She's my neighbor."

Seijun put his guitar down and sat up.

"Geez, I'm sorry."

"What's the deal, what are we up against? How many want to pull their money out?"

"Here, take a look:"

He swung his MacBook around and showed Chad the numbers. Chad studied them for a second. This job was the best thing he'd had in a long time, and he knew he'd need to keep it if he wanted to keep Vanessa. He'd be damned if he'd leave this and go back to a cubicle.

"Dude, five of these guys live in the area. Let's clean you up and meet each one face to face. Then we have a few scattered out on the West Coast. We could fly out tonight."

"What are you talking about?"

"Dude, we don't need Lars anymore, we haven't needed him since you paid the rest of his mother's loan in the last quarter."

"But he brought in some of these people, we can't—"

"The numbers speak for themselves. We go there, face to face, show these figures and projections, tell them we're done with Lars, that all he was was some initial start-up cash and connections, but now it's you and me. Come on, tell me this isn't worth fighting for, not when we're so close! If your projections pan out—"

"Not if, when. I've studied this quite a bit. I'm not just playing *Galaga* all day you know."

"Come on, you wanna go bankrupt, or you wanna fight for this?"

Seijun looked at him for a second. Wow, he was serious. This is Chad? This is the guy who'd never been to Vegas before, didn't know what he was doing out there? Had no wardrobe to speak of until Lars and I took him out and picked out his clothes for him? He's the one telling me I need to cut the shit? And he's *serious*. Yes, he's right.

He hit the intercom button on his phone.

"Betty, I'm going to need you to call some people, tell them we need to see them ASAP."

Yes, Chad thought, let's do this.

Within a few minutes, Seijun had reestablished the old pecking order. Chad marveled at the ease and speed with which he went from disheveled, hair all over the place, rocking five o'clock shadow, a V-Neck and nurse's scrubs, to clean shaven, nattily attired in a suit that made Chad's look like he bought it at JC Penny's, and his hair looking so perfect, you'd think he spent three hours on it alone putting each follicle in place. No one would believe that just ten minutes ago he was a drunken mess singing Brittney Spears songs in a gruff singer/songwriter's voice.

"I think I still smell like booze, what do you think?"

"Hard to tell with your cologne. I wouldn't worry about it."

"All right, let's do this."

Seijun had Chad drive them in his Jetta over to the lawyer's office first. They were stuck in traffic.

"Jesus, we probably should've walked. I forgot about the construction on 16th."

Chad nodded.

"I'm thinkin' Lars won't want to be bought out so easily, especially since he knows what we're on the verge of here; but we have a clause in our business agreement about actions detrimental to the fund, which I'm hoping we can invoke. The other thing I'm thinking is, Lars's mother is probably mortified by this whole thing, and we did just pay her loan to us off, meaning she's not out anything as far as we go. I bet if we go to *her* with the buyout offer, instead of Lars, she'll think it's better to only have to fight on one front—the criminal charges that could carry potential jail time, and are already dragging her family's name through the mud. If she can be done with us, all the better."

When Chad blurted out to Seijun that they didn't need Lars anymore, he didn't consider Lars having a legal stake in the company, didn't consider that cutting ties with him might be tougher than just removing his name from his office door. But this was why he admired Seijun, because Seijun did consider that, and in a very Machiavellian way, thought of using Lars's mom as the quickest route to get them out from under him.

The lawyer agreed, and drew up the paperwork to present to Lars's mother's attorney, saying he hoped he'd get an answer in a few days. They chatted with the lawyer for a few minutes about the craziness of the situation, then left to meet the first of the investors.

"Alan Kroger, 55, owns Kroger Landscaping. He has three daughters, 2 right around your neighbor's age, and according to Betty, he was the first to call this morning and demand his money out. If we can get him, we'll have an in with the others, because we can say 'if Alan's back in, and he has three daughters....' "

Alan was a clean cut, distinguished man, one of those fiftysomethings that people call "mature" instead of "old". He was the kind of guy that one couldn't picture as a child, as an infant, as having ever been younger than he was now in his fifties. His business office was on an upper floor of the building, and had a nice view of the water. He was ready to take a hard line, and thought the visit from Seijun and Chad was rather dubious. That was until he was introduced to Chad. He knew Chad's mother.

"Are you the war hero son or the son that saved the girl from the pedophile?"

"Um… the second."

He put out his hand to Chad. Seijun could hardly contain his excitement. He had no idea what Chad did, but whatever it was it looked good. Chad was nonplussed at Alan's change of tone too, and in that state, he wasn't prepared for Alan's firm, hardy handshake, which crushed his fingers and hurt his wrist. It was the kind of handshake that told him Alan Kroger was a much better man to have on his side than against him.

"Why don't you two have a seat. Would you like my secretary to get you some coffee or something?"

Chad couldn't believe what was happening, but seeing how cool Seijun was playing it, he wanted to follow suit. Seijun felt the same way, but he knew he wasn't out of the water yet.

"Let's cut right to the chase: we're in the process of buying out Lars's interest in the hedge fund. We know, as you know, that we can't go forward with him."

"You understand my position Seijun. He's met my two youngest daughters, and after hearing what was said about him on the news last night, I can't in good conscience have my money in a fund run by someone like that. Now, if you're replacing him with a guy like this fella, well…"

"I should point out Alan, that Lars did absolutely nothing as far as the day-to-day running of the fund. I make all of the investment decisions, and Chad here has been with us since December doing the administrative work. You did like the return on our initial short sales, right? And the projections I sent you for the next quarter aren't any different after what happened last night. If the only issue is Lars, then I can say with all assuredness that his departure will do nothing to affect the return we're expecting on your investment." He handed Kroger a print-out of the figures. "It's up to you, and if you still want to pull your money out, we can do that for you, I just want to make sure any decision you make is done with a full recognition of the facts and what the ramifications of pulling your money out now could mean for your bottom line."

Kroger saw the potential money laid out for him on the sheet, and he thought about what he and his wife and kids could do with that.

"And you're no longer associated with Lars?"

"Our attorney is faxing the buyout agreement to his mother's attorney as we speak. We're hoping she'll want to settle this quickly, because I can't imagine she'd want a legal battle with us while Lars deals with his criminal charges."

He stood, and Seijun and Chad did with him, Chad mimicking Seijun buttoning his coat as they did so.

"Okay, I'll keep my money in for now, but I want confirmation next week that Lars is no longer a part of your operation."

"Absolutely."

There were more firm handshakes, and Kroger saw them out.

"Jesus Chad, have you been holding out on me? What did you do that made him think so highly of you?"

As they went back to the Jetta, Chad told Seijun about MacKenzie and Hestermann.

"Wow, how did I not know this?"

"You never asked, I guess."

Seijun laughed.

"All right man, let's go get some lunch. I want to let Kroger call his pals around town, put in a good word for us, before we go over and sell them on staying in. You did great in there, Chad, but we still have some work to do."

As they were eating at a 50s themed diner downtown, Chad tried to find in Seijun the distraught, disheveled man who was singing Brittney Spears that morning, while Seijun was trying to find in Chad the person who saved a girl's life ten years before. There was a faint sense over both of them that they were closer to equals than either thought. Not equals though. Chad was missing something that kept him from being Seijun all the time, and Seijun had something that kept him from being Chad for too long. But they saw that crack, Seijun saw that Chad could sometimes step up to the plate like him, and Chad saw that Seijun could sometimes breakdown like him, but even then it was foreign to the other. When Chad stepped up to the plate, he wasn't as smooth and crisp as Seijun was, there was something messy and uncouth about it; and when Seijun faltered, he didn't just sit at home in his pajamas and watch *Maury*, he sang Brittney Spears in a raspy voice—there was something cool about it, as if even in his worst moments he was cooler than Chad, and even in his best moments, Chad couldn't be as cool as Seijun.

But they fit together like Michael Jordan and Scottie Pippen, knocking out the other four investors, who, as Seijun predicted, were much more amenable to keeping their money in the fund after talking to Kroger. After the fifth one, Seijun had his secretary book them tickets to LA.

"LA?"

"Yes. Two of our biggest accounts are out there, and one of them wants to pull his money. I want to be able to see him first thing tomorrow morning, then visit the second one to reassure him."

But...

"Tonight?"

"Of course. Why? It was your idea, remember?"

No, he didn't remember. At that moment, he would've said anything to keep him from that dreaded cubicle, but now.... He thought about Vanessa. Would she be upset? He wanted to see her. That's what his days were now, waiting for them to end so he could see her.

"Okay, Betty has tickets for us, the plane leaves in a couple hours. We'll go back to office, grab a few things, then head straight over there. You don't mind parking at the airport? I can pay for it if you want."

"Um, no... I just... I need to uh..."

"Need to what?"

He looked at Seijun. Seijun was married, and didn't think twice about this—Chad didn't know she was in New York securing funding for her next film project, so it wasn't the same as Vanessa waiting at home to hear from him. They were going to LA. Then what? Vegas? Dallas? Where else did they have investors? When would he get back? But he wanted this, wanted Seijun to fight for this, and now he was all in. It was either this or the cubicle. He could handle a few more nights without Vanessa.

"Um, I need to call my girlfriend and let her know what's up."

"Sounds good, you can call her from the office."

Chad had already called her to let her know what he was doing and that he'd be late. By this time it was going on 7, and Vanessa thought his phone call was just to tell her he was on his way, and did she need him to get anything.

"Um, so Seijun and I are flying out to LA."

"Oh, when?"

"In a couple hours. We need to hurry actually."

"Oh, wow... more business stuff?"

"Yeah, Seijun wants to see some investors first thing tomorrow."

"Wow, okay... well, be safe. When do you think you'll be back?"

"Hopefully tomorrow, right after, but I have no idea. There's a few other clients scattered around the country, Vegas, Dallas, Chicago, I don't know if Seijun will want to see them too."

"All right, you do what you have to do, and we'll see you whenever you get back, okay?"

"Yes, that sounds good."

"Okay, be safe honey, and I love you."

"I love you too."

He thought about her as he and Seijun drove to the airport, got their boarding passes, and went through security. All of the crap that went along with flying that Chad didn't have the energy for. How did Seijun have the energy for it? How did Seijun book flights to LA, pack a suit and briefcase, and go through security at an airport in a matter of a couple hours like it was nothing, like other people ran to the store to pick up a few groceries? Is this what Chad would have to do if he wanted this hedge fund to work? Was this the alternative to living a quiet life in a cubicle? If he was still at the insurance firm, he'd be home with Vanessa right now, not taking off his shoes and any metal out of his pockets. But would Vanessa have wanted him when he was at the insurance firm? What did he want? This morning when he saw Seijun playing Brittney Spears on his guitar, the cubicle was a death sentence, a living hell, and he would've done anything to keep himself from it; and now he's sitting on a bench next to Seijun, sliding his wingtips back on, thinking that maybe that cubicle wasn't so bad.

No! No, he lost five years of his life to that cubicle. Look at him now. Look at how cool and together he and Seijun looked walking through the airport, taking seats at the bar, ordering microbrews. Look at the bartender taking their orders, she knows Seijun and Chad are doers, not grunts working in cubicles. Our suits are better, we carry ourselves with more confidence, we're more sophisticated. Fuck that cubicle, fuck that insurance company, and fuck...

He almost thought fuck Vanessa. Fuck Vanessa? It's because of her that he was even thinking of going back to that cubicle. Maybe Lars was right, maybe he was settling too easily. Look at him, ready to go back to a cubicle so he could be with Vanessa. He should be stoked to be flying out to LA. He'd never been there before. Maybe he could go to Hollywood tomorrow.

Shit, Lars is right? It's because of fucking Lars that he and Seijun were even in this airport bar waiting for their flight to LA. What the fuck did he know? And Vanessa wasn't angry with him for going to LA, Chad was the one who was angry. He was angry because he'd be sleeping alone tonight, because he wouldn't have Vanessa's flesh against him as he slept, but it wasn't Vanessa's fault, or the cubicle's.

"You know Chad, there will be Lars's share of the performance fees to consider. You've acquitted yourself very nicely here today, and I think it's only fair that when we get back we talk about bumping up your share."

Seijun, in his Machiavellian way of thinking, assumed all along that this was Chad's motive for pushing Seijun out of his funk to save the hedge fund. He didn't know—couldn't possibly know, because it was so foreign to him—what Chad's life had been for the five years before he met Seijun. The fear of returning to that life was motive enough.

But if Seijun was going to offer him more money, well, who was he to turn it down.

"I was thinking I'd bump my 10 and ½ up to 11, and give you a full 8. We'll probably have to deduct some from both of our shares to buy out Lars for this quarter, but I'm hoping that'll be nominal considering the circumstances."

8 percent? That would mean six figures for this upcoming quarter alone, and maybe over a million through next year! Seijun could tell he was happy with that offer. He lifted his glass.

"To us."

"To us."

They tapped glasses. Fuck that cubicle.

Over 65 years before Seijun was flying with Chad across the country to save his hedge fund, his grandfather Takeshi owned a fish shop in Seattle, until he and Seijun's grandmother Setsuko were forced into the internment camps. When they were finally released after the war, they decided to move to the Northeast and start over. Their new hometown was not initially welcoming either, but once they saw how well Takeshi knew seafood, he earned their respect, and became an integral part of the coastal community.

Kazuo, Seijun's father, was Takeshi and Setsuko's first child and only son. From a young age he loved spending his days at the movies, watching old Bogart, Cagney, and Robinson films. Takeshi wanted Kazuo to know the great film makers of Japan too, so he bought a small film projector and sent away to Japan for some of the films. Kurosawa, Ozu, Mizoguchi, they were all nice, but it was the Nikkatsu Noir films of Seijun Suzuki that really piqued his interest. These were the gangster films he loved, but with Japanese stars. Who needed Cagney when he had Jo Shishido?

He went to Dodge State to study film—which initially disappointed his father, but then he thought Kazuo might be the next Ozu. Kazuo's cousin Makoto flew over from Japan to help in the fish shop, which left Kazuo free to follow his dream. His junior year though, he met a beautiful exchange student, Ayako, and they fell in love.

They married and moved back to his hometown. He still had his dream to be a film maker, and Ayako supported him, but she got pregnant with Seijun, and that changed things. To make a little money, Takeshi offered to pay him to shoot a TV commercial for the fish shop. That led to other local businesses asking if he could shoot theirs too. With each new offer—and two more children that also needed to be supported—Kazuo's dream went to the backburner, to off the stove, to stored in the basement freezer and all but forgotten about; but his business producing local television advertisements flourished.

Seijun knew he and his family were different, being the only Japanese family in town at that time; but they were so well established in the community, first through his grandfather, and later through his father, that no one really treated them differently. He didn't know that being good at math was supposed to be a stereotypically Asian trait, not until he got to Harvard, and as a freshman in Micro a white male classmate made a comment that he must be good at math since he was Asian. Later, as he tried to make friends and build connections, it was other jokes. Lars one time made a crack about him being a bad driver, and when Seijun was angry about it, Lars said he was just kidding around and not to take it personally.

He remembered the first time he went out to Vegas with Lars and some other guys from Harvard. At one point he got separated from them, and all alone, decided to try something. He did his best impression of his mother or Makoto, pretending to not know a lot of English, and sat at one of the $10 blackjack tables. No one suspected a thing, it was easy money.

It was just like he described to Chad, he'd make a trip out there, either with Lars and his buddies from Harvard, or on his own, and make thousands of dollars counting cards. He eventually went to the well too much though, and the casinos shut him down, but not before he'd made a lot of money and tried his hand investing it. He studied trends, looked at what worked and what didn't, and developed his own algorithm.

After he met Noriko, the plan was for them to move to New York after school and start their life there; but later he found out Lars and his family were moving near his hometown. He knew that Lars's family knew people, and he could use Lars to get some of those people to invest in his hedge fund idea. It didn't take much to play on Lars's vanity to get him on-board, and Noriko, while initially keeping their apartment in New York on her own and splitting her time between two places, grew to miss her times away from Seijun's family—both his father who loved talking film with her and whom she sometimes needed to be rescued from during their moments in the basement theater room watching his old films on his projector, or now on VHS, laser disk, and DVD; and his mother who reminded her of her parents that were both immigrants living in San Francisco. After a year she moved in with him full time in their luxury condo downtown with it's nice view over the water.

And Lars worked his magic as well, using his parents' connections to get them a large stable of investors. The problem was Lars, of course. He was a loose cannon, whether it was making a racial slur while trying to endear himself to some investors, or the women and the partying, or just the fact that he didn't know what he was doing but thought he did. When he came to Seijun to suggest Chad as someone to do all the back-end functions Seijun was having trouble keeping up with, Seijun was dubious: not only was Lars making the suggestion, but he came as a recommendation from Kovacs, whom Seijun knew since he was very young because Seijun's father did the commercials for Kovacs's father's car dealership.

Chad surprised him right away, from their first meeting, just by how knowledgeable he was; but he also seemed to be with a lot of women too, and enjoyed partying with Lars. He remembered the relief he felt when Lars complained to him that Chad was becoming "pussywhipped" by that Vanessa chick. Seijun had been surreptitiously taking over from Lars when it came to molding and grooming Chad to be the partner he needed to take this fund to the next level, with the idea in mind that he would force Lars out eventually. As luck would have it, two things had happened in one day: Lars gave him the opportunity to force him out, and Chad proved that he was more than ready to step up and be the person Seijun needed him to be. Now it was a matter of seeing how he did on this trip around the country to see the rest of their investors.

The Today Show wanted to interview Amy and her mother on Friday morning. Her mother was very excited, but Amy could've done without it. All day Thursday there were calls from local news outlets, national shows like *Nancy Grace* and *Dr. Phil*, and all kinds of family and friends. Amy didn't sign on for any of this. She didn't like Lars, but didn't think he was *that* bad of a guy; and she hated the implication that he completely manipulated her, as if she didn't have any say in wanting to be with him. Then there were the people calling into question her mother's parenting skills, which Amy couldn't deny—she'd be the first to tell you her mother wouldn't win any Mom of the Year awards—but Amy prided herself on being self-sufficient. And the depictions of the party she went to, the horrible college kids she fell in with, how scary that must've been. Scary? That was the best moment of her life, it wasn't scary.

Thursday also marked a change in her mother. She wanted to make up for lost time, which at first made Amy happy, but then became overbearing. Brittney called and told Amy that their YouTube video views had spiked due to all the publicity, and she wanted to go to the computer to see. That led to a series of questions: what are you doing on there? Who are you talking to? I want to see what you're doing. What does it mean when it says that? Who is that guy?

"Mom, Jesus, I know what I'm doing. Just, go, do something else, please."

"I'm your mother, you can't talk to me like that."

"You've been my mother for like ten minutes, just…"

Now her mother was crying. Jesus, Amy thought, it was easier when she was too drunk to care. She left her and went to Brittney's, where she had to rehash the whole story to *her* family. She spent the night there, and went to school the next day instead of doing *The Today Show*, but the principle decided to send her home because she was a distraction to all the other kids. That meant she had to go back and see her mom, who was passed out on the couch with a half-empty half-gallon bottle of vodka tipped over on the floor in front of her. She covered her up with an afghan bunched up near her feet. She thought about Dirk, and what it would be like to be his girlfriend, parties, ski trips to Goose Eye Mountain, making out with him in the hot tub. She sighed.

"I'm not signing this mother, do you know how much he's expecting to make next quarter?"

"This is nonnegotiable Lars, you don't go around with little girls and get arrested and expect us to clean up the mess and still get to play around with your little investment scheme. Besides, Tom said you'll probably lose in court anyway and end up with much less."

"Tom doesn't know what the fuck he's talking about. Seijun exaggerated how many investors were pulling their money out so he could screw me out of this deal."

"I trust Tom a lot more than I trust you, I can tell you that. And he knows those people that invested in your little fund—if *he* says they were pulling their money out because of you, then they were pulling their money out because of you. You're lucky he's even taking your case at all, considering a lot of those people don't like that he's defending you in court. And your father and I can't show *our* faces around those people either after what you did. What were you thinking?"

"It's not that big of a deal. So what, she's fifteen. That would be legal in Sweden."

"Good! Sign the paper, then do what Tom tells you, and when this is all settled you're going back there!"

She handed him the pen and the buyout proposal Seijun's lawyer had sent Tom, and he signed it.

Lars couldn't believe any of this was happening. That stupid bitch! He didn't even get a chance to fuck her, and look at all the shit she's got him in. And Seijun, that bastard! He'd been looking for an opportunity like this to cut him out for a long time now. Short selling my ass, he was stalling, just wanted to get enough to pay off his mother so he could cut him out before the bigger money came in this summer. He was also jealous that I was the better *Galaga* player, I know it.

And then that bastard Chad! After what he did to his buddy Kovacs, I should've known anyway. I shouldn't have yelled to him at Kinkos. I treated him like my little bro, showed him the ropes, got him laid, and this is the thanks I get.

Tom was working out a plea bargain. They were threatening to charge him with things like kidnapping. Kidnapping? I took her on a fucking train for Christ's sake! These small town Tea

Baggers were just looking for something to get up in arms about, and now that the whole thing was on TV it made them even hungrier for the publicity. He was a poor Swedish aristocrat at the mercy of this populist, draconian, bloodthirsty, justice system run by pub hungry ignoramuses.

Tom knew though that the kidnapping charge, along with the various sexual assault on a minor charges, were meant to scare Lars and Tom into making a plea bargain, and after talking to Lars's mother, Tom knew that she wanted a plea bargain too. It didn't take long to bang out an agreement to plea out to some lesser charges that carried only a month in jail, of which three weeks were suspended, plus a year probation and some community service, the latter two that he could serve back in Sweden. Two weeks later, he had his day in court, and was in jail that night. He never saw Seijun or Chad again.

LA was not the place Chad expected. He was thinking Hollywood and Beverly Hills, and instead they were in office buildings in a downtown city that looked like all the other big cities he'd been to. But they were nice office buildings. Everything was nice. He was a VIP with Seijun and their investors. They got into exclusive restaurants, had courtside seats to the Clippers—the Lakers were on a road trip, but still, courtside seats!

They were on the road for a week, going from LA to Vegas, then Dallas, Chicago, and finally New York. It was a world Chad had only dreamed of. Golf—which he sucked at—at exclusive courses, luxury box seats to hockey games or courtside seats to basketball games, fancy restaurants, entry into members only clubs, yachts, spas—this was his future, and he needed to learn to play ball. He needed to be better at golf, needed to know what to wear for every occasion, what fork to use, how to smoke a cigar or drink a glass of cognac. He did his best to follow Seijun's lead, and Seijun was willing to teach him. Seijun was seeing Chad as the valuable asset he'd hoped he'd be. While Lars might have had a better golf game, Chad had more business savvy, and that counted more with these people. He understood the nuts and bolts of Seijun's investment strategy, and knew when to step in and take over when they were in front of clients, and when to back off and let Seijun do the talking. Lars always wanted to show the investors that he and Seijun were equals, when they weren't, and that friction, combined with the fact that Lars often had no clue what he was talking about, or was likely to say something offensive, turned their clients off, and meant Seijun always felt like he was working uphill to keep things at even par. Now with Chad, they were excelling. Seijun may have had more experience with the luxury they were both enjoying, but these investors weren't inviting he and Lars along the way they invited he and Chad—he never let Chad know that though.

That first night in LA, Chad talked to Vanessa for a few minutes. He missed her, and wanted so bad to tell her what Seijun said about raising his cut of the performance fee, and what that money meant, but they hadn't heard from the lawyer yet on whether or not Lars had signed off on the buyout terms, plus they needed to make sure all the investors weren't pulling their money. He could tell Vanessa was a little melancholy, especially when she found out they'd be gone for a week, and he told Seijun as much.

"Send her a postcard."

Wow, that was pretty cold. Was he that nice to Noriko?

"I'm not being facetious, I'm serious, send her a postcard."

"What, a postcard?"

"Yes, of course, she and her daughter will love it. Send one from every place we go, it'll let her know how much you're thinking of her."

"Wouldn't she know that by me calling?"

"Jesus Chad, a phone call is expected. This is going the extra mile, you're taking the trouble to buy a postcard and a stamp, and hand write a personal message. She'll be touched, her daughter will be excited, she'll tell all her friends at school where you are…"

"Yeah, but what do I write?"

"Just what you did that day, 'Dear Vanessa and… and…'"

"Edie."

"Right, Edie. 'Dear Vanessa and Edie, went to see so and so today, ate at this really nice restaurant, went to see so and so play, yadda yadda yadda, I miss you so much and can't wait to get back, love you, Chad.' "

Chad couldn't remember the last time he'd done anything like that. The next night, after the Clippers game, he bought three postcards. He also bought souvenirs at the game for Edie—another one of Seijun's suggestions. He bought three postcards in case he screwed up on one, which he did right away.

"Chad man, this isn't rocket science."

"But dude, my handwriting is messy, and I have no idea what to say."

"First off, you only write on the left side, you save the right for the address."

"Oh."

"Look, just start with dear Vanessa and Edie, then say 'we went to a Clippers game today', 'we saw our two investors today, the meetings went well, and one of them gave us courtside seats to see the Clippers. I got Edie some souvenirs. LA is nice, maybe we can all come out here together some day on vacation. I bet you'd love it. Hope everything is good at home. I miss you and I love you. Chad.' "

"Wait, can you start again from 'gave us courtside seats'?"

By Dallas he had the hang of it, and by Chicago the lawyer had finalized Lars's buyout, and by New York Chad needed a new suitcase for all the things he'd bought Vanessa and Edie. They got back on Friday, and he went straight to Vanessa's. Edie tore into the suitcase of their stuff, while Chad sat on the couch with Vanessa on his arm watching her. All of it felt right and worth it. He was home.

That same day, across town, Amy received a call from a representative of The TeenGo Channel. She missed the call because she was at school and her mother was sleeping, but she returned it right away when she got home. What could a guy from The TeenGo Channel want?

"My name is Robert Adkins, creative director here at The TeenGo Channel's teen sitcom programming division. I've been following your story pretty closely, Amy, and I was wondering if maybe we could do something together."

"Um, yeah, that sounds great. What?"

"I was thinking of a sitcom about a girl, like yourself, who inherits her father's business or maybe has to take care of some younger siblings, something like that, where she would need to do like you did, and dress like an older woman in order to fool everyone. I see a lot of comedic potential with her having to straddle two worlds, that of an adult and a child."

Holy shit! A TV show? Me?

He flew in that Monday, and met Amy and her mother out for lunch. He had her bring her business suit with her, which Amy had to get cleaned over the weekend, something her mother was all too happy to pay for.

"This is so exciting, my little girl meeting a TV guy."

"God mom, don't embarrass me!"

Mr. Adkins was already at the restaurant—the same one Chad met his mother at before Christmas—, and they did some handshakes and sat down. Amy's mom couldn't believe the menu, everything was so expensive. This was a restaurant she'd always wanted to go to. What should she order? Would it be bad to get something that cost too much with him paying? Maybe she should've worn a skirt instead of jeans. She didn't want to embarrass Amy and ruin her big shot—then she could eat here all the time with her rich and famous daughter!...

Mr. Adkins wasn't there to cast Amy, all he wanted were the rights to her story so he could use it as the basis for his sitcom, and wanted to get it before Disney or Lifetime or someone else took it to make a TV movie or another show; but he wanted to make sure this whole idea was possible and would really work on TV. He had her retell what happened, which made her mother upset to have to imagine it all again, but she concealed that too for Amy's sake.

"I gotta say, sitting here across from you, it's impossible to believe you could pass as an adult just by changing your clothes. I need to see this. Do you mind?"

"Not at all."

Mr. Adkins and her mother tried their best to carry on some desultory conversation in Amy's absence. Yes, she was scared when Amy turned up missing, yes she's very proud of her daughter now too. What did she do for work? Well, she's kind of between things…. Adkins saw on TV the week before that Amy's mother was accused of being negligent in her duties as a parent, and he was trying his best to tiptoe around anything that could upset her and jeopardize what he hoped would be a fruitful trip. Then Amy emerged from the bathroom. They both stood to meet her.

"Oh my God," he said. "I wouldn't have believed it if I hadn't seen it with my own eyes. You really do look ten years older." He spun her around. "The heels are a big part of it, you go from like 5'4" to 5'7" in those. But you walk in them so well, not at all like a 15-year-old would. And the make-up is excellent. And your hair. Wow. How did you learn how to do all this?"

"The internet."

"Wow… all right, I want to see this in action with someone who doesn't know what we're doing. I want you to order a drink at the bar."

"A drink? But I don't…"

"Honey, just do it for the man, it's no big deal."

"You don't have to drink it, just order it and see if they'll sell it to you without carding you. If they ask for your ID, just say you forgot it and come back over, no biggie. The thing is, I want to see if you can do this. Those bartenders aren't the bumpkins at that mountain village who think any woman in a suit must be important. They see people in suits all day."

"Okay Bob, I'll give it a shot. Can you give me a ten-spot?"

She held out her hand. A ten-spot? Did this girl just ask for a "ten-spot"? My daughter is 16, and she has never asked me for a "ten-spot". And she called me "Bob" to boot. She sounded like one of my college buddies or something. This is a unique girl. I can't wait to see this.

Her mother went to scold Amy for being so impertinent—calling him "Bob" instead of "Mr. Adkins"—, but things happened too fast in front of her, and before she knew it Amy was on her way. She was nervous. She was proud that her daughter could look so distinguished, but nervous that she wouldn't succeed. Please sell her the drink, please sell her the drink, come on…

They couldn't hear, only watch from where they were standing in the dining room. They saw her joking with the bartender, show her how she did her make-up—at least that was the best guess when they saw the bartender lean over and Amy point out something around her eyes, then pulled some make-up containers out of her purse. She was handed a glass of white wine, and Amy told her to keep the change, and walked back over to them.

"Here you go, how'd I do Bob?"

"Amy! Be more respectful to the man!"

It was Amy's mother making up for her missed opportunity to reprimand her daughter before, and Amy went to reprimand her back, but Bob jumped in.

"Ma'am, if you don't mind my saying, your daughter is very special. I mean, that was amazing, you had that woman eating out of your hands up there. I wish I had gone with you to hear what you said, but I was afraid my being older and in a suit too would make things too easy for you, you know?… what did you do?"

"I just sold it Bob, that's all there is to it. It's all about being confident, but not cocky, not being a snob. I learned that while I was with those college kids—once they thought I was a big deal, everything after that was gravy—but being snobby would've turned them off, right?"

"So are you selling me right now?"

"Hey Bob, you asked to see the show, and I'm only givin' you what you wanted."

She giggled. The giggle snapped him back. She really did have him believing she was older, even when he knew all along how old she really was. He regretted not bringing a talent scout with him, because they'd know for sure, but he thought they might have something here.

"What's your school schedule like? You probably just had February vacation, right? And you missed all that school last week—and today, which I know is probably not a good thing… I just wanted to see if you and your mother would like to come down to Orlando and meet with me and my talent scouts. I want you to go dressed like this though. We'll pretend you're her agent, and the 'girl' hasn't arrived yet, get it? We won't tell them it's you, or any of that… what do you think, can we do that?"

"What do you think mom?"

Oh my God, that's right, she's the mom here, it's ultimately *her* decision. She wanted to shout out Yes!, but she didn't want to embarrass Amy or make Bob think she was uncouth.

"Well, honey, it's up to you. I'm sure we can talk to your school about any stuff you miss, right?"

"Oh yeah, Britt will take notes for me. We're in Bob."

They flew down that Friday, and met Bob at a restaurant, doing exactly as he asked. The talent scouts had no idea, Amy fooled them all. And after that, she won them over too.

There were formalities like contracts and other paperwork before it would be official, and Amy's grandmother's lawyer would help them with that back at home; but before that, Amy and her mother had the weekend together at Disney World, all expenses paid by TeenGo. It was the most time they'd spent with one another ever, and it was the happiest either had ever been. Amy scared her mother though. She couldn't believe the baby she gave birth to had so suddenly become a 15-year-old young lady. Now she'd be making more money than her, had completely earned this TV show on her own, and at times seemed more mature than her, like in deciding what restaurant to eat at, or what attractions to see, or even asking for help from one of the staff. She was supposed to be this girl's mother, but could she tell her what to do? Discipline her? Make decisions for them both?

Amy was scared too. What would happen to Brittney? Would she still see her? And as great an opportunity as this was, could she trust all these people? This wasn't something someone could look up on the internet: type into Google "signing your first TV show contract"? Or could she? Her grandmother's lawyer would take care of it though. She trusted her grandmother to do adult things. Since she and her mother moved to Chad's apartment complex a few years ago, she'd seen less of her grandmother, but she also needed her less. Amy was learning to take care of herself. And the past few weeks had shown her that she was pretty good at taking care of herself; but fooling a bunch of people into thinking she's an adult was different from contracts and agents and stuff like that. Part of her was excited and felt like this was everything she could've dreamed of, but another part of her wished none of this had ever happened, that she was back home thinking of another silly YouTube video with Brittney and staying with Miguel and Julía while her mom brought back some weird guy, then finding her mother the next day passed out on the couch.

She wanted to tell her mother she was scared, but she couldn't. These were decisions that were difficult for someone twice Amy's age to make, and Amy shouldn't have had to make them; but Amy didn't make sense as a 15-year-old to her mother anymore, and her mother couldn't see that, couldn't see that there was even a decision to make. How could she not want to be a TV star, especially with her talent?

With everyone in her life telling her this was a great opportunity, Amy convinced herself that it was too, and said yes to the TV show. She had no idea what she was getting herself into, but everyone's excitement at the opportunity rubbed off on her enough. She would begin screentests in a month.

Epilogue

It was now late June, and Chad and Vanessa were sitting at the reception of Mackenzie's wedding. Chad didn't know any of the people around him at the table, and wanted to talk to Vanessa about what they were going to do with the rest of their weekend since Edie was away with her father; but everyone at the table knew him and knew what he did, and knew that none of them would be there at that moment if not for him, and they wanted to talk to him about it. Vanessa wasn't expecting to be such the center of attention, and was glad she put in the effort to lose that fifteen pounds—help she had by going to the gym with Haley, who was training to go to Denali. The toasts and other perfunctory wedding events were all sign posts Chad checked off in his head telling him he was closer to getting out of there and out of this suit and relaxing by the pool with Vanessa. The maid of honor's toast included Chad though, and he had to stand and be applauded.

"My guy, the hero."

Chad liked it when Vanessa joked about it. He was worried, after what Gwen told him, that Vanessa would be exposed to all of this and feel the same way Gwen did and wonder why he wasn't Superman. But Vanessa understood it. Though she wouldn't diminish the impact of what Chad did—he really did save that girl's life—she understood that Chad wasn't breaking down doors or beating guys up. He just happened upon a situation and did the right thing. It was much more Clark Kent than Superman, and she loved him for that.

Maybe it was knowing Chad for longer than Gwen did that made the difference. Whereas Gwen had trouble comprehending that the guy who saved MacKenzie's life was the same guy that could only exist as Gwen's Chad, Vanessa had trouble comprehending that the same guy whom she went on a date with in January, and who ended a ten-year-long string of heartache and failed relationships for her, was the guy she knew from high school. Rich guys, poor guys, bad guys, nice guys, she'd tried them all, even tried a woman, and none of them worked; but then here comes a guy that she dated in 8th grade, whose house she used to go to afterschool because his mom wasn't home and made-out with him and watched MTV, and then who made-out with Julie Sludowski after she was caught by her parents and grounded because he thought that meant they'd broken up. Life is funny sometimes, but now it was like those ten years didn't happen, other than watching her daughter grow up. That's the only thing she had for so long, just her daughter's life to live through, and when she'd resigned herself to that being her fate, that she'd never find a guy that would want her, Chad came around. And he looked at her that way in his kitchen when she was wearing his shirt. And as she sat on his lap at MacKenzie's wedding reception, he was still looking at her that way. She was no longer just Edie's mother, she was Chad's Vanessa.

Chad couldn't have been happier either having Vanessa sitting on him. Vanessa always felt good sitting on him, leaning against him, lying on him when they were in bed. He didn't know feelings like these were possible when he was with Gwen, but now that he knew them, he didn't want to stop feeling them, and fortunately Vanessa felt the same way when he asked her to marry him two months ago.

It seemed like everyone in his life was doing well too. Haley successfully summated Denali a month earlier, to which Chad still thought "fuck that", but she was happy, and she was happy with Dave. They had had a very awkward double date with Chad and Vanessa in March, where Haley in her extreme positivity lightened the mood and made everyone cordial. Now, much to Chad's chagrin, Vanessa wanted to take up hiking too. Steve had had a great first season as the Oak Grove lacrosse coach, and he and Sara were expecting another child in August. This prompted Vanessa to suggest that Chad might one want too, which was a little unnerving—Edie was enough for right now. And of course Amy, who had moved out of the apartment a week before to go down to Orlando with her mother. Miguel and Julía had a going away party for her, which was the first time Chad had been back to his old complex since he'd moved into Vanessa's house in April.

Then there was the hedge fund. With the quarter almost ending, the returns were even bigger than Seijun's predictions. In a few weeks he would have almost $300,000 at his disposal. Vanessa wanted to buy a new house, but he was just getting used to living at hers, and Edie also loved their house, so she didn't argue, especially after the size of the engagement ring he gave her. If staying where they were made them happy, then she was happy too.

Chad wanted to relish this happiness as much as he could. He knew what he didn't have for the past five years, knew how miserable he was, and felt like he couldn't enjoy these changes enough, couldn't feel Vanessa against him enough, couldn't lie on the couch with her and watch shows he hated like *The Bachelor* enough, couldn't practice soccer with Edie so she could make the traveling team enough, couldn't sit in his office and recognize that it was *his* office enough; in short, couldn't be happy enough.

But maybe, just being happy was enough. He had found his bowl of life on the floor.

Made in the USA
Middletown, DE
01 May 2020

91742907R00139